Bye, Baby

Also by Carola Lovering

Bye, Baby

A NOVEL

✳

Carola Lovering

ST. MARTIN'S PRESS
NEW YORK

First published in the United States by St. Martin's Press, an imprint of St. Martin's Publishing Group

BYE, BABY. Copyright © 2024 by Carola Lovering. All rights reserved. Printed in the United States of America. For information, address St. Martin's Publishing Group, 120 Broadway, New York, NY 10271.

www.stmartins.com

Library of Congress Cataloging-in-Publication Data

Names: Lovering, Carola, author.
Title: Bye, baby : a novel / Carola Lovering.
Description: First edition. | New York : St. Martin's Press, 2024.
Identifiers: LCCN 2023027214 | ISBN 9781250289360 (hardcover) |
    ISBN 9781250289377 (ebook)
Subjects: LCSH: Best friends—Fiction. | Female friendship—Fiction. |
    Kidnapping—Fiction. | LCGFT: Thrillers (Fiction) | Novels.
Classification: LCC PS3612.O855 B94 2024 | DDC 813/.6—
    dc23/eng/20230612
LC record available at https://lccn.loc.gov/2023027214

Our books may be purchased in bulk for promotional, educational, or business use. Please contact your local bookseller or the Macmillan Corporate and Premium Sales Department at 1-800-221-7945, extension 5442, or by email at MacmillanSpecialMarkets@macmillan.com.

First Edition: 2024

10 9 8 7 6 5 4 3 2 1

For Lila. We wrote this one together.

Each friend represents a world in us, a world possibly not born until they arrive, and it is only by this meeting that a new world is born.

—ANAÏS NIN, *THE DIARY OF ANAÏS NIN*

Darkness has a hunger that's insatiable, and lightness has a call that's hard to hear.

—INDIGO GIRLS

Prologue

October 13, 2023

The baby stops fussing, settling into my arms like a sleepy puppy. The soft weight of her. Her lips pucker, then relax, her little chest rising and falling almost to the rhythm of my own. She is back to sleep, her face peaceful as a porcelain doll's. That wasn't hard.

The living room window is open; fevered voices carry in from the terrace of the apartment above. Commotion. Mania. I shouldn't be surprised.

I recognize the sound of Cassie's screaming, obviously—I've heard her scream dozens of times. Horror movies (she love-hates them); the afternoon we picnicked upstate and she got stung by a whole swarm of bees; the time in high school when she walked in on her ex-boyfriend Kyle and our semi-friend Ashton, manically fucking in her basement during a party. *Manically fucking* was the way Cassie described it afterward, so that's how I remember it.

Anyway, Cassie is screaming now the way she did then—except even more psychotically this time, and who can blame her? Her baby is gone.

I picture her one story up, her blue eyes swimming with tears, already swollen even though it's only been fifteen minutes since Ella went missing. Five since anyone noticed.

In the midst of Cassie's wailing, I hear her friends banding together. I recognize Ava's voice, McKay's. I don't know the others' voices by heart, but some of them sound familiar, probably from Cassie's Instagram stories. Evelyn, maybe Blake? The one who speaks with an upward inflection.

"I just called the cops," someone says.

"Hold on, where's Grant?" It's McKay, panicked. "Someone get him. Someone get Grant!"

"No," says Cassie, and I hear her sniffle. Eight stories below, there's a series of violent honking. A siren blares, a high-pitched wailing that climbs into windows and bounces off buildings. Part of the soundtrack of the city.

"Billie," she says, and I freeze. "I need Billie."

"*Billie? Why?*" McKay is the one challenging this statement. Of course. Dumb bitch.

Just then, my phone begins to vibrate on the couch. Carefully, I remove one arm from where it supports the baby and reach down for the phone, silencing the vibration as I drink in the sight of her name on the caller ID. *Cassie Barnwell.* She's been married for well over a year now, and I still haven't gotten around to adding her new last name.

For a moment, I let myself bask in the fact that she's calling me. *She* is calling *me.* How many months has it been since that happened? I study the picture of the girl on my screen—Cassie's contact photo for as long as I can remember. Straight brown hair, wide blue eyes, one of her dark eyebrows raised as she puckers goofily at the camera. A stupid selfie from another lifetime.

I let the call ring. I screen it. What else am I supposed to do? Still, the warm glow behind my chest lingers. I hear her words. *Billie. I need Billie.*

Cassie needs me. She wanted *me.* Before Grant, even. I feel high, victorious.

I move a little closer to the window.

"She's not picking up." Cassie begins to cry again, her sobs punctuated by a low moaning. "My baby, my *baby*!" She's growing more hysterical now, her screams piercing the cool air, the oblivious city night.

"The cops are on their way," someone assures her. The voice is consoling, maternal.

"But who would take her? Who would take Ella? *WHO*?"

I look down at the sleeping bundle in my arms, the dark sweep of a tiny set of eyelashes. Long and thick, just like Cassie's.

"*Who took her?*" the voice of my best friend echoes.

I realize with a jolt, as though I'm just re-remembering the past fifteen minutes, that it was me.

Part

ONE

Chapter One

Billie

I'm not a baby person. I used to assume I'd become one, eventually, like most of the girls-turned-women I've known in my life, their voices rising in pitch at the sight of a chubby baby arm, the creased rolls of a tiny wrist cuff. I kept waiting for it to happen. But it hasn't. I am thirty-five years old, and I've never felt that particular tug.

Alex doesn't ask about kids, thank god. It's only our third date, but you'd be surprised by the number of conversations that veer in that direction when you're in your midthirties.

Alex chews his grilled calamari and comments on my upcoming trip to the Azores. It'll be my second time traveling to the archipelago off the coast of Portugal, my first to the coveted Formigas Islets.

"You have the dream job," he says, swallowing his bite. "Staying at top hotels in the most beautiful destinations around the world, and all comped? Sounds like I should've been a luxury travel consultant instead of a boring cop."

He smiles, and something in his face reminds me of James Franco. A less objectively hot James Franco, but still. I have the sudden urge to text Cassie and tell her this—she's been obsessed ever since we saw *Pineapple Express* in college—but we haven't spoken all summer. I've tried to reach her, plenty of times, but she never responds. About once a month, she texts something like, Things have been so crazy with the baby, I'll call you back soon. But she doesn't. I've started to feel like an unrequited lover, desperately trying to get in touch with my own best friend.

I cast a warm look at Alex. His job isn't boring, and he knows it, but still, I always appreciate humility in a person. It's a rare quality.

"How did you decide to become a cop?" I ask.

"Runs in the family." He drums his fingers against the wood surface of the table. "My dad, my brother. My grandfather was a detective, and that's my real aspiration." He pauses. "I know it might seem unoriginal, following in their footsteps, but I love the work. I really can't imagine doing anything else."

Our waitress drops the bill. She has long, stemmy legs and pouty lips, and Alex hasn't checked her out all night, which I give him credit for. But he doesn't shoo me away when I lay my Visa on top of his, which I consider a potential red flag. Yes, he paid for our happy hour drinks on the first two dates. But this isn't an eight-dollar glass of pinot grigio; it's dinner, our first shared meal. I imagine the way Cassie would roll her eyes at the scenario. *You love to think of yourself as traditional, Billie,* she'd say knowingly. *You want a man to pay for you, but you get all weird when it comes to marriage and kids? That's some warped kind of feminism.*

I leave a 20 percent tip and scribble my signature on the receipt. I hate that I'm always thinking about Cassie, especially when I know she's not thinking about me. I sigh audibly, unconsciously, prompting Alex to lift his eyebrows.

"All good?"

One side of his mouth curls, forming a dimple that makes my whole body hum. I nod, push the bill-splitting out of my mind. I'm not actually a stickler for etiquette—that's Cassie. I'm fooling myself when I pretend to be.

"That was delicious," I tell him once we're out on the street. It's a humid night, the end of August. Seventh Avenue is busy, a wave of traffic rushing by.

"Very delicious."

I step toward him, one strap of my sundress slipping from my shoulder down toward my elbow. Alex touches his hand to my arm, lifts the strap, secures it back in place. His fingertips linger on my shoulder, tracing the constellation of freckles there, the one Remy used to say looked like Orion. Then his hand moves lower, settling against the middle of my back in a way that turns the humming feeling into a churning. A magnetic force. My knee joints are melting.

"Billie." Alex's voice is slightly raspy. We're both a little drunk. "Is it a family name?"

"Sort of." I tip my chin up toward his. Alex isn't as tall as Remy, but he's got a few inches on me, at least. "My mom's dad was William. And my mom was convinced I was going to be a boy, so she'd planned to name me after him."

"Really?" He smiles, and there's a shimmer in his green-brown gaze. "What made your mom so sure you were a boy?"

I shrug, swallowing hard. I don't want to talk about Mom.

"Can I convince you to get one more drink?" he asks.

I bite the inside of my lip. More than anything, I want to wrap my arms around him. I want to run my hands up the back of his neck, through his fine brown hair, press my body to his like we're a pair of Pringles. God, it's been so long since I've been held.

But it's our third date, which isn't nothing, and there's a familiar question in his eyes, in the hopeful way they're studying mine. And the voice is there again, the one that nags at the back of my brain during these sorts of moments. *Leave this guy alone, Billie. He's nice. He's good. You need to walk away now, before it's too late.*

"I have an early morning," I tell him, half hoping he can sense the lie. "There's a ton of work stuff going on before I leave Saturday." And then, even though I don't mean it, perhaps only because I wish I *did* mean it, "Rain check?"

"Sure." The light in his gaze dims a little, but he doesn't push. "When are you back from Portugal?"

"The week after Labor Day."

"Cool. I hope you have the best time." The vibe feels perfunctory, suddenly, something between us deflated. It's my fault, no doubt.

"What are you doing for the long weekend?" I ask, because I still have no idea how this man spends his free time. Alex is unlike any other guy I've gone out with; I can't fill in the blanks with him.

"I'm going to my parents' out on Long Island."

"You said you're from Port Washington, right?"

He nods. "My mom always hosts this big end-of-summer barbecue. She gives me and my siblings hell if we don't come home for it." He laughs softly. "My family can get pretty rowdy."

As I watch Alex hail a cab, it feels unlikely that he'll call me again. I'll be away for almost two weeks, which is long enough to let this fizzle if either of us wants it to. I know it's for the best, but it stings. I walk home thinking of his James Franco squint, his kind voice.

My apartment is only four blocks away, a true one-bedroom on Christopher Street that I could never have afforded in my twenties.

I think back on all the crappy spots I've inhabited in this city—the basement unit in Greenpoint, the Craigslist roommates and bedbugs in Chinatown, the four-hundred-square-foot studio that Cassie and I shared in Alphabet City our first few years out of college—and I know I'll never take this place for granted.

I don't need more alcohol, but I pluck a cold bottle of rosé from the fridge and pour myself a glass. I flop down onto my plush West Elm couch—the nicest piece of furniture in my apartment, by far. It cost me a whole paycheck, but a good couch is important, and I was due for an upgrade. It's white, because it can be, because I don't have to worry about anyone spilling on it but myself. I pull a soft beige blanket from where it's draped over the back and curl up with my wine. The AC is blasting, just the way I like it. I take out my phone.

I haven't opened Instagram in hours, which means a surge of new Cassie content. Goody.

Sure enough, a pink ring glows around her avatar at the top of my feed, her username in small letters underneath: @cassidyadler.

How pathetic that I actually take pleasure in this: drinking alone while watching my best friend on earth—who has all but stopped speaking to me—narrate her life on Instagram.

I click her avatar, the circular sphere that grants me—and forty-eight thousand others—access into her daily world. Cassie's face appears on the screen; it is flawless, her pores sucked away by a filter. She wears a white linen nightgown, cap-sleeved and eyelet.

"Okay, I'm such a grandma, it's not even eight thirty and I'm about to climb into bed, *but* I just had to hop on here and show you guys this nightgown that I'm literally obsessed with; it's this *amazing* brand Celestine, and *yes,* we're carrying it in the store, online and brick-and-mortar, and I'm just . . . guys, I'm obsessed. It's so soft, so delicate, so comfy, so feminine. Ella will probably spit up all over it any second, but it's *not* hand-wash only like a lot of my favorite nightie brands, so that's a huge plus to be able to throw it in the wash, though I would hang dry if you can. Anyway, I've linked it here. Sweet dreams."

Cassie's voice on camera oozes friendliness, and is higher in pitch than I've ever heard it in real life. I take a long drink of wine, addicted, transfixed. It's my only access to her these days, and I'm not ready for it to be over. Thankfully, there's more.

In the next story, she lies in bed, nestled into her scalloped shams, which are propped against her cream upholstered headboard. I know where everything in her apartment was purchased; she's told us, all forty-eight thousand of us. She's provided links to every piece of furniture, every monogrammed hand towel.

The makeup is scrubbed from Cassie's eyes, and her shiny chestnut locks fall in two even sheets past her shoulders. I think of her hair in high school and college, that tumble of curls she now smooths and straightens with religious frequency. She looks so different. She's always been beautiful, but her beauty used to have an edge, a wildness. Now, she's perfect, like a brunette Barbie doll. How does a person look this flawless going to bed at night? How is it possible?

"Hi, guys, sorry I'm whispering—Grant's asleep—*but* I got a bunch of questions about nightgown sizing, so wanted to hop back on here real quick. I'm wearing an extra small . . . this brand is a pretty billowy fit, there's a lot of fabric to work with. I also just have to say, on a completely different note, my skin literally feels like silk right now. Tatcha sent me their new moisturizer, and it's *heaven*. I'm having total mom brain and blanking on the exact name. It's in, like, a mint-green jar, but I promise I'll link it in the morning and get you guys my discount code, too. I just know this is gonna be my new favorite moisturizer; it's totally clean *and* safe for breastfeeding, which you know is my jam these days. Speaking of which, Ella will be up in a matter of hours, so I'm *actually* signing off now. Mwah."

Cassie's narration ends, and Instagram skips over to the next story, some girl I went to college with, a boomerang of her baby in a swing. It's like I blinked and everybody has babies now.

I navigate back to Cassie's profile so I can watch her stories again, this time from the start of the past twenty-four hours. In her profile avatar, she wears a white strapless maxi dress, her thin arms crossed, her smile inviting. She stands beside the storefront of Cassidy Adler, the retail shop she opened in SoHo two summers ago. Underneath the photo is her bio:

Cassie Adler
Mama, wife, founder of Cassidy Adler
We're a curated clothing boutique in NYC, coming soon to East Hampton!
Shop online: cassidyadler.com

Her store was originally called "Cassidy's Closet" before a publicist deemed the name too quirky, said it evoked a Midwestern vibe that bordered on second-rate. The opposite of what Cassie was going for with her curation of cashmere sets and offensively priced cocktail dresses. The publicist, perhaps to detract from the notion that there could be anything tasteless about Cassie's own vision, advised she make the switch to "Cassidy Adler"—both the store name and Instagram handle—in an effort to put her "whole self" into the brand. Cassie was engaged to Grant by then; that she would take his last name and incorporate it into her new identity came as no surprise to me.

I click the avatar, watch her stories play through. I catch a clip of the night before, a video of Cassie and Grant out to dinner with another couple, people I don't recognize. A stylish woman wearing multiple gold-chain necklaces and a man with a flabby jawline in an expensive suit. Cassie seems to have more and more new friends.

"Parents' night out!" she sings into her phone, clutching a martini with her free hand. Grant smiles awkwardly beside her, and I know him well enough to know that it must wear on him, the endlessness of her social media use, the perpetual exposure of a life lived on camera.

There's a series of photos of their sushi dinner. Shiny slabs of yellowtail sashimi, battered tempura. The restaurant is tagged—a trendy new place in Nolita. There's a screenshot of the baby monitor app, a grainy black-and-white picture of Ella sleeping peacefully, over which Cassie has captioned: *Parents' night out = two martinis deep and staring at my baby at dinner! Take me home to her* 🍼

There is an eight-hour period of inactivity—even micro-influencers sleep. At 7:00 a.m., she's back. I rewatch her morning, the smoothie she makes while Ella naps against her chest in a rose-colored sling. Ella sleeps through the noise of the Vitamix, and Cassie laughs about what a good, easy baby she has. Cassie links to the protein powder in the smoothie. She links to the Vitamix. She links to the sling. She films herself breastfeeding while giving an update on the store's amended hours over Labor Day weekend, Ella suckling away at her chest.

Later in the day, she gives us a tour of her powder room, which she and Grant are in the process of renovating. She shows us the wallpaper she's chosen. The light fixtures. The vanity. She links it all. Expensive things in her beautiful apartment that have nothing to do with her clothing store.

Rosé-induced thoughts swirl through my head.

I hate her.

I miss her.

Who the hell is this internet caricature, and what did she do with my best friend?

I exit Instagram and scroll through my text messages. There's nothing new. I'm not really in touch with many people on a daily basis. Today it's been Alex, my boss-turned-soul-sister, Jane, and my group chat with Becca and Esme, my two closest friends from college.

I keep scrolling down. A month ago—that was the last time I reached out to Cassie. I cringe at the message I sent.

> How's everything going?! I miss you and Ella, she's the cutest. Love seeing all the pictures and videos on Insta. Lunch next week? I can bring over takeout if that's easiest! I'm free any day!

Cassie never replied, which hadn't come as a total shock. These days, there seems to be about a one-in-four chance she responds to my texts. I like to tell myself it's because she has a new baby, but on nights like tonight—when I have enough alcohol in my system—the truth reaches me. It isn't about Ella. Becca has two kids, and she always answers.

I've only met Ella once, back in May, just after she was born. I'd texted Cassie that I had a gift to drop off, could I leave it with her doorman? Shockingly, she'd invited me up.

I remember the sight of Cassie, curled into a corner of the couch, her hair piled on top of her head in the kind of messy, lopsided bun she'd never dream of showing on Instagram. She wore pajama pants and an old Harvard T-shirt, tiny Ella swaddled like a burrito in her lap.

"It was so hard, Bill," she'd said, her eyes growing honest, tears pricking them. The real Cassie.

I remembered us in high school, how terrified we'd been of childbirth.

"Billie and I are *one hundred* percent getting surrogates," Cassie would declare to her mother, usually just after we'd finished watching *Nine Months*, a movie that constantly seemed to air on TV in the early aughts. I'd nod in emphatic agreement.

"Don't be so dramatic, girls," Mrs. Barnwell would say, an eyebrow raised in amusement. "Labor isn't as bad as Hollywood makes it out to be."

That May afternoon, I'd nestled beside Cassie on the couch. I'd glanced down at Ella, whose smooth head was the size of a cantaloupe. "I can't believe you birthed her."

"I know."

"Was it as crazy as it looked in *Nine Months*?"

Cassie had frowned. Around her, I no longer seemed to be able to say the right thing.

That was the last time we saw each other. Three whole months ago. I sigh, thinking of how much has changed. Not just in three months, but over the past few years.

I stare at my phone. I miss her. I want to text her so badly.

I think of what Jane would say, what Jane *has* said when I get like this. *Stop giving her the time of day, Billie. Why do you bend over backward for this girl when she clearly doesn't want or need you in her life?*

But she does need me, I tell myself. She does. She always has. Just like I need her.

I start typing. There's a one-in-four chance she'll answer. Why not try again?

Chapter Two

Cassie

August 25, 2023
49 days before

Grant puts his finger in my mouth. It's meant to be a turn-on, but it isn't. Just bony flesh, the hard smoothness of his nail. Worse, it makes me think of Ella, the way she nestles her fingers on the inside of my lips when she feeds. Since having a baby, so many things that once felt sexual now just feel like a function of biology. I push Grant away.

"Honestly, babe, I'm exhausted."

He sighs. "You're always exhausted."

"It's not even seven. I need coffee."

"It's been almost four months, Cass. I'm going crazy."

I stifle a groan, closing my eyes as I sink back into the pillows. My OB cleared us for sex six weeks after Ella was born, but I wasn't ready then. I haven't felt "ready" since, but still. I can't make Grant wait forever.

"Okay," I acquiesce.

His eyebrows shoot up in surprise. "Really? Are you sure?"

"I said *okay*." I reach for him, pulling his body on top of mine. If he wants it this badly, he can do the work.

Grant does want it. Badly. He practically rips my nightgown over my head—the linen one from Celestine that I showed on Instagram last night—and his boxers are already down around his ankles. I'm not warmed up—I'm still half-asleep—but he's wedging my thighs apart with his knees, and then I feel him, all too suddenly, tearing me apart in a shock of pain that sends me straight back to the delivery room, straight back to the visceral memory of the stitches that held me together for weeks after Ella's birth. I had to sit on a fucking inner tube for the better part of a month.

"*Jesus*, Grant!"

He stops thrusting. I'm his wife; he knows my cries of pleasure, and these aren't them.

"Shit. Cassie. Are you okay?" His eyes are wide with concern, his dark bangs falling over his forehead.

I feel tears rushing to my throat. I blink them back. "Fuck."

"What is it, baby? Is it painful?"

I nod. "Yeah. I just—" I'm really crying now. The damn hormones. "I want everything to be normal, but it's not."

"Babe. It will be." There's concern and sympathy in Grant's voice, but something else, too. Frustration.

I dab the inner corners of my eyes with the pads of my fingers. I study Grant, the sharp line of his jaw, the slight furrow of his brow. He's good-looking, but not quite handsome. There are certain weak qualities to his face, like his chin. The slight fleshiness of his nose. I notice them more and more as time passes. Still, he's Grant Adler. He could've picked any woman, and he picked me.

"Our sex life, though . . ." I sniffle, blinking up at him. "You have needs. What if you . . . I mean, is this why men cheat?" I don't entirely *mean* to be manipulative, but sometimes I can't help it. Sometimes it feels like my duty as a woman to fuck with the opposite sex, just a little.

"Cassie." Grant's face falls. He brushes a few strands of hair off my face, looks deep into my eyes. "I would *never* cheat on you. How could that thought even enter your head?"

Told you.

Grant kisses me, then disappears into the bathroom, and I hear the shower running. He's most definitely jerking off in there, but who can blame him? I tore badly when Ella came out. It's going to be at least another month before the man sees any action, especially if he keeps skimping on foreplay.

Down the hall, Ella starts to stir. There's a light, heady feeling low in my stomach that spreads up into my chest at the sound of her sweet little noises. I may be permanently tired, I may be scarred from ever having sex with my husband again, but for Ella, it's worth it. A trillion times over.

I pluck her from her crib, holding her warm, snuggly body against mine, nuzzling my nose into the soft roll of her neck. I walk back down the hall with her and climb into bed. I slide the top of my nightie down and feel her latch onto me, instinctively, the two of us locked in a rhythm more primal and intimate than anything I've ever known. *This* is how I like to start my mornings.

While Ella feeds, I check my phone. I have dozens of Instagram notifications, per usual, followers complimenting my nightgown and begging for my Tatcha discount code. My "mommy group" chat is blowing up; Allegra has a clogged duct and everyone is offering their favorite home remedies. A piping-hot washcloth; coconut oil; thinly sliced organic potatoes laid all over the affected breast.

I have a message from Mara trying to organize an anniversary dinner for our parents in September. And lastly, there's a text from Billie.

> Hey, stranger, I miss you. Let's get something on the books? Lunch, dinner, coffee . . . I know your life is crazy right now, so whatever's easiest. x

Guilt wobbles through me as I switch Ella to the other breast. It isn't just guilt, though. With Billie, it's more complicated than that. It's anxiety. Mild distaste. A discomforting, aged-out kind of love, and something else fraught. Billie just doesn't get my life. As the years have passed, the gap between us has only grown wider. Now, we exist on separate islands.

I scroll up through my older texts with Billie, realizing that I never responded to her last few messages. I can't remember now if ignoring her was even conscious, but it's possible. I haven't exactly been *eager* to talk to Billie. My armor is that I've been swamped. I have an infant, not to mention a chaotic entrepreneurial job. She can't take it personally.

Grant emerges from the bathroom, freshly shaven, a thick white towel hooked around his waist. He rakes his fingers through his damp hair.

"Nice shower?" I raise an eyebrow. I can't help it.

Grant gives a demure smile. He looks his best just after he's shaved off the stubble. He comes over to the bed and smooths my hair, then leans down to kiss Ella's tiny cheek.

"My beautiful girls."

"Question for you."

"Yeah?" He digs through his dresser for boxers. I watch the towel fall from his waist and land in a heap on the floor, where it will stay all day unless *I* pick it up. I open my mouth, then close it, resisting the urge to nag him before either of us have had coffee.

"Well, Billie texted me."

"Billie? You haven't seen her in a while."

"I know." I groan. "So I'm thinking I should just grab a drink with her tonight. Get it over with."

Grant chuckles. "You know she's not exactly my favorite person, but she's not *that* bad. But if you're asking if I can watch Ella later, the answer is yes. I'll be home before Lourdes leaves."

"Just for an hour or so." I pick at the pale pink polish on my thumbnail. I peel off a whole strip without thinking. It's a bad habit. Manicure ruined.

Grant yanks on a pair of blue boxers dotted with little sail-boats. "Of course. Stay out longer than that, if you want. Is there an occasion?"

I shake my head. "Just that I haven't seen her since Ella was like, a week old, and I can't ignore her forever."

"Well, you shouldn't really ignore your best friend at all."

"Billie isn't my best friend." I bend my knees and prop Ella up against my thighs. She smiles, all gums, a little milk dribbling down her chin.

"Well, she was when you and I met. And that was only three years ago."

I watch Grant as he buttons his dress shirt, and I can't believe it's been just three years. One year of dating before the proposal, one year of planning the wedding, one year of being pregnant and having a newborn. We moved quickly, in retrospect. But I was almost thirty-two when we met. I knew what I wanted. I didn't have time to waste.

"Feels longer than that, huh?" Grant poses, reading my mind.

"I just can't believe I'll be thirty-five soon." I make a face.

"Thirty-five is young, Cassie." He winks at me in the floor-length mirror while knotting his tie. "Plus, you look hotter than ever." He grabs his jacket from where it's draped on the back of the armchair. "I'll put the coffee on before I go."

"Thanks."

Grant notices the angst on my face. "Don't stress about Billie. I know you guys have drifted apart, but she's harmless."

I chew my bottom lip, then tap out a response before I can change my mind.

> Sorry I've been MIA! Miss you, too. We're actually around this weekend, not going out to Hamptons bc painters are there. Free for a glass of wine tonight? 6:30?

Her reply comes thirty seconds later. YES!

After Grant leaves for the office, I stick Ella in her bouncy chair on the kitchen floor and pour myself a cup of coffee. The second the first sip hits my bloodstream, I feel better. The tiredness dissipates, replaced by a feeling of ignition, a spark. One of the things I adore about Grant is that he shares my love—my *need*—for great coffee. Not the crappy, pre-ground pencil shavings you buy at the supermarket. The real stuff. Whole bean, home ground, French pressed. He makes it for us every morning—it's part of our routine. For some reason, it's never as good when I do it.

I take a selfie for my followers, clutching the steaming mug in front of my face. I caption: *My husband makes the best coffee in the world. And without caffeine, I am nothing.*

I have several new DMs from more people asking for the Tatcha discount. I jiggle Ella's chair with one foot while I scroll through my email, digging up the message from Tatcha's company rep. I find the code, then navigate back to Instagram. I study myself in the camera. I haven't washed my face yet, but I don't look bad. My skin is dewy from sleep and sun-kissed from spending most of the summer out in East Hampton. Thin lines run across my forehead and crack into the edges of my eyes, but it's nothing a filter can't fix. I hit the white circle at the bottom of the screen to record a story.

"Morning, guys, I'm just here having a little coffee with my tiny best friend. . . ." I flip the camera around for a moment to show Ella, happily sucking on her pacifier in the bouncy chair. "Anyway, sorry for the delay, but I got you my code for twenty percent off *anything* from Tatcha; it's CASSIE20, all caps. The moisturizer I tried last night is called the Water Cream; it's *super* light, so if you're like me and get oily in the warm weather, this one's for you."

I upload the story, take another sip of coffee. People often assume it's draining, the incessant attention this app requires of me. Almost fifty thousand followers, hungry for my content. Grant pokes fun at me, mostly for my abysmal screen time. My mom calls, confused as to why I'm sharing the details of Ella's birth story on social media. How is that helping business for Cassidy Adler, she wants to know. In recent months, I've noticed that a handful of peers from high school and college have unfollowed me. I know what they think: *Just another dumb, shallow girl on Instagram assuming everyone cares about her day-to-day life.*

But here's the thing: people *do* care about my day-to-day life. A lot of people care. And that's why I ignore Grant's remarks about my phone usage. I ignore the fact that my mom's generation can't grasp that it's not just the store I'm selling—it's me. I box the haters from high school out of my mind. Because the more I post, the more followers I acquire. And if I'm being honest, the sight of my following climbing higher and higher each day is a rush, a dopamine hit I wouldn't trade. The fact that all these people legitimately care about my life isn't draining; it's invigorating. And the real win is, the more followers I acquire, the more awareness I'm bringing to Cassidy Adler. It's good—no, it's *great*—for the store. Soon to be *stores*, plural. Which reminds me. I hit the Record button again.

"On another note, let me give you guys a quick update on Cassidy Adler East Hampton, because I've had a bunch of you asking. So, we found an amazing space right in town—which, in full transparency, used to be a FedEx—so we're undergoing a bunch of renovations. I *hope* those will be finished this fall, but you know how these things go. It's going to be stunning, though; I'm trying to be patient, but I seriously can't *wait* for you all to see it. If everything goes according to schedule, I'm hoping we'll open early next spring. I promise to keep you guys looped in, and in the meantime, come visit us in SoHo, because we have tons of cute stuff in for fall. Okay, my stomach is growling; Mama needs her morning smoothie, but I'll hop back on here later and show you guys some of my favorite new fall pieces. Bye for now!"

I smile and wiggle my fingers at the camera. I rewatch the story before I upload. I'm rambling; it's not my best. But my stomach is actually eating itself—breastfeeding has sent my metabolism into overdrive—and I don't have the patience to film it all again.

Less than a minute after I post, the DMs are flying in, messages from strangers that fill me, feed me.

> *HOW ARE YOU THIS GORGEOUS*
>
> *Literally obsessed with Cassidy Adler SoHo and so excited for the Hamptons store. My fam has a place in Quogue!*
>
> *You rock that Celestine nightgown sooo well, I've been influenced, purchasing asap*

And then, a familiar name in my inbox. Her.

> *billie_west: can't wait to see you tonight!*

I cringe, my heart sinking for a reason I can't quite articulate. It didn't used to be this way. But lately, it feels impossible to be around Billie without going back, without feeling the heaviness of everything that happened in that past life.

And I can never go back. Not now, not when I've come this far.

Chapter Three

Billie

Summer 2000

The sun is sizzling, scorching. The town pool is the only relief, even if it's so chlorinated it leaves my skin so dry it starts to crack.

My friend Ashton says the pool has to have that much chlorine, since the little kids pee in it. There's even the occasional turd floating in the shallow end, bobbing along the bright aqua surface like a small river log until one of the lifeguards fishes it out with a net. This pool is a dump, but it's cheap for town residents. The one at the country club half an hour south is much nicer, but I overheard Mom say it costs thousands of dollars to belong there, and we don't have that kind of money to throw around.

Ashton hands me the Hawaiian Tropic, and I rub some onto my stomach, where it forms a greasy puddle in my belly button. Mom berates me for using tanning oil without a shred of SPF, warning that I'll look like a wrinkled leather handbag by the time I'm her age. But at twelve, that's far enough away to be irrelevant, and besides, all that really matters is getting as tan as possible.

Ashton tells me she's going to the snack bar to get lunch. I lie back on the chaise and close my eyes, inhaling the banana-coconut scent of the oil and savoring the heat of the sun on my body. I tilt my head to the side, and when I blink my eyes open, a girl is sitting there who isn't Ashton. She's in a magenta bikini, her dark brown hair in two long braids that fall past her shoulders and end at her midsection. When I catch her watching me, her eyes flicker away, settling into the magazine on her lap.

I pick up the bottle of Hawaiian Tropic from the dry grass below my chaise, hold it out to her. "Want some?"

She turns to me, her wide mouth spreading into a smile. "Thanks."

She's startlingly pretty, but in a way that takes me a minute to register. She has an elegant sort of nose that's long and slopes up at the tip, and her cheekbones are sharp, jutting out like knobs below her wide-set eyes. Her olive skin is smooth, poreless.

I watch her rub the tanning oil into her long, chopstick legs, envying her stick-thinness. My own body has recently been hijacked by new pockets of flesh: curvy hips, breasts that spill out of my Gap training bras.

"I bought this same stuff at the pharmacy, and my mom freaked out and said it would give me skin cancer." The girl hands me the bottle of Hawaiian Tropic. "She dumped it straight in the trash. She's such a massive bitch."

"My mom says the same thing."

"But she doesn't take it away from you like you're a little baby." The girl scrunches her nose. I notice that her hair—where it's loose above her braids—is curly. "I'm Cassie, by the way. We just moved here last week."

"I'm Billie."

"Billy? Isn't that a boys' name?"

I feel a stab of self-consciousness. "It's spelled with i-e on the end."

"Like the Michael Jackson song?" Cassie grins. "'Billie Jean'?"

"Ugh. That's what my mom's awful boyfriend calls me."

She raises an eyebrow. "Noted."

I smile. "I like your bathing suit."

"Do you? It's my sister Mara's. But I hate her and would totally lend it to you."

"Why do you hate her?"

"I dunno. Mostly because she thinks she's better than everyone, and she talks down to me even though she's only a year and a half older."

Ashton wanders back from the snack bar, balancing a plate of chicken fingers and a can of Mott's apple juice.

"Hey." She looks from Cassie to me, then back to Cassie. "Uh, that's where I was sitting. My bag is right there."

Cassie gives a wry smile, then swings her long legs over the side of the chaise and stands. "All yours."

Ashton leans over and dangles a soggy fry in my face. "Want one, Billie?" She pulls it away, stuffs it down her own throat. "Kidding," she says, her mouth full. "Fried food is the last thing you need."

I feel my face turn hot, beet red. I bite the inside of my lip, bottling my shame.

Ashton rolls her eyes. "Oh, come on. You were just telling me your jeans don't fit."

Cassie pulls on drawstring shorts, slides a white tank top over her head. She glances at me. "I'm ready to walk into town, if you're still coming?"

I stare at her. Something warm and sudden blooms in my chest, blotting out the humiliation and anger. "Right. Yeah." Cassie's bright blue eyes latch onto mine, and it's like we're in on a secret. I shift toward Ashton without really looking at her. "I told Cassie I'd show her around town. She's new here. See you later."

"Right now? But I—um, okay. Whatever, I guess." Ashton shrugs, her expression wounded.

When we're out of the pool gate, Cassie hooks her elbow through mine like it's something we've done a thousand times.

"That girl is vile," she says. "Who drinks apple juice from a can?"

Chapter Four

Billie

August 25, 2023
49 days before

We meet at a wine bar near her apartment in Gramercy. I'm in actual shock that Cassie is available the very day I text her. A few years ago, we always used to meet up on a whim. But that was a different time. That was before she got so evasive. So goddamn hard to pin down.

Tonight, her availability feels like a gift. Something precious and rare.

I wish it were darker in the bar. I don't want Cassie to see my flushed cheeks, my greasy roots that I didn't have time to wash. Sweat pricks the nape of my neck as I slip between the tables, moving to where I see her sitting in the back. I hate how excited I am, how desperate I know I appear. I am a self-sufficient woman with a busy life, other friends. Around Cassie, I turn to putty.

She flashes her wide smile, white teeth glowing, spreading across her face like a string of lights. "Hey, Bill." She stands, hooking her arms around my shoulders. It's a flimsy hug. She's wearing a dress, something long and gauzy that probably retails for $800 and looks like everything else in her store. Her sharp, floral perfume—Viktor & Rolf's Flowerbomb, the same scent she's worn for years—seeps into my nostrils.

"Hey, Cass." I slide into the seat across from her. "It's been forever."

"I know, right?"

The truth sits between us, heavy; the elephant in the room. All the texts I've sent her, most of them unanswered. The voicemails I've left. My blatant effort. Her blatant disdain. Or perhaps it's her indifference. I'm not sure which is worse.

"The summer, it gets away from me every time. And with Ella, it's just been . . ." Cassie sighs, twirling a lock of hair around her pointer finger. She doesn't need to say more. The baby is the excuse.

"Well, it looked like an incredible summer," I offer, forcing another unspoken truth into the space between us. The fact that she puts her entire life on social media for all to see. The fact that if anyone wanted to know how Cassie Adler's summer went, all they'd have to do is glance at their phone. Through the thirteen square inches of my screen, I've seen every corner of the lavish second home she and Grant recently purchased in East Hampton, where they've spent nearly every weekend since Memorial Day. I've witnessed every trip to the farmers' market, every dinner party, every beach walk, every Melissa Wood exercise class. Every element of her existence is documented—at least, the bright and shiny parts.

If Cassie feels a flicker of self-consciousness, or if anything is less than perfect about her life, she doesn't show it.

"Grant and I come here sometimes," she says, changing the subject as she gestures to the bottle of wine in the cooler between us. "I ordered our favorite white Burgundy." Her sleeve slips to her elbow and two shiny bangles clink—gold, matching. I may live under a rock when it comes to fashion, but even I know what a Cartier Love bracelet looks like. The last time I saw Cassie, she was wearing only one.

Our glasses are already filled; I reach for mine and take a sip. The wine is dry and tart, ice cold. I haven't eaten since lunch, and it rushes straight to my head, dulling the hard edges of my thoughts, leaving my stomach toasty.

"It's good," I tell her, because it is. It's probably an expensive bottle.

"You look thin." She raises one of her thick, dark eyebrows in a way that tells me it's a compliment.

"Do I?" I know I do, a little bit. Work has been nuts, and when I'm slammed, I do a poor job of feeding myself. I forget to eat for hours during the day, then crash on the couch around dinnertime with a bag of popcorn, too zonked to make an actual meal. It's a bad habit.

Cassie spins her wineglass around in her fingers. I notice her manicure, pale pink and glossy, a single strip of polish peeled from her thumb. Cassie's bad habit is picking at her nails.

A diamond the size of a tooth glistens against her knuckles. It screams: *I'm taken. I'm married to someone phenomenal who can afford these four gargantuan carats, no problem.*

No shit, Grant is rich. He's a hedge fund guy, with serious family money on top of that. He's swimming in more wealth than anyone will ever actually need, and that's exactly what Cassie wanted. I'm perpetually reminding myself that I shouldn't be surprised by the life she's ended up with.

Cassie has come a long way from the girl she was when we met—frizzy-haired, forced to shop at Old Navy and Marshalls like everyone else in our small, middle-class town. And I wonder, not for the first time, what it's like for her now. To be loaded to the point of total disregard for dollar amounts. I steal a glance at the menu. There's only one white Burgundy on the wine list, and the bottle is priced at $165.

"You look pretty, Billie." Cassie smiles. "Tell me how you are. What's new?"

What she really wants to know is if there's a guy. So I tell her about Alex, omitting the fact that there's a high probability I'll never see him again. I explain how we met on a dating app, how he's a cop who lives in Chelsea.

"A cop?" Cassie wrinkles her nose—just slightly, but I notice. "Interesting."

"He's hoping to become a detective," I say as if this will change her opinion of him. I know Cassie well enough to be sure that in her mind, any kind of law enforcement job is strictly blue-collar.

"He's super sweet," I add. "Genuine. A really good guy." There's a tender glow behind my rib cage, and I wonder if it's about Alex or if I'm just happy to be sitting in front of Cassie, talking to her, after so many weeks and months of wishing I could talk to her.

She laughs. "So the sex is good?"

I love this about Cassie, the way she blows through any barriers I've envisioned in my head, proving that all the time in the world can pass and we'll still be us. We'll pick up right where we left off. The distance between us—all that space, the two of us off living our own lives—is rapidly shrinking.

"Well." I laugh, too. My head feels buzzy and light.

She rolls her eyes playfully. "Let me guess. You haven't had sex yet."

"It's only been three dates." I don't tell her about our last date, how badly I wanted to sleep with him. How I made myself walk away. The memory of his face—hopeful, respectful—picks at something inside of me.

"Fair."

"So why is that funny?"

"I don't know." Cassie sighs, reaching for the bottle and refilling our glasses. "I miss you, Bill."

There's a puncture of shock at my chest, followed by burgeoning relief that floods my body like a drug. Cassie has been my best friend since I was twelve—that's twenty-three years. The bulk of my life. For better or for worse, I've never felt whole without her.

"I miss you so much, Cassie."

"I know I've been all over the place." She gives her head a little shake. She looks like she might cry.

"Well, you have Ella. You have the store."

"I know. Life is insane with a baby. I mean, I'm so happy, but . . . it's a shit show sometimes. I'm just so fucking tired—" She presses her index fingers to the corners of her eyes.

"Hey." I reach across the table for her hand, tears of my own swimming in my throat. "I love you."

"I love you, too." She sniffles. "Jesus, what the hell is wrong with me? I don't know why I'm getting so emotional. I'm such a lightweight."

"It's okay, Cass. It's just me."

She blinks, nodding softly. "Hey, what're you doing the weekend after Labor Day? McKay and Tom are coming over for dinner that Saturday."

I swallow hard, an image of McKay filling my mind. Her glossy, platinum curtain of hair. Pert little nose. Saccharine smile. Grant's cousin. The girl who wrapped my best friend tighter and tighter around her finger, until one day I woke up and it was McKay, not me, who Cassie was asking to be her maid of honor.

"Why don't you come, Bill?"

"Huh?"

"To dinner. At our place on the ninth." Cassie stares at me with wide, expectant eyes. "Bring Alex."

The corners of my mouth lift on instinct. I have zero interest in fraternizing with bitchy McKay and her dull-as-cardboard husband, Tom, but it's been almost a year since Cassie invited me over.

"I'm not sure about bringing Alex."

"Uh, you were just telling me how great he is." Cassie rolls her eyes. "Billie. You're going to have to let someone in eventually."

Why? I want to challenge. *Because that's what you did?*

I tear at the edge of my cocktail napkin. In this vulnerable, wine-induced moment, I want to tell her. I want to let the cooped-up torrent inside me tumble out like a flash flood. *Alex is like Remy,* I'd start. *I just know he is. Close with his parents and siblings, you know the type. And I can't let history repeat itself. I can't even chance it.*

I imagine the relief of sharing this with Cassie, and for a moment, it's almost enough.

But Cassie is looking at me hopefully, with such optimism. This is the best—well, the only—night we've had in months, and I can't fuck it up with a confession she won't understand. If only I could be what she wants me to be. If only it were that easy.

"I get back from Portugal that Thursday, so yeah, Saturday sounds fun." I hesitate. "And I'll ask Alex if he's free."

"*Portugal.* You little world traveler. God, I'm envious." She wrinkles her nose in a way that reminds me of teenage Cassie, pesky and rebellious. So much rougher around the edges than she is now.

"We're scouting a new property in the Azores. I'm excited."

"You seriously have the coolest job. I'm so proud of you, Billie. You have a career most people dream of."

I watch the locked smile on Cassie's face, the familiar set of her ocean-blue eyes. Her flattery feels genuine, and I'm propelled to match it.

"I'm proud of you, too. The incredible business you've built, and all while becoming a mom? It's so badass." I pluck the wine from the cooler, tilting it in her direction. "We've got some work to do on this bottle."

Cassie presses her lips together, rolling them inward. She glances down at her phone on the table, then lifts her gaze. I already know what she's going to say. "I should really get back. Ella's been waking up at the crack of dawn, and I need to be in bed early." Her voice trails, spinning off into silence.

I despise this—the fact that women with children have a permanent, incontestable excuse to bail. Cassie and I have been at the bar for less than an hour.

"Right." I swallow my annoyance as I scan past her shoulder for our waitress, waving for the check. "If you need to run, I can Venmo charge you."

"Do you mind?" Cassie stands, gathering her phone and black Hermès bag, tiny dots puncturing the leather to form the coveted *H*. "Sorry to rush out. I get worried about Grant, leaving him alone with her."

I want to challenge this—I want to make her clarify which thing she's concerned about: Is it getting to bed on time, or is it Grant? I want to remind her that Grant is Ella's father, that he can deal with his kid for one goddamn hour—but I can't. I have zero authority on the subject.

"It was great to see you," I say instead.

"Bill." She leans down and gives me a tight hug. I inhale the sharp jasmine-and-rose notes of her perfume. "It was *so* great. I hope you come to dinner on the ninth. We need to see each other more. We need to do better."

The way she holds on to the hug a few beats too long tells me that she's sorry for something she'll never articulate. When she pulls away, the apology is there on her face, in her eyes. It's refreshing. It's the old Cassie.

I nod, my heart pulsing with old, loyal love. "Get home safely. Give Ella a squeeze for me."

The minute she's gone, our waitress drops the check next to my glass. More than $200 for the wine with tax and tip. I cork the remaining half of the overpriced bottle and stick it in the old *New Yorker* tote bag I've been using as a purse.

I drink the rest at home, my legs tucked underneath me on the couch. A dark nostalgia courses through my body, but I'm not exactly sad. I don't know what I am. I want to text Cassie, to call her, to tell her to come over and finish the wine with me. That an hour together in three whole months isn't enough. But it's a ridiculous thought, and I push it out of my mind.

I grab my phone from the coffee table and google "Cartier Love bracelet." The search results tell me that the piece of jewelry retails for $6,900. I open the RealReal app and find a used one for $6,000 flat, minimal scratches on the exterior. I consider whether I could ever be the kind of person who justifies spending that amount of money on a bracelet. Two months' rent. Seven round-trip tickets to Bali, my favorite place on earth. Four hundred and sixty-three Kale Caesars from Sweetgreen.

I exit the app and scroll through my texts with Alex. He hasn't reached out since I cut our date short the night before, and for the first time all day, I let myself feel what I actually feel: disappointment. A wrenching, wringing feeling in my stomach that won't subside. I think of Cassie's words: *Billie. You're going to have to let someone in eventually.*

And my next thought, involuntary: *What if?*

Maybe it's the wine, but I tap out a text, hit Send before I have time to convince myself otherwise.

> Hey! I know this is a ways off, but my best friend is having a small dinner party at her apartment on Saturday, 9/9, just after I get back from Portugal. It might be kind of a boring crowd (mostly new parents), but any chance you're free and want to join?

I sink back into the couch and open the *New York Times* Crossword app. I'm addicted to doing the puzzle—like Mom was—and almost always finish it daily, even on weekends. *It makes me happy,* I think to myself as I consider a Japanese noodle spelled with four letters. My habits, my work, my time. The tower of novels on my nightstand that never incites an iota of guilt, because I know I'll read all of them. The freedom to live life for no one but myself, on my own terms.

Soba. It clicks with a jolt of satisfaction, just as my phone vibrates. Alex's response heats the space behind my collarbone, and it's something stronger than consolation.

> If you're there, it won't be boring. Count me in.

Chapter Five

Cassie

August 26, 2023
48 days before

McKay waits for me at the corner of Twenty-first and Lexington. The sight of her—long buttery hair, linen blazer, palms resting on the handlebar of her stroller—quite literally warms my heart. I'm so lucky she's my best friend. My go-to person. Ella's godmother.

She hands me a Starbucks cup and grins, and I think of the first time we met, outside Annenberg Hall on move-in day freshman year. She wore athletic shorts and a T-shirt with HOTCHKISS stamped across the front in navy block letters, her face flushed pink from exertion, blond wisps coming loose from her ponytail. It was clear she'd just been for a run.

I'd worked up the courage to ask her where she was from, because *she* was the kind of girl who I knew—even in sweaty workout clothes—would be good to know.

"Marblehead." She drank from her Nalgene. "You?"

"Greenwich," I'd answered quickly, without a thought. It was mostly true, anyway.

She'd considered me then, a smile playing over her mouth, and I could almost see the conclusion running through her mind. *A pretty blonde from Marblehead and a pretty brunette from Greenwich. It makes sense for us to be friends.* But her next question caught me off guard.

"Did you go to Greenwich Academy?"

"I—no." I closed my mouth, suddenly anxious. It wasn't like I could just lie to this girl. "I actually went to high school in Red Hook, in the Hudson Valley?" I hated the insecurity in my voice, the way it spun off at the end to turn a clear statement into a question. "My family moved upstate. I'm originally from Greenwich, I should have clarified."

"Oh." McKay had folded her arms, the Nalgene dangling from the bend in her pointer finger. I remember the way she scrunched her nose just a little, but I don't like to think about that. "I should get upstairs," she'd said, glancing toward the dorm. "I have a lot more unpacking to do."

A friendship with McKay didn't happen overnight. It took a while for us to develop our now sister-like closeness, but the greatest things in life are always earned. Seventeen years later, here we are. Best friends—cousins by marriage—living in the same Manhattan neighborhood, married to the loves of our lives, with babies just six weeks apart. Finn is McKay's second. Her oldest, Juliette, is almost three. The fact that McKay is already a mother of two gets under my skin if I let myself think about it. I'm almost thirty-five, and Ella is my first baby. If only it hadn't taken me so long to find Grant.

"*El!*" McKay reaches down into my stroller and touches Ella's pillowy cheek. "She really is more beautiful every time I see her."

I gratefully accept the oat-milk latte, and we exchange a quick hug, even though we see each other multiple times a week, and most weekends. McKay and Tom have a place out east, too. This is the first Saturday we've both been in the city all summer.

"You're saving me with this coffee. One was not enough this morning." I glance down into the bassinet of McKay's stroller. "Hiii, Finny. Sweet boy." McKay and I never get sick of gushing over each other's kids.

We fall in line side by side and push our matching Bugaboos west on Twenty-third Street, toward Madison Square Park. It's not yet ten, but the sun beats down in splintering rays. McKay sheds her blazer, tosses it in the basket of the stroller.

"It's *hot*," she whines. "Remind me never to spend an August weekend in the city again."

"Yeah, I'm shocked you guys stayed."

McKay groans. "Tom's college roommate is getting married at the Carlyle tonight."

"*Oh.* I forgot. Woof."

"I absolutely detest when people have weddings in the city in the middle of the fucking summer. Like, in what world?" McKay sighs, then launches into a venting session about the hurdles of planning this year's Young Fellows Ball at the Frick, where she's on the board. McKay sits on several boards; she left her job at Sotheby's after Juliette was born.

"I feel like I might need to give up my seat after the ball this year," she's saying. "It's too much. I want to focus on redecorating the apartment, you know? I've been trying to switch out the wallpaper in Juliette's room for months. And it's just like . . . I haven't had a moment. Even with Mariana here thirty hours a week. Who knew volunteering would be this much of a time suck?" She laughs, then thinks better of it and touches my arm. "Wait, sorry. Here I am complaining about having no time, and you're, like, in full entrepreneur mode."

"Don't apologize. You're allowed to vent." I stifle a yawn, take another sip of my latte.

"Tired?" McKay eyes me. "What'd you do last night?"

"You won't believe it." I groan. "I got a drink with Billie."

McKay raises an eyebrow. "How'd *that* happen?"

I shrug. "You know she's always bugging me to get together. I just had to check it off my list."

"I get it." McKay glances to our left, where a man is sitting on a bench playing a familiar Sinatra tune on the accordion, his case an open tip jar at his feet. Her gaze flickers back to me. "But you can't do *everything* for *everyone.* You're a mom now. Your life is insane."

I nod. "That's what I always tell Billie. She just has this way of making me feel . . . guilty."

"That's fucked up. She doesn't get it. She doesn't have kids."

"Right?" Chatting with McKay is like a tonic.

We plop down a few benches away from the accordion guy. I jostle the stroller back and forth with my foot as I sip my coffee. The caffeine is sharpening my vision, dulling the headache that sits behind my eyes.

"Sometimes we outgrow people," McKay says. "Like jeans."

"Like *jeans.* You're so right. I don't think I'll ever fit into my favorite Agoldes post-baby. It's like my hip bones have moved."

"They probably have."

"I accidentally invited her to the dinner party we're having on the ninth."

"Billie? *Why?*"

"I don't know." I run my tongue across my teeth. "Honestly, I was tipsy and getting weirdly sentimental, and I blurted it out. She's seeing some new guy she's going to bring."

"Great."

"I obviously regret inviting her." A prick of self-consciousness creeps in. "But she's harmless," I add, echoing Grant's words from yesterday.

McKay adjusts Finn's sock over his tiny foot. "I just don't love being around people who explicitly dislike me."

"She doesn't dislike you," I say, even though we both know it's a lie. Billie has been cold to McKay ever since I asked her to be my maid of honor. She'd never admit it, but she can't stand the fact that it was McKay instead of her.

"She absolutely dislikes me." McKay gives a wry laugh, crosses her legs. "But honestly, whatever."

I fiddle with my necklace, the delicate gold chain with an *E* charm that Grant gave me after Ella was born. I can't help but think of all the things I haven't told McKay about Billie. Things I'll *never* tell McKay about Billie.

"I just feel like she gives off this holier-than-thou vibe," McKay continues. "Like she's silently judging us for making the life choice to have children. Like it's basic or something."

"Exactly." I pick the rest of the polish off my thumbnail. "Last night, she rolled her eyes when I said I had to go because I need to be in bed early, since Ella gets up at the crack. As if I'm using my baby as a pretext to be lame."

"God, that's rude."

"It's like nothing I do is ever enough for her."

"Because it *isn't* enough for her." McKay shoves her sunglasses—the black Celines we both own—down over her eyes. "Because she has nothing going on in her life besides work. It's sad. Is she still at that travel company?"

"Yeah. It's actually kind of amazing, the trips she gets to take. She left for Portugal today. She's going to Cuba later in the fall. I swear, she's in a different country every month."

"I'm sure it gets old, Cassie. It *sounds* glamorous, but she'll never be able to have a real life if she keeps that up. Marriage? *Kids?* Forget about it."

"I know." I adjust Ella's pacifier, which has fallen from her mouth. "I worry about Billie. I want her to find stability. I want her to be happy."

"Of course you do." McKay casts me a knowing smile. "Because you're a good person."

"Billie—she just, she makes me feel like I'm not. She makes me feel . . . self-involved. And superficial. I *hate* that." A fervent mixture of frustration and resolve tightens behind my ribs.

"Honestly, at the root of it, she's probably jealous of you."

I shake my head. "Billie's not the type to get jealous of other women."

"I'm sorry, but you have *everything* any woman could ever want. Amazing husband, beautiful baby, flourishing career as a smoking-hot and brilliant influencer slash small-business owner."

I shoot her a look, though my chest glows warm from the praise. McKay knows how to indulge me like this. She's uniquely capable of making me feel like the superhuman version of myself, and I love her for it. "Isn't *influencer* a stretch, Mick?"

"Not these days, babe. You're basically famous. Thousands of people are obsessed with you, with the store, with your life." One corner of her mouth curls. "And who's obsessed with Billie? *No one.*"

I drain the rest of my coffee, ready to change the subject. The Billie bashing is starting to feel like overkill, but this is the other thing about McKay. If you're not on her good side, she can get a little wicked.

I pull out my phone and open Instagram. "Let's take a pic."

McKay pushes her sunglasses on top of her head. "*Yes.* Only if you tag me. My famous best friend."

I snap a selfie of the two of us, our cheeks pressed together, our smiles relaxed—no teeth. I tilt the screen toward McKay so she can approve the picture before I post.

She grins. "It's cute."

I flip the camera around and film a short video of the babies side by side in their strollers: Ella sucking on the paci, Finn conked out peacefully, his heart-shaped lips parted. *If these two weren't related, they'd 100% be betrothed,* I caption with a winking emoji. It isn't my best—it might even be weird—but I'm too sapped to think of something genuinely clever.

As I upload the stories, I can't help but envision Billie's reaction when she watches them. Despite her compliments last night, I know she'll inevitably cringe. Billie has been flouting social media since Facebook became a thing in the aughts. She *has* an Instagram account, but almost never posts.

Ella begins to fuss in the stroller, her little face scrunching. I feel a wave of love for her as my nipples tingle on instinct—my milk coming down. It's crazy, the biology involved in motherhood. At the end of the day, we're all just animals.

I turn to McKay, clutching my chest. "I should go back and feed her before I ruin this shirt."

She nods—she gets it; neither of us expect our morning coffee dates to last long—and I thank my lucky stars for mom friends like McKay. We exit the park the way we came, winding our way through the paved path and out on Twenty-third.

"You guys will be out east for Labor Day, right?" McKay pulls her hair back into a low pony. Beside us, the street is clogged with traffic. A cabbie blares his horn, leaning out the window to curse at a pair of jaywalkers.

I nod. "The painters will be finished on Tuesday, thank God. So I think we'll head out Thursday. There's someone coming to give us a quote on a pool—I'm still trying to persuade Grant—and I desperately need to check on the store."

"*Do* the pool. You won't regret it." McKay unfolds the pale blue canopy of her stroller, shading Finn. "I'll have Tom convince Grant. Our pool in Amagansett changed his life. You think you don't need one in the Hamptons, but I'm telling you, the beach with kids—once they're mobile—is sheer hell."

I laugh. "Oh, I don't doubt it."

Ella is really fussing now, her legs kicking violently, and this is our cue. I wave goodbye. "Let's walk on Monday?"

"Yes! Let's rope Blake in and do Gramercy Park. I'm so endlessly jealous their new place has a key."

"Ooh, that's right. Okay, I'll text you. Have fun at the wedding, Mick."

It's quiet and empty back in the apartment, and I feed Ella on the living room couch. She curls into me, instantly calming as she begins to suckle my breast. It's a relief for both of us, her feeding, and a sense of deep contentment washes through me, smoothing over the hard edges of the anxiety that's cropped up since I saw Billie.

I worried about breastfeeding, before Ella came. I'd heard horror stories of the agony, of mothers with bloody nipples shredded by tongue-tied infants. But Ella and I fell into an easy rhythm almost instantly; there was initial discomfort, acclimating, but never pain.

I gaze down at her profile, the dark sweep of her eyelashes against her cheek, her milky mouth suckling, and I'm struck by our mammalian connection, more intimate than anything I've ever known. I am her mother, her literal sustenance, and she is my young. It's a wild, pre-language kind of love—primal and boundless.

At its lucid root, I know one thing: if another being ever tries to hurt her, I'll do everything in my power to destroy them.

Chapter Six

Billie

Fall 2001

Mom takes Cassie and me to the mall one Friday after school. Limited Too is having a sale. I don't care about clothes as much as Cassie does, but when Mom offered to take us, I knew it would make Cassie happy.

"Your mom is so nice." Cassie's voice is tinged with longing. "Mine refuses to set foot in the mall."

We're in the dressing room trying on jeans. Cassie pulls on a pair of dark-wash bell-bottoms with rhinestones lining the pockets, examining herself in the full-length mirror. She wants a new outfit for the high school homecoming dance on Saturday. We're only in eighth grade—still confined to the lameness of middle school—but Kyle Briggs, a freshman, invited Cassie over AIM.

U n ur friend r cute, *he typed last week.* Stop by homecoming this weekend. Jon is working the front door at the dance, he'll get u 2 in.

Cassie spins around. "What do you think?" She glances over her shoulder in the mirror, checking out her ass.

"I don't know." I fold my arms. "The rhinestones are a bit much."

Cassie purses her lips. "You're right."

"I mean, you look good, obviously," I add, because she does. Her dark curls fall almost to her belly button, her skin still golden brown from the summer.

She sighs. "Everything in here is tacky. We should go to Ralph Lauren."

"The Polo store? It's so expensive. They charge like triple the price just for that little horse logo."

Cassie frowns. "Their clothes are great, Billie. I have tons of Polo shirts." A beat of silence passes. "I guess I'll just steal Mara's Solow skirt for homecoming."

"She'll murder you if she finds out."

"What are you gonna wear?"

"I don't know. I need to dig through my closet."

"Let's go back to your house."

"How's it going in there, girls?"

Cassie pulls the dressing room curtain back. Mom is leaning against the wall, reading The New York Times. The news seems to be everywhere since the Twin Towers fell in September, and at home, Mom always has CNN on. The thought of what happened puts a pit in my stomach. A girl in our grade lost her uncle; he was one of the firefighters.

"These jeans are tacky, right, Mrs. West?" Cassie's voice is too loud; the sales girl glances over and frowns.

"For the millionth time, Cassie, Mrs. West is my ex-mother-in-law. Call me Lorraine." Mom looks up and wrinkles her nose. "But I'm not a fan of those shiny stick-on things."

"Rhinestones." I roll my eyes. "Can we go, Mom?"

She closes the paper. "I thought you'd never ask."

We stop for burgers on the way home. Cassie orders a black-and-white milkshake and slurps it down in the car.

"I'm forever jealous of your metabolism," I say.

"I'm forever jealous of your hair," she counters, pulling at a strand of her curls, her mouth bowing into a frown.

"Be proud of your curves, Billie," Mom urges. "We're a family of strong, voluptuous women."

Cassie giggles in the back seat, flexing her bicep. I make a face and steal her milkshake, chugging the last of it.

At home, Mom's boyfriend, Wade, is in the leather recliner watching football, as per usual. He's a big lump of a man, too lazy to do anything but drink beer and eat Ruffles straight from the bag. His beard always has little pieces of food stuck in it. Mom met him a year and a half ago, at the dental practice where she works as a hygienist. He was in for a teeth cleaning, which is ironic because he seems to have no other regard for personal hygiene. I don't know what Mom sees in him. Cassie thinks maybe Mom was just lonely, which could be true. Wade is the first man she's been serious with since my dad left us for a Southern woman named Melody. I was four at the time. I have an early memory *of Mom crying in her bathroom, and when I asked what was wrong, she told me her heart was broken.*

Wade glances up from the television, giving Cassie and me the once-over. "Hey, Billie Jean, Billie Jean's friend."

"It's Cassie," I tell him, even though I know he knows her name.

"You girls buy some nice new clothes?" Wade gives us a creepy grin.

When we don't respond, he sits up straighter. "Yoo-hoo? Anybody home?"

Cassie shrugs. "I almost got jeans, but I didn't."

"That's a shame." Wade's eyes linger on Cassie's long, thin body. "You'd look good in a new pair of jeans."

Next to me, I feel Cassie stiffen. The door to the kitchen swings open, and we're saved by Mom, who's carrying a plastic tray with Wade's re-heated cheeseburger.

"Here you go, baby." She hands Wade the tray, leaning down to kiss his greasy lips. "Extra bacon."

"What did I do to deserve a woman like you, Lorraine?" Wade gives her ass a little smack, then grabs a fistful of fries.

Later, after Cassie leaves, Mom comes up to my room to say good night. I'm in bed reading a Judy Blume book, and she sits at the edge of my mattress, pulls the covers up over my chest. The fact that she still tucks me in makes me feel like a baby, but I secretly love it. Mom is my favorite person in the world, tied with Cassie.

I inhale the familiar, fresh scent of her cucumber face cream. I close my creased paperback copy of Deenie.

"Mom. I know you love Wade, but he's kind of a perv."

Her eyebrows lift. "A perv?"

Guilt wobbles in my stomach. "I just mean . . . he says weird things to Cassie. Like, he told her she'd look good in new jeans and was checking her out." I don't mention the fact that I sometimes catch him checking me out, too. It feels like overkill.

"Bill." Mom sighs, smoothing the front of my hair. "Wade is a genu-inely friendly man. I'm sure you're misinterpreting whatever he said. I know it's hard, me being with someone other than Dad—"

"What? That's not it. I barely have a relationship with Dad."

"Billie." She looks sad, but then something in her caramel eyes hard-ens. "I want you to give Wade a chance."

I pick at a scab on my arm, a late-summer mosquito bite that refuses to heal. I glance up at my mother. She's forty-two, but she looks younger. The skin around her face is supple and smooth. A few threads of silver run through her honey-brown waves, but you can't see them unless you get close. When people tell me I look like her, it's the best thing on earth.

"I want you to give him a chance," she says again.

There's a bolt of anger in my throat—a raw lump—but I swallow it down. "Fine."

She gives my wrist a gentle pull. "Don't pick that scab."

"Can Cassie sleep over tomorrow? After the homecoming dance?"

"Of course. Wade and I are going to the movies. That new comedy with Ben Stiller."

"We can get a ride home."

"Just don't get in the car with anyone who's been drinking. You know that."

"I won't."

Mom brushes a lock of hair off my forehead. "Does Cassie like that high school boy? The one who invited you guys to the homecoming dance?"

"Kyle Briggs?" I shrug. "Maybe. He likes her."

"How do you know?"

"Because everyone likes Cassie, Mom."

My mother stands. She reaches to the left of my bed and pulls down the white pleated shade. It taps against the window.

"Cassie is a beautiful girl, but don't sell yourself short." Mom leans down, plants a kiss on my temple. "You look like me."

Chapter Seven

Billie

August 26, 2023
48 days before

Jane and I fly business class to Lisbon. I feel more alive on a plane than anywhere else. It's freeing, the knowledge that I have zero control over my circumstances when in flight. Jane feels the same, which is why we're kindred spirits as well as coworkers.

Technically speaking, Jane is my boss. The Path is Jane's company, a boutique luxury travel service she founded after working at several larger establishments in the industry. I was her first hire when The Path opened its doors three years ago, and we've since grown to a small but mighty team of fifteen. My title hasn't changed since I started—I'm still a luxury travel consultant—but Jane isn't the kind of entrepreneur to adhere to corporate lingo. What matters, she reminds me constantly, is that I'm her right-hand woman. Everyone at the company gets to travel, but not as much as Jane and I. We jet all over the world together, scoping out the hottest new hotels and restaurants and experiences around the globe, everything comped. Cassie wasn't wrong—my job is cool. I'm lucky. Most people dream of seeing the most beautiful and exotic corners of the planet; I actually get paid to do it.

It's early morning—barely 6:00 New York time—and Jane and I are both clicking away on our laptops as we speed across the Atlantic. I'm finishing up an itinerary for a client who's booked a vacation to Bora Bora—he's surprising his wife for their anniversary, and I'm working with the Four Seasons to have a pitcher of coconut mojitos waiting in their suite when they arrive. This kind of special attention is what we pride ourselves on at The Path. We don't just piece together the perfect itinerary; we take it a step further than that. My client didn't *ask* for

in-room coconut mojitos, but he did mention that was the cocktail he
and his wife drank on their first date, and I ran with the idea.

A flight attendant informs us we'll be landing in an hour and
smiles politely as she refills our coffees. I stir in two creams and a
packet of sugar; Jane drinks hers black. She takes a sip, then frowns.

"I swear, all airplane coffee is secretly decaf. I drink endless cups
of this shit, and it doesn't do a damn thing."

"Shh." I roll my eyes. Jane is not a morning person; she's notori-
ously grumpy before ten. "I'll get you a big strong cup of Portuguese
coffee when we land."

"We land at noon. By the time we make it to our hotel, I'll be ready
for a martini and a nap." She tilts her computer toward me. "What do
you think of this?"

It's a StreetEasy listing, like I knew it would be. Jane and her wife,
Sasha, have been apartment hunting for months. They've put in half a
dozen offers, but every single place they've liked has gone for well over
ask. Manhattan could not be less of a buyer's market at the moment.

I squint at the screen. "Two-point-two mil and it only has *one*
bathroom? That's highway robbery."

Jane groans. "Don't I know it. We're destined to grow old in our
East Village walk-up."

"The East Village isn't so bad."

"Yeah, if you're twenty-three and perpetually raging. I'm serious,
though. I'm starting to think we're never going to find a place. All the
good ones go like that." She snaps her fingers.

I give her a sympathetic smile. "Well, the good news is, you can't
fuck up what's meant for you."

The edges of her mouth play at a grin. "Wow. I love that."

I pick my phone up from where it sits beside my laptop on the tray
table. I'm not even bored, but at this point, opening Instagram is as
instinctual as scratching an itch.

A pink ring glows around Cassie's avatar—no surprise. I touch
it to see that she's already awake, stirring oatmeal on the stove while
Ella sits in a baby chair contraption on the counter, bouncing lightly
as she sucks her pacifier.

"This little girl has been up since five," Cassie narrates peppily.
"Thank God she's cute, is all I have to say!"

"Volume, please?"

I jerk up to see that Jane is watching me, annoyed.

"Sorry." I put my phone down, turn back to my computer.

Jane sips her coffee. "It's too ungodly an hour for me to endure the sound of Cassie Adler's voice."

I smile. Jane knows all about Cassie. They've only met twice, but Jane listens to me vent about Cassie all the time. Sometimes we watch her Instagram stories together and cringe. It makes me feel a little better.

"She invited me over the weekend after next," I say. "She's having some dinner party."

"Oooh." Jane's voice drips with sarcasm. "Sounds exclusive. Lucky you."

"I said I would go."

"Of course you did. She doesn't reach out to you for months—ignores your calls and texts—and the second she offers a bread crumb, you pounce."

"Weird analogy."

Jane shrugs, her expression tinged with frustration. "We both know I'm right."

The seat belt sign flicks on overhead, followed by a *ding*. The captain's voice comes through the loudspeaker, low and clear as he tells us to store our carry-on items as the plane makes its descent into the greater Lisbon area.

"Thank fucking God." Jane shuts her laptop, and it closes soundlessly, like an eyelid. "I'm ready for vodka and Egyptian cotton sheets."

"Can I ask you something?"

"Anything, my apprentice." Jane always jokes that I'm her "apprentice" since she's my boss, even though she's two years younger.

"Do you want kids?"

Jane's eyes widen in genuine surprise. It's not often that I catch her off guard. She presses her lips together, considering the question. "I do." She pauses again. "It's more complicated for Sasha and me, obviously. But when we're ready, we'll figure it out."

I nod. Jane has been married to Sasha for almost a year. Their wedding was at a beautiful lake in the Adirondacks last fall. I read a Mary Oliver poem during the ceremony, right before the vows.

"Sorry, I just—"

"What is this about, Billie? Is it Cassie?"

"I don't know." I sigh, swirling the chalky brown remnants of coffee around the base of my paper cup. "She's just so in my head."

"I *know* she's in your head. It isn't healthy."

"When we got drinks the other night, she just . . . I can't explain it. She doesn't say it out loud, but I know she's silently judging me for not . . . living the kind of life she is."

Jane snorts. "You mean, for not being married to a scummy trust fund man-child and birthing his babies and telling the whole world about it on camera? *Please.* She can claim that her store is a successful business—and maybe it is—but Cassidy Adler wouldn't exist without Grant, and everyone who knows her knows that."

"True." I swallow, my ears popping as the plane descends. "I just feel like she's become this completely different person. And if I don't figure out how to fit into her life the way she wants me to, she's going to drop me for good."

"Who cares? You don't need her, Billie."

But I do, I think, the heaviness of the conviction a stone in my heart. I close my eyes and I'm seventeen again. I'm sitting on the floor of Cassie's bedroom with my knees tucked into my chest, tears dripping down my face like rain, Alanis Morissette playing lightly from the speakers.

I'm sad, but I'm laughing
I'm brave, but I'm chickenshit

Cassie is beside me, her hand on my back, her voice like a healing balm. *I'm here, Billie. I'm here. I'll always be right here.*

The memory wraps around me like a fungus. I shake it off, suddenly cold.

"Cassie told me to bring Alex to dinner," I tell Jane after a moment. "So, I invited him."

"Well, that's good, right? You like Alex." Jane searches my face. When I say nothing, she sighs. "Bill. Not every story leaves off like yours and Remy's. You deserve a happy ending. You know that, right?"

I nod, but only so Jane will stop looking at me like that. "I just—I need armor when it comes to Cassie. I wish I could bring *you* to dinner."

Jane gives a thin laugh, tucks a lock of strawberry-blond hair behind her ear. "As *thrilling* as that sounds . . ." Her smile drops, her gaze grows serious. "You know I'm never getting within ten feet of Grant Adler again."

A roiling wave of dread crests and falls in my stomach. Sometimes I forget about what happened with Jane and Grant. I like to push it out of my mind so I don't have to think of it, don't have to remember the reason why my friendship with Cassie grew even more fraught than it already was.

The wheels of the plane touch down in Lisbon, my body lurching forward with a jolt. I love the adventure of being in a foreign place—it's my true passion—but landing always comes with a pang of sadness, too. Already I miss the sensation of being suspended in the air, caught between time zones and cities in a way that tables reality, that offers an interlude from the weight of my own existence.

Jane, on the other hand, is always relieved to be back on solid ground. She turns to me and smiles, her eyes bright. "Here we are."

Chapter Eight
Cassie

August 31, 2023
43 days before

We drive out to East Hampton on Thursday after lunch to beat the rush-hour traffic. Once we're on the Long Island Expressway, Grant hits the gas on his beloved BMW. We're going almost ninety.

"Slow *down!*" I yelp from the back, where I'm sitting next to Ella in her car seat. "Baby on board. Jesus."

Grant eases his foot off the pedal, but only slightly. "Relax, honey. This car cruises. Why don't you sit up front so you can actually enjoy the ride?"

"Because I like sitting back here with Ella," I protest, annoyed. "Seriously, slow *down*, Grant. You're making me nervous."

He sighs. "You're always nervous, Cassie. You need to fucking chill."

"Don't swear in front of the baby."

"You're one to talk. You always swear in front of the baby."

We bicker like this on and off for the duration of the two-and-a-half-hour drive. Once Grant and I fall into this rhythm of fighting like cats, it can be hard to break. By the time we reach the house in East Hampton, I'm so pissed I pluck Ella from her car seat and storm off, holding her close to my chest as I rush down toward the water. Grant can deal with the bags.

Grant has been coming out east since he was a kid; his parents own the house next door. Sometimes the proximity is too close for comfort, but luckily, my in-laws only spend the summer months here. When the home next to theirs went on the market, they snatched it up and gifted it to Grant and his brother, Reed, as part of their trust fund. But Reed is a surf instructor in Santa Barbara, so Grant bought him out last year, and now the property is fully ours. A five-bedroom, shingle-clad, light-filled colonial, nestled against Hook Pond with views of the ocean. It reminds me a little of my grandmother's house in Cape Cod. Grandma Catherine passed away when I was in college, but I like to think she would be proud of me for marrying a man like Grant. For living this kind of life.

I sit down on the grass and wedge Ella between my thighs. I take a selfie of us, my chin touching the top of her perfectly round head. *Out in the Hamptons with my girl for Labor Day Weekend,* I caption. *And checking on the store! Stay tuned for updates!*

The DMs flood in immediately.

OMG SHE'S SO CUTE

Yayyy! Can't wait for store updates

Ella is a beauty angel babe and so is her mama :)

The rush of praise never fails to lift my mood when I'm down, like the first sip of a strong cocktail after a bad day. In truth, I can't even remember why Grant and I are fighting. This tends to happen when we argue; in the aftermath, the specifics evade me with surreal speed. What I'm left with is the potent feeling of knowing I'm mad, the chemical residue of the anger in my body.

I wish he would come outside and find me—find *us*—but he doesn't. Eventually, Ella starts to fuss, and I catch a whiff of her diaper, and I have no choice but to surrender my own self-will and venture indoors.

Grant is sitting at the kitchen island, nursing a glass of scotch and looking at his phone. He hasn't bothered to unpack the cooler.

"Here." I thrust Ella in his face. "Why don't you go change a poopy diaper for once in your life."

"Jesus, Cassie," he snaps. "Why are you so *on me*? I thought we'd have a nice, relaxing weekend out here as a family, and you just have to make everything a fucking problem." He catches his mistake, sticks out his palm. "I'm sorry, I'm sorry, I swore in front of a three-month-old with no language comprehension. Take me out back and shoot me."

Grant and Ella disappear upstairs. I pluck a bottle of my favorite bone-dry Riesling from the wine cooler and pour myself a generous glass, fighting back tears. I want to run upstairs and tear Grant a new one for speaking like that about our daughter, as if she's brainless just because she's an infant, but for what? To argue all night, to be miserable for the rest of the weekend? Miserable forever?

The sun hangs low over Hook Pond, on the verge of torching the horizon. I open the french doors off the den and snap a picture of my wineglass against the sherbet sky.

Perfect way to start the long weekend, I caption. No one has to know it's the polar opposite of perfect.

When Grant and Ella come downstairs fifteen minutes later, I'm already on my second glass of Riesling.

"Fresh diaper, *and* I got her in her PJs." Grant gives me a small smile, his attempt at a peace offering.

Do you want a medal? I feel like asking.

"She needed a bath tonight," I say instead. I shouldn't, but I can't help myself. I'm sick of Grant's ignorance, of being the only parent who knows what's going on. "Don't you remember she had a blowout right before we left the apartment? She's dirty."

Grant presses his lips together, puffs air into his cheeks to let me know he's had it. "Okay, then. I'll go give her a bath."

He turns back toward the stairs, but I swoop in and grab her. "Just forget it. I'll do it."

"Why are you so stubborn?" he calls after me.

"Why are *you* so stubborn?" I parrot, indignant, shooting him a glare over my shoulder.

I give Ella a bath in her blue whale tub, her chubby legs kicking happily. She loves the warm water. I shampoo what little hair she has on her head—sandy blond, like Grant's was when he was young—while tears stream down my face. I smile through them, gazing down at my beautiful baby girl, grateful that she won't remember this moment. Her mess of a mother bathing her, eyes raw from crying.

In the morning, things feel mildly better. Grant gets up with Ella and lets me sleep, and when I wander downstairs just before nine, he hands me a mug of coffee. His hair is rumpled, the lines around his eyes sharp. He looks older than the man I fell for three years earlier.

"Hopefully someone woke up on the right side of the bed today." He gives a strained smile. It's the wrong thing to say, but he's trying. We're both too exhausted to keep fighting.

"Thanks for letting me sleep." I sit down on the edge of Ella's play mat and drink my coffee, watching her observe the colorful objects that dangle above her, cooing merrily. Clear lemony light streams in through the kitchen windows. It's a beautiful day.

"I have a noon tee time at Maidstone with my dad and Tom," Grant says. He cracks an egg against the side of the cast-iron pan. It hits the hot butter with a sizzle.

I frown. "I didn't know you were playing golf today. I need to—"

"You need to check on the store, I know. Why don't you go this morning? I'll stay with Ella."

I consider this. "All right." I nod. "Let me feed her first."

It's been over twelve hours since I've posted to Instagram, so after Ella nurses, I snap a few shots of our house and add them to my story. I make sure to highlight the most recently decorated spaces—our new Lee Jofa wallpaper in the entryway, the freshly painted living and dining rooms, the Restoration Hardware patio furniture that finally arrived after being back-ordered all summer.

"Decorating our Hamptons home has been endless fun," I narrate. "I hope some of these nooks and crannies bring a little sunshine to your Friday."

I tag the relevant designers and companies, including the name of the interior design firm we hired for the project.

One follower DMs me almost right away.

> *Nooks and crannies??? Umm u live in a fucking palace.*
> *Come back down to earth where the rest of us are.*

A knot of shame forms low and tight in my stomach. I consider taking down the story and revising my wording, but it's already been posted for a couple of minutes. Hundreds of people have already viewed the video. And I think of what McKay would tell me: *Once the haters come, that's when you know you've made it.* I know she's right. So I let the shame sit there, heavy and churning as I drive into town through the tree-lined streets, the edges of the green leaves dry and tinged with gold. End of summer. An old Alanis Morissette song is on the radio, and even though it reminds me of Billie, I blast it, feel my limbs loosen, wind rippling against my face through the open windows.

The Cassidy Adler storefront is primely located smack on the main drag of East Hampton, wedged between SoulCycle and a popular French restaurant. I've already hired a store manager, Wendy, a fortysomething divorcée who lives in Sag Harbor year-round and who is overseeing the renovation. She's there when I walk in, bright-eyed and bushy-tailed, our dispositions a clear clash. But seeing the store's progress instantly boosts my mood; I inhale the scent of sawdust and primer, admiring the pale wood beams that run along either side of the sloped ceiling. They're a new addition—just decorative, but they really elevate the space.

"The queen herself!" Wendy sings. She flips her chin-length hair, platinum blond, pin straight. "You look adorable, Cassie. So put together."

"Do I?" It's a rhetorical question. I know I look polished. These days, with more and more followers stopping me on the street, I can't afford to leave the house in less than my best. I smile at Wendy and smooth my hands over my hips. These Theory jeans were my go-tos before Ella was born; now, I'm just able to squeeze back into them. But I'm severely uncomfortable, the button straining against my still-doughy stomach. I should've worn Lululemons or a billowy sundress and spared myself the pain.

Wendy and I are flipping through a booklet of paint colors from Farrow & Ball—we're leaning toward a soft blue called Borrowed Light for the interior—when my phone vibrates in my back pocket. When I dig it out, *Mara* flashes across the screen. It's the third time she's called this week. Fuck.

I tell Wendy I need to take it and pace to the front of the store, pressing the phone against my ear. I forgot my AirPods at home.

"What do you need?" I keep my voice hushed.

"*That's* how you greet your one and only sister? Who you haven't spoken to in six fucking months?" Mara gives a sardonic laugh.

"I'm kind of working, okay?"

"I'd love to know what *kind of working* means. Is that what rich white women do?"

"Jesus, Mara. Don't act like you're not a white woman." I can feel Wendy's gaze on me from behind the desk. I swing open the front door and step out onto the sidewalk.

"Not a rich one," Mara says.

I lean against the store's white brick exterior. "Why are you calling?"

"I've been trying to reach you. Did you get my text? Mom and Dad's fortieth wedding anniversary is next weekend."

"Okay." I squint into the bright sky, wishing I'd remembered my sunglasses.

"So, it's kind of a big deal."

"Is it? Do they even like each other?"

"Cassie." Mara lets out a long breath. "I didn't *want* to call you, but it would mean a ton to them if you came for dinner on Saturday. Mom finally got Instagram, so they're fully updated on your life now, but still. Social media isn't a fix for everything."

I imagine my parents huddled on their twenty-year-old plaid couch watching my stories, a window into my life without them. The Cassidy Adler stores and Ella and my stylish friends and Grant and our multiple fancy homes. The thought makes me squirm.

"They'd love to see their granddaughter for a second time, too," Mara continues. "And Jack's never met his cousin."

I close my eyes, which burn with fatigue. I picture Mara on the other end of the phone and I see my own face, the exact set of my eyes on another person. My same fiery spite. Even though we haven't had a relationship in years, Mara still knows how to crawl under my skin and sit there.

I clench my back molars so hard pain shoots through my jaw. "We're busy next Saturday," I say, thinking of the dinner party Grant and I are hosting. I hesitate. "But we can make dinner on Sunday work."

"Wonderful." Sarcasm oozes from the word. "You're an angel for squeezing us in."

"Mara, you don't need—"

"One more thing," she says, cutting me off. "Just . . . keep it low-key when you're here, okay?"

"Huh?"

"Like, maybe leave the Hermès bag in the car. Try not to persuade Mom that an eight-hundred-dollar dress from your store will bring a little sunshine to her Friday."

My insides twist at her reference to my Instagram story from earlier. The shame rejigged, coursing through my veins like poison.

"Fuck you, Mara." Tears push up my throat.

"Fuck you, Cassie." I hear the derisive smile in her voice, the pulsing contempt. "See you next weekend."

The phone goes dead.

I'm wiping my face when the door swings open and Wendy appears beside me.

"Are you okay?" The concern in her question sounds genuine, maternal. Wendy's husband got the loft in SoHo, but she has full custody of her fourteen-year-old twins.

I glance down at my phone, at Ella's chubby, perfect little face spanning the lock screen. Her luscious pink mouth. Her eyes liquid blue and wide-set, like mine. Like Mara's.

"Cassie? Are you okay?" Wendy repeats the questions.

I look up at her and nod, swallowing the lump in my throat. "Yes," I say, because it's true. As long as I have Ella, I will be.

Chapter Nine

Billie

Fall 2002

A lot happens the fall of our freshman year: Wade moves in. I lose my baby fat. Cassie loses her virginity.

Cassie and Kyle have been an item for a year, since homecoming. When they first started going out, there was a part of me that wondered if she actually liked him, or if she just liked the idea of having a boy-friend. But now, I'm convinced otherwise. Whenever Kyle walks into a room, Cassie's whole face lights up, her eyes get even bluer. And now that they're having sex, they're more all over each other than ever. I like Kyle. A lot of his friends are jerky, but he's actually a genuine guy. He always stops when we pass each other in the hallway, makes a point of asking me how I'm doing.

In October, the three of us drive an hour and a half to Greenwich to have lunch with Cassie's grandmother at her fancy yacht club. Cassie does these lunches once every few months, but her grandmother usually sends a car. But today, since Kyle and I are invited, he takes us in his dad's Subaru. When we stop for gas, Kyle goes into the convenience store for a Gatorade. Cassie watches him stroll across the parking lot, the broad line of his shoulders, his long, even stride.

She turns to me from the passenger seat. "Is it embarrassing that I'm with someone who dresses like that?"

I watch as Kyle pulls open the swinging door and disappears inside. He's wearing khakis and a red-checkered button-down. The same back-ward Yankees cap that seems to be permanently affixed to his head of floppy brown hair. Kyle is the best-looking boy in the sophomore class.

My eyebrows knit together. "What's wrong with the way he's dressed?"

"Billie." Cassie sighs, deep and dramatic. "I told him to look nice today, and do you know where he bought that shirt? Costco." She makes a face, her nose scrunching. "And those aren't even real khakis—they're polyester. And don't even get me started on his weird loafers. They're his dad's from the eighties. What will Grandma Catherine think?" She taps her fingers against the center console. She seems uncharacteristically flustered.

"Are you nervous about seeing your grandmother?" I ask gently.

"Of course not." Cassie adjusts the collar of her dress, a navy-blue shift with a pleated skirt that reminds me of Pollyanna. Her curly hair is ironed straight, which makes it even longer. "Grandma Catherine and I have always been close," she adds. "She used to pick me up from school every Friday to run errands on the Ave. I just don't see her as much since we moved. But once I get my license, that will change. I'll go down to Greenwich more. I'll start visiting her on the Cape in August, like we used to."

"Doesn't she ever come to Red Hook?"

Cassie snorts. "She's estranged from my parents. Besides, why would she ever want to visit a place like Red Hook?"

A long moment of silence sits between us.

"At least Kyle made an effort," I say eventually. "I think his clothes look fine."

Greenwich is as striking as Cassie described: the houses are huge, immaculate structures with pristine rolling lawns, bright green and manicured. The driveways are set with Belgian block, the hedges trimmed just so. I can't imagine how rich you have to be to own a house here. Cassie gazes out the window longingly, her forehead pressed to the glass.

"Crazy that you used to live here, babe." Kyle rests one hand on the back of her neck, his other steady on the wheel.

"Once upon a time, before Eric blew every dollar to his name."

Eric is Cassie's father. I don't know the exact details of how he lost all their money, though I've heard the terms high-risk investment *and* options trading *floating around the Barnwell home. What I do know is this: Grandma Catherine's late husband, Harold, made a killing in oil. When Harold died, he left a quarter of his wealth to Catherine and a quarter to each of their three sons. Eric had a history of bad investment decisions—he was addicted to the rush of risk—and after being bailed out one too many times by his mother and brothers, the family made a pact: no more helping Eric.*

It was only a matter of time, then, before the bank would seize Cassie's parents' home in Greenwich. Cassie's mother had grown up in Dutchess County, and when she found a small medical building for sale in Red Hook, she convinced Eric to make one final plea to Catherine to help him buy it. Catherine obliged—and also supplied the down payment for the new house—but she vowed it was the last time Eric would see a penny from any of the Barnwells. Now Eric owns the medical building and collects rent for income, and Cassie's mother seems glad to live closer to her roots.

"It's almost too sad coming back here." Cassie rolls down the window and sticks her neck out, lets the wind smack her face.

"Your parents ever come with you?" Kyle asks.

"Nope. My mom was always overwhelmed by Greenwich."

"And your dad?"

"He'll never forgive Grandma Catherine for cutting him off, which is ridiculous, because she obviously had no choice."

"So you're not mad at your grandma at all?"

"My father is a reckless, selfish man-child, Kyle." Cassie turns up the radio, a Pearl Jam song we all love. "I seem to be the only one in my family who sees that."

"What about Mara?"

"Mara is brainwashed by my parents. Grandma Catherine stopped inviting her down to Greenwich. Here—" Cassie waves her hand, motioning for Kyle to slow down. "This is our turn on the left."

The clubhouse is east-facing, with sweeping views of Long Island Sound. White-hulled sailboats cling to their moorings, dotting the inky harbor like stars. A thick American flag flaps in the midday breeze. Inside, the dining room is all white tablecloths and glass, the wood floors polished and dark. The ceilings are lofted, with pale pine beams that Grandma Catherine explains are structural, not decorative. She drinks white wine and tells us about the history of the club for what feels like an hour. I'm so bored I want to scream. I watch Kyle picking at his napkin, little paper shreds falling to his lap like snow. Grandma Catherine has barely said a word to either of us. When Kyle gets up to use the bathroom, she turns to Cassie, an eyebrow raised.

"His fingernails are very dirty. Does he bathe, Cassidy?" Grandma

Catherine is the only person I've ever heard call Cassie by her real name. She is eighty years old, but looks younger. Her short, fluffy hair is dyed chocolate brown, a quarter inch of silver stemming from the roots. "I speak in jest." Grandma Catherine gives a wry grin, her mouth pinched like a prune. "I'm sure he showers on occasion. The real problem is his attire. But I'm sure you know that."

Cassie's smile wavers, the corners of her eyes shining. We've been best friends for two years now—inseparable, the other's shadow—but it's the first time I've seen her cry. I resist the urge to rip open a packet of salt and dump it in Grandma Catherine's chardonnay.

"You need to get him to a Brooks Brothers, dear," the old lady counsels, patting Cassie's arm. She turns to me, suddenly, for the first time all afternoon, and I flinch.

"You have beautiful hair, Billie." She reaches over and takes a clump in her fist, pulling a little, a shot of pain at my scalp. I study her face, the cracks around her eyes that branch out like tree roots.

Cassie seems to have recovered. She looks from me to Grandma Catherine, a small smile on her lips. "Billie does have the best hair, doesn't she?"

On the drive back to Red Hook, Cassie is silent. She pretends to be napping, her head nudged between the seat and window. But I can tell she isn't really asleep, the way she keeps fidgeting. When Cassie is truly out, she doesn't move a muscle. She's like a dead body.

Kyle turns on Z100 and talks to me in the back seat. He has a soft voice and a friendly, easy way of being. The Subaru smells faintly of wet dog, but I crack the back window and don't complain while we make conversation about various classmates, gossip from school. He tells me his friend Travis thinks I'm cute.

"Maybe we can go on a double date," he offers.

An image of Travis drifts into my mind. Stocky, hairy, big beak of a nose. Ashton kissed him at the movies last summer and said his saliva tasted like onions.

"Maybe," I tell Kyle.

It's almost four by the time Kyle drops Cassie and me at my house. I watch her lean across the center console to kiss him goodbye. Their mouths open slightly; his tongue slides in to touch hers. Kissing is still so foreign to me. I've only made out with one boy, one time. Todd Clemmons, in the basement at one of Kyle's parties. I was so drunk on Jell-O shots, I barely remember it.

"How was lunch?" *Mom asks when we walk through the kitchen door. She's sitting at the table, tackling the Sunday crossword with a steaming mug of Constant Comment—her favorite tea—and a box of Triscuits.*

"It was fun," *I say, even though it wasn't.*

"It was fine." *Cassie shrugs.*

"I'm sure it was nice to see your grandmother."

"Yeah." *Cassie's mouth is a thin line. There's a heaviness in her eyes that I've never seen before.*

"The food was delicious," *I add.* "We all got the poached salmon."

"Yum." *Mom smiles, sipping her tea.* "Cass, are you hanging around for a bit, or do you need a ride home?"

Cassie shakes her head. "Mara can pick me up after her shift at the diner."

"Ah." *Mom turns back to the paper, picks up her pencil.* "Well, I know you just ate, but if you girls are hungry, there's vegetarian chili on the stove."

"Vegetarian *chili,"* Wade parrots. *I hadn't noticed him lying there, on the couch in the alcove off the kitchen.* "Your mother is plotting to get me on some kind of diet, I swear." *He sits up and yawns, stretching his meaty arms overhead. I hate that he lives here. I hate that the kitchen smells like beer and that he never flushes his pee, and that when Mom asks me to fold the laundry, I now have to touch Wade's disgusting tighty-whities. Most of all, I hate the way I can always feel him watching me. But Mom is happy, and that's what matters. So I keep my mouth shut.*

"It wouldn't hurt us all to make healthier choices." *Mom smiles as she fills in a clue. She's addicted to the crossword.*

Wade is studying Cassie and me in that creepy way, his dark eyes scanning the length of our bodies. Blatant and secretive at the same time, with Mom in the very same room. His gaze lingers on my chest for a moment, then his eyes clip to mine. When he winks, there's a prick of fear in the pit of my stomach.

"Cassie," *Mom calls, her eyes still glued to the newspaper.* "Do you need a ride home?"

Cassie and I exchange a puzzled look.

She swallows. "Uh, no, thanks, Lorraine. Mara is coming to get me. In an hour or so."

"Ah." Mom nods. "Good."

In my bedroom, Cassie and I sit cross-legged on the floor and flip through issues of Cosmopolitan. *I buy them with my babysitting money and hide them under my mattress—I don't want Mom to know I'm interested in reading about sex positions. She'd get the wrong idea.*

"What's it like to give a blow job?" I ask Cassie. I ask her all the time—every day, practically—and she laughs.

"Why don't you find out? Kyle says Travis likes you."

"Gross. I'm not hooking up with Travis."

"I don't blame you. He's kind of an ogre. Even if he is lacrosse captain."

"There are no attractive boys at school." I tuck my knees into my chest. "Kyle's really the only one."

Cassie's expression is blank. She says nothing for a few moments. Then, she sighs. "I'm not sure how I feel about Kyle."

"What?" I let out a small laugh. "That's a joke, right?"

"Not really." Cassie's voice is soft, almost a whisper. She stares at the magazine. "He's starting to annoy me."

I study her. "Please tell me this doesn't have anything to do with what your grandmother said at lunch."

Cassie glances up at me. Her eyes are hard. "You don't know my grandmother, Billie."

I swallow, speechless, but the moment is interrupted by a light rapping on my bedroom door. Seconds later, Mom's head pokes through the crack.

"Hey, girls." She grins. Mom is constantly cheerful, her calm, upbeat demeanor rarely waning. She's the opposite of Cassie's mother, who always seems to be in some sort of tizzy.

"Hi." I slide Cosmo *under the bed. "What's up?"*

"Just checking in. Cassie, are you hanging out for a bit, or do you need a ride home?"

"Mom!" I exclaim, suddenly annoyed. "You've asked her that three times. Jesus."

Mom's smile drops, her expression wounded, almost fearful. The blood drains from her face, paling her soft cheeks. "Have I?"

I don't recognize my mother in this moment. She looks like a child who's been scolded, regretful and afraid. If I could go back now and alter my reaction, I would. But I can't. And it doesn't matter, anyway. It wouldn't have changed anything. What happened next was out of everyone's control.

Chapter Ten

Billie

September 9, 2023
34 days before

The Saturday of Cassie's dinner party, it's eighty degrees outside, even though it's early September.

"I like this weather," Alex says as we stroll up Irving Place toward Cassie and Grant's apartment. "I'm not ready for summer to end."

His knuckles brush my fingers, and for a moment, I think he might try to hold my hand. There's a prickle at the base of my spine.

"I'm a fall girl," I tell him. "Always have been."

"Really? Fall always makes me a little sad, with the dying leaves, et cetera."

I smile. "You sound just like Cassie."

"Cassie, as in . . . your friend who's hosting this dinner?"

"Right." I pause, unsure of how to even begin explaining my relationship with Cassie to Alex. "She's my oldest friend. My best—well, she was my best friend, for a really long time." My throat feels swollen, my voice breaking a little. *God, Billie,* I think. *Get a grip.* "Anyway, things are different now. She's married. She has a baby."

Alex frowns. "You're no longer best friends because she's married with a kid?" He sounds genuinely confused.

"Not exactly. I mean, it's more complicated than that."

We walk the rest of the block in silence. I like this about Alex, that even though we hardly know each other, he doesn't feel the need to fill every minute of our time together with chatter and noise, the way most men do. Around him, I feel like I can breathe. I can think.

We reach the entrance to Cassie's building in Gramercy. It's older than many of the buildings that have sprung up in the area—a nine-story wedding cake–style charmer that's been around for at least a century. Cassie and Grant have been here for as long as they've lived together, and even though she complains about it—her super's slow response rate, the ancient plumbing, the rickety elevator—theirs is still one of the most beautiful New York apartments I've ever stepped foot in. I've looked it up on StreetEasy; they bought their penthouse unit for $7 million.

Alex turns to face me on the sidewalk, and I drink in the sight of him. He wears a short-sleeve button-down pulled taut by the span of his shoulders, a soft green color that matches the flecks in his hazel eyes. Sandy-brown stubble crawls down to the soft part of this throat.

"Billie," he says, and the sound of my name on his lips makes the base of my spine feel gooey, like it's melting in the heat. "I thought about you when you were in Portugal." He blinks, gives a soft laugh. "God, I even got drunk at the family barbecue and told my sister about my crush on you."

There's something so genuine about this man, about the verity of his words. I feel buzzy but heavy, rooted in the weight of my own body.

"Anyway," he continues. "I've been . . . looking forward to this. To seeing you again."

An easy smile spreads across my face. "So have I, Alex."

He smiles back, and this time he takes my hand as we walk inside the building. His fingers feel solid and warm as we ride the elevator up to the ninth floor. The door to Cassie and Grant's apartment is cracked, and when I push it open, a rush of voices floods my eardrums.

It isn't just McKay and Tom here; there are at least three other couples gathered in the Adlers' immaculate living room, cradling cocktails. The only women I actually know are McKay and Ava, from our college days in Boston, but I recognize Blake, a brunette I've met twice through Cassie in recent years.

"*Billie.*" Cassie appears in the foyer, her arms looping around my shoulders—the same limp hug she gave me at the wine bar. "This must be the *famous* Alex."

I pin her a look. I've hardly told her about Alex—she knows we've only been on a few dates—but she just shrugs and flashes an innocent smile before batting her long eyelashes in Alex's direction. "I'm Cassie Adler. It's wonderful to meet you."

"Alex Jensen. Likewise. Your place is stunning." He gestures through the foyer and living room toward two tall windows with sweeping views of the park. In between the windows is a set of french doors open to a large terrace that wraps around the corner of the building, the western end overlooking Lexington and the former Gramercy Park Hotel. As far as Manhattan real estate goes, the Adlers' place is essentially as prime as it gets.

"Sorry to be totally anal, but do you guys mind taking off your shoes if you've been on the subway or anywhere icky? I'm a germaphobe these days." Cassie rearranges her face into an apology, but I can tell she relishes the role of careful-bordering-on-obsessive new mom.

Alex nods obligingly; he kicks off his Allbirds, and I slip out of my leather sandals, the same Banana Republic pair I've worn every day this summer.

"Before I forget." Alex hands Cassie a bottle of wine. "It's a red Bordeaux."

Cassie takes the wine, admires the bottle like it's a pair of fuzzy socks. Negligibly thoughtful, fully unnecessary. "This is great. Thank you."

We follow her to the bar; on the way, I catch a glimpse of the renovated chef's kitchen. A petite Hispanic woman I've never seen before is bent over the counter, assembling a platter of smoked salmon.

"That's Lourdes," Cassie says, following my gaze. "She's a total life-saver."

"I didn't realize you had a housekeeper."

"Nanny . . . housekeeper . . . she's part-time, but Lourdes does it all, really." Cassie smiles, pressing her palms together.

I'm caught off guard. Cassie holds nothing back in the narration of her days on social media, and not once has there been a mention or even a glimpse of Lourdes. I'm not surprised to learn she has help, but still. I can't shake the irritation that simmers below my collarbone.

"What can I get you two to drink?"

I'm too distracted to decide, so when I hear Alex ask for a gin and tonic, I mumble that I'll have the same. I watch Cassie mix the cocktails, studying her in detail. She wears white jeans that make her legs look small and sculpted, and a cornflower-blue top with oversize puffy sleeves—a trend I don't understand. Cassie has always dressed well, but since launching Cassidy Adler, her style has become more ambitious, toeing the line between classic and aspirational. Thanks to Grant, she can afford to buy whatever she wants now and it shows; I steal a glance at her Chanel espadrilles, the back-to-back Cs interlocked over each toe. The shoes are flashy, but that has to be the point, right?

Cassie presses the drinks into our hands. "I didn't know you were a gin drinker now, Bill." Her long hair is pulled back into a sleek pony, and shiny gold hoops swing from her ears. I can feel Alex checking her out, too. Bringing him here suddenly feels like a huge mistake.

"Sometimes." I take a generous sip. The liquor burns the back of my throat before it settles warmly in my gut. "I didn't realize there'd be so many people here. I thought it was just McKay and Tom."

"You know how it is." Cassie swats at the air, then picks up her own drink. "It started *out* as McKay and Tom, and then McKay invited Ava and her husband, Ned, and then I figured, why not add a few more to the mix? Make a real night of it." She gestures toward the terrace, where most of the guests have converged. "You met Blake at the wedding, I think, but in case you need a refresher, that's her and her husband, Preston, and that's Evelyn and her husband, Harvey—they just moved back to the city after a brief stint in Palm Beach. Preston is Tom's best friend from grad school, so that's how we know the Lawrences. And Blake used to work at *Vogue* with Evelyn, and now we all live in Gramercy and have babies under a year, so yeah, we've kind of formed a little unit."

I study the group, lost. Three of the men are wearing velvet loafers. I recognize the stylish woman from Cassie's Instagram story at the sushi restaurant—that must be Evelyn. She's wearing an orange dress with beaded sleeves, and wire-frame glasses that somehow complete the outfit perfectly. She looks like she still works at *Vogue*.

"I swear, having kids is such a great way to meet people. You'll see, one day."

My breath sticks in my chest. I take another sip of my gin and tonic—I'm practically chugging it—and this helps a little. I force myself to smile. "Where's Ella?"

Cassie lets out a small laugh. "Asleep, thank God."

"Really? Darn. I haven't seen her since she was just born."

"Well, she's a baby, Billie. She goes down at seven." Cassie sips her cocktail. A tequila soda, no doubt. She's been drinking them since college, claiming that tequila is the least caloric spirit. "Although we're thinking of pushing her bedtime back a couple of hours so she sleeps later in the morning. Anyway, you'll see her next time."

Next time. *And when will that be?* I want to demand. But I don't, obviously. The fact that Cassie and I have gotten together twice in two weeks feels like nothing short of a miracle. Maybe this is a new beginning for us. I just need to play it cool, not seem so desperate.

"You have an open invitation to babysit, Billie." Grant appears out of nowhere, slinging his arm around Cassie's neck as he winks in my direction. He holds a tumbler of scotch, which is all he drinks. Scotch and now white Burgundy, apparently.

"Hey, Grant." I try to sound pleasant, but the sight of him fills me with dread.

He gives a smug smile that makes me clench my back molars—a habit my dentist would like me to break. He introduces himself to Alex, because I'm too numb with revulsion to do so.

I study Grant in his pressed khakis and dress shirt, the top three buttons undone to reveal a dark patch of chest hair. His face is freshly shaven, his eyes more gray than blue today. He isn't conventionally handsome, at least I don't think so. His nose is slightly bulbous, his chin lacks definition—but for a man like Grant, it doesn't matter. He has money; he's beguiling. But he's slippery. I've never trusted him. Still, he's Cassie's husband, and I have to pretend to think he's a decent guy. Especially after what happened three years ago.

Cassie reaches for my hand. "I'm stealing Billie for a sec," she tells Alex. "Make yourself at home."

She leads me through the living room, toward the other end of the apartment. Even though it's older architecture, the design feels contemporary—all sleek wood floors and white furniture with soft pops of color in the form of accent pillows and coffee table books, a Rothko above the fireplace. Cassie hired a decorator when they first moved in—some sought-after woman regularly featured in *Architectural Digest*—and it shows. The apartment is striking, accentuated by the high ceilings and oversize windows. It makes my spot in the Village feel like a college dorm.

Cassie pauses outside one of the bedroom doors. "This is Ella's nursery," she whispers, and it strikes me as strange and sad that I'm only just seeing Cassie's baby's room for the first time. Yet another indicator of just how far apart we've drifted.

Cassie must read my mind. Something regretful flashes across her face, and for a brief moment, she looks more like her old self. "I'm sorry it's been so long," she says. "It's been . . . weird. Not having you around. And somehow Ella is already almost four months."

She pushes the door open before I have time to respond. Ella's room is dark, filled with the static sound of white noise. But there's enough light seeping through the roman shades that I can make out the crib in the corner, the outline of Ella sleeping peacefully on her back.

"She's beautiful," I whisper.

Cassie's eyes shimmer in the dimness. "She really is, isn't she?"

We're quiet for a few moments.

"You'll have one, too, one day." Cassie looks at me. "Sooner than you think, I bet."

I'm still holding my near-empty drink in one hand. I clasp it tightly, the pads of my fingers pressing into the cold glass. "I don't know," I say, feeling honest, woozy from the gin on an empty stomach. "I don't know if I want kids." It isn't the first time I've told her this.

Part of me expects Cassie to appear offended, but she just gives me a knowing smile, her expression tinged with sympathy. "You're only saying that because of all the shit with your own parents. Plus, you haven't met the right person yet. But Alex . . . he seems great."

You've barely exchanged two words with him, I want to challenge. But I don't. Around Cassie, I no longer seem to be capable of saying what I mean. In fact, me *not* saying what I mean seems to be the one thing still gluing our friendship together.

"I don't think I've met a cop in real life before," she adds. "You know, off duty, I mean." Cassie clicks the bedroom door shut. "Oh God, remember that time in high school I got pulled over for speeding in Mara's car, and later, we realized there was a huge ziplock bag of her weed in the back seat?" She laughs, clinks the watery ice around in her tumbler. "I need a refill. Seems like you do, too."

Dinner is served in the dining room, another tastefully decorated space—grass cloth wallpaper, faded Persian rug. The table is covered in a cloth I recognize from Cassie's Instagram—something floral and periwinkle, block-printed in a way that reminds me of the market linens Jane and I saw in Jaipur during a trip to India last year. The plates, napkins, and water tumblers all match perfectly, complementing the tablecloth in various shades of blue. In the middle of two glass hurricanes sits a china vase filled with white dahlias, the petals fat and gleaming.

"This is a *vision!*" sings McKay, who's unfortunately seated to my right.

"Like, straight out of *House Beautiful.*" Ava studies the tablescape with a look of intense longing. She touches her napkin carefully, like she's petting a small animal.

Blake picks up a turquoise water tumbler and turns to Cassie. "I am *seduced* by these glasses."

"Smile, everyone!" Cassie stands on her chair at the head of the table, her phone tilted down. "Gotta get the bird's-eye view!"

I lean into the frame and force a grin, keeping my eyes as wide as possible so I don't accidentally close them. I'm terrible at photographs. Cassie used to tell me I look much better in person than in pictures, which is probably true.

She angles the phone in my direction. "Cute, right?"

It's a vertical shot of the table, each of Cassie's guests craning their necks in toward the center. My strained smile is a bit lopsided, but at least I've managed to keep my eyes open. Alex's hand rests on my back, his own smile natural and relaxed.

"It's good."

Cassie steps down and slides back into her chair. "I'll post it later."

We dig into the food—wild rice, teriyaki chicken, a green salad with lemon vinaigrette. Everything is delicious; excluding Portugal, it's the best meal I've had in weeks. I'm about to ask Cassie if she did all this herself, when Ava's voice rings across the table.

"Lourdes is the best fucking cook. Can she come over and give our nanny lessons?"

"Yes, please." Ned shovels a bite of rice into his mouth, muffling his words. "That woman can barely make scrambled eggs."

"*Literally* all Mariana makes is macaroni and cheese," Blake whines. "The kind that comes in a box. Olivia is actually going to get scurvy."

"Oh, that reminds me." McKay whips toward Blake. "Can we switch Mariana's days next week? I need her on Thursday for the family photo shoot."

"Sure." Blake flips her shiny chestnut hair, and it bounces against her shoulders. "Just remind me via text, because I can't keep anything straight these days. Wait, where are you doing the photo shoot? I need to book ours for the Christmas card. Ugh. How is it already September?"

"Central Park, where else?" McKay cackles. "Our photographer is an actual wizard. Last year, Juliette had this huge rip in her sweater because she snagged it on a branch *right* before the pictures, but this guy, he photoshopped the whole thing out."

"*Really?*" Cassie's eyes bloom with intrigue. "They can do that?"

"Oh, he's a miracle worker. I was *so* stressed—of course Tom was like, just have Juliette take off the sweater, McKay. And I'm like, Tom, do you *realize* how much time and energy I've put into choosing everyone's outfit for the Christmas card? The colors don't coordinate themselves."

"Okay, you just recited a literal conversation between Harvey and me." Evelyn adjusts her glasses on the bridge of her nose. "Sorry, boys, but this is where you are fundamentally clueless." The five women erupt into robust laughter.

Preston rolls his eyes. He rakes a hand through his thinning brown hair, peppered with gray strands. "Yeah, Blake orders me seven new dress shirts a full month before our photo shoot, all in *slightly* different shades of navy."

Grant knocks back the rest of his scotch. He shakes his head, but he looks amused.

"*Because,* Pres, your shirt needed to match the piping on Olivia's dress!" Blake laughs, but there's an underlying severity in her voice. "These are photos we're going to have forever. The right shade of navy *matters.*"

There's a sip of wine left in my glass, and I tip it down my throat. I feel as though I'm having an out-of-body experience, listening to Cassie's friends emphasize the gravity of outfit coordination in holiday card photos. Next to me, Alex is silent. How could I have agreed to bring him here?

Across the table, Blake catches my eye. She seems to notice that neither Alex nor I have spoken since the meal began. "How do you all know Cassie again?" she asks.

Like the rest of the women at the table, Blake is put together and polished. Her makeup is pristine, her forehead glassy and unmoving. The diamond on her ring finger is even bigger than Cassie's. It catches a shard of light, momentarily blinding me.

"We, um—we grew up together." My voice feels strangled, reaching over a lump in my throat.

"You probably met Billie at Cassie's wedding, Blake," McKay says.

"Ah, probably. It's all such a blur."

I'm tempted to remind Blake that we also met last year, at Cassie's birthday dinner, but my vocal cords are tied.

Blake tilts her head, still trying to place me. "Were you a bridesmaid in the wedding?"

"Cassie didn't have bridesmaids," McKay reminds everyone.

"*Right*. It was just you, McKay?"

She nods, the apples of her cheeks dewy with pride.

"Remember McKay's maid of honor toast?" Ava glances around the table. "I cried ugly tears."

"Technically, I was *matron* of honor." McKay smiles. "Even then, I was a married old hag."

The lump in my throat slides down into my stomach, forming a pit that extinguishes my appetite. I force myself to look at Cassie. She's staring past her plate, a muted half smile glued to her face as she pushes rice around with her fork.

The memory slams into me. That sloppy Saturday when we were twenty-four, maybe twenty-five. It was springtime and some friend of a friend had invited us to a charity event on the East River—a cruise boat, open bar, DJ on deck. The party started at noon, and I remember how wasted we got, how impossible it was to *not* get wasted when the drinks were free. We ended up on the floor of our tiny apartment, binge-eating pizza from Artichoke at four in the afternoon.

"You'll be my maid of honor, right?" Cassie's question was so out of nowhere, I'd started laughing hysterically.

"I'm serious, Billie." She'd stopped eating her pizza, staring at me intensely. Grease on her chin, mascara-smudged eyes.

"Uh, are you getting *married*?"

"I meant *one day*." She'd spread her arms wide like wings, tossed her head back drunkenly. "Whenever I do find someone in this crazy world who will have me." Her head lifted, blue eyes locking on mine. "It'll be you, right?"

I'd smiled, my heart filling with warmth. "Duh."

"And I'll be yours?"

"Who else would be mine?"

She'd grinned, satisfied, and we'd polished off the rest of the pizza. Drunk, oblivious, happy.

Alex touches my arm, pulling me out of the memory. It may as well be from another lifetime. "Hey." His voice is hushed. "You okay?"

At the end of the table, Cassie looks up, her smile broadening. She reaches for her wine. "God, it's hard to believe our wedding was only a year and a half ago."

"And now you guys have a *baby*," Blake squeals.

"A perfect baby." Evelyn raises her glass.

McKay turns to me. "You've met Ella, right?"

The pit in my gut deepens, sawing itself into the lining of my stomach. "Once. Just after she was born."

"Twice." Cassie swallows her sip of wine. "Including tonight."

I clench my molars. It's almost a relief to feel the anger rising in my chest. "I don't think tonight counts. She was asleep."

Cassie blinks. Beside her, Grant looks bored, gazing longingly at the other end of the table where the other men are deep in conversation.

Ava clears her throat. "Well, Billie, you'll have to get your hands on little miss Ella soon. Because she is just *delicious*."

"I'd love to," I say pathetically. "Anytime. Maybe later this month?" I search Cassie's face, but she's smiling at Ava.

"Aw, Aves." Cassie beams. "Charlie boy is delicious, too."

Ava shakes her head. "Not like Ella. I *live* for your Instagrams of those thigh rolls. No matter how much I feed Charlie, he's still so darn skinny."

Evelyn nods knowingly. "I feel you. When Leo was Charlie's age, he was this long string bean baby. What I always did, to try to fatten him up, was pump at night, then give him the extra milk the next . . ."

Evelyn's unsolicited advice launches the table into an enthused discussion on breast milk and formula and pumping and cluster feeding, and I'm so lost that at some point I stop listening entirely. I stare at my plate, at the uneaten half of my delicious dinner that Lourdes spent all day preparing.

"Billie." Alex touches my forearm again, lowering his voice to a whisper. "You want to get out of here?"

Cassie doesn't seem to mind that Alex and I duck out before dessert. She walks us to the front door, shooting me a knowing look on the way. *He's cute,* she mouths, and I try not to think about the fact that she didn't ask Alex a single question all night.

"Sorry about all the baby talk." Cassie gives me a credulous grin.

"Don't apologize. I kind of love it."

She smiles, too far off the ground to know I'm lying.

Out on the street, it's humid and dark, only a few degrees cooler than it was before dinner. Alex and I walk half a block in silence.

He turns to me at the corner. "What was that?" The way he's looking at me sends tears rushing to my throat, stinging the back of my nose.

I shake my head. I'm so pissed off I can feel myself trembling. "Those aren't my friends, Alex. I'm not friends with people like that."

"Okay."

"I'm not like that."

"I know you're not."

"It's just, Cassie—" My voice catches, and his arms are around me. They feel strong, safe, encompassing. *Like home,* I think, though I'm not sure I know what that word means. I press my head to his chest, listen to the thumping beat of his heart through the cotton of his shirt. "She used to be my family."

Alex holds me. He smells like soap and warm wind. "People change."

"So I'm told."

"That apartment was massive. I've never seen anything like it."

"Yeah."

"Cassie seems like kind of a snob, Billie." A beat passes. "Sorry. I shouldn't say that. I hardly know her."

"No. You're not wrong." I pause. "She is a snob. She didn't used to be." I swallow, debating whether the last part of that statement is true.

"But you love her?"

"I wish I didn't."

Alex pulls back from me, uses his thumbs to swipe the tears from my eyes. "How about one more drink?"

I gaze up at him, heady with attraction, my entire body fizzing with a longing that sways me, that blots out the anger and sadness and pragmatism. I don't want to think.

"I have a better idea," I say.

Chapter Eleven

Cassie

September 10, 2023
33 days before

The temperature drops overnight, and there's a noticeable chill in the air, even with the sunshine. As Grant and I drive farther north toward Red Hook, the tips of the leaves become burnt orange, like they've been dipped in fire. I used to hate the onset of fall—the new binders from Staples, back-to-reality time of year—but now, I don't mind it. Now, I can actually appreciate autumn's bright, bucolic beauty.

The drive has been hellish; it took us an hour of bumper-to-bumper just to get out of the city, and Grant is berating me for agreeing to a dinner upstate that coincides with Sunday traffic. It doesn't help that we're both hungover from last night. McKay and Tom stayed late; Tom and Grant fell into a passionate competition over who mixes a better Manhattan, and by the time they left our apartment at two, all four of us were seeing double.

I ignore Grant's complaining and force him to take a selfie at a red light—our faces squished into the frame, Ella's car seat visible between us in the background.

Sunday adventures with the fam ♡, I caption.

While Grant drives and Ella naps, I knock back two more Advil and take the opportunity to check in with my followers. I post an Ask Me Anything button to my story and record a quick video: "Husband's at the wheel, baby's sleeping in the back, and I have some time in the car, so . . . ask me anything!"

"Jesus, Cassie," Grant mutters from the driver's seat. "Can't you put that thing down for a minute of peace?"

I don't gratify him with a response. We've been on-and-off squabbling since our fight in the Hamptons last weekend, and I know he's just trying to push my buttons. Instead, I scroll through the questions that are rolling in at the speed of light.

Do you eat carbs?

When will you and hubby start trying for baby number two?

Your skin is amazing, you MUST do Botox?

How long will u breastfeed?

Where'd you get Ella's pink sweater? The monogrammed one from the other day in the park.

What does your husband do? Seems like u guys are rolling in it!

How long did you date before your man proposed? Worried my guy never will . . .

I laugh, eyes glued to the screen. "Actually, Grant, I'm doing an Ask Me Anything, and a bunch of the questions are about you."

"Me?"

"Yeah."

"Why are they about me, if your Instagram is supposed to be about the store?"

I frown, sifting through more of the questions. So far, none of them even mention the store. It's just strangers wanting to know what size jeans I wear post-baby.

I glance out the window as we drive across the Kingston-Rhinecliff Bridge, the surface of the Hudson River shimmering in the early-evening light. I snap a quick shot of the view, and it's too pretty not to add to my Instagram story. *So nice to be out of the city,* I caption.

"Can you put your phone away and help me navigate?" Grant flicks on his blinker. "We're almost there."

My parents' one-story ranch in Red Hook is a middle-class artifact, frozen in time. This, among other reasons, is why I avoid coming back here. The light gray paint on the exterior is peeling but intact, and the inside is a collection of frugal decisions from the nineties: linoleum floors, brown plywood cabinets, floral drapes from Home Depot that look like shower curtains flanking the windows. Mystifyingly, none of it has ever bothered my mother. She's always been oblivious to the home's drabness—or perhaps content with it—and so has my father. Since they left Greenwich for Red Hook twenty-three years ago, neither of them has ever hinted at missing that old life. Sometimes I can't believe I'm their daughter.

We step into the foyer, and I'm flooded with the familiar smell of the house—lemon wax and mothballs. It isn't Grant's first time here, but still, I can feel him physically recoil.

The first thing my mother does is grab the baby from my arms.

"She's *beautiful*." My mom cradles Ella horizontally, like she's a newborn. I watch her round eyes blink open, fresh from sleep, her mouth puckering. I expect her face to scrunch and redden at the sight of a stranger, but she's calm in my mother's grasp. She reaches up and bats at her nose.

"Awww." My mom gives a soft chuckle. "She's getting to be such a big girl. The last time I saw her, she was just a few days old." She looks up at me, her eyes glazed with tears that are meant to make me feel guilty. I won't fall for it. "Cassie, Grant, I would hug you both, but I'm never letting go of my precious granddaughter." She laughs again, as if her jokes are legitimately funny. "Thanks for making the trip."

"It was long," I mumble. "Over three hours. Horrible traffic."

"Happy anniversary." Grant gives a stiff smile and hands my father a bottle of vintage Dom Pérignon. Grant doesn't think much of my parents—why would he?—but he never forgets his manners. Grandma Catherine would've adored him.

"Wow." My father stares at the champagne like it might sprout wings and fly away. "This is very nice."

"Just a little vintage Dom." Mara appears in the front hall, a snarky smile spreading across her face. She's wearing a black ribbed dress with long sleeves, and her hair is shorter than I remember, just grazing her shoulders. A little boy's arms are looped around one of her legs. My nephew, Jack. "Nothing five hundred dollars can't get you, Dad."

"Mara." My mother sighs, still gazing dreamily at Ella. "Be pleasant. If only for today."

Since we're so late, we sit down to eat almost right away. If my father has a meal later than six thirty, he gets heartburn.

Dinner is served in the dining room, a small space with a swinging door right off the kitchen. Being here, at the oval pine table with the blue gingham napkins, eating off my parents' ancient wedding china, I feel as though I've traveled back in time. It's only the sight of Ella, babbling in her portable bouncy chair at my feet, that reminds me I'm not thirteen again. That my life has evolved so far beyond this place, I can barely see it in the rearview. It doesn't mean anything anymore.

I sit beside Jack, who tells me about kindergarten, how he's learning to read. He has Mara's bright eyes and fine hair, the same dusting of freckles across his nose.

"My dad's picking me up from school on Friday," Jack says blithely. I nod and take a sip of champagne—which my mother has poured into an old set of dusty flutes—and resist the urge to ask any questions. Brandon, Jack's father, has been in and out of rehab since Jack was two. He fell off a ladder working construction, and a doctor prescribed opioids for his back injury. Brandon got addicted, and he's never been the same. I'm not even sure if he and Mara are still married, but I don't want to ask.

I find her eyes across the table. My eyes. Ella's eyes. Jack's eyes. The haunting reality of genetics.

"We're not together, if that's what you're wondering," she says evenly.

Jack looks from me to Mara. "But when Daddy gets better, he'll move back in. Right, Mama?"

Her smile falters, pain etched into the contours of her face. "We'll see, baby."

"How's business, Cassie?" my mother asks, helping herself to another piece of buttery garlic bread. At sixty-four, her body is still as svelte as it was in college. Mara and I both inherited her fast metabolism, and if there's anything I thank her for, it's that.

"It's great," I say. "Cassidy Adler has been insanely busy. Online and brick-and-mortar, both."

"That's wonderful." My mother smiles. "I've been on your website, but everything is so expensive. Four hundred dollars for a blouse, my. Is that what the high-end stores are charging these days? Anyway, you must be proud of her, Grant."

"Of course." Grant places his hand over mine, the pads of his fingers wedged between my knuckles. "It's fun what she's doing."

"Fun?" Mara raises a dark eyebrow, and in that moment, something in my heart reaches for her.

Grant swallows a bite of steak and nods casually. "Most women in Cassie's position give work a rest when they become mothers. So it's cute to see her get jazzed about something other than the baby."

"Cute?" Mara blinks, her wide mouth expressionless. My sister is demonic, but she's stunning. She always has been, even with her atrocious style. "Well, I'm a mother, and it never occurred to me to give work a rest. But I suppose I'm not in Cassie's *position*."

Grant presses his lips together, rolling them inward in a way that tells me he's severely uncomfortable. "Remind me where you work again?"

Mara says nothing, her eyes cold. Then she stands, smooths the front of her dress. "I'm going to stick the pie in the oven."

"Pie!" Jack squeals with delight. "Is there ice cream, too, Mama?"

"There's ice cream, too, baby."

I excuse myself to use the bathroom, but really, I follow Mara into the kitchen. I find her leaning against the sink in front of the open window, where a stream of cool air rolls in. Through the upper glass, I can see the crescent moon, a fingernail clipping pinned low in the indigo sky.

"You don't have to be so hard on him," I say.

Mara turns around slowly, pressing her elbows against the white laminate counter. A long moment passes before she speaks.

"I wonder how you can be with a man like that." She gives her head a little shake, her jaw held tight. "A man who belittles you, who's objectively sexist. But then I think, it isn't my problem."

I swallow the mass that's formed in my throat. "No, it isn't."

She reaches for the cabinet above the sink and takes out two small tumblers. Juice glasses from our childhood. There's an open bottle of wine on the counter, and she pours some into the tumblers, hands one to me.

"I mean, *I* can tell you that what you're doing is ridiculous," she continues. "Sharing your pricey skin-care routine with a bunch of strangers online. Inviting them to ask you anything they want about your personal life. And why, all because you own a clothing boutique?"

"Disparage my business all you want, Mara. It won't get to me." I sip the wine, which tastes sugary and instantly reignites my headache. It's the cheap sauvignon blanc my mother buys in bulk.

"I'm not trying to get to you. I'm trying to get *through* to you." Mara glances over my shoulder, tips her chin toward the dining room. "I can be the one who's snarky and disparaging. But your husband—*he* should have your back."

I close my eyes, the backs of my lids burning. I won't let Mara make me cry.

"You don't even know him." It comes out as a whisper, gravelly and weak.

"I just want you to be happy, Cassie."

"Do you?"

"Let me ask you something." She places her wine on the counter. "What does Billie think?"

"*Billie?*" I snort. "Why?"

Mara shrugs. "I'm asking what your best friend thinks of your husband."

"Billie isn't my best friend."

Mara folds her arms, her eyebrows knitting together. "That's news to me."

"We haven't been close in years, Mara."

"What happened?"

"Nothing." I run my finger across the chipped rim of my glass. "We're fine. I saw her last night, actually." I pause, remembering how strange it felt to have Billie in my apartment, her presence somehow tainting the space, the otherwise buoyant vibe. I was glad when she and the cop left early. I sigh. "People change, Mara. People grow apart."

"Okay."

"If you don't believe me, I don't care."

"Oh, I believe you. It just makes me sad, that's all."

"It makes *you* sad that Billie and I are no longer best friends?" I give a thin laugh. "Since when do you care about Billie? You never even gave her the time of day."

Mara is quiet for a few long beats. Then she sighs, and I can feel the cynicism draining from her demeanor. Her eyes clip mine. "Something tells me Billie is the only person in your life who loves you for exactly who you are."

My throat feels raw and compressed, cinched by an invisible rope. "You don't know anything about my life," I hiss. "Just because *you're* miserable about your own shit circumstances, about Brandon, whatever, it doesn't give you the right to—" I pause, wine sloshing over the rim of my glass and onto the floor. "Jesus, Mara. This is the first time I've seen you in months. This is the first time you're meeting my daughter."

"And that's *my* fault? You've made it clear you want nothing to do with us."

"I never said that."

"Actions speak louder than words, right?" Mara's thin shoulders slump. She chews her bottom lip and glances away. When she turns back to me, her eyes are clear. "You have no idea how much it means to Mom and Dad that you came tonight. It's all Mom has talked about for an entire week."

I shake my head. "Don't try to guilt-trip me. It won't work."

Through the swinging door, I hear Ella begin to fuss. I hear Grant pluck her from her bouncy chair and shush her.

Sweet girl, he coos, and I picture the way he holds her against his chest. *Shhh, it's okay. We'll go in a minute, baby.*

Our cue. Thank fucking God.

I set my glass down on the counter as the door to the kitchen flies open and Grant comes in, Ella propped on his hip. Her face is pink, her little fists balled, and I can tell she's on the verge of a meltdown. I take her from his arms and hold her close, inhaling the sweet, milky warmth of her skin. She settles against me, and my heart feels full again.

Grant touches my arm. "I think she's hungry."

Over Ella's shoulder, I study Mara—her smudged mascara, her cheap polyester dress, the cringey infinity tattoo below her collarbone. Her blatant disdain for me, for being smart enough to choose a bigger life than she did before it was too late.

My gaze moves to Grant. Polished, wonderful, polite, generous Grant. How did I get so lucky? I press my nose to the top of Ella's head, smooth as velvet.

"I'll feed her in the car," I tell him. "It's time for us to go."

Forty minutes later, we're cruising south on I-87, Ella passed out in her car seat. I scroll through my phone, willing something, anything on the screen to stamp out the residual anger at Mara that curdles behind my chest. There are several DMs in response to my Instagram stories from earlier, and I'm sifting through them when a message from an account I've never seen before catches my eye.

birchballer6: *Returning to the scene of the crime, are we?*

I stiffen. It's a reply to the photo I posted of the river, when we were driving over the bridge into Red Hook.

There's no geotag—I didn't include one. Goose bumps prickle my arms. I close my eyes, and even though it's the last image I wish to conjure, his face appears. His eyes, the way they taunted me, dared me to prove my own self-worth.

The scene of the crime.

I must make a noise, because Grant looks over from the driver's seat.

"You okay, Cass?"

No, I think. *I'm not okay. If there's one thing I never want to remember, it's this.*

"I'm fine," I lie. "Just tired."

I place my phone down on the center console and stare ahead at the dark highway, dread coursing through my veins at the realization that someone might be watching me. Someone who knows.

Chapter Twelve

Billie

Fall 2004

Junior year, I'm still a virgin. Ashton starts going out with Kyle, and Cassie shit-talks Ashton behind her back every chance she gets. It doesn't matter that Ashton is—technically—in our friend group or that Cassie dumped Kyle before they got together. We made the mistake of showing up to one of Kyle's parties, and when Cassie went looking for more beer in the basement, she found him ass-naked having sex with Ashton.

"I never liked her," Cassie proclaims at lunch, munching on Doritos. We're perched at our usual corner table, spying on Ashton and Kyle at the other end of the cafeteria. She ruffles his hair; he offers her a sip of his Coke. I watch her shake her head, wrinkle her pert little nose. Ashton only drinks Diet.

Cassie is relentless. "From that first day I met her at the town pool, when she was with you, and she told you that you shouldn't be eating fried food . . ." Cassie narrows her eyes, indignant. "Well, guess what? Ashton is the one who shouldn't be eating fried food. Have you seen her thighs? Cellulite city."

"Cass." I turn to her. She is driving me out of my mind, and she knows it. "You're the one who broke up with Kyle, remember?"

She sighs. Of course she remembers. We have the same conversation every goddamn day.

"But Kyle looks like shit lately, doesn't he?" She tucks her dark hair behind her ears. It's so long these days. When she straightens it, it hits her butt.

"Definitely," I say, even though I don't think Kyle looks like shit at all.

She eats the last Dorito, then balls up the bag and arcs it into the nearest trash can.

"Three-pointer!" Shane Baxter exclaims, flashing Cassie a double thumbs-up. Like every other guy at school, Shane has an enormous crush on Cassie, especially now that she's single. A hot commodity.

She ignores him and nudges my shoulder. "Let's ditch seventh and watch Dirty Dancing at your place."

Lately, we're obsessed with Dirty Dancing, especially because of how hot Patrick Swayze is. We watch the movie at least once a week and have started to call each other Baby after Jennifer Grey's character, an in-joke that really makes no sense. But that's the beauty of friendship.

I hesitate. "I shouldn't skip Western Civ. Mr. Ennis is giving us a test Friday, and I did horribly on the last one."

"Horribly as in, you got an A minus?" One side of Cassie's ripe mouth curls as she hops up from the orange plastic chair. "I had Western Civ with Ennis this morning. You can have my notes. C'mon, Baby." She stretches her arms overhead, her cropped sweater rising to reveal a generous sliver of her perfect stomach. I can feel every guy in the cafeteria staring, drooling. It's not easy being Cassie's best friend. But I wouldn't change it for the world.

When we reach my house, Wade's truck is in the driveway. He should be at his job at RadioShack in Kingston, where he's assistant manager.

"Ugh." My stomach sinks. "Why isn't he at work?"

"The only person I despise more than Ashton"—Cassie kicks the front tire of his rusted Chevy—"is Wade."

The second we step through the door, I can tell something is off. Tea candles line the front hall table, a dozen little flames flickering in the dim light. A single red rose is strewn across the ivory shag carpet. Etta James blares through the speakers singing that her love has come along.

My lonely days are over
And life is like a song

"Hello? Mom?"

I find her in the den, slow dancing with Wade, still in her flannel nightgown. When she notices Cassie and me standing there, she startles, her shoulders jolting. Her face is flushed pink, her honey-brown hair wild and unbrushed. Disheveled, but beautiful as always. My beautiful mother.

It's been almost two years since she was diagnosed with early-onset Alzheimer's at the impossibly young age of forty-three. Two years since her short-term memory started evaporating like morning mist, sucked away by some powerful, inevitable force against which she stands no chance.

Some days are better than others. On good days, it's easy to pretend that everything is normal. On the bad ones, I pretend not to notice that Mom asks me the same question five times in the span of ten minutes. Either way, I'm pretending.

And somehow, Wade is still here. Awful Wade, with his fishy, beery smell and creepy stare, has not been scared off by Mom's diagnosis. Even when she was forced to leave her job at the dental practice, where she worked as a hygienist. Even when the doctor told us, his expression solemn, that she might have five good years. Might.

A giddy smile spreads across Mom's face, her eyes brightening. She teeters a little on her bare feet. If she notices we've ditched school early, she doesn't seem to care.

"Mom, what's going on?" I swallow hard. This is how I live now—in a perpetual state of agonizing worry, waiting for the other shoe to drop. "Why are you still in your pajamas?"

Beside me, Cassie slips her hand in mine and squeezes my palm. She sees it before I do. But I shake her off. My heart is thrashing like a hammer in my chest.

"Oh, Bill. I'm so glad you're home." Mom presses a hand to her collarbone, and that's when I see it, too. A diamond glinting on her ring finger. Smaller than the one Dad gave her in the eighties, but it's there, winking at me like a cruel joke. Wade's eyes drop to mine, his lip curled above his teeth—a gummy, victorious sneer.

A wrenching mix of horror and shock unfurls low in my belly as Mom wraps her arms around me—a tight, familiar hug. I feel like I'll disintegrate. Like my body is made of sand, on the brink of collapsing into something formless.

"Sweetie." She pulls back, her hands on my shoulders, her face an explosion of joy. "Wade surprised me this morning. Breakfast in bed, mimosas, the whole nine yards. He proposed, Billie." Her eyes are shining, tears pooling at the corners. "We're getting married."

"Mom." My voice is strangled, hoarse. "Wow." A headache crawls to

the front of my brain, slinking into the space around my sinuses, tight-
ening. Blood pounds in my ears, a heavy thump that distorts the sound
in the room. Mom says something about champagne, about us being old
enough for a splash, and disappears into the kitchen.

My eyes find Wade, my heart in my throat as the anger slowly settles.
"How can you marry her?" I shake my head. "Tomorrow she might not
even remember that you asked her."

"So I'll ask her again." He smirks. "C'mon, Billie Jean. The least you
can do is give your future stepfather a warm embrace." He lumbers toward
me, his thick, heavy arms encircling my shoulders. His grip is suffocat-
ing; he smells like sour sweat and sardines. I try to pull back, but I'm
trapped—he won't let go. Slowly, I feel his hand slide down my back, his
fingers tracing each knob of my spine.

"Get off me," I spit, trembling.

But he doesn't stop. When he reaches my tailbone, he keeps going.
Icy fear pricks my body as he cups my ass, squeezing over the thin cotton
of my leggings.

"Mmm. You have the same juicy ass as your mother." His whisper
is a growl, hot and damp in my ear. "You know, I'm genuinely looking
forward to having a daughter." He squeezes again.

"Get the fuck off her." Cassie's voice is hard, irate. She yanks at
Wade's arm, but she isn't strong enough.

"Don't listen to your friend." Wade snickers. "I bet all the boys at
school think she's the hot one, but if the choice were mine, I'd have me
some Billie Jean." He cackles. "Hell, maybe I will."

I'm numb with terror, too frozen to react. I hear the creak of the
kitchen door swinging and Wade's hand jumps north, landing on the
back of my turtleneck. A normal hug.

"What a sweet sight." I can hear the smile in Mom's voice. "I could've
sworn I had another bottle of champagne, but I can't find it any-
where . . ."

Wade releases me. I stare at the floor, at the worn fibers of the ori-
ental rug that's been in our house for as long as I can remember. It used
to be in the master bedroom, back when my parents were still married.

"That's okay, Lor." Wade kisses her cheek. "I'll run out and get some.
We need more Bud, anyway."

"Thanks, baby. My credit card is in the center console."

I open my mouth. I want to ask Mom why Wade can't use his own credit card, but there's a painful knot at the base of my throat.

Mom is studying me. "You okay, honey? You look pale."

"We had some nasty cafeteria tacos earlier," Cassie says, saving me. "We've both been queasy since. Come on, Bill, let's get some air." She turns to Mom and flashes an innocent smile. "We'll be right back, Lorraine."

We escape to the widow's walk on the roof of the house. It's been our spot for years, even though Mom hates us coming up here. She says it's dangerous, since one side of the railing has a few rotten posts. She's been bugging Wade to fix them since he moved in.

"Fuck, Billie." Cassie presses her palms to her forehead. "Fuck."

I'm lying horizontal on the wooden slats, my vision lost in the overcast sky, the thick tangle of clouds that shields the sun.

She lies down beside me. "I'll kill him if he touches you."

"He just did."

"You know what I mean." She pauses. "You have to tell your mom."

My throat is hot, full of tears. "I can't."

"You have to."

"There's no point, Cassie. She'll forget. Her short-term memory is essentially gone."

"I know, but this is serious."

I shake my head. "I refuse to keep reminding her, to keep making her miserable over and over again. She's literally losing her mind, and Wade is the one thing that seems to be distracting her from that. Did you see how happy she was just now? God . . . I haven't seen her like that in months."

"Fine. Then tell your dad."

I think of my father, living in a Dallas suburb with Melody, who thinks my name is Millie. They have three kids I've never met. He doesn't call on my birthday.

"No way. He doesn't even know about Mom." I turn to Cassie, my eyes leaking. "You know what's going to happen, right? Wade is going to marry her, and then, when it gets so bad that she has to go live in a home—because the doctor said it's only a matter of time—then it'll just be Wade and me. And he'll have all her money and he'll be able to do whatever he wants."

"*That's not going to happen. What about your mom's family? Can't they help?*"

I shake my head, thinking of Mom's mother and her sister, Christine, both living in Vancouver, Mom's hometown, thousands of miles away. Mom only talks to them a few times a year, and neither of them have any money. They live together in a tiny double-wide, with Christine's husband, Ron, and their adult son, my cousin, Dylan, who has yet to get his own place. I tell Cassie as much.

She takes my hand again, knotting our fingers. "*Then you'll come live with me.*"

"*Cass . . .*"

"*I'm serious. I'll get bunk beds, or we'll take Mara's room when she goes to college.*"

The clouds darken, ominous swirls of charcoal. A drop of cold rain lands on my cheek, mixing with my tears.

"*Billie.*" *Cassie blinks, and there are tears in her eyes, too.* "*I love you so much. You're my best friend.*" *Thunder cracks through the sky, a warning.* "*I swear on my life, everything is going to be okay.*"

Chapter Thirteen

Billie

September 10, 2023
33 days before

Alex has magic hands, I decide as he presses against me, his fingers tracing the inside of my thigh. Liquid light filters in through the slatted blinds, dappling our skin.

Before last night, I hadn't slept with anyone in ten months. Not since Dean, an accountant I went on four dull, perfunctory dates with last fall. We had sex on the fourth one, and only because I thought I should. I hadn't liked anyone in ages, and I thought doing it might make me feel something. Afterward, Dean spooned me for thirty seconds before scrambling out of my apartment, claiming he needed to get home for night seven of a two-week teeth-whitening regimen. I think we both knew we'd never see each other again.

It strikes me now, as Alex plays with the hem of the oversize T-shirt I slept in, how much better his touch feels than Dean's, than anyone I've been with in longer than I can remember. Maybe even better than Remy's. I close my eyes, a potent pressure weighing in my stomach at the thought of Remy, my last and only serious relationship. A blurred image of him appears in my mind—nut-brown curls, light gray eyes; taller than Alex, but lanky, missing his strength.

I push the image of Remy away and grip Alex harder as he draws his hands higher, running them up my thighs.

I didn't sleep in underwear, so it's easy. He slides two fingers inside me, slow at first. I let out a soft moan and fall back onto the pillows, pulling him down with me.

The sex is so much better this time, in the morning, without the alcohol dulling our senses. When it's over, Alex kisses me, his lips soft but solid at once. My mouth works its way into a smile against his.

"I haven't had sex like that in a long time." They're the words running through my head; I don't realize I've spoken them out loud until it's too late. They sit between us.

But Alex just grins, falling onto his back beside me. "I like you, Billie." He tugs my baggy sleeve. "And I like you in my shirt."

My whole body is dense and buzzy as I prop myself up on one elbow, blinking, absorbing the sight of Alex's apartment.

"So this is where you live."

His place is technically a studio, but it's big—more spacious than I'd anticipated. I admire the charming details: high ceilings with coffered moldings; tall windows overlooking tree-lined Twenty-third Street; wide pine floorboards; a wall of built-in bookshelves. I scan the rows of hardbacks; there's a lot of Gladwell, Grisham, Baldacci, Bill Bryson, a few surfing books. I have to smile. Alex is such a guy.

"My brother and I surf the Rockaways whenever we get the chance," he says, following my gaze.

"Cool. Does he live in the city?"

"Brooklyn." Alex takes a pair of horn-rimmed glasses from his nightstand and secures them over the bridge of his nose. "He and his wife just bought in Prospect Heights."

I nod, glancing around. "Well, your place is amazing. Not your average studio."

His eyes wander to the kitchen at the far side of the apartment— it's all stainless steel and clean white countertops. "Yeah, it's sweet. I've lived here for six years and it's rent-stabilized, so I really lucked out."

I smile and touch the edges of his glasses, which make him look more like a hot professor than a cop. "I'm into these."

He leans over and kisses me again, more deeply this time. "I could kiss you all weekend," he says.

I stay at Alex's until the next morning, wrapped in his silky sheets and his strong, warm limbs. We emerge from bed only for coffee, and for Amstel Lights from the fridge, and to answer the door when Chinese takeout arrives. We dunk dumplings in soy sauce and watch *Ted Lasso* and laugh at all the same parts. And after thirty-six hours at his apartment, I feel like walking sex.

"Don't go," he says, when I untangle myself from his grasp Monday morning. I've showered and brushed my hair with Alex's tiny man comb. I got lucky with my hair—it air dries thick and shiny, with just enough of a natural wave to give it volume, never frizz. I have an old Revlon dryer that I've used maybe twice.

I shimmy out of my towel and pull on the same dress I wore to Cassie's dinner party, now wrinkled from spending two nights in a crumpled ball on Alex's couch.

I grin at the sight of him lounging on the bed in boxers, hands interlaced across his torso. There seems to be a permanent look of appeasement on his face, as if his lips will break into an easy smile at any moment.

"Some of us have work," I tell him. "You included."

"Not till three. I have the evening shift on Mondays."

I poke my arms into my jean jacket—an old one from J.Crew I've had since college. "Well. Thanks for letting me squat."

He yawns. "Thanks for inviting me to that terrible dinner party on Saturday."

An uneasy feeling wobbles through me. I've been too distracted with Alex to think much about Cassie's dinner, but the memory comes roaring back.

"I'm kidding." Alex climbs out of bed, wraps his arms around me. "You smell like my shampoo. I like it."

"I like that you like it."

"Come back tonight? I'm not off till eleven, so maybe that sounds like a booty call."

I laugh. "That definitely sounds like a booty call."

"Tomorrow, then. We'll go out. A proper date." He smooths my hair, still damp from the shower. "Don't make me beg, Billie." I love the way he says my name.

I press my chin to his chest. "We might be past the stage of proper dates. Besides, I don't think I can wait until tomorrow."

"Neither can I."

"I'll come back tonight," I tell him, knowing the promise of it will carry me through the day on a cloud.

On Seventh Avenue, I dip into a Starbucks, where I order a Venti latte and one of their breakfast wraps. There's a crisp quality to the early-morning air that makes the hot, milky coffee taste especially good.

Walking back down to Greenwich Village with my AirPods in, Taylor Swift's *Lover* album blaring, I'm in heaven.

An incoming call interrupts my trance.

"Jane."

"Where the hell have you been? Ever heard of responding to texts?"

"Hmm. Did you text me?"

"What's wrong? Why do you sound all light and airy? Did Cassie poison you on Saturday?"

I laugh. "No."

Jane is silent for a moment. "Wait. You had sex."

"Jesus, Jane."

"You had *good* sex. With Alex."

"*Jane.*" I cross Bleecker Street, pushing myself through a swarm of commuters darting for the subway. I'm almost home.

"Yes?"

"How do you know *everything*?"

I feel Jane grinning through the phone. "Call me later this morning, after you check your email. That *fucking* client Yvette—you know, the crazy woman who wants to book a monthlong safari for her and her senile husband—"

"Gold digger Yvette?"

"That's the one. She's on our case about the contract. Feels twelve percent is a bit steep."

"Christ. People with money—"

"Are terrified of losing it. I know."

I can't help but smile. Jane and I truly do finish each other's sentences. I pull open the heavy door to my building, careful not to spill my coffee. "I just got home. Let me read her email and I'll call you back."

Upstairs, my apartment is quiet and clean, just how I left it on Saturday. I leave my purse on the lacquered chest by the entryway and wander into my "office," which is really just a small nook off the living room with a desk and a Herman Miller chair that was worth every penny. All fifteen of The Path's employees work remotely, from a variety of cities around the country. It's an ideal situation in my book—I cherish the freedom and flexibility of not being chained to an office. Jane and I get together multiple times a week when we're not on a trip, but mostly because we want to. If we weren't such close friends, we'd probably just limit our relationship to Zoom like the rest of the company.

I sink into my swivel chair and power on my laptop. While it revs to life, I check my phone. I already have a text from Alex: My apartment feels weirdly empty without you . . . It makes my stomach flip.

I open Instagram. I didn't check the app all weekend, which feels like a personal record. Cassie has a whole slew of stories I haven't watched yet, so I click her avatar while my computer continues to boot. There she is yesterday morning, walking through Madison Square Park with McKay and Ava. The three of them are drinking iced coffees and pushing strollers. They're all dressed the same: black leggings that accentuate their pin-thin legs; lightweight sweaters; cat-eye sunglasses.

I watch Cassie go back to her apartment and put Ella down for a nap. I watch her make a smoothie in the kitchen: frozen banana, spinach, chia seeds, almond butter, oat milk. I watch her try on a new dress that the store will carry starting in October. It's taupe, smocked, puff-sleeved—it looks like every other dress in every other store. Six hundred dollars.

Cassie drifts into her walk-in closet, keeping the camera close to her face as she gives a lecture on the importance of investment pieces.

"A couple of good blazers, Chanel slingbacks, diamond studs, you get the gist." The way she smiles into the phone reminds me of a jack-o'-lantern, her teeth glowing. "Timeless items you'll wear forever and ever."

My computer has finished booting. Dozens of unread emails wait in my inbox, but I can't stop watching Cassie.

She plucks an avocado from a white ceramic bowl on her kitchen counter.

"I think I'll make guacamole tonight," she tells the world. "Ella *loves* her guac."

"Yeah, right," I mutter out loud to no one. "Lourdes will make guac while you film yourself taking a giant shit."

Now Cassie is holding a bottle of red wine next to her face. On the label, a cat dressed in a tuxedo dangles a bunch of grapes.

"I've been meaning to tell you guys about this wine, because I just bought some for a dinner party I hosted on Saturday, and it's *so* good.

Like, will be stocking this in bulk at the Adler residence going forward." She laughs like a hyena. "And it's only sixty, so very well-priced for your house red."

Only sixty. As if that's an attainable amount of money for the average person to spend on an everyday bottle of wine. I think of the sauvignon blanc Cassie's mother used to drink when we were kids— piss-yellow magnums from Barefoot Cellars for under ten dollars. We used to take swigs from the fridge when she wasn't looking, savoring every sour, acetic mouthful.

"Oh, and here's a photo from my dinner party that I meant to share earlier. It's the only pic I took, believe it or not. I guess that's the sign of a good party."

The next story shows the picture Cassie snapped while standing on her chair—the bird's-eye view of the table. She's tightened the photo to better fit the frame, but when I search for my face, it isn't there. A hard knot forms behind my collarbone, sliding down into my stomach like a stone. Everyone who was at the dinner is in the photo—Grant, McKay, Tom, Ava, Blake, Evelyn, the velvet-loafer-clad husbands—but not me. Not Alex. She's cropped us out.

The best night with the best friends, Cassie has captioned. Underneath, everyone is tagged except me.

I fight the tears that come instantly, automatically, knowing my reaction is overkill. If Jane were here, she'd tell me to get my shit together. *It's just a fucking picture on Instagram, Billie. You can't overthink this stuff. You're going to make yourself crazy. Besides, Cassie is a narcissistic she-devil. What do you expect?*

I stare at the photo for too long, a gnarled web of emotions clawing inside me. I wish I could hate Cassie for her unique ability to make me feel objectively unwanted, for giving me the physical sensation of shrinking, of invisibility. But I can't. There's an old stubborn loyalty I cannot fight, a love that lingers in my soul, that's woven into the fabric of my systemic rhythms. Like knowing how to swallow, how to cry, how to breathe. How do you forget something like that? How do you push a love like that out of your physical body?

I wish I could ask Cassie.

Chapter Fourteen

Cassie

September 18, 2023
25 days before

McKay, Ava, and I take the 6:00 a.m. Yoga Sculpt at CorePower on Monday morning. The time is brutal, but we agree that if we don't get it done bright and early, it won't happen. Life is too fucking crazy these days.

I'm desperate for a workout, too. Desperate to get out of my mind, into my body. I can't shake the anxious, ominous feeling that's lingered since reading that creepy DM last Sunday.

Returning to the scene of the crime, are we?

Nine words that echo in my head. I've looked into the username, but birchballer6 is a private account with only two hundred followers, and there isn't a bio or a profile photo. I keep trying to convince myself that the paranoia isn't warranted. That what happened back then is so far in the past, it's nothing but a dead, forgotten nightmare. There isn't a way for it to reach me now.

The Yoga Sculpt instructor, Madison, really works us this morning. We do double sets of mountain climbers and burpees, and by the end of the class, my leggings and crop top are completely soaked through with sweat.

"Christ," Ava says, mopping her face on the way out of the heated studio. "I won't be able to walk tomorrow."

"As if you don't work out daily, Aves." McKay hands her a fresh towel from a stack beside the lockers.

"Not anymore. I *still* can't sit on the Peloton because my crotch is so fucked up."

I wince. Ava gave birth to her son in July and had a fourth-degree tear. That was ten weeks ago, and her stitches aren't done healing. No one talks about what a bitch postpartum can be—my friends and I have had to figure that out for ourselves.

A girl who looks like she's still in college is staring in our direction from a few lockers over. Her skin is tight and lineless, dewy with youth and sweat. I recognize her from class; she was on the mat to the left of McKay's.

Ava catches the girl staring and frowns. "Sorry if you overheard that graphic detail. Tell your friends to use birth control unless they want a vagasshole."

I laugh—Ava is ruthless in her sense of humor—at the same time the girl's brow raises in confusion. "Um, sorry," she says, and I notice then that her eyes are fixed on me. "I just wanted to say that I'm a huge fan."

"*Oh*. So this isn't about my desecrated nether regions. It's about my famous friend, Cassie Adler." Ava gives me a soft jab in the ribs. "Shoulda known."

I study the girl. Her body is small and toned, her raven hair scraped up into a topknot. "Thank you," I say, flashing a smile so big it hurts my mouth.

"I *love* following you," she gushes, her eyes brightening. "Ella is *so* cute, and my friends and I are obsessed with Cassidy Adler. I live on Mercer, so I pop in all the time."

"That means a lot," I say, genuinely grateful that she mentioned the store and not just my Instagram. I study her pale, poreless skin with a twinge of envy. Billie and I spent too much time in the sun as teenagers.

"I love meeting followers in person," I add, because it's true. The feeling of meeting people who are genuinely interested in my life and in my business never gets old. I'm not a celebrity by any means, but I'm on the spectrum of being someone *known*.

"Can we get a picture?" The girl blinks up at me, hopeful.

I get asked for pictures every now and then—once or twice a month, maybe—not often enough that I can justify saying no, even when I'm drenched in sweat.

I slip the elastic band from my ponytail, fluff my hair over my shoulders. "Of course."

The girl beams. Presumptuously, she hands her phone to McKay, who raises an eyebrow in my direction. I shrug as if to say: *Just take the damn picture so we can go get coffee.*

"I'm Sam, by the way," the girl offers as if I'll remember or care.

She sidles up next to me, and I pose for the camera. Lips curled but touching, no teeth, like I'm sucking on a mint. My abs are exposed in my crop top, and I make sure to tighten them, pulling in the low part of my stomach that's still fleshy from pregnancy.

"Thanks," Sam says, taking her phone back from McKay. "My friends are going to *die* when I tell them I met you. We're literally your biggest fans." Her gaze moves down the length of my body. "You look *hot,* by the way. I can't believe you just had a baby."

Ten minutes later, McKay, Ava, and I sip oat milk lattes at a table outside Ralph's, our go-to breakfast spot after a CorePower class.

"It's kind of crazy how celebrity you've become," Ava is saying. She picks at her yogurt bowl. Ava has always been afraid of food, even the healthiest choices. "Not to say I don't enjoy watching college girls drool over your post-baby abs, because I definitely do. We need more of that."

I smile, swallowing a bite of my avocado toast. I hold my phone above the table and snap an artful shot of our meal.

Nothing beats a morning of @corepoweryoga and @ralphscoffee with @mckayadlermorris and @avab_nyc, I caption.

McKay's and Ava's phones both buzz with the notification that I've tagged them on Instagram.

McKay checks her screen. "Basic, but lovely."

I clink my mug against hers. "My vibe precisely."

A cloud passes over the sun, shading our table. I reach down and grab a gray Alo hoodie from my yoga bag. I slip my arms into the soft sleeves and pull the sweatshirt overhead, adjusting my hair around the collar, and that's when I see her. Thick, honey-brown locks, a familiar stride I could never mistake. Heading right toward us.

McKay squints. "Isn't that Billie?"

Ava zips her Lululemon jacket up to her chin, peering down the street. "That *is* her."

I chew my bottom lip, averting my gaze. I haven't spoken to Billie since she came to dinner at our apartment. She texted to thank me for having her and Alex, but I forgot to respond. That was a week ago.

McKay frowns, lowers her voice. "She was weird at your dinner party. Barely said a word."

"Well, we were probably talking about baby stuff the whole time," Ava points out. "And she doesn't have kids."

"No, she was totally weird." I glance at McKay and nod. "I regret inviting her, honestly. And her *cop* boyfriend. I can't believe Billie is going for the type of guy who could've gone to our high school."

Ava giggles, raises an eyebrow. "You're mean, Cass."

"Shh." I shake my head at Ava, a silent order to table the conversation. Billie is more than halfway down the block, mere feet from us now.

"Cassie." She says my name first, stopping short when she sees us, waving to McKay and Ava. She wears loose linen pants and the same jean jacket she's had forever. Grungy white Vans, no makeup, a *New Yorker* tote bag hanging from her shoulder.

"Billie!" I rearrange my face into a smile. "What are you doing in this neighborhood? And so early?"

Billie checks her watch. "It's quarter of eight. It's not that early." She looks up, her hazel eyes locking mine. "Even childless women have to wake up in the morning."

A typical Billie dig. Underneath the table, McKay kicks my foot.

"Alex lives in Chelsea, and I have an errand to run in Union Square," she adds. "This is my route home today."

"Ah." An awkward silence engulfs the space between us. If I were a kinder person, I'd invite her to join us for a coffee. But I'm not a kinder person. At some base level, subconsciously, I know this. And I'm fine with it. Because the more years that pass, the more I've come to understand my own limits. And how to effectively *implement* those limits. Just because I run into Billie doesn't mean I need to invite her into my day. I'm not required to love her as much as she loves me. I'm not required to love her at all.

"What are you doing for your birthday, Cass?"

The question catches me off guard. "It's like a month away."

Billie shrugs. "Yeah, but your birthday is your thing."

"My thing? Not really." Irritation pricks my chest. "I stopped loving my birthday halfway through my twenties. Same as most people."

"No way," she presses, and the statement is more of a query. "You plan something every year. Remember your thirtieth? We had that party on the rooftop of the Delancey, and then afterward, everyone went to the St. Lucia concert at Bowery Electric, and we told the band it was your birthday and they pulled you up onstage. Remember how obsessed you used to be with St. Lucia?"

I feel McKay and Ava staring between us, uncomfortably digesting this secondhand awkwardness. Neither of them was present for my thirtieth birthday. That was a different time. A different *me*. In this moment, I can't stand Billie. I just want her to leave me the fuck alone.

I give a thin laugh. "God, Bill, is there anything you *don't* remember?"

I watch her deflate. But then, something in her face changes. I can almost see the defiance rise behind her rib cage.

"You're about to turn thirty-five, Cass. I just figured you'd be doing something. It's a big one."

"Don't remind me." I frown, tapping my fingernails against the wooden surface of the table. I look up, meet her gaze. "I'm thinking I'll keep it low-key this year, but if I change my mind, I'll obviously let you know."

Billie adjusts the bag on her shoulder. "Well, if you want to have a quiet dinner or something, I'm around?" Her sentence spins off into a question, her eyes searching mine. "Maybe Balthazar, like old times?"

I want to laugh in her face. I feel a kind of wickedness move through me, absent of shame. Balthazar was our spot years ago, before everything changed. We used to sit at the bar and order escargot and champagne and relive our high school trip to Paris with Grandma Catherine, speaking in terrible French accents. Two giddy twenty-five-year-olds. Another lifetime. Is she kidding?

I want to remind her that we haven't been to Balthazar in half a decade, that it isn't like that between us anymore, that I have a husband and a baby and best friends like McKay and Ava, and that if I were going to spend my birthday with anyone, it would be them.

But I don't say any of this. Instead, I will myself to remain pleasant, harmless. I remember that if I stay in that lane with Billie, she can't touch me.

"Balthazar. What a throwback." I force a wistful smile and pick at my manicure, little chips of cherry-red polish falling to my lap.

Billie folds her arms and says nothing, her weight shifting from one foot to the other. For a passing moment, I almost feel sorry for her.

McKay gives my foot another kick under the table, then taps her phone screen. "It's past eight." She sighs. "I need to get back. Tom has a call in twenty minutes, which means I'm on kid duty."

I know McKay is fibbing—she has Mariana on Mondays—but in this moment, I'm endlessly grateful for her smooth white lie.

Billie holds up a hand. "I should get going, too. Nice to see you, ladies."

The three of us wiggle our fingers. "Bye, Bill," I call. "Let's *please* get together soon."

When Billie has crossed the street, McKay turns to me. "You are *so* good at being fake nice to her."

I roll my eyes. "It's easier that way. God, that was brutal. Thanks for saving me. I know you have Mariana today."

"I do, but I still need to get back. I have a call with a caterer about this damn Frick event." McKay spots our waiter, waves for the check. "But first, let's clear one thing up. You're *having* a thirty-fifth birthday party."

I laugh. "Is that so?"

"You must!" Ava claps her hands together. "McKay and I will talk to Grant. You won't have to lift a finger."

I cross my legs, considering for a moment. "*If* I have a party—"

"Which you *will*—"

"—it's easier if Billie doesn't come. Okay? I'll just be stressed if she's there."

"After that extreme discomfort just witnessed by all, message received." Ava licks a speck of yogurt off the end of her spoon. "Childhood friendships are fucking weird. I feel badly for Billie, honestly. Midthirties, single, no kids. That's tough."

I dig my credit card out of my wallet. "She doesn't seem to want kids."

McKay snorts. "That's a load of crock. Everybody wants kids."

The three of us pay the bill, then head east toward Gramercy. We part ways at Twentieth Street, where McKay and Ava both live, promising to do lunch or a walk later in the week. I continue north, quickening my pace, the anxiety kicking back in now that I'm alone. Perhaps it's due to seeing Billie, but all I can think of is the trip to Red Hook, the message from birchballer6. *How* could someone know? And if someone knows, what could that mean?

All I want, in this moment, is to be with Grant and Ella. As the worry encroaches—dark, ravenous, churning through me like a parasite—I'm running up Lex without realizing it, my yoga mat bouncing against my back in its cotton bag.

My heart is pounding by the time I reach the apartment, sweat beading my temples. Grant sits at the kitchen counter, baby spoon in hand, Ella beside him in her clip-on chair. He's feeding her puréed sweet potatoes—the ones Lourdes made from scratch now that we've introduced solids. Orange driblets run down Ella's chin, smearing her chipmunk cheeks. She smiles when she sees me, and I'm flooded with such intense relief that tears spring to my eyes. I drop my bag, press my face to hers.

"Whoa, babe." Grant touches my arm with his free hand. "You're out of breath. You okay?"

I nod, smothering Ella with kisses, so many that she starts to whine. I know I'm covered in sweet potatoes, but I couldn't care less.

"I'm okay." I pull back, my eyes still glued to Ella, my heart still beating fast. I want to tell him: *I'm scared.*

But I don't. I can't.

Instead, I wrap my arms around his neck and lean down to kiss him, and he doesn't care that I'm covered in sweet potatoes, either. "I'm okay," I say again. "I just really missed her. I missed you both."

Chapter Fifteen
Billie

2005–2006

Senior year, Wade and Mom get married in a small courthouse cere-
mony, even though her long-term memories have started to disappear,
too. She goes for a walk and winds up on the other side of town, unable
to find her way home. She calls me from her cell phone, sobbing and
afraid.

She calls me, not Wade, so that's something. Still, he's my stepfather
now. My disgusting pervert of a stepfather, who touches my ass every
chance he gets—when I'm removing a casserole from the oven, or rinsing
dishes at the sink, or checking my reflection in the front hall mirror. I feel
his big meaty hand on the back of my jeans, the nauseating, inevitable
squeeze.

One night, when Mom is already asleep, he comes into the bathroom
when I've just gotten out of the shower. I clutch the towel tighter against
my chest, goose bumps pricking my skin. He gives a sly smile, reaches
for me.

"Get away." My voice melts in my windpipe, barely audible against
the whirring of the fan.

His finger traces my jawline, stopping in the center of my chin.

"You are so beautiful, Billie Jean. A teenage version of Lorraine." His
hand moves south, grazing my rib cage, all the way down to my hip. I
close my eyes in terror as he presses against me, all of him, swollen and
throbbing. All that separates us is my flimsy cotton towel, his boxers.
Bile shoots up my throat, and when I turn to heave in the sink, he laughs
and wanders away.

When I tell Cassie, she says it's only a matter of time before he does
something worse. She says I need to alert the authorities. But I can't do

that to Mom, not in her fragile state. I was there when the doctor told us to keep things easy and happy and peaceful at the end. Before she slips away for good. Added stress could send her over the edge too soon, into an impressionless void from which she'll never come back.

When I explain all this to Cassie, she watches me with heavy eyes. "But, Billie," she says, unblinking. "She's already gone."

In that moment, I hate her. Pure and deep. I run home from school, my body searing with panic at the thought of losing Mom. Inevitable, true.

She's already gone.

I find Mom in her bed, resting. She spends most of her days there. I kick off my Converses and crawl into bed beside her like a little girl, feel the warmth of her, the beating life of her. I burrow into her side and sob silently, staining her nightgown with my tears.

In December, Cassie gets accepted early decision to Harvard. She's a double legacy there—her grandfather and father both attended—and Grandma Catherine is paying her tuition.

"Why doesn't Grandma Catherine pay for Mara's college?" I ask. Mara goes to state school an hour north. She has a boyfriend named Ace, who deals weed.

Cassie huffs. It's Saturday, and we're sitting on her bed painting our nails. She examines hers—metallic purple—then reaches for the clear bottle of topcoat. "Mara hasn't spoken to Grandma Catherine in years. You know this."

"But still. You're both her grandchildren."

"But I'm the only one who makes an effort. I call her. I send birthday cards. I go down and see her in Greenwich. Mara doesn't." Cassie shrugs. "Mara doesn't care if she goes to some dumpy state school. She doesn't care about Harvard."

"You think she could've gotten into Harvard?"

"She *did* get into Harvard. My grandfather basically paid for the library."

"For real?" I study Cassie. I can't imagine turning down an Ivy League college for a state school.

"Yup. My dad called Grandma Catherine for the first time in years and asked her to pay Mara's tuition. But she refused." The expression on

Cassie's face is almost smug. "She told my dad the only person in our family she feels any allegiance to is me."

"Wow."

"That's why she gave me the Tiffany heart bracelet for my birthday. And it's real—unlike the fake one Ashton bought in Chinatown."

I suppress the urge to roll my eyes; Cassie still can't resist a dig at Ashton. "Yeah."

"My parents and Mara are really so dumb for cutting ties with her." *Cassie blows lightly on her nails.* "So much of life is about being in with the right people, you know?"

I don't know, but I nod, anyway.

"I'm sure you'll get into Northeastern." *Cassie hands me the topcoat, giddy.* "Then we'll only be ten minutes apart."

I say nothing for a moment, imagining this potential reality. It's far from fair, the fact that Cassie will attend the top university in the country while the best school I applied to is barely mid-tier. My grades are better than hers—substantially. Cassie would've failed Algebra II if I hadn't been her tutor most of junior year.

But I don't have a rich grandmother. My name isn't on any building.

I feel Cassie's eyes on me. "What're you thinking?" *Her voice is soft.*

I sigh. "Even if I get into Northeastern . . . that doesn't mean I get to go."

"It depends how much financial aid you get. I know."

"It depends what Wade decides he wants to do. He's my guardian now." *A queasy wave rocks in my stomach.*

Cassie frowns. "But it's not his money. It's your mom's. I thought you said she had a college fund saved."

"It doesn't matter."

"Billie, your mom is still—"

"She's already gone. You said it yourself."

"I didn't mean—"

"Cassie." *My voice is thick with tears. They slide from the corners of my eyes and leak down my cheeks.* "Can we just . . . can we not talk about this right now? Can we go for a drive or something?"

Cassie takes her dad's Saab without asking. We stop at Holy Cow for ice cream, even though it's frigid, and eat our mint chip cones driving south on Route 9. It's Saturday afternoon, and there isn't any traffic. The trees are bare, and the sun sets at four thirty, the sky morphing from cobalt to navy to black, a line of neon orange singeing the horizon through the skeletal forests. We get cold from the ice cream, so Cassie blasts the heat. A CD plays from the speakers—it's mostly Alanis Morissette and Third Eye Blind, an old mix I made junior year. I don't know how long we drive, but at some point, Cassie turns down the music, and I know she's about to break the silence.

"I love you, Bill," she says. "No matter where we end up next year, you'll always be my best friend." She keeps her eyes on the road, but I can see the edge of her smile in profile. "And nobody puts Baby in a corner, right?"

It's the bleak brink of winter, the landscape is miserable, and it's dark when it should be light, but I'm crushed with gratitude. For Cassie, for walking into my life, for choosing me for some enigmatic reason that escapes me. Or maybe that's just how friendship works when you're young. Maybe the choice to tether yourselves to each other isn't a choice at all but an unconscious pull that doesn't require an explanation, a response to shared circumstance, joined with something in your heart that feels good and right. The loyalty that follows feels inherent, lasting, tamperproof.

"Nobody puts Baby in a corner," I echo, blinking away tears. "And I love you, too."

The low beat of "Hand in My Pocket" thrums through the speakers, and Cassie cranks the volume.

I'm sad, but I'm laughing

I'm brave, but I'm chickenshit

Cassie knows every word to every Alanis track, and she sings along at the top of her lungs like we're in a karaoke bar. I laugh. I love her so much.

We turn around at the next intersection, head back the way we came.

"Wanna sleep over?" she asks. "I found a six-pack under Mara's bed."

"Sure. Will your parents let us go to Owen's party?"

Cassie makes a face. "You want to go to that?"

I shrug. Owen is the captain of the basketball team, and I sort of have a crush on him, but Cassie thinks the basketball guys are losers. According to Cassie, the only "cool" sports are hockey and lacrosse. And squash, but I don't know what that is. She says it's a big thing in Greenwich. But it isn't just the basketball guys. Since senior year started, Cassie never wants to go to parties anymore.

"Sort of." I put my feet up on the dash, stretch my hamstrings. "I haven't kissed anyone since Todd Clemmons freshman fall. That's pathetic."

Cassie sighs. "It's only because our school is full of dweebs. Let's just drink at my house and watch Dirty Dancing and focus on the fact that this time next year, we'll be somewhere way more exciting. Where the men look like Patrick Swayze."

The last Saturday in March, a thick manila envelope comes in the mail. It's an acceptance packet from Northeastern, but it isn't good news. They're only giving me half the financial aid I applied for. Out of pocket, half tuition is still almost four times as much as a state school. Plus, I've already been offered a full ride to SUNY New Paltz, excluding student housing. Wade is thrilled about this. New Paltz is only thirty minutes from Red Hook. I could live at home, and the cost would be totally free.

Wade laughs in my face when I show him the packet from Northeastern.

"I'm not paying twenty grand a year for you to go to college." He stares at the television, scratching his balls through his sweatpants.

"It's not your money. It's Mom's."

He laughs again. "Child, are you out of your goddamn mind? Your mother is going to need a live-in nurse soon. Do you have any idea how expensive that is?"

"Fuck you."

One half of his mouth curls, his voice lowers. "Not if I fuck you first."

I call my father in Dallas. Melody answers the phone and tells me my father is out running errands.

"Have him call me back as soon as possible, please." I'm shaking. I hate Melody, but I try to sound polite so she'll do what I want. "It's about college, and it's an emergency."

Melody scowls. "It better not be some crap about needing money. Because he's never missed a goddamn child support payment, not in fifteen years, Millie."

I open my mouth to reply that this isn't true and that isn't my name, but she keeps barking.

"You tell your mother y'all won't be seeing an extra dime from him. He's given her thousands. Thousands! Don't call back here." The line goes dead in my ear.

Mom's out to lunch with her friend Lois. When Lois drops her at home, I make us a pot of Constant Comment, and we drink it at the kitchen table. Wade is outside spreading grass seed, making himself useful for a change. Mom watches him from the bay windows overlooking the backyard, a beholden smile on her face.

"Wade's such a help around here, isn't he?" Mom sips her tea. "This is good. Thanks, Bill."

"Mom." I place the acceptance letter in front of her. "I got into Northeastern." I will the tears back—knowing she won't remember tomorrow—but it's no use. They come, anyway, salty lines sliding down my cheeks.

"Billie!" Mom's face breaks into a look of pure elation, of genuine pride. "This is amazing! Oh, I knew you'd get in. I just knew it." She reaches for the nape of my neck, gives it a gentle squeeze. "Whoa. Why are you crying?"

I swipe the corners of my eyes. "I—well, the financial aid package isn't great." A lie that is also the truth.

Mom glances down at the letter, reading it carefully. "That's not true, honey." She picks her head up, her eyes brightening. "They're giving you half," she tells me as if I don't already know. "We can afford half."

"Are you sure, Mom?"

She nods fervently. "Of course I'm sure. It's the reason I've saved, Billie. You know your education is more important to me than anything. There's money set aside for this."

"I know, but, Mom—" I press my lips together, my throat throbbing. I can't say it.

But she's looking at me like she knows. "Billie. Wade will support this, too. He's a good man."

I study Mom, her chin pointed forward, the conviction in her eyes that tells me she believes her words are true. Swirls of panic and anger and something else—inevitable grief, maybe—churn through my veins. It's helpless agony, feeling her slip away from me, knowing there's nothing

I can do to stop it. And how can she leave me with him? *How can she not see who he is?*

I think of The Merchant of Venice, *which we read for AP English in the fall. Of how Jessica says of Lorenzo:* For I am much ashamed of my exchange, but love is blind and lovers cannot see. *Mrs. Vaughn told us Shakespeare wrote of love's blindness in three different plays. I see it now, the transcendence of that message.*

"Wade says you need a live-in nurse, Mom. He says that's expensive."

"No." *She shakes her head, but I watch her eyes fill.* "That's ridiculous. I'm fine. I'm fine."

"That's what I said," *I tell her, though we both know it isn't true.*

Mom sets her mug down on the table, so hard tea sloshes over the rim, seeping into the pine surface of the table. "Look at me." *Her voice is suddenly hard, on the verge of anger. She almost never gets mad, so I know it's serious.* "I saved that money for your college education. I've been saving it for seventeen years. It's money that's not going anywhere else. Do you understand?"

I nod.

She swallows. "I'll make sure Wade knows that."

Later, Cassie is over, and we're cooking chicken Milanese for dinner. She's sous-chef, since I've been watching Mom make this recipe my whole life. I pound the cutlets till they're tender, then Cassie dusts them with flour and panko bread crumbs while I slice a few lemons. Per usual, Wade is a fat lump on the sofa, half a dozen empty beer bottles littered around him while he watches his fourth hour of March Madness. After ten minutes of tossing grass seed around the yard, he deserves it.

"Smells delicious, girls." *Mom drifts into the kitchen. She's just out of the bath, wrapped in her pink kimono robe, her damp hair combed straight. She kisses my cheek, then Cassie's, peering over our shoulders.* "Really, is there a better scent than roasting garlic?"

She wanders over to the round table, riffling through a pile of mail when she lets out a yelp. I drop the knife. Lemon juice burns the raw cuticle on my thumb.

"What happened?" *I spin around to see Mom holding my Northeastern letter, her jaw on the floor.*

"Billie!" *Her eyes find mine, sparkling with delight, and I already know what comes next. "I'm so, so proud of you." Her arms are around me, tight; the ends of her hair drip water on my shirt as I drown in the notes of her cucumber face cream. "You got into Northeastern. I knew you would, baby." She holds the back of my head, her voice bursting with pride.*

I rest my chin on her bony shoulder, too sick to cry. Wade is watching me from the couch, a slow grin moving across his frightening face. He winks.

Chapter Sixteen

Billie

October 2, 2023
11 days before

I gulp hungry sips of air, hands pressed to the tops of my thighs as I heave forward, catching my breath. Between the railing slats, the Hudson River shimmers like liquid gold in the early-morning light. Alex hands me a bottle of Poland Spring. His forehead is slicked with sweat, but he's barely out of breath. He's in much better shape than I am.

"Four miles today." He grins.

I take a swig of water. "I'm going to be so sore."

Running the path along the West Side Highway before work has become our routine over the past couple of weeks. I like this about him—that he's active, that he brings out this side of me. I wasn't surprised to learn he's a runner—being fit is part of the job description for a patrol officer. Still, it's a romantic dynamic I'm not used to. All I know is what I had with Remy.

When Remy and I were together, we never worked out. We'd get deli bacon egg and cheeses every morning, eat them in bed like a couple of logs. For years, I smelled of bacon grease and Remy's beloved acrylics.

Alex hooks a hand around his ankle to stretch his quad, wincing a little. I admire his body, the sculpted muscles of his tan legs, the way his New York Rangers T-shirt pulls taut between the span of his broad shoulders. Something stirs deep and low inside of me, an insatiable thrumming. I move close to Alex, wrap my arms around his middle, and inhale the scent of him, salty sweat and Old Spice.

He kisses my forehead. "Maybe we should train for a half marathon."

I laugh. "Slow your roll. I just barely ran four miles."

When he smiles, a small dimple creases one of his cheeks. "Baby steps."

We stroll back to the Village hand in hand, stopping for cart coffees on the way. Mine is hot and milky with just the right amount of sugar—exactly what I need. The jolt of caffeine combined with post-cardio endorphins is a delicious, potent combination. The day is mine to conquer.

We're south of Chelsea, so Alex walks me to my building before heading back to his place. On Christopher Street, shopkeepers are beginning to open, iron-chained gates lifting from the storefronts. Alex tosses his empty cup in the nearest trash bin, then loops his arms around my neck.

"You look hot all sweaty. If I didn't have a call with this guy from the detective bureau at nine . . . I would totally follow you upstairs."

I bite my bottom lip, the thrumming sensation reigniting between my hips, stronger this time. "Don't tease me."

"So." He pauses. "I was thinking."

"You were thinking."

"My best buddy, Mark, is in town this weekend with his wife. Are you free Friday to meet them for dinner? I think my brother, Dave, and my sister-in-law are joining, too. We were all close in high school."

I don't mean to hesitate, but Alex sees the wavering look on my face.

"I promise it won't be totally boring," he adds. "Dave and Hailey are a blast; they're the ones who live in Brooklyn. And Fiona—Mark's wife—is very cool. She owns her own gallery in Seattle, where they're based now. I think you two will hit it off."

"It isn't that." I give a strained smile, digging through my brain for a way to articulate what, exactly, *it* is. A beat passes. "It feels serious, right? Meeting your best friend? And your brother?"

I watch Alex's face fall and know I've said the wrong thing.

"That isn't—I didn't mean that's not what I want." I sigh, nerves swimming in the pit of my belly. "I'm sorry. I'm so bad at this."

Alex leans against the stone rail of the front stoop, watching me. "Billie, if it's too soon—"

"Have you ever been in love?"

I can tell right away I've surprised him. We haven't discussed past relationships. It's a topic we've never even skimmed.

"Once," he says evenly. "We were together seven years." A pause. "She cheated on me."

"God. I'm sorry."

"Have you?"

An image of Remy forms in my mind. Beautiful Remy, the slender slope of his nose, his mess of Botticelli curls. Gentle gray eyes that felt like home, that held my soul. The first and only man who made me feel safe after what happened. He didn't save me—that was Cassie—but he did open my heart again.

"Once." I nod. "Also for a long time. I . . . screwed it up."

Alex's eyebrows knit together, creasing the space between them. "Did you cheat?"

"No." I shake my head. "In the end, I couldn't be what he wanted me to be. It caused both of us so much pain."

Alex's expression softens. "So, you're scared."

"I just—" My voice catches. "I don't think I can handle hurting another person that way again. It's the reason I've been on my own for so long."

"Billie." Alex reaches for a strand of hair that's come loose at the front of my ponytail and pushes it back behind my ear. Goose bumps prickle my cheekbone, the line of skin his fingers touched. I can't lose him.

He withdraws his hand, shrugs. "For what it's worth, I don't want you to be anything but what you are." His eyes find mine; I can see the disappointment, new and heavy. "You can think about dinner. Let me know. There isn't any pressure."

Alex gives my hand a quick squeeze, but he doesn't kiss me good-bye before he walks away. I feel gutted as I trudge the three flights of stairs up to my apartment, as I run the shower as hot as it will go. I step under the scorching water, let it scald the dried sweat from my skin.

Afterward, I wrap myself in a towel and sit down on the edge of my bed, the ends of my hair dripping water on the duvet. I call Jane.

"What if I'm sabotaging my relationship with Alex?"

Jane groans. I hear her fumbling around for something, the squeak of a mattress.

I stifle a laugh. "Did I wake you up?"

"Did you go on another crack-of-dawn run?" Her voice is raspy, hoarse.

"Maybe."

"Psychopath."

"It's quarter of nine, Jane."

"I know." I hear her chugging water through the phone. "Sasha and I had a late one. Two bottles of wine at dinner, lost count of how many Negronis at the Marlton. Didn't get to bed till three."

"Wow. I was asleep before ten."

"I despise you." There's the sound of the faucet turning, water filling up a glass. "Anyway. Continue. What's the deal with Alex?"

"He invited me to dinner with his best friend on Saturday. And his best friend's wife. And his brother and sister-in-law."

"Tell me there's more to this story."

"It just feels so . . . *serious*."

"Heading in that direction, maybe. Does it not feel right?"

"No, it does." I put the phone on speaker and toss it on the bed so I can dress while we talk. "But maybe I should tell him now that I'm not sure I want kids. Before things go any further in that direction. Right?"

"Wrong. You're scarred by what went down with Remy a million years ago—I get that. But you and Alex have been dating for, what, a month?"

"A little longer."

"Just . . . try to take the pressure off. Go to dinner. Meet his friends and family. Have fun. The right person fits into *your* life, Billie. Not the other way around."

"What are you saying?" I yank on a pair of high-waisted jeans, clasp the button.

Jane sighs. "I don't know when you'll finally forgive yourself for not rearranging your life to fit exactly what Remy wanted." She pauses. "You're such an inherently selfless person, but did you ever stop to think that it was mutual? That Remy refused to accommodate what *you* wanted just the same?"

I clip my bra and pull the straps up over my shoulders. "Honestly, no. I was the one who couldn't commit to having children."

"And in our culture, being childless by choice makes you a terrible person."

"A leper, basically. A woman with no real place in society."

Jane sighs again. "If there's a place in society for gay mothers, there has to be a place for straight non-mothers."

"You would think."

"And you never know. Maybe you'll change your mind."

"Maybe."

"Fuck." She winces. "I need a coffee the size of my head. And ten Advil."

"Poor Jane. Any occasion for all the Marlton Negronis?"

"Just in the mood to embrace the functioning alcoholic I could have been."

I laugh, riffling through my closet for a decent shirt.

"*Actually,* there was an occasion." Jane's voice springs to life. "I meant to text you last night. Sasha and I got the apartment."

"*What?* The one you showed me on StreetEasy the other day?"

"No, no. That place went for way over ask. But *this* place—hang on, I'll send you some pictures—is insane. Prewar, great Gramercy location, sick terrace. Our Realtor told us about it before it even went on the market, and we put in an offer right away. That's the only reason we got it, no question. The owners have already moved, so I think they just wanted to sell as quickly as possible."

"I didn't realize you were looking in Gramercy."

"We weren't originally. Okay, check your texts."

I pluck my phone from the bed, scroll through the images Jane has sent. The apartment is a two-bed, two-bath with high ceilings, inlaid oak floors, custom millwork on the moldings and doorways. The kitchen is huge and newly renovated, with a wine cooler and a walk-in pantry.

"Holy shit, Jane. It's stunning. I'm sorry, but . . . how can you afford a place like this?"

"Our little company is doing quite well, if you haven't noticed." I can feel Jane grinning through the phone. "And being married to a dermatologist in a city that's rabid for injectables helps, too."

I pull a blue-and-white-striped button-down from a hanger. The sleeves are wrinkled, but it'll do. "I'm thrilled for you guys. You've been apartment hunting for longer than anyone should have to."

"Don't I know it. Thank *god* this nightmare is finally over. And we close in two weeks."

"That seems quick."

"That's what I said, but it's because the apartment is already vacant. And our current lease is up in December, so we'll break early. Sayonara, Avenue A. See you never."

"I can't believe you'll be neighbors with Cassie."

"I forgot she lives in Gramercy. Gross." Jane pauses. "Have you talked to her since the dinner party from hell?"

I dig through the box of jewelry on my dresser and find a pair of small, thick silver hoops. I prefer gold over silver in general, but these are still my go-tos. They were a gift from Mom—the last Christmas present she ever gave me.

"I ran into her on the street a couple of weeks ago," I say, poking the hoops through each ear. "It was weird. I have this fear that she's planning some big thirty-fifth birthday party and not inviting me."

"Why do you think that?"

"Because I'm a paranoid freak who's still stuck in middle school? I don't know."

Jane sighs. "You're not a paranoid freak." The line is silent for a long moment. "But I'll never understand why you can't let that girl go."

I close my eyes, memories I can never erase rushing to the muddy blackness behind my lids. Of course Jane doesn't understand. Jane is the kind of person who doesn't look back, who would never let the past sink its claws in. But I'm not wired that way. And so everything that happened then lives in me now—defining, festering, haunting. Mom. Wade. Cassie. The secrets I can never share. If I could, I'd tell Jane just how much she doesn't know.

"Bill, I have to hop." Jane's voice rips me back to the moment. "We have that call with Le Sirenuse at ten, and I need to pull myself together."

"Right." I yawn, hit with a wave of fatigue, my muscles tender from the run. The post-caffeine buzz is already fading; I need more coffee. "Speaking of Le Sirenuse, what I wouldn't give to go back to Positano. If only for the espresso. And the tomatoes."

"Let's hope the call goes well, and maybe they'll host us in May or June."

"Fingers crossed."

"Oh, and, Billie? Text Alex. Tell him you'll do the dinner. Don't ruin this thing."

I hang up the phone, knowing Jane is right. I wander into my tiny kitchen and stick two pieces of sourdough in the toaster, put water on to boil for the french press. I gaze out the small window to the left of the sink, never not grateful for my view. Charming, tree-lined Christopher Street, the leaves bright flashes of yellow and red. Fall is well underway.

I think of my first New York apartment again, that tiny studio on East Eleventh Street that Cassie and I *shared*. It hardly seems possible, in retrospect. There were two windows in the whole place, both of which looked out at the brick exterior of the adjacent building. It was like living in a tunnel, but we were ecstatic to be there. High on life, on its possibilities, on the endless hypothetical paths that all held the legitimate potential to become real. And the freedom of being young enough to avoid choosing for a while longer.

The toaster dings, and two slices of browned sourdough jump through the slots. I reach for my phone and text Alex before I have the chance to overthink it.

> Forget what I said earlier. Dinner Friday sounds great.
> Can't wait to meet everyone.

I think of Jane's words: *The right person fits into* your *life, Billie. Not the other way around.*

I let myself imagine, for a passing moment, that perhaps she isn't wrong.

Chapter Seventeen

Cassie

October 3, 2023
10 days before

Grant finds me in bed in the middle of the day. Lourdes has taken Ella out for a walk, and I'm too zonked to move. An overflowing Zara shopping bag sits in the corner of the bedroom—yesterday's haul. I'd planned to do a try-on for my followers—people genuinely appreciate seeing the stuff I find at Zara—but I have zero energy. I can't even bring myself to work from my desk like a normal person. Instead, I'm propped up on a wad of euro shams with my laptop, drinking mint tea that I wish were a latte and worrying about the identity of birchballer6.

I've just typed *birchballer* into Google, but all that's come up is an online store that sells balls made of white birchwood. *Great for making models and crafts,* the description reads.

"Honey? You working?" Grant pokes his head through the doorway. He's wearing a gray blazer and his hair is combed back, slicked through with the gel he overuses.

I click out of the search results window. "Yes," I lie, because what I should be doing is browsing the Johanna Ortiz resort line. It's past time to order for spring/summer, and Violet, my SoHo store manager, emailed this morning to let me know we're running behind.

"Are you okay? You look a little pale."

"I'm tired, Grant." I close my laptop. "Ella was up three times last night."

"I know." He sighs and walks into the room, hands in his pockets. "This four-month sleep regression is killer. I'm completely wiped, too."

I scowl, remembering Ella's cries through the monitor. The agony of dragging myself out of bed while Grant snored obliviously, his face smashed into the pillow. The exhaustion isn't helping my anxiety.

"You didn't even wake up," I tell him.

"Yes, I did. Maybe not all three times, but I did. You're not the only one who gets to be tired, Cassie. We're both her parents."

In this moment, I despise this man. I clench my teeth, knowing we're on the brink of a blowout fight. But my eyes feel like paperweights. I don't have the energy to go there.

I swallow my anger, change course. "What are you doing home?"

"I have a lunch meeting at Eataly. I figured I'd swing by, check on my girls."

"Ella's with Lourdes until five thirty, every day except Friday. You know that."

Grant rubs his jaw. I can see the exasperation in his expression. "I figured they might be home, Cassie." He sits on the edge of the bed. I study his face—the small bags under his eyes, the rough, dull pallor of his skin. I feel empty of love for him in this moment, and I wonder, briefly, if our spark has just extinguished, or if there's someone out there who I could've loved more. Or perhaps going through a sleep regression with an infant is simply so draining that I'm sapped of all feeling.

One side of his mouth curls into a playful smile. "The last time I found you in bed in the middle of the day, you were pregnant."

I frown. "I'm certainly not pregnant, if that's what you're implying. We've barely had sex since Ella was born."

"Well, that can easily change . . ." He reaches for my hand. His fingers trace up my arm and underneath the sleeve of my T-shirt, fiddling with my bra strap.

I push him away. "Cut it out, Grant. I'm so tired I'm sick."

"Cassie." He sighs. "You need to get out of this funk. I blame your family. You've been in a mood ever since we were up there for dinner."

I close my eyes, let my shoulder blades drop back into the pillows. If there's one minuscule reason that I love Grant in this moment— that I can access my love for him through this haze of resentment and worry and sleep deprivation—it's the reminder of this: he's my lifeline away from Mara and my parents. He's my forever ticket to happiness, even if I sometimes forget it.

Grant clears his throat. "I know you hate surprises, so I'm telling you now, and I'm making an executive decision. You're having a birthday party, here at the apartment. Everything will be taken care of. All you have to do is show up."

I fight a smile. "Did McKay and Ava call you?"

"No comment."

"If you invite my sister, I'll kill you."

"I'm under strict orders to keep Mara off the list. Billie, too. It's your party. I'm not asking any questions."

"Thank you."

He winks, and I feel that tiny pocket of love bloom larger in a corner of my heart. A relief: I do adore my husband. I am exorbitantly, unthinkably lucky to have him.

"What are you up to?" Grant plucks his phone from his jacket pocket and begins to scroll through email.

"Buying for the spring and summer lines. I'm behind. Violet is on my case."

"Ah." Grant purses his lips, still staring at his phone. Finally he looks up, blinks. "How's the store doing, by the way? I'd love to see the numbers from last quarter, before you order for spring."

"The numbers were fine."

"Can I see them?"

"Why? Please don't micromanage me, Grant. This is my thing."

"Cassie." He exhales. "This business is a huge investment for me. I want to make sure . . . we're on track."

A headache slinks to the space behind my eyes, pain that distracts me from the anger replenishing in my chest. Even now that we're married, Grant will never stop doing this—subtly reminding me that the money is his, not ours. He's the wealthy husband who bankrolls my business. I'm the blue-collar wife who signed a prenup.

He catches his mistake. "I didn't mean—"

"I'm trying to build something here, you know? For *us*. And I've really grown a following."

"On Instagram, yes. But does that translate to a profit?"

"The more followers I have, the more brands will pay me for sponsored content."

"Come on, Cassie. You make, what, a couple of hundred bucks for a sponsored post here and there? Besides, I was asking if it translates to a profit for the *store*."

"What's your point, Grant?"

"My point—" He pauses, hesitant. "My point is that a lot of young women seem to enjoy following a beautiful, stylish new mom with a cute baby and a glamorous life. They watch you put almond butter in your smoothies and push Ella through the park while you recommend skin-care products and tell them about your day. But are these same young women dropping thousands at Cassidy Adler the way we need them to? Somehow, I doubt it. But you won't let me see the numbers."

My throat tightens, tears pressing against my windpipe. More than the unsettling suspicion that Grant is right is the shock that I feel—the betrayal—that he's been spying on me. Grant doesn't use Instagram. He made an account in his twenties, but the last time I checked, he didn't even have the app on his phone. He thinks social media is a Gen Z time suck.

I close my eyes. I remember the night I first met Grant, three years ago now. McKay and I slumped at a table at Dorrian's, drunk off Dirty Shirleys, picking at a plate of greasy fries. Somehow it was just the two of us left at the end of birthday drinks for Adair, a girl from college who was more McKay's friend than mine.

McKay had smiled down at her phone. *My cousin lives up here; I told him to swing by. He's on his way home from some work event.* Her eyes lifted, liquid turquoise. Model-pretty McKay Morris, née Adler. The It Girl from my class at Harvard. A peripheral friend whose attention I'd never fully managed to capture. *He works too much, but he's cute.* She giggled, downed the rest of her drink. All of a sudden, her fingers were grasping the ends of my blowout. She seemed to really consider me for the first time all night. *Your hair looks good. Mine would never grow this long.* The corners of her lips twitched. *I don't want to jinx it, but I could see you two hitting it off, Cassie. You and my cousin. He used to play the field a little, but now he's a grown-up. You're totally his type.*

And then: our moment. Grant brushing through the swinging doors in a navy suit, dark hair tousled, tie loosened, cheeks slightly reddened. A smile breaking across his face, slowly, like a wave rolling toward the shore, his eyes latching upon mine. Good, straight teeth. A dimple on his chin. McKay's first cousin. The pedigree was top-notch, unbeatable. I felt a dip in my stomach, a warm shiver running up my spine.

And now, here we are, with so much to show for our three years together. The wedding pictures, the penthouse apartment, the beach house, the baby. The life of my dreams.

I blink my eyes open and leave the memory, tears beading the ends of my lashes. I glance around the bedroom for Grant, but he's gone. I throw the covers back and climb out of bed, dizzy with the uneasy feeling I can't seem to shake. I call for him, but my voice echoes around the apartment, bouncing back to me. The reverberations sound like laughter.

Chapter Eighteen

Billie

2006

For April break, Grandma Catherine is taking Cassie on a trip to Paris. At the last minute, Catherine says she's allowed to bring a friend, so Cassie invites me to come along. My jaw hits the floor. I've only been out of the country once, when I was in seventh grade and Mom and I flew to Vancouver for my grandfather's funeral.

I'm supposed to go to Ashton's family's place in the Catskills for April break, with a bunch of other seniors. When I tell Ashton that my plans have changed, she looks like I've just slapped her in the face.

"Your priorities are so out of whack, Billie."

"Ash." I fiddle with my hair, pick apart a split end so one strand becomes two. "It's Paris."

"You and Cassie don't hang out with anyone but each other."

I shrug. I can't argue with that.

"You guys think you're above everyone."

"I don't think that, Ashton."

"Well, Cassie does."

I say nothing. I can't argue with that, either.

We fly to Paris on a Friday evening. Our tickets are first class, which means the flight attendants bring us extra snacks, and our seats recline all the way down when it's time to sleep. I watch Grandma Catherine chase a small blue pill with chardonnay, then conk out almost immediately. Her mouth is open, her breath a gentle snore.

The minute we touch down in Paris, everything feels like magic. Something light and buzzy fizzes in my chest, and it isn't just the relief of landing thousands of miles away from Wade and the horrifying reality of my life in Red Hook. It's more than that. It's visceral and heady, the bright intoxication of being somewhere new that makes my mind feel stretched and open, that turns each of my senses on high. Wandering the streets of Paris, I've never felt so alive.

We stay at the Ritz in the first arrondissement. Cassie and I have our own room, with a king-size bed and a marble fireplace and a balcony overlooking the Place Vendôme. It's a dream. I can't stop laughing. Cassie and I wrap ourselves in the matching hotel robes and drink champagne on the balcony. We speak in dramatized French accents and toss our flutes into the air, little drops of gold bubbly falling from the sky.

For breakfast, we eat freshly baked croissants with jam, then take endlessly long walks around the city. Grandma Catherine spends a lot of time resting, so it's mostly just Cassie and me. We visit the Louvre and the Musée d'Orsay; we see Notre Dame and the Arc de Triomphe; we wander through the Marais and Saint-Germain. A few Frenchmen stop to tell us that we're magnifique, and though I'm inclined to think they're speaking to Cassie, they're looking at both of us as they clutch their hands to their chests in feigned, melodramatic heartache.

One of the only times Grandma Catherine leaves the hotel is to take us shopping. She's promised Cassie a special French bag as an early graduation present. The brand is Goyard, which I only know because Cassie hasn't shut up about it. I feel like a misplaced puppy as I follow them into the department store, where fancy leather totes are enclosed in glass like museum artifacts. The one Cassie chooses is brown and beige and looks like kitchen floor tile. I sneak a look at the price tag; I have no idea how it could possibly cost one thousand euros, but I've never seen Cassie giddier than when we exit the shop, the shiny new bag slung over her shoulder.

On our last night, Cassie and I scramble up the Eiffel Tower at dusk, passing the slow tourists, only stopping to catch our breath when we reach the top. The view of Paris and beyond is majestic, glittery, vast; it leaves me speechless. We're silent for several minutes as we watch the sun torch the horizon, bathing the city in a liquid tangerine glow.

I turn to Cassie. "Do you still love Kyle?" I'm not sure why I'm asking now; it's been two years since they broke up. But here we are in the city of love—perhaps I wonder if she'll lie to me.

She laughs, but I can feel her climbing onto some metaphorical high horse. "Jesus, Billie. No. Kyle's a fucking loser."

I blink, swallowing my disappointment.

"You know he's going to a state school," she adds.

"Your sister goes to a state school."

"My sister is an embarrassment."

"I'm probably going to a state school, Cassie."

"That's not true." She turns to me then, her eyes piercing.

"What if it is?" I challenge.

"You're going to Northeastern."

I pick at the cuticle of my thumb, pull a thin strip of skin across the nail bed. Blood pulses underneath, red and raw.

"I'm serious," she presses. *"It's where you deserve to be. You earned your spot there. Don't let Wade take that away from you. This is your future—your whole fucking life."*

"I might not have a choice." I feel helpless, the pain of this reality rushing back to me. I clutch the railing of the Eiffel Tower, wishing I could stay in Paris forever. Wishing Mom weren't sick. Wishing everything were different. *"There's nothing I can do."*

"There's always something you can do." A flicker of darkness moves across her face, but only for a second, and then her mouth is breaking into that wide, luscious Cassie smile, and she grabs my hand. *"Come on, Baby. It's our last night in Paris. Let's go get a sidecar before we meet Grandma Catherine for dinner."*

That's the other phenomenal thing about Paris. I'm eighteen, and even though Cassie isn't yet, nobody cards us. We can drink wherever and whatever we want.

I dream about France for a full week after we get back. The pastries, the cheese, the wine, the art. Laughing with Cassie at corner cafés; the lightness of being somewhere new. Somewhere uncharted.

I bring Mom a postcard—a picture of the Seine with the Eiffel Tower spearing the backdrop—but she doesn't remember where I've been, and she doesn't seem to recognize Paris. She doesn't even seem self-conscious about forgetting, the way she did when her short-term memories first started going. She just smiles at the postcard and says it's pretty, then pats my head like a child petting a dog. That's what she reminds me of more and more each day—a child.

One afternoon, near the end of the month, I come home from school to find Mom sitting out on the porch swing, knees tucked into her chest, her chin cradled between them.

"It's chilly, Mom." I hand her a fleece blanket, tucking the edges around her. It rained earlier, and the air is damp and cold. Spring has been a tease this year.

Mom looks up at me, her caramel eyes wide and innocent. And in that moment, I know. It just hits me. I know before the words leave her lips.

She blinks, the edges of her mouth twitching into a curious smile. "Who are you?"

Wade comes to me later that night. I'm in bed, flipping through the May issue of Travel + Leisure, which I bought with a roll of quarters I found in Wade's truck. I've been reading the magazine since Cassie and I got back from Paris. She says I've caught the travel bug.

Wade sits down on the edge of my mattress, which squeaks and grinds from his weight. I flinch, goose bumps sidling up my spine. "Get out."

He rubs his temples, lets out a long stream of air. Breath that smells like pickled onions and Budweiser. "We need to discuss your mother."

I think of Mom, asleep in her bed down the hall, not knowing my name.

"It's getting bad, Billie Jean." His dark eyes look almost black, the whites around them slightly bloodshot.

"I know." I fight back tears. I won't let Wade see me cry.

"There's a nursing home that'll take her. It's upstate. An hour and twenty without traffic."

"No." I feel the blood leave my face, cold panic filling my cells.

"It's a tragedy, Billie, but we can't just sit by and watch while she loses the rest of her mind. She could get hurt. She needs full-time care."

"But—you said—you said . . . we could get her a nurse." I'm choking on the words, my eyes filling whether I like it or not. "Someone to live here."

He laughs. A deep, genuine belly laugh. "You want to go to college, right?"

"What?"

"We can't afford a live-in nurse. The price is astronomical. It's out of the question."

"But you said before—"

"I don't care what I said before."

"How much does it cost?"

"Too much."

"Give me a number."

"Why?"

"She's my mother, Wade. She's forty-seven. You can't send her away to a nursing home with a bunch of ninety-year-olds in diapers."

"I can do whatever I want," he snaps. "It's my money."

"It's her *money."*

He laughs again. "She's my wife. Remember?"

I say nothing. Hot, heavy tears stream down my face.

"Please don't send her away." I screw my eyes shut, imagine my mother in a nursing home upstate, the sickly sweet smell of death all around her. How scared she'd be during the moments when random memories resurfaced. Fighting to remember, clawing her way up the slippery crag of her shrinking mind. Confused. Terrified. Alone.

Wade reaches for me, the rough surface of his index finger swiping a tear from my cheek. Like sand on my skin.

"Please don't send her away," I repeat, my voice barely a whisper. "Forget Northeastern. I'll go to a state school. I'll live here, and then we can afford a nurse for Mom. Please. Please."

Wade is silent for several long beats. Then his lips curl, moving toward my face. "That's a start." He slides his finger down my chin, over my throat, into the hard dip of my collarbone. I'm not breathing. I'm too scared to move. He leans closer. His rotten smell overpowers my airways. "But there's always a price, Billie Jean."

His hand slides lower, into the V of my snowflake pajama top. I'm numb with fear as he unclasps the buttons, then cups my breast in his palm. He groans.

"Wait." I pull back. There's a sudden clearing in the fog of my panic— the fear dulling enough for me rationalize, to negotiate. "If I do this . . . Mom stays here?"

He nods, slow. "We all stay here. The three of us." He reaches for his belt, and I hear the clink of the buckle, the purr of his zipper. "No Northeastern."

"Fine. But there's one condition."

"Oh yeah? What's that?" He hovers above me, bulbous and massive, a bushy eyebrow raised in amusement.

"No sex. No intercourse."

"Intercourse." He chortles, mocking me.

"Or else I go to the cops."

"You go to the cops, it's your word against mine. Besides, you turned eighteen in March. It's legal."

I swallow, knowing on some fucked-up level that he's right. That there isn't a way for me to help Mom without making a sacrifice.

"We'll start slow," he growls, his eyes hungry as he reaches down between his legs. "Take off your clothes. For now, I just want to look at you."

Chapter Nineteen

Billie

October 6, 2023
7 days before

The cemetery is empty except for me. The sky is a wash of gray overhead, light rain drizzling from the ashy clouds.

I'm glad it isn't sunny. The day she died was, blindingly so, the rays so strong and the sky so flawlessly blue it felt like mockery.

I pull the hood of my rain jacket over my head, tuck my knees into my chest in front of her gravestone. *Lorraine Angela West.* I trace my fingers along the etched letters of my mother's name. I can't believe it's been seven years today.

I close my eyes and think of her. Shiny honey-brown hair, like mine. Pale skin that was so unblemished, it always made her look ten years younger. The gentle way she engaged with the world, soft-spoken, forgiving. Sometimes I wish she could've been stronger, more combative, but I loved her trusting soul.

There are moments when I still can't believe Mom is gone, that she left the world as young as she did. After she died, I underwent testing to determine whether I had the gene mutations that increase the risk of early-onset Alzheimer's. I remember waiting for the results, the anxiety that shot through my body, all the way to my fingertips. But when the doctor called, I heard the relief in his voice. *You have nothing to worry about, Billie.*

I open my eyes. The chrysanthemums I brought are nestled against the base of the silver granite. Mom hated fall flowers. At least the shop had them in white.

She's buried at the top of a hill, under a tall oak tree with limbs that fan out in so many directions, it looks like the tree is stretching. I gaze out over the rest of the cemetery, tombstones dotting the expansive lawn that slopes down into a mist of fog. She wouldn't have minded it here.

My phone vibrates in the pocket of my jacket, and I pull it out to see another text from Alex.

Here if you need me.

I remember his words from earlier today, just before I left his apartment to catch my Uber to Grand Central. *You don't have to do everything alone, you know.*

Alex is running errands on his day off, but he'd offered to bag them and come to the cemetery. But how would it have been, with Alex here? Alex, who never knew Mom, who couldn't remember the cucumber scent of her face cream, or the way her eyes got teary when she laughed. Cassie is the only one who's ever come to the grave site, her hand in mine those agonizing first few years, when getting through Mom's anniversary felt like trying to exist without oxygen.

I scroll through the rest of my messages. I've heard from Jane, Becca, Esme, my aunt Christine in Vancouver. Even Mom's mom—my ninety-six-year-old grandmother—managed to leave a voicemail, and her vision is so shot, she can barely use the phone. Remy texted, too—he does every year, even though we'd already broken up when Mom died.

Thinking of you, Bill, he wrote.

I heart Remy's message, grateful that we've found a way to stay in each other's lives, even in the smallest capacity. Our love story wasn't for nothing.

I navigate back to Alex's text. *I'm not alone,* I want to tell him. Or maybe I am alone, but it's easier that way.

I stand, wipe the grass from the back of my jeans. The rain is falling faster now, a steady pitter-patter against the damp earth. The air smells musky, fresh. I could walk around—I usually do—but the sky is filling with darker, denser clouds. I open Uber and request a car to the train station. I might as well head back to the city. I can get to Alex's early; we can spend some time together before our group dinner.

I kiss the top of Mom's wet grave, whisper that I love her, that I carry her. My Uber rolls up—a white Acura—and I don't let myself look back as we drive away from the cemetery.

On the train, I get another text—a thoughtful message from my cousin, Dylan. The only close friend I haven't heard from is Cassie. I hate that I'm acutely aware of this, and of the fact that she reached out last year, that she's blatantly pulling away from me even though she pretends she isn't, and that I can't do anything to stop it. I gaze out the window at the blur of trees and strip malls. Cassie knows the pain of this day better than anyone.

My train doesn't get in to Grand Central until four, and it's half past five by the time I grab a change of clothes at my place and make it to Alex's apartment. When I walk through his door, he just holds me, a wordless hug that absorbs at least a little of the day's sorrow.

"Mark made a reservation at Emily in Williamsburg. Are you okay going to Brooklyn?"

I nod into his chest.

"I feel terrible," he says. "If I'd known what today was before, I never would have scheduled this dinner."

"No, no. I'm looking forward to it. I just need to change."

"The reservation isn't till eight. I figure we can take the L train over, grab a drink by ourselves before?" Alex's eyes soften. "I want to hear more about your mom."

I glance up at him. "She would've liked you."

He smiles. "Need a shower? I'm about to hop in."

"I think I just want to lie down for a minute. Long day."

"Sure." He kisses my forehead. "My bed is all yours."

While Alex showers, I nestle into his plush pillows and pull out my phone. My heart bounces in my chest when I see what's on the screen: a text from Cassie. Finally.

> Thinking of you and Lorraine ♡ Miss her always.

I reply right away. I can't not. Hearing from Cassie is like medicine, instant relief that smooths the harsh edges of this day. She's the only person in my life who knew Mom—who *really* knew her. Before.

> Thanks, that means a lot. How are you? Did you change
> your mind about your birthday next weekend?

The year Mom died, Cassie didn't want to celebrate her birthday, but I insisted. So we took the subway out to Coney Island; we drank vodka mixed with Fresca from a Nalgene and ate Nathan's hot dogs and rode the Cyclone roller coaster so many times we both ended up puking on the beach. Laughing and crying at the same time.

Cassie's response comes thirty seconds later.

> Nah, just going to lie low this year. Takeout and
> Succession on the couch with Grant!

I send a thumbs-up emoji. I'm not sure I believe her. Cassie *always* celebrates her birthday—even last year when she was in the throes of first-trimester morning sickness, she hosted a dinner at Bobo—but there's nothing more to say. The conversation has hit a dead end. I feel like an idiot for even bringing it up again.

I open Instagram for the first time all day, catch up on Cassie's stories while I wait for Alex to get out of the shower.

There she is, perched in the back seat of a taxi, wearing oversize sunglasses that look trendy and expensive. The chunky frames are a rich olive green.

Per usual, she's talking into the camera like she's gabbing with a friend, and I suddenly wonder what the cab driver thinks. Maybe he assumes she's FaceTiming. Or perhaps he doesn't notice at all.

Cassie goes on about her morning, raving about the fabulous brunch she had at Sadelle's—"If you don't get the bagel with lox at Sadelle's, what are you even doing"—and the fabulous Balmain boots she found at Intermix—"We will definitely, definitely be stocking these lug soles at Cassidy Adler"—and the fabulous hat she bought for Ella at Bonpoint—"She's going to look like a little cream puff, you guys, I can't."

Fabulous, fabulous, fabulous.

I don't even notice that Alex is out of the shower until I hear the sound of his dresser drawers sliding open beside the bed.

He glances over his shoulder, peers at my screen. "Who's that?"

I immediately close Instagram, place my phone facedown on the duvet. "No one. Just something dumb on TikTok."

"Ah."

I watch as he yanks on a pair of boxers, his clean skin effusing the fresh scent of Irish Spring. I reach for him. "Come here."

He sits on the edge of the bed and leans down to kiss me, a flop of his damp hair tickling my nose. When he pulls back, a grin plays at the edges of his lips. "I thought about something in the shower."

"Oh yeah?"

"I was thinking, when we meet everyone for dinner tonight, I'd like to introduce you as my girlfriend."

The air in his bedroom stills. It's one of those moments that's perfect in tone, in how natural it feels, nothing about it cheesy or contrived.

Alex blinks down at me, the green flecks in his eyes shining like tiny emeralds. His cheeks are slightly pink, and I'm so attracted to him that heat wraps around my thighs and I have the urge to do something uncharacteristic and girlie, like yelp out loud.

"What do you think, Billie?"

My smile spreads toward my ears as I nod, pulling him closer, knowing I'm going to answer from my heart, not my head, and that afterward, there won't be any turning back. In this moment, I'm at peace with not knowing whether it will all be okay.

Chapter Twenty

Cassie

October 13, 2023
The day of

McKay hands me a shot of tequila. Two fingers of gold liquid in a clear tumbler. I sniff the rim, sure I'm going to gag. In six hours, I'll be thirty-five years old.

"A double for the birthday girl," she sings, raising her own glass. I'm reminded, then, of twenty-year-old McKay at Kappa Sig parties. The way she'd knock back shots in some short dress, her skin permanently tanned from constant family vacations to St. Barts, frat guys drooling at the sight of her. *Me* drooling at the sight of her, desperate to make my way into her inner circle. Wishing so fervently that I could break down whatever invisible barrier stood in the way of that happening.

And look at us now.

The tequila burns going down, sour and stinging, an instant rush to my head.

"Shit." I laugh. "I can't be drunk before people get here."

"You can do whatever you want." McKay smiles. I adore her, forever in awe of her *zero-fucks-given* approach to life. "And you just pumped, so you're good for the night." She leans against the kitchen counter, her ivory crêpe top slipping to reveal a sliver of nonexistent cleavage. McKay is flat-chested unless she's pregnant—this makes her look phenomenal in all clothes. She sucks on a lime wedge, then tosses it into the sink. "Did Grant say how many people are coming?"

"Fifty, I think."

"Perfect." She squints, tilting her head. "Love that dress, by the way."

I smooth the black silk that hugs my body, a new arrival at the store. "Thanks. You know I'm a sucker for a good slip dress."

In the living room, the makeshift bar is fully stocked and ready to go. Grant has hired two bartenders and several waitstaff from our favorite caterer in Gramercy. Lourdes is on Ella duty.

"What can I get you?" the male bartender asks. He's cute—messy blond surfer hair, playful smile—the kind of guy I would've gone home with in my twenties.

"Two vodka martinis. Grey Goose. Extra dirty." McKay knocks her hip against mine.

"Shaken?" Cute Bartender winks.

"Not stirred." McKay winks back. She's unconditionally devoted to Tom, but she still flirts like a sorority girl.

We wander out onto the terrace to drink our martinis before the guests arrive. The sun sits low in the sky, nestled behind the skyscrapers in the distance. Gramercy Park looks like a painting, the foliage on fire even in the low light, the trees an impressionist wash of brilliant yellows and burnt oranges.

"Fall." McKay sighs. "I don't know if I'm ready for it. It just means winter is right around the corner."

I rest my elbows on the railing, gaze out at our unbeatable view. "Winter means St. Barts, Mick."

"*True.* You guys are coming for Thanksgiving this year, right?"

McKay and Grant grew up vacationing at their grandfather's villa in St. Barts. When he passed away, the house went to Grant's father, Jamie, McKay's father, Everett, and their younger sister, Cecilia. The family still spends the winter holidays on the island, which means McKay and I get to be together for most Thanksgivings and Christmases, unless she's with Tom's parents. I haven't spent a holiday with my own family since I met Grant.

"That's the plan." I sip my martini, envisioning the clear turquoise water, the white beaches with sand as soft as butter. "God, I can't wait."

My phone chimes on the teak coffee table. I balance my martini on the surface of the railing and reach for it.

"Fuck."

McKay peers over my shoulder, reads the text from Billie that's just appeared on the screen.

> Happy (almost) birthday, Cass! Love you and hope you
> have a relaxing day with Grant and Ella tomorrow. You
> deserve it!

"God. Can't she leave you alone?"

I chew my bottom lip, irritation swarming in my chest.

"Billie has this weird *thing* about my birthday." I shake my head. "Like she obsesses over it, just because that's what we did when we were kids. It's like she needs to prove that she cares about my birthday more than anyone else, as if that somehow means we're still best friends."

"How lame." McKay sips the last of her martini, then pops the olive in her mouth. "Is she going to freak that you didn't invite her?"

I laugh, my frustration replaced by a sudden, tequila-vodka-infused giddiness that makes me realize: I don't even care.

"I don't even care!" I belt, stretching my arms out wide, spilling my drink. A little splatters on the floor of the terrace, narrowly missing my hot-pink Jimmy Choo pumps.

"That's my girl." McKay shimmies her empty glass, indicating that it's time for a refill. "I'm getting another before the bar crowds. Give me yours, too."

Van Morrison begins to play through the speakers. I sway to the familiar beat while I wait for McKay to come back with our drinks. The sun rests on the horizon now, magenta light swirling through the cobalt sky. I feel giddy and free, drunk and happy, grateful for this uninhibited sensation that's so rarely available to a breastfeeding mother. Better yet, I don't care about birchballer6. I don't care about what happened back then, about whether it was wrong or if someone besides Billie knows the truth. For the first time in weeks, anxiety can't touch me.

Grant finds me on the terrace, bopping to "Days Like This."

When all the parts of the puzzle start to look like they fit
Then I must remember, there'll be days like this

"Our wedding song." He winks, and there's a playfulness to his grin that tells me he's had more than one scotch. Everything about Grant is looser when he drinks; he reverts to the mischievous frat boy I imagine I would've encountered in college, if we'd met back then.

"Come on." He grabs my hand and twirls me, then dips me low, catching the small of my back like he did during our first dance. I throw my head back and laugh, lost in the moment for a change. Grant is a great dancer—confident and spontaneous but always in control. I'm never more attracted to him than when we're dancing.

He picks me up and spins us in circles, then slides me down the front of his body, his hands grazing my hips. He looks handsome in a pressed dress shirt with the collar undone, his face freshly shaven, his hair a little windswept from the dance.

"This dress is so hot. My wife is so hot." He cups my ass, presses his mouth to the space below my ear in a way that pulls goose bumps up the side of my neck.

"Let's fuck tonight," I whisper into his collar.

A slow grin spreads across his face. "I love you."

"I love you, too."

"Hey." He glances to the side, and I sense the gears turning in his head as he tries to remember the reason he came to find me. "Lourdes just left. I paid her for the week."

I pull back from him. "Wait, she *left*? We need her to stay tonight."

"I know."

"Where's Ella?"

"My mom's giving her a bottle inside. She just got here."

"Grant, you said you were taking care of everything—"

"I forgot, all right?" He rubs his forehead. "It's been an insane week at work, and I forgot to ask Lourdes in advance if she could stay late. And she can't—she has a recital or something for one of her kids. She had to go."

I reach for Grant's wrist, yank his watch toward my face. "It's not even seven. Ella doesn't go down for two more hours. We pushed her bedtime back, remember?"

"I know. I fucked up. I'm sorry, Cass." His eyes lock mine, and I see the exhaustion and stress that sits in the deep cracks around their edges. It isn't worth picking a fight over this. Not tonight.

"It's okay. There's been a lot going on." I glance inside. A few more guests have started to arrive. I see Ava and Ned chatting with Lisette, my old colleague from Intermix. I turn back to Grant and give an appreciative smile. "And you planned all this."

"Look, I'm not worried. We'll stick Ella in the stroller with the paci and that crinkle toy she loves. She'll be fine in the living room, or even on the terrace. It's a nice night."

I press my lips together, trying to think. "She might get over-whelmed inside. We have fifty people coming."

Grant nods. "I think the terrace is best. It'll be quieter out here, not as many people, and we'll turn the outdoor speakers down."

I glance around the terrace. It's big—it wraps around the corner of the building, extending the whole length of our apartment. And it's private. It's safe. It was a big selling point when we bought this place.

Van Morrison morphs into Taylor Swift's "22," and I smile. I may be on the cusp of middle age, but I wouldn't relive my twenties for all the money in the world.

"Okay." I blink up at Grant. "But *you* have to be out here supervising. It's my birthday. I'm off duty."

"Deal. You just relax, have fun. I've got it. I'll give her the milk you pumped earlier at bedtime." He leans down and kisses me. He tastes like smoky scotch.

"And you'll come get me before you put her down? You know I always need to say good night."

"Of course, babe."

"Okay." I grab my phone from the table. "We're taking a selfie in front of this insane sunset, and I don't want to hear a word of pushback."

Grant chuckles. "I forgot how bossy drunk Cassie is."

I crack a smile. "I'm not drunk."

He presses the side of his face against mine as I tilt my phone horizontally and extend my arm in front of us.

"Liar," he whispers, then turns to kiss my cheek just as I snap the shot. It's a perfect selfie—the cotton candy sky, this moment of genuine love between husband and wife.

When Grant goes back inside, I post the picture to my story. I'm not even thinking of what to write for a caption when it comes to me.

If the sun has to set on the first half of my thirties, I'm happy it looks like this. Let the celebrations commence!

Chapter Twenty-one

Billie

Spring 2006

Cassie finds the letter to SUNY New Paltz on my desk. The one notifying the university of my decision to accept their offer of admission.

"What the fuck?" She picks it up, waves it in my face.

My insides cramp. I haven't yet planned what to tell Cassie.

"Billie?" she presses. "What about Northeastern?"

I shrug. "I have no choice. New Paltz is giving me a free ride. We can't afford Northeastern."

"Since when? You got aid there, too."

"Not enough."

"But your mom has a college fund saved."

"Like I said, not enough." I know I'm being short with her, but I'm not in the mood for these questions.

"Why are you being snarky and weird?" Cassie sets the letter down on my bed. "What's going on?" Her eyes watch me closely.

"Cassie! Just stop."

"Stop what?" She stands there, arms open at her sides. I study her—her thin body looks perfect in dark jeans and a crisp white tee, her long, glossy hair falling past her shoulders. She uses the straightener almost daily now. She and her Tiffany bracelet will fit right in at Harvard, no questions asked. She can forget these six weird years at public school in Dutchess County, pretend they never existed. Anger bubbles through me.

"Not everyone has a rich grandmother who can buy their way into an Ivy," I spit. "Not everyone gets handed a future like that." I watch my words land, Cassie's face momentarily wounded, then twisting into a scowl.

"*Screw you, Billie.*" She grabs her hoodie from the back of my desk chair, swings her backpack over one shoulder. Before she storms out of my bedroom, she turns back to look at me, her gaze narrowing. "*You're better than this.*"

We've argued before, but those were just squabbles, like when she borrowed my True Religion jeans and ripped the knee, or when I ate Mara's Sour Patch watermelons and Cassie got blamed for it.

But this feels serious. The spite, which felt satisfying spewing out of me moments earlier, leaves a hollow pit in my stomach.

In May, the weather finally turns, the chill of a lingering winter chased out by warm air and pale sunshine. Cassie spends the last month of our last year of high school avoiding me. She sits with Ashton and Maureen and their crew at lunch, and I nibble on Ritz crackers in the parking lot behind the cafeteria. I haven't had an appetite since Wade and I began our nightly ritual, which requires me meeting him in the basement after Mom is asleep.

I think of sexual assault victims around the world and try to focus on the fact that it could be worse. Most of the time, Wade just touches himself while I lie naked on the grubby leather couch. If I'm lucky, I screw my eyes shut and he's done in under ten minutes. If I'm unlucky, he commands that I keep them open and watch. If I'm really unlucky, he puts his hands on me, groping parts of my body that have never been touched by anyone before him.

Afterward, when I lie in my bed, sleepless and trembling, I tell myself I'll ask for help. That I won't wait another day. I vow to tell my father or Cassie or my aunt or a counselor at school, but in the morning light, my conviction resets. I think of Mom, and I can't do it. Even if they believe me, I'm a legal adult; the acts I engage in are my choice. It's not like there are charges to press. Nothing will happen to Wade except he'll know I snitched. He'll send Mom to the nursing home, and all of it will be for nothing.

Nurse Sandra starts two weeks before graduation. She's tall for a woman—close to six feet from the looks of it—with frizzy silver hair and a kind smile. Mom seems to like her. But she isn't a live-in nurse, like Wade promised, and I protest.

"*She's in the house fourteen hours a day,*" he counters that night in the basement. He unzips his jeans, and his fat stomach jiggles over his legs. "Seven to nine, that's standard for full-time care. She might as well live here."

I say nothing, but I know the truth. Wade doesn't want anyone else around at night. He needs the undisturbed darkness of a near-empty house to do as he pleases, and me all to himself.

The last Monday of high school, Cassie finds me outside at lunch. I'm slumped against the school's brick exterior, picking at a granola bar that tastes like cardboard.

"You look like shit," she says. "Like you haven't slept in a month."

Something sick in my heart makes me laugh at the truth. "Yeah. I haven't."

"What?" Cassie folds her arms, looks at me funny. I've missed her so much. I close my eyes, and a tear slips through.

"Billie. What's going on?" She takes a step toward me.

I press my pointer fingers to the inside corners of my eyes, which burn with dozens of sleepless nights. "I'm so sorry for what I said to you about Harvard. It was terrible."

She shrugs. "Maybe you were right. Maybe that's why it hit a nerve."

"I wasn't right."

"Billie." Cassie sighs, and when her wide blue eyes meet mine, they're brimming with concern. "You'd tell me if something was wrong, yeah?"

The bell rings then, sounding through the open windows. Lunch is over.

I nod, swallowing my tears as I stand and brush gravel from the backs of my thighs. I glance away. I can't bring myself to look at her. "I have to get to English. We're getting our final papers back. I—I miss you, Cass. I really am sorry."

"I miss you, too." I feel her watching me as I disappear inside the building. "Bye, Baby," she calls behind me.

When I arrive home from school, I find Mom in the backyard. She's sitting cross-legged on a red-checkered picnic blanket in front of Sandra, who is braiding her hair.

Mom looks up at me. "Hey." She squints into the sun. "You're pretty. Who are you?"

It never fails to make me wish I were dead, Mom not knowing my *name. I feel Sandra looking at me, but I avert my gaze. If I see the sympathy in her eyes, I'll crumble.*

After dinner, I tell Wade I'm sleeping at a friend's house. It's a lie, obviously, but I can't bear the thought of another basement session. I need a night off. I figure I can take Mom's car and find a parking lot somewhere, camp out in the back seat.

Wade sips his Budweiser and lets out a small belch. When he looks up from the television, he has foam on his lip, and his eyes meet mine, ravenous. "You're staying here." His voice is gravelly, low. He runs a hand over his head, the overhead light reflecting off his bald spot. "Don't cross me, Billie Jean."

Two hours later, we're in the basement, and Wade is telling me I can leave my clothes on. He sits beside me on the couch and begins to stroke my hair. His breath smells like the tuna casserole Sandra made for dinner.

"You're a good girl, right? You want to do something nice for me?" Wade takes my hand, sliding it underneath the drawstring of his sweatpants. It's the first time I've ever had to touch him.

"Grip it," he commands.

I reach down, my fingers working through wiry hair and flesh, then squeezing around him. It's solid but rubbery. Bile shoots up the back of my throat.

"Now move your hand up and down."

When I do, he groans. "Faster," he says through choppy breaths.

At some point, Wade reaches for his waistband and yanks his pants all the way down. They fall to his ankles, and his dick boings up toward his navel. "Now get on your knees and suck it."

"No." Involuntary tears spring to my eyes, cold panic behind my ribs.

"Don't be a little bitch." He spreads his legs wider, and I see a dark line of hair at his crack. I know if I put my mouth on him, I'll never recover.

"You want me to fire Sandra tomorrow? Drive your mom upstate?" He presses his hands to my shoulders, shoves me south.

I close my eyes. I think of Paris.

When I leave for school the next morning, I find Cassie waiting at the end of the driveway. She's standing beside the mailbox, wearing jean cutoffs and holding a paper bag from the Bagel Shoppe.

"I thought you might want breakfast." She holds out the bag. A truce. Her eyes search mine.

I open my mouth to speak, but no sound emerges. Only tears; sudden, erupting, running down my face like a salt river.

"It's Wade, isn't it? He did something, didn't he?" The set of her jaw tightens. "Billie! You have to tell me."

I say nothing, nodding as I let Cassie catch me in her arms. Let myself sob against the safe, familiar beat of my best friend's heart.

Chapter Twenty-two

Billie

October 13, 2023
The day of

"Do you feel different?" Jane asks, one of her eyebrows arching. We're having a Friday morning catch-up over cronuts and cappuccinos at Dominique Ansel. I haven't seen her in two weeks, which is rare for us, but she's been busy with the move, and I've been in La-La Land with Alex. Last night was the first one we've spent apart since he asked me to be official. I already miss him.

"Different?" I take a bite of my cronut—half croissant, half doughnut—which is sweet, buttery heaven in my mouth.

"You know, all coupled up now."

I shrug. "It's going well, but it's still early days."

"It's *exciting*, Billie. You're allowed to feel excited about it, you know." Jane sips her coffee.

"I am excited. But I don't want to get ahead of myself." I stare into my mug, foam dissolving into milky espresso. Then I glance up, tap the top of my laptop with my pointer finger. "Enough about my love life. Can we talk work for a minute? I have something I want to run by you."

Jane interlaces her hands across the table. "What is it?"

I draw in a breath, suddenly nervous. What I'm about to say has been on my mind for a while, but I hadn't uttered it out loud—not to anyone—until I ran it by Alex the other night. He thought it was brilliant.

"Billie?" Jane prompts.

"So." I exhale. "We book luxury vacations for the one percent."

She nods. "We do."

"And I love my job—no, I'm *obsessed* with my job. You've built a phenomenal company, Jane. You truly have."

"Wait." She holds up her palm. "You're not—"

"I'm not quitting, don't worry."

"Christ. Don't scare me like that."

"But I do have a proposition for you." I pause, gathering my thoughts. "The majority of our clients—they're loaded. They value memorable, luxurious experiences and high-end amenities. But they also value philanthropy, altruism. So, I'm thinking, what if we added a charitable component to our services?"

Jane tilts her chin forward, listening.

"We earn anywhere from ten to fifteen percent commission from various vendors—hotels, rentals, boutique tour operators, whatever. What if we—I mean The Path as a company—pledge a given portion of our commissions as charitable donations? We can partner with select charities around the globe, make it localized. So if we're booking a safari in Tanzania, for example, the donation would go to a Tanzanian cause that we vet and choose."

Jane studies me, silent, her eyebrows inching closer together. For once, I can't read her expression.

"This differentiates us in the industry in a way that I think will attract more eyes, more business," I continue. "It makes us the Toms or the Bombas of luxury travel. And there are ways to play around with this concept, increase our impact. Like maybe—maybe we give clients the option to match whatever we donate? Rich people love this shit. It makes them feel less guilty about spending thirty grand on a swanky trip to New Zealand while most of the world's population never leaves their own backyard."

Jane takes another sip of her cappuccino, peering at me over the mug's rim. "And it would make you feel less guilty, too?"

"Of course. I love what I do, but some days, it feels shallow. That part I don't love."

"I feel the same way." A small, slow grin spreads across Jane's face, breaking into a full-blown smile. She nods, her eyes shining. "I adore this idea, Billie."

My heart lifts. "I hoped you might."

She rolls her lips inward, thinking. "I'll need to crunch some numbers and run it all by Craig—you know, the consultant I meet with twice a year? It would require new marketing, which isn't nothing, so I need to look at all the angles." Jane reaches across the table, pats my hand. "But you're onto something. I wouldn't say it if I didn't mean it." She glances at her watch—a Cartier tank, an anniversary present from Sasha. "Shoot. I have to bounce."

"Go. I'm gonna stay for a bit."

Jane shoves her laptop and wallet into her bag. "Oh! I almost forgot, Bill—*I* have something to run by *you*. Not work-related."

"What's up?"

She sighs. "You know Sasha and I leave for Iceland later today? That's why I have to run home and pack."

"*Today?* I knew you were going soon, but that crept up fast."

"I know. And our goddamn cat sitter just bailed. No reason given. We just got a cancellation email from rover-dot-com and that's it." Jane huffs, tucking a strawberry-blond lock behind her ear. Her hair is constantly spilling out of its ponytail. "Anyway, Sasha found another one, but this new girl is out of town until tomorrow, so this is me, begging." She presses her palms together, widens her eyes like the nut that she is.

I laugh. "Are you asking me to feed Willie Nelson?"

"Just tonight. We leave for the airport at two thirty, so I'll top off his kibble, but since this chick can't come till four tomorrow, can you pop over sometime this evening and just make sure he's good on food and water? He's a diva. I'll love you for eternity."

I wave a hand. "I got you. Don't stress."

"*Lifesaver.*" Jane stands, gathering her leather jacket from the back of the chair. She pulls a small gold key from the pocket and places it on the table between us. "Here's the spare. I'll text you our new address, and *please* don't judge the horrifying state of the apartment. I haven't unpacked a single box except some random clothes. It's a disaster."

"As it should be. You just moved in a few days ago."

Jane swings her bag over one shoulder, blows me a kiss. "I love you. And I love your idea. I promise I'll schedule a call with Craig as soon as I'm back."

"Have the best trip." I kiss the air. "Can't wait to see pictures."

After Jane leaves, I flip my laptop open and spend some time catching up on email. I have a few hours till I meet Esme at Grand Central; we're ditching work early and taking the train out to Bronxville to visit

Becca in the suburbs, something we haven't done enough since she moved there. I haven't seen either of them since before I met Alex.

I order a second cappuccino and respond to a client who's reached out about honeymooning in Thailand, then another who wants to surprise his father with a trip to Patagonia. Time ticks by unnoticed, the way it always does when I'm crafting sample itineraries. My mind escapes to foreign lands: exotic Thai beaches and jagged Chilean mountain ranges, Buddhist temples in Bangkok and Argentinian glaciers that span hundreds of square miles. Building a trip is the perfect balance of creativity and structure—the ideal task for a brain like mine that craves both.

At quarter of one, I order an Uber to take me to midtown. I pack up my computer and toss a couple of dollar bills on the table.

Out on the street, the sun sits high and bright in the sky. The sidewalk shimmers, dappled light catching bits of silver mica buried in the concrete. I locate my Uber at the end of the block and climb in the back seat as my phone vibrates in my pocket. I haven't checked my messages in hours, and I read through them as the car speeds uptown.

There's a new text from Alex, who has the day off and is surfing Rockaway Beach with Dave. He's asking what time I'll be back from Becca's—he's craving the turkey burger from Westville and wants to know if I can meet there at nine, when it's not as crowded. We both love Westville, but they don't take reservations, and it's a madhouse on the weekends.

I will never say no to Westville or to you, I write back. I picture Alex in his black wet suit, hair damp and tousled from the salty waves. It's crazy how much I miss him after just one night apart, how far away tonight's dinner already feels.

My only other message is from Jane. She's sent the address of her new apartment, along with instructions on where to find Willie Nelson's kibble.

I reread Jane's text, subconsciously making a mental note of the address so I can figure out how far she lives from Cassie now that she's in Gramercy. And that's when I register what exactly I'm seeing. Jane's address—27 Gramercy Park South, 8A. My body goes numb with hot, prickly shock.

27 Gramercy Park South is Cassie's address. And not only that—Cassie's apartment is 9A. Jane moved to Cassie's building, to the unit *directly* below Cassie's. Of all the buildings and all the apartments in New York.

A pit burrows into my stomach. *How?*

I call Jane, but there's no answer. The Uber pulls to a stop at the curb in front of Grand Central, and I climb out in a daze. Crowds of people brush by me on Forty-second Street, knocking into me as they hurry into the terminal. One man looks over his shoulder and scowls at my lack of motion. So many New Yorkers are just looking for reasons to be angry.

I make my way inside, find Esme waiting at the clock tower. She's wearing a cream trench coat, and her brown hair is pulled halfway back, the way she almost always wears it. She moves her hand in little circles, gesturing at me to hurry. The familiar sight of my old friend is a comfort.

"We're so late!" She grabs my arm, and we run downstairs to our track, slipping through the sliding doors of the train just as they're beginning to close. We find a vacant row of seats and plop down onto the shiny red leather, catching our breath.

Esme glances at me with wide eyes, still panting. "Where *were* you? We almost missed the train."

Esme is mostly the same as she was when we met in college: a slightly neurotic perfectionist with a heart of gold.

I lean my head against her shoulder. "Sorry, Ez. Weird morning."

"Want to talk about it?"

"Not really," I say, because I'm trying my best not to think about the fact that Jane lives in Cassie's building, and that I have to go there later to feed Willie Nelson, and that tomorrow is Cassie's birthday. "Tell me about you."

Esme does. She fills me in on things with John, a private wealth advisor she's been seeing for a year and a half. It's the longest relationship Esme has had since I've known her, and she's over the moon. She has reason to suspect he's looking at rings. Esme wants everything that Becca has: the house in the suburbs, the Metro North husband, the two-point-five kids. Even though the two of us remain the only unmarried women in our orbit—and possibly in Manhattan—Esme has never lost sight of this goal, and I'm jealous of her certainty. I can only imagine the peace that must come from knowing exactly what you want out of life, even if it's not a guarantee.

Becca's house in Bronxville is white brick with black shutters, the door painted a glossy navy with a brass knocker. Her neighborhood is the epitome of suburban, the properties squished close together, a neat row of homes with boxwoods and window planters. I can feel Esme salivating as we make our way up the bluestone walk and ring the doorbell. The brass knocker is decorative.

Becca squeals when she sees us, her knees bouncing. The three of us have been close since Northeastern, when we were all assigned to the same hall of the same freshman dorm. Becca and Esme were always slightly closer with each other, since I spent so much time at Harvard with Cassie. In retrospect, Cassie almost never visited Northeastern. It's always been me at her beck and call.

Becca leads us into the house, which is an objective mess, and I love this about her—the fact that she isn't trying to prove anything by cleaning up for us. The kitchen is littered with dishes and there's a blue handprint on one of the white walls, streaked at the fingertips. She catches me looking.

"Yeah, turns out washable paint isn't washable when your kid decides to use the *walls* as a canvas."

I trip over a plastic dump truck on the way into the family room, where Becca has laid out a cheese plate and a basket of crackers.

"Sorry," she says. "This is the best I could do for lunch."

Milo, Becca's two-year-old, runs out of the playroom singing "Old MacDonald Had a Farm" at the top of his lungs. He's wearing a T-shirt that says ONE MAN BAND in block letters, and nothing at all on the bottom.

"Oh my God." Becca chases after him. "Milo! Mommy said *no* taking off your diaper! *No* pee-pee without a diaper." She glances over her shoulder. "There's a bottle of La Crema in the fridge. Can one of you open it? I'll be right back."

Becca disappears upstairs. When she returns, Milo is fully clothed, and Esme and I have finished our first glass of wine. Becca sticks Milo in front of something on the TV in the playroom and plops down on the couch next to Esme. She looks exhausted, dark circles ringing her eyes. I hand her a brimming glass of La Crema and tell her she looks beautiful.

"Two is a nightmare," she sighs. I'm not sure if she's talking about the age or the number of children, but I give a sympathetic nod.

"Where's Frank?" Esme asks.

"He golfs on Friday afternoons."

"Every Friday afternoon?"

"Don't get me started." Becca shakes her head, pouring more wine into all of our glasses. "Tell me about *you* guys. What's new?"

We gab into the afternoon, catching up on the important stuff. Esme talks about John and the recruiting firm where she works and her sister's upcoming wedding; I tell them about Alex and The Path and my idea to make the company more philanthropic. I don't mention Cassie, because there's too much backstory, and besides, if I bring it up now, I'm just going to be focused on Jane's new apartment, on the anxiety that riddles my body when I think about going there later.

Our conversation flows, though there's a slight strain I can't help but notice—a lack of seamlessness that wasn't present the last time we were all together. Becca's eyes keep darting to the playroom and the baby monitor, and when she goes upstairs to check on Mac, her napping eight-month-old, Esme and I sit in silence. She scrolls through her phone, and I look around the room, absorbing the details of a home that is chaotic, but cultivated. I notice a spread of fabric swatches on the window seat, small squares of different tasteful prints, and maybe it's the wine, but it takes me a moment to reconcile the Becca that I knew six years ago—dancing on the bar at Southside, ponytail swinging—with a woman who reupholsters furniture in the house where she lives with her husband and children. How fast everything changed.

Suddenly, I feel a foreign object poking up my nose; I look down and it is Milo's finger.

"You have boogie," he says in a small, husky voice.

"Milo!" Becca reappears with Mac on her hip, shooing Milo away from me.

"It's okay, Becks." I smile up at her, at the sight of my dear friend and her precious second baby. Mac curls his hand into a little fist, rubs it against his eye.

"It's *not* okay, Milo. We don't touch people's faces without asking." Becca shakes her head for emphasis, and I start laughing when I imagine anyone *asking* if they can touch a person's face.

Mac begins to babble, and Esme stretches out her arms. "Give me that delicious baby."

She bounces him on her lap and presses her nose to his head, inhaling sharply like she's smelling a candle. Then she reaches for her purse and digs out a small package wrapped in cellophane and pale blue ribbon, hands it to Becca.

"If it's too small, you can exchange it," she says, and I feel a stab of unwarranted annoyance toward Esme for bringing a gift when I didn't. Now I look like an asshole.

Becca unwraps the present and gushes over the little onesie covered in blue stars. Mac begins to fuss on Esme's lap.

"I should feed him." Becca pushes her shirt down and unclips her bra, revealing a melon-sized boob that could've swallowed one of her pre-baby breasts. Milo starts running around the coffee table in circles, whining for snacks, and this is our cue to leave, though Becca is too kind a friend to push us out.

"You're welcome to stay!" she exclaims when we stand and clear the empty glasses and mention the train schedule. She switches Mac to the other boob and offers to drive us to the station, but it's a seven-minute walk and we tell her not to be ridiculous.

Esme falls asleep on the way back to the city, her cheek smashed against the window. I gaze past her at the suburban sprawl backing onto the train line, a blurred scene of rusty swing sets and chain-link fences. Eventually, I let my eyes flutter closed, digest the afternoon. I think of the tiny blue handprint on Becca's wall and the fabric swatches and the baby monitor and imagine Alex and I living a life that encompasses those things. Instantly, the thought feels wrong, glaringly so, and I'm relieved that the train is pulling into Grand Central, Esme blinking her eyes open with a wide yawn as the conductor announces our arrival.

Esme and I part ways on Lexington. We promise to grab drinks next week, but the plan is flimsy, the fact that it'll likely get rain checked an unspoken truth between us. *That's just how friendships become in your thirties,* I think as I head south. The love is still there, but the urgency for that constant companionship fades, replaced by something else—romantic partnerships, yes, but maybe we also just get tired. This makes me think of Cassie, of the stark difference when it comes to her. Becca and Esme were never my family, not like Cassie was. And the irony is that now, when I truly need them, Becca and Esme are the ones who answer my calls.

It feels good to stretch my legs, and I end up walking all the way down to the West Village. I left Jane's key at my apartment, so I decide to shower and change, then stop and feed Willie Nelson on my way to meet Alex for dinner. The steady movement of my legs almost makes me forget how anxious I am about going to Jane's building—to Cassie's building.

It's past six by the time I reach my neighborhood, and the streets are buzzing with Friday energy. In front of me, a little girl in a plaid coat is holding her mother's hand, skipping to keep up, her blond braids swinging. For some reason, the sight makes me think of what Cassie used to say about maternal instinct whenever I expressed my hunch that it was something I lacked. She told me it would come, that it was probably delayed because of my parents' divorce and Mom's illness and the trauma of Wade, but that one day it would just appear and take hold of me forever, an inexplicable, everlasting purpose that I'd know in the marrow of my bones.

But I'm thirty-five years old. I've been waiting. And this instinct hasn't arrived. I watch the girl and her mother, and my heart feels full, just like it did watching Becca and Mac this afternoon. But my heart feels for *them,* not for me. I appreciate motherhood. I respect it—God, I respect it. But I don't want it for myself.

Tears prick my eyes as I pull open the heavy double doors to my building, and I wish, for the billionth time, that I could talk to my own mother. That I could crawl into her lap and let her stroke my hair, let her soothe me with her voice, the one that always held answers, that made me feel safe for no other reason than that it belonged to her.

In my apartment, I flop down on the unmade bed, let a fresh batch of tears slide from my eyes, crushed by the weight of so much that I don't understand.

I don't know why I don't want to be a mother.

I don't know why it bothers me that Jane unwittingly moved to Cassie's building.

I don't know why I can't stop remembering that tomorrow is Cassie's birthday. I don't know why I care that it used to be a day I cherished and celebrated but isn't anymore because it can't be, because she won't let it be. She won't let me care about her, and I don't know why.

I breathe in and out, reach for the bottle of water on my nightstand. I drink some down, calming a little. *I can do this,* I tell myself. *I can go to Jane-slash-Cassie's building and feed Jane's cat. It'll take ten minutes, then I'll grab a cab down to Chelsea and meet Alex at Westville. It's not like I'm going to run into Cassie in the elevator—what are the chances of that? And if I do, I'll explain why I'm there. It's not like I'm stalking her.*

I close my eyes. Even though my life feels more together than it has in ages, I can't help but wish that so many things were different.

Chapter Twenty-three

Cassie

October 13, 2023
The day of

By eight, my birthday party is in full swing. I have to hand it to Grant—he did a phenomenal job. The drinks are strong, the food is a hit, the playlist is an ideal mix of mellow favorites and pump-up bangers, and most importantly, he nailed the guest list. Everyone I care about is here: our city friends, our Hamptons friends, the women from my mommy group at the Y, old coworkers I still keep up with, the small but mighty team employed at Cassidy Adler, and Grant's extended family of borderline-alcoholic WASPs who make everything more fun.

Ava, McKay, and I giggle in the corner watching my mother-in-law, Lillian, flirt with the hot bartender, who can't be a day over twenty-five. He pours her a shot of bourbon, and we watch as she insists he pour one for himself, too. They click glasses and knock them back. Lillian starts gagging dramatically, grabbing onto the bartender's arm for support. McKay is on the floor.

"Aunt Lillian is fucking crazy," she chokes through her laughter. "I'm so sad my parents aren't here," she adds with a pout.

"Me, too. Where are they again?"

"A wedding in Sun Valley. You know the Larkins' son Henry? His."

Ava holds up her empty glass. She purses her mouth, which makes it look like she's sucking in her cheeks. "I'm not nearly drunk enough. Another round?"

The ground is starting to feel wobbly beneath my four-inch pumps. "I've had two martinis and a shot," I say. "I'd better switch to wine."

A Dua Lipa song blares through the speakers. At the bar, Lillian moves her hips in a continuous loop, her arms raised overhead while the poor bartender forces an amused smile.

"Yikes." Ava shakes her head. "Someone save him."

I gesture to Ava and McKay. "C'mon. The good wine is in the kitchen. Plus my phone. Oh my God, guys, I've taken *no* pictures or videos all night."

"God forbid!" McKay's hand flies to her mouth, and we all laugh. She drapes her arm around my shoulders. "You know I'm kidding. You've gotta give the people what they want."

In the kitchen, we open a bottle of expensive cab. We find a box of artisan cheese sticks, and Ava is inhaling them at lightning speed. I know she's going to beat herself up for this later, and I wish she wouldn't. I wish she knew how beautiful she was, even with a few pounds of baby weight left to lose. I take a selfie of the three of us, faces mashed together. McKay puckers her lips in a way that makes her look like a Victoria's Secret model. I feel like we're back in college, except this time, McKay and I are best friends.

She wraps her arms around my middle, and I can tell she's on the verge of saying something sentimental. "I'm so fucking lucky you're my cousin!" she yelps. I laugh, chugging my wine. All three of us are drunk as hell.

I take my phone and my glass of red and wander around the party. I film snippets of everything happening: the caterers replenishing the extensive charcuterie board, Ned and Tom looking like grade A fools twerking to a Nicki Minaj remix, my mommy group friends Allegra and Kate sharing a cigarette on the terrace.

"Tell me you didn't get that on film!" Kate exclaims in her adorable British accent, stubbing the cig on the stone railing. "I haven't had a smoke since before Joss was born!"

I smile innocently, scrolling through the newly captured content on my phone. I post it all to Instagram.

"You look cool, promise." I blow Kate a drunken kiss, sidling up beside her and Allegra and seamlessly joining their conversation about the four-month sleep regression. We're all in the thick of it, and we agree it's hell.

Chatter about baby sleep morphs into a candid heart-to-heart about postpartum sex life, which morphs into a venting session about the ineptitudes of our husbands when it comes to some of the most basic principles of childcare. These are the kinds of conversations that I love, that I lose myself in—conversations with other moms who get it, who see me, who validate what are sometimes irrational feelings from a place of empathy.

The three of us talk for so long that I lose track of time, and when I glance down at my phone, I see that it's already nine fifteen. Jesus. Did Grant put Ella to bed without telling me?

I apologize to Allegra and Kate and excuse myself, scanning the terrace for Grant. It's crowded out here—more so than I'd anticipated it would be—and it takes me a minute to find him. Finally, I spot the familiar line of his shoulders near the corner of the terrace, his back to the wall of the building as he nurses a beer, deep in conversation with his younger brother, Reed, who's in town from Santa Barbara.

Reed notices me approaching them and grins. His face is a near replica of Grant's, except for his eyes, which are the same grass-green hue as Lillian's. "Hi, birthday girl," he says. "You look great. Not a day over twenty-seven."

I flash Reed a distracted smile, pulling on Grant's arm. "Hey." I lower my voice. "Did you put Ella to bed?"

"Not yet." He glances at his watch. "Shoot. I lost track of time."

"Seriously?" A sliver of panic lodges itself behind my ribs. "Where is she? The stroller isn't out here." My heart is suddenly racing so hard, I can hear its thumping beat in my ears.

"Relax, babe, she's right over there. It was getting loud on this side, and she was falling asleep, so I moved the stroller around the corner."

Relief floods me like a narcotic.

"I'll go put her down now," Grant says.

I shake my head. "It's fine. I want to do it."

"You sure?" He rubs his chin. "We agreed you were off duty tonight."

But I'm already walking away, waving off Grant's overture, too relieved to be irritated. In the haze of my drunkenness, a single, clear-cut desire consumes me. I just want to be with my daughter. I want to hold her soft, chubby body in my arms and give her one more bottle and tuck her safely in her crib.

I round the corner, and there's the pale blue fabric of her stroller, just visible in the semidarkness. My heart bounces in my chest as I move toward Ella, my hands reaching down into the bassinet, ready to scoop her up.

But the bassinet is empty. Ella is not in her stroller. My body turns to stone.

"Grant!" I call, frantic. *"Grant!"*

I run back around the corner, yanking Grant away from Reed. "Where the fuck is Ella? She's not in her stroller."

"What?" He turns to me. "Are you sure?"

"Of course I'm sure!" Fear clobbers my chest.

"Okay, she's probably inside, then. I bet she was fussing and my mom or someone picked her up. Come on."

Grant leads me indoors, where we scan the room for Ella, for the sight of someone holding our baby. We are both calling her name, pacing the apartment, checking every corner, asking every guest.

"Lillian!" I find my mother-in-law in the powder room, reapplying makeup. "Have you seen Ella? We can't find her anywhere."

Lillian turns away from the mirror, peach lipstick smudging the corner of her tooth. "Ella? No, I haven't seen her—"

I run back to the terrace before Lillian can finish her sentence, my stomach in my throat. I feel as though I've been pushed off the side of the building, and the fall won't end.

When I scream, it's unconscious. A jarring, mammalian howl that expels from me, piercing and foreign as it rips across the night.

Time freezes. Or maybe it accelerates. I fall to my knees as Grant reappears beside me, as the music stops.

"Where could she be?" he is shouting, panicked now. "I've asked everyone! Where's our daughter?"

I can't speak. My maternal instinct knows—even as Grant rushes inside to look again—that he isn't going to find her. She's been taken. I know it in my gut, in my soul.

McKay drops to her knees beside me, frantically asking questions. She blots my face with her sleeve, and I realize I must be crying.

The voices around me are rising in pitch, frantic. I hear someone announce that they're calling the police. Ava, I think.

"Cassie, you're shaking." It's McKay again, her hand icy cold on the back of my neck, an alien object. "Hold on, where's Grant?"

"He went inside," I croak.

"Well, someone get him! Someone get Grant!"

"No." The tears are pouring from my eyes like a vicious rainstorm, and I know who I need. Her face appears in the center of my mind, her gentle hazel gaze, the person who knows me better than anyone on this earth, whether or not I want it to be true. And the only one who will understand my fear that the worst thing I've ever done has come back to haunt me.

"Billie," I call to anyone who will listen. "I need Billie."

Chapter Twenty-four
Billie

Spring 2006

Cassie and I ditch school and sit on a bench in the town park with our bagels. I spare no details when I tell her everything—about Wade, the basement, turning down Northeastern, his threats.

She's a mess by the end of it. We both are.

"This has to stop." *She wipes her face.* "You have to go to the police."

"I can't, Cass. Technically, I'm not a minor."

"That's bullshit. He's ruining your life, Billie. Think about what your mom would say, if she knew. If she knew he was keeping you from your dream school, trapping you at home, raping you every fucking night . . ." *Cassie shakes her head.* "She'd kill him."

"I know." *I swallow the last of my everything bagel. The confession has made me ravenous, hungrier than I've felt in weeks. I ball up the aluminum foil.* "But if I try to get Wade in trouble, he'll take Mom away. He'll let her die in some miserable nursing home."

"He won't, 'cause he'll be in trouble."

"Not necessarily."

She sighs, turning to me, her eyes pooling with consternation. "There has to be a way out of this."

That night, I don't go home. Cassie won't let me. She brings me to the safety of her house, where her mother hands us warm bowls of spaghetti on the couch. I thank her and dig in immediately, starving again.

Mrs. Barnwell clears her throat. "Principal Mattis called earlier. She said both of you girls skipped graduation rehearsal today."

"Shit." Cassie looks at me, raises a dark eyebrow. "Our gowns. We forgot."

"Language, Cass." Mrs. Barnwell sighs, rubbing her forehead. "Girls. You have less than a week left of high school. You graduate on Saturday. Just . . . try to end this chapter on a high note, okay?" She pivots toward the kitchen, then looks back over her shoulder. "I picked up your graduation gowns. They're hanging in the front hall closet."

Cassie rolls her eyes, but I smile. I like Mrs. Barnwell. She's not nearly as insufferable as Cassie makes her out to be.

I sleep in Mara's room, since it's empty and Cassie only has a twin bed in hers. Mara is obsessed with Prince; she has an entire wall covered in posters and memorabilia. I prop myself up against the pillows and study the Purple Rain album cover. It's iconic—Prince in his purple trench jacket and white ruffled shirt, a faraway look in his eyes.

I think of Mara an hour north at SUNY New Paltz, where I'll be in a matter of months. Maybe she could be my friend. Cassie has never gotten along with her sister, but maybe Mara, like their mother, isn't actually so bad. Anyone who loves Prince has to be cool. Maybe Mara has her reasons for not sucking up to Grandma Catherine the way Cassie does.

My phone vibrates then—a text. I know who it's from before I check the screen.

Where the fuck are you Billie Jean?

I shiver and power off the phone, huddling under the covers. Fear churns through me like a giant worm, coursing its way through my insides. I will pay for this tomorrow, I know. He will make me pay. I fend off sleep for as long as I can manage, savoring the Wade-less safety of Cassie's house. Dreading the light of day.

"I have an idea," Cassie says in the morning when we're walking to school. "What if I sleep at your house tonight? Then Wade won't be able to do anything."

"Aren't you afraid to sleep at my house?"

"I'm not scared of him, Billie. I'm scared to leave you alone with him."

I glance at her, gratitude flooding my heart. "Okay." I nod. "But . . . just tonight? Then what happens tomorrow?"

She chews her bottom lip. "Let's just take it one day at a time. We'll think of something."

The mood at school is restless, celebratory. Exams are over; teachers have stopped assigning homework; summer vacation is—literally—hours away. Meanwhile, I'm jittery as hell. I call the house line during lunch, and when Sandra answers, I'm so relieved I could cry. If Sandra is there, that means Wade hasn't taken Mom to the nursing home.

"Sorry I didn't see you last night," I tell her. "I slept at a friend's. Mom's doing okay?"

"She is," Sandra sings, and I hear the sound of the television in the background. "We're just having some soup and watching When Harry Met Sally."

In spite of everything, I smile. "That's one of her favorites."

After I hang up with Sandra, I'm grabbing a book from my locker when Ashton corners me.

"Hey." She smacks her gum. She's wearing bright blue eyeliner that makes her look like Gwen Stefani on the Love Angel Music Baby *album*. I understand why Cassie thinks she's trashy.

"Hey."

"I see you got your best friend back."

"Right." I set my combination and close the lock.

"Are you okay?" Ashton crosses her arms, blows a wisp of dyed blond hair off her forehead. "You look really . . . wrecked. And I heard you had to turn down Northeastern."

"I'm fine, Ash."

"That really sucks. But hey, at least we'll be at New Paltz together."

I give a joyless smile, say nothing.

Ashton looks me up and down. "You have to do something about your appearance before Saturday. You seriously look like garbage, and graduation pictures last a lifetime."

Cassie and I buy cigarettes at the gas station after school. When we reach my house, Wade's truck isn't in the driveway. I exhale a sigh of relief.

"Come on," I tell her. "We can smoke up on the widow's walk."

It's a warm, windless day, only a few clouds dotting the rich blue sky. From the roof of the house, we can see Sandra pushing Mom in the hammock between the two maple trees out back. Mom's eyes are closed, her hands clasped peacefully across her chest.

"She looks happy," Cassie observes. She fishes two Parliaments from the box and lights both at the same time.

I hate the smell of cigarettes, but I need something to take the edge off, and we're not old enough to buy alcohol. Cassie hands me one, and I take a deep drag, feel the smoke burn the back of my throat, then all the way into my lungs. The rush of nicotine that follows leaves my head light and dizzy.

"She does." I lean against the railing, gazing down at Mom dipping back and forth between the trees. She looks like a little girl.

"Fuck Wade." Cassie exhales a long stream of smoke, sunlight bouncing off her sharp cheekbones. She looks darkly beautiful, like an old Hollywood movie star.

"Do we have to talk about Wade?"

"At least you didn't have, like, actual sex with him."

"Yet."

Cassie shakes her head. "Billie. I won't let you."

"What the fuck am I going to do here when you're gone?"

"I'm not going anywhere yet."

"You're moving to Boston in three months. That's soon."

Cassie says nothing. Her eyes land on mine, heavy and desolate. She takes another drag of her cigarette, the coals at the tip glowing orange.

I stare up at the sky. A plane weaves across the mass of cerulean, a stream of white contrails in its wake. "I wish we could go back to Paris."

Cassie laughs. "God. Me, too."

We stay on the roof for hours, talking and chain-smoking until I'm so light-headed I need to lie down. Cassie lies beside me, the weathered slats of the widow's walk digging into our shoulder blades. It's dusk now, the last of the light slipping behind the full trees.

"It's getting late," I say. "Are you hungry?"

"Not really. Cigs curb my appetite. It's so peaceful up here."

"It is." I admire the sight of the perfect fingernail moon, an illuminated crescent against the darkening sky.

"I thought only places on the sea had widow's walks."

"We're close enough to the Hudson that you can see the river when it's clear. Mom always thought that was why the house had one."

Cassie is quiet for a long beat. "You talk about her in the past tense."

"I don't mean to."

"It must be so hard. Her being . . . gone but not gone."

My chest feels like it's loaded with bricks. "It's torture. Actual torture."

Cassie is quiet for a moment. Then, she reaches for my hand. "You're the best daughter. I'll be lucky if my kids love me half as much as you love Lorraine. You know?"

I say nothing. I don't know. Cassie talks about her future kids all the time, like they already exist. It's different for me. When I think about the future, I don't see children as a given. I don't see anything as a given. I never have.

"Billie," she says, reading me. Her voice sounds strangled, squeezed. "You're going to get out of here."

As if on cue, the creak of the attic ladder sounds below, heavy footsteps weighing on its rungs. The roof hatch swings open, and there he is: sweaty, sneering, his meaty fingers gripping a can of Budweiser. Cassie and I scramble to our feet.

"Look who I found." Wade glances down at the cigarette butts, the near-empty pack of Parliaments. "Smoking will kill you, you know."

"So will sitting on your ass all day, drinking your weight in Bud Heavy." Cassie folds her arms, her eyes glacial.

Wade gives a wry smile. He looks at me, one bushy eyebrow darting toward his sparse hairline. "This friend of yours is a real pistol. Did her mommy forget to teach her to respect her elders?"

Cassie glowers. "Did your mommy forget to teach you not to rape high school girls?"

I watch Wade's face turn a deeper shade of red, the vein in his temple bulging. "Careful with that word." His eyes are pinned to me. "It's time for your friend to leave now, Billie Jean."

"I'm not going anywhere."

Wade turns to Cassie, his upper lip curling. He grips his can of beer so hard it crinkles. "You know what your problem is? You think you're better than this." He opens his arms and peers from left to right; he seems to be gesturing to the panorama around us, the sleepy houses of Red Hook that stretch into the horizon.

"What?" Cassie's eyes narrow.

"You think you're better than this town. Than everyone in it, Billie included. It's been written on your smug little face since the day she brought you over. Her new friend from Greenwich whose daddy blew all their money."

"That's not—"

"But you only think you're better; that's what makes you so insufferable. You think you have an exit plan, that you can skip off to a rich-girl college and that your years here won't matter. But guess what? This place . . . this shit town that you want to forget? It runs in your fucking blood now, Cassie Barnwell. It's who you are. Whether you cover it up or not."

The air falls silent around us, a pair of whistling robins drowned out by the beating blood in my ears. I look from Wade to Cassie, then back to Wade, my head spinning, fighting to understand how he knew exactly what to say to get under her skin. Wade has been cruel, yes, but never perceptive. I'm astonished. I didn't even know he knew Cassie's last name.

From the corner of my eye, I see Cassie's arm drop to her side, her fingers clenching into a fist. She steps toward him. "Fuck you. You're a rapist." There's venom in her voice. "You belong in prison."

The sky is indigo now, a shade away from black. Lights from neighboring houses glow beneath us, but it's dark up on the roof, harder to see. I can just make out Wade draining the rest of his beer. He tosses the can on the floor of the widow's walk, crushes it under the heel of his boot.

"I didn't rape anyone," Wade spits. He glances at me, the whites of his eyes shining in the dimness. "Billie. Your friend needs to go now. Don't make me say it again."

Cassie shakes her head. "I told you, I'm not going anywhere."

"Oh, but you are." Wade lumbers toward her, tripping over something at his feet—Cassie's backpack, I think. She dodges him, and he lands against the railing, near the part where the posts are rotten through. On instinct, I open my mouth to tell him to be careful. But the words don't come. I let him stay there, half his weight supported by the crumbly wood.

"Fuck," he mutters, reaching for the rail's corner post.

It happens in slow motion. Cassie glances at me, only for a split second, but I see it in her eyes—her frosty rage, her decision. If I grab *her wrist, hold her back for a beat, Wade will have time to hoist himself up, to recover. But I don't. Instead, I watch as she steps toward him. I can feel the story taking shape between us, tightening like a secret knot as I watch her place her hands against his chest—up high near his shoulders—and push him into the place where she knows the wood is rotten, too.*

I don't see his face before he falls, and I'm glad—I'm glad I don't have that image to carry with me. I only hear the heavy thud of his body when it hits the ground, thirty feet below.

Chapter Twenty-five

Billie

October 13, 2023
The day of

I haven't seen Alex in thirty-six hours, but it feels like much longer. I miss him acutely; my skin is practically vibrating with the urge to see him, to press my body against his, run my fingers through the hair at the nape of his neck.

It's after seven by the time I shower and blow-dry my hair, dusk settling through the small window in my bathroom. I'm dabbing concealer under my eyes when my phone buzzes on the ledge of the sink; the sight of Alex's name on the screen lifts my heart. I almost can't believe how much I like him.

> Hey, you. Want to grab a drink around 8, before Westville? Maybe Fiddlesticks?

Desire singes the length of my spine, drenches my chest. All I want is to be in a dimly lit bar with Alex, to order a strong cocktail and feel his hand slide up my thigh while we sip our drinks.

Wish I could, I text back. But I have to feed Jane's cat (she's out of town) and I'm running late already. I'll see you at the restaurant at 9 ☺

Below my text box with Alex is my most recent exchange with Cassie, a message I sent thirty minutes ago, after deliberating in the shower.

> Happy (almost) birthday, Cass! Love you and hope you have a relaxing day with Grant and Ella tomorrow. You deserve it!

I figure if she answers quickly, I can mention Jane's new apartment and that I'm stopping by to feed the cat on my way to dinner. Maybe

I can give her a quick birthday hug. Despite everything, it still feels strange to be going to Cassie's building without letting her know.

But half an hour later, when I'm dressed and walking out the door, she still hasn't answered, and I regret sending the text at all. I feel stupid and anxious as I ride the subway uptown, nerves swimming in my stomach as I grow closer and closer to 27 Gramercy Park South.

I'm wearing a midnight-blue maxi dress and black leather ankle boots, extra mascara, and some shimmery eye shadow I found in the back of my medicine cabinet. For me, this is really doing it up, but it's Friday night, and I want to look good for Alex.

I feel the man across the subway aisle checking me out. He's at least sixty, and when he winks, I avert my gaze and dig my phone out of my clutch—the silver beaded one Cassie got me for free when she worked at Intermix, the one I save for nice occasions. Somehow, I have service, so I open Instagram without thinking. A pink circle glows around @cassidyadler, and my thumb is already tapping it before my brain has time to catch up. Tap, tap, tap. Check, check, check. A habit so ingrained in me I wouldn't know how to stop if I tried.

Yet again, I find myself watching Cassie's day unfold. There she is making her morning smoothie, her hair tumbling past her shoulders in two perfect, effortless curtains. There she is having coffee with Grant and Ella at Irving Farm, then swinging by the store to "check on things." There she is in her white marble bathroom, telling the world about an eye cream that's changed her life. There she is with McKay and Ava, their faces pressed together, lips painted red, smiles wide, wineglasses raised. I notice something in the background—a bundle of white, gold, and pink balloons.

I press my thumb to the middle of the screen, pausing the picture. My heart shrivels, slides down into my gut. I just know.

I should close Instagram, forget what I saw, quit being so pathetic and obsessive. The subway car begins to slow, sliding to a halt at Fourteenth Street. I almost don't notice where we are; I almost forget that this is my stop, that I need to get off and transfer to the L train.

I slip through the doors just as they start to close, my eyes still glued to my phone. Cassie's next story, posted just ten minutes ago, is a video of what appears to be an elaborate cocktail party at her home. There are caterers in ties arranging brie and olives on a dark wood cheese board. There are people everywhere, packed into the apartment, drinking and talking, the drone of voices competing with the music. I recognize a couple of preppy men with receding hairlines from Cassie's dinner party—dancing, laughing at themselves. In the next story, there are two women I've never seen before—both thin, elegant—sharing a cigarette on the terrace, tendrils of smoke curling into the darkening sky.

As it hits me, as it pierces me, I find that I'm not even surprised. It's exactly what I've been expecting.

Despite what she'd said, Cassie is having a birthday party.

At this very minute.

At her apartment.

At her building.

Where I'm headed right now.

I don't remember transferring to the L train, but suddenly we're speeding east, and before I can process my thoughts, the doors are opening at Union Square. I follow a clogged swarm of New Yorkers up two flights of tall concrete steps until a rush of cold air hits my lungs. Outside, the streets are crowded, like they always are in this part of the city, especially on the weekend. I pull my phone out of my bag, fingers trembling. I'm about to google *how long can cats survive without food* when I remember that Willie Nelson needs water, too. And regardless, I can't bail on Jane. I can't turn into a selfish, unreliable asshole just because that's what Cassie has become.

I feel something hard and bright charge through my sternum, bolting me forward, forcing my legs to move. I head north. A myriad of images passes through my mind as I walk faster, darting around slow pedestrians, skipping across streets while the crosswalk blinks red. In my head, I see Cassie's eleven-year-old face at the pool the first day we ever met, the wrinkle at the top of her nose when she smiled at me with such assurance, such magnetism. I see the two of us walking through the hallways at Red Hook High, our elbows linked, our heads pressed together, so many years of being literally connected. So many moments shared, trivial and important. And then, the most important moment of all. Cassie, high up on the widow's walk of my childhood home, her hands pressed to Wade's shoulders, the resolve in her force. The way her eyes locked on mine while we waited for his body to hit the ground.

I hook a right on Nineteenth Street and recall Cassie's text, the one she sent last week when I'd asked if she'd changed her mind about her birthday plans.

> Nah, just going to lie low this year. Takeout and
> Succession on the couch with Grant!

I hate her. It feels like fire in my body. Fire that can't breathe, that's suffocating, cracking, screaming inside of me.

I turn left on Irving Place. I'm so close now, a single block away. Before I know it, I'm rounding Twenty-first Street, and my body is numb with shock and rage, and I see the entrance to Cassie's building—*Jane's* building—and there's a man a few paces in front of me. I follow him inside, and he waves to the doorman, says he's going up to the Adlers'. The lobby is warm; it smells of clean rubber and perfume, and the marble floors are polished. The walls are black paneled with gold trim. I can't believe Jane lives somewhere like this.

The doorman nods; he must assume we are together, because he pays no attention as I follow the man into the elevator.

The doors click closed, and the man glances at me expectantly, his hand hovering above the rows of numbered buttons. He has a weak chin and close-cropped, salt-and-pepper hair, and I recognize him from Cassie's dinner party. He's Evelyn's husband. Hank? Harry?

"What floor?" he asks, evidence he doesn't remember me. If he did, he would've assumed I was going up to the Adlers', too.

"Eight." My voice is hoarse, barely a whisper. "Thanks."

The elevator is rickety, old. It shakes to life, then begins its ascent. Hank or Harry is reading something on his phone. Neither of us says anything when I slip out on the eighth floor. I fumble in my clutch for the small gold key and let myself into Jane's apartment.

Jane wasn't lying—she and Sasha have hardly unpacked. Even though the kitchen and living room are chock-full of boxes, I can tell right away that the space is beautiful. It boasts high ceilings and tall windows and the same elegant crown moldings as Cassie's apartment above. Willie Nelson appears from nowhere, snaking through my legs in figure eights, his spine rounding. He gives a loud purr.

"Hey, buddy." I lean down and scratch the base of his ear. "You must be hungry."

I work on staying focused, locating the cat food in the pantry per

Jane's instructions. I scoop some into Willie Nelson's dish, then fill his water bowl from the tap. He goes for a drink first, lapping thirstily.

I walk through the living room toward the windows, rest my forehead against the glass. It's eerie, the sense of déjà vu I experience being here. The view is exactly the same as Cassie's—of course it is. I watch the cars crawl across Twentieth Street below, pedestrians on the sidewalk who look like ants, even in the dark. The lamplit square of Gramercy Park glows on the other side of the street. Without really thinking, I walk over to the french doors and unlatch them open onto the terrace. The outdoor space is not as refined as Cassie's—there's no teak furniture, no row of potted boxwoods. Still, it's a beautiful terrace. In wedding-cake style buildings like this one, only the top few floors have them.

I'm admiring the stone features, and that's when I hear it. Thumping music. High-pitched peals of laughter. A chorus of animated conversations. Cassie's party, happening right above me. Instagram doesn't lie.

Anger climbs in my abdomen, burning high in my chest, near my throat. The question pounds inside my head, a single word that throbs against my skull.

Why?

Why would my oldest, closest friend in the world have a birthday party and not invite me? Why would she lie to me about her plans when I asked, then put the entire thing on social media where she *knows* I'll see it? Or maybe—maybe it doesn't even occur to her that I'll see it, because that's how little she cares. Because that's how little she considers my existence in this city, on this planet. I feel my jaw clench tightly like there's a screw there. Years of rage simmer inside me. It's so far from being about just this.

I lean over the rail of Jane's terrace. For some reason, I think of Wade. Did it hurt when he fell? Did he die instantly, or did he lie there for several minutes while his brain bled out on the slate walk, suffering, knowing the end was coming? How can you love someone so much that you kill for them, then forget them? How can a human heart be capable of that kind of operation?

A gust of wind hits my face, whistling as it blows across the terrace. When it subsides, I hear a different noise. It sounds like the wind but sharper, even higher in pitch. Someone is crying. No, *wailing*. It's coming from directly above me, from Cassie's terrace, edging out the music and drunken laughter in its earsplitting frequency.

I know what the sound is. I may not be a mother, but I know that it's a baby. It's got to be Ella. How does no one hear her?

I open Instagram again and instantly click Cassie's avatar when I see that she's uploaded new content. She's posted a series of selfies with the two women smoking on the terrace, their mouths open in amused laughter, then serious, then puckering, then clinking their empty martini glasses. The last one is from thirty-two seconds ago. How does she not hear her own baby crying?

I pace the length of Jane's terrace. Like Cassie's, it wraps around the corner of the building. It's big. It's possible that the guests are gathered on one side—the side I'm seeing in her Instagram stories. It's possible that over the music, Ella can't be heard.

But Ella is *screaming* now. The sound is bloodcurdling, raw. My heart thumps against my chest, anxious. I'll wait five minutes. If five minutes pass and Ella is still losing it, then . . . *Then what, Billie?* I shake my head, forearms pressed to the railing, the city lights around me twinkling like jewels. I need to get a hold of myself.

I'm still gripping my clutch, which suddenly starts to vibrate. My phone. I pull it out, check the screen. Alex.

Getting on the subway. See you soon!

I glance at the time. *8:40.* We're meeting in twenty minutes. If I don't leave now, I'll be late.

Ella's screams are piercing, intolerable. The sound makes my heart feel fragile, exposed, and I have the sudden, acute feeling that I'm in the wrong place at the wrong time. That I should just get the hell out of here, not let this become my problem.

But some mysterious force keeps my feet frozen where they are. I navigate back to Instagram, just to see. The pink ring circles Cassie's name again. Is this a joke? She's drunk and posting incessantly to social media while her baby is hysterical, mere feet away.

I walk to the end of the terrace where I can hear Ella the loudest. The terraces are tiered, but she must be almost directly above where I'm standing. I notice a fire escape attached to the building, something I didn't register before. I reach for it, my palm wrapping around the cold metal. I hoist myself up to the base without really thinking, and then I'm there, standing on the first step of the ladder. All I'd have to do is climb up.

My phone vibrates again, and I realize I'm still holding it. Alex.

What's your ETA? Can't wait to see you.

8:51. Nine minutes. But dinner at Westville doesn't seem important now.

Ella lets out a guttural wail. I take a deep breath and lean down, dropping my phone and clutch to the floor of Jane's terrace. I pull off my ankle boots and ditch those, too.

Something takes over. Something primal, unstoppable. Perhaps it's the anger in me finally roused, responding, snapping like a burning branch. Perhaps it's the fight for a personal justice I believe in but can't quite articulate—the fight to prove to myself or maybe to Cassie that I'm still here, that those decades of sacred friendship mean more than this. Or perhaps I'm just genuinely worried about Ella.

Either way, I'm climbing, ascending. I'm moving with momentum, decision, purpose, my socked feet gripping the stairs of the fire escape, my dress blowing lightly against my legs. Ella's wails grow louder with each step.

And then I'm there, level with Cassie's terrace. I see lights glowing through the windows indoors, but the drapes—at least on this side of the apartment—are closed shut. I hear the party going in full force; the music is more deafening that I'd realized. A Wilson Phillips song blares, an old favorite of Cassie's.

I know there's pain (I know there's pain)
Why do you lock yourself up in these chains? (These chains)

There is no one on this side of the terrace. The stroller is right there, just a few feet from the ledge, the blue canopy I've seen a thousand times on Instagram, winding through Madison Square Park and the quiet, hedge-lined roads of East Hampton. I stand on my tiptoes and squint, and there is Ella's little body writhing in the bassinet. Her throat must be raw by now.

No one is there to witness what unfolds in these next thirty seconds: me, hopping over the rail of the terrace and plucking Ella from the stroller. Ella, in my arms, already beginning to calm. Me, holding Ella tightly against my chest as the two of us slip back down the fire escape, as I descend the steps till I'm safely on Jane's terrace again. I catch my breath, grab my clutch, phone and boots and slip back into the apartment.

I look down at Ella's face, her mouth suckling on nothing. I notice a pacifier clipped to her onesie, and I place it between her lips. Instantly, her eyes flutter closed.

The only furniture in Jane's living room is an L-shaped couch and a pair of club chairs. I crack open a window, then settle onto one end of the couch with Ella. Her mouth is still suckling the pacifier, but she's asleep—I'm almost sure of it. She's warm in my arms. She has that indescribably good baby smell, like sweet, hot milk.

Willie Nelson leaps up on the couch beside us, curling into a ball against my thigh. He startles me; for a second, I've forgotten why he's here. And then it all comes rushing back. What I'm doing at Jane's apartment. Feeding the cat on my way to dinner with Alex.

Alex.

I tap the screen of my phone, which tells me it's quarter past nine. I have a missed call from him and several new texts.

> I'm here, snagged us a table in the back.
>
> All good?
>
> ????

I swallow hard.

Suddenly, through the cracked window, I hear someone scream. It's Cassie—I know right away. The music stops.

I stand and move toward the window, Ella secure in my arms. For a full minute, it's all I hear. Cassie's violent, animal screams from one story above. I can't believe I thought Ella was loud—that was crickets compared to this. I'm afraid Ella will wake up, but somehow, she doesn't. She must be exhausted from crying.

Someone announces that they've called the police. I move closer to the window, press my ear against the screen.

"Hold on, where's Grant?" It's McKay's voice, desperate. "Well, someone get him! Someone get Grant!"

"No." It's Cassie speaking now, and I imagine her face in this moment. Blotchy red, tear-stained, mascara running down her cheeks. "Billie," she says, and I freeze. "I need Billie."

"Billie? Why?" McKay again.

Before I can process what's happening, my phone is vibrating on the couch. I back away from the window and reach for it, silencing the buzzing, staring at the name flashing across the screen. *Cassie Barnwell.*

My heart swells, a tide rising in my chest. The moment feels like a miracle, a victory. Cassie, in her deepest pain, needs *me.*

I hear someone say that the cops are on their way. I glance down at Ella's peaceful, sleeping face. Even with her eyes closed, she looks like Cassie. Much more so than I'd ever realized from pictures.

The cops are on their way. There's a sudden pang of pure, unfiltered panic in my stomach as this piece of information lands. I study Ella in my arms, the dark sweep of eyelashes against a creamy white cheek.

The cops are on their way to find a missing baby. A baby who *I've* taken.

I feel as if I'm slowly waking from a trance, a lucid dream. What the hell have I done?

Part

TWO

Chapter Twenty-six

Billie

Spring 2006

A woman's scream echoes from below. It sounds like Sandra.

"Oh my God. Oh my God." I turn toward Cassie, but she isn't looking at me. She's staring straight ahead at the crumbling gap in the railing, the place where she's just pushed Wade.

"What just happened, Cassie? Is he dead?"

She yanks my arm, pulls me toward the open hatch. "Come on." Her voice is steady, but urgent. "We have to get off the roof. Now."

We grab our backpacks and the empty carton of Parliaments and make our way down the attic ladder, back into the house. Fear pounds in my chest, and I force myself to breathe. Cassie seems to know what she's doing. She seems to have a plan.

Once we're back in my bedroom, she turns to me, and it's then that I see it: the fear swimming in her eyes. She's scared, too.

"Billie. Listen to me." She clutches both my wrists. "We weren't on the roof, okay?"

"But—"

"We were here in your room the whole time. We were studying."

The door is ajar, and we hear Sandra's voice from downstairs. "Hello, this is 911? There's been an accident at the house where I work. River Road, across from the Episcopal church. A man—my employer—I think he fell from the widow's walk. I think"—Sandra's voice breaks—"I think he might be dead."

My stomach lurches.

"Did you hear that?" Cassie whispers. She grips my wrists harder. "It was an accident. That's what Sandra thinks, and that's what we'll tell the police when they get here."

"But, Cass, what if they—"

"Billie." Her gaze hardens, and there's something in the way she's looking at me—a silent directive that resembles a threat. She swallows. "What I just did up there . . . I did it for you."

"I know."

"You can't ever tell anyone."

"I won't."

"Promise me."

"I promise, Cassie."

We go downstairs and find Sandra in the kitchen. She's sitting at the round table, shoulders hunched, her expression glazed over.

"We heard someone scream," Cassie says. "Is everything okay?"

Sandra glances up at us, her eyes watery. All the color has drained from her face. She shakes her head. "Wade had a fall. The police are on their way."

"What? Holy shit." Cassie's shock sounds as real as it gets, and I have to hand it to her—she's a good actress. "Is he . . . is he all right?"

"I don't know, honey."

It strikes me that I should contribute, say something. I dig for words and force myself to speak them, to be as convincing as Cassie. "Oh my God, Sandra. We were—we were in my room, and we heard that scream. I thought it might've been you. Where's Mom?"

"Your mom is already in bed, thank the lord."

"She's asleep?"

Sandra nods. "I'd just left her room when I heard the noise from outside. This terrible sound, like a thud, but also a crack . . ." She screws her eyes shut; her hand flies to her mouth. "I went out the front door, and that's when I saw him on the slate walk. Don't go out there, girls. Please don't go out there."

A cop car arrives minutes later, an ambulance in tow. A middle-aged officer with a red beard introduces himself, but I'm too shaken to register the name he gives. Cassie and I listen as he asks Sandra questions, her voice wobbly as she reiterates what she told the dispatcher on the phone.

Eventually, the cop turns to Cassie and me. His eyes are kind, with *soft lines around the edges. He asks about Wade, if either of us spoke to him when we got home from school. If we heard or witnessed anything out of the ordinary.*

This is my cue, and thankfully, the words come easily, as if this moment has been mine all along. As if it's my destiny to protect her, the same intrepid way she's protected me.

"No," I tell the officer, my tone solemn. "Neither of us saw Wade today. He would go up to the roof sometimes; he'd drink up there. It wasn't unusual." I pause. "Cassie and I were in my bedroom studying. We didn't hear him fall."

Just then, an EMT comes through the back door. She's young—early thirties, maybe—and her expression stays neutral as she folds her arms across her uniformed chest. She must do this all the time.

"I'm so sorry," she says, her voice lowering to just the right degree of sympathy. "There's no pulse. He's gone."

At the table, Sandra emits a small whimper. I force my face to fall, drop my head to the floor, but in the charged space between Cassie and me, I can feel what's really there, the mutual sensations that wash through both of us.

Gratitude. Relief.

Wade is gone. He isn't coming back.

Chapter Twenty-seven
Cassie

October 13, 2023
30 minutes after

Falling. The sensation of my stomach lifting to my ribs and flipping around, suspended, sick. The drop that follows is never-ending. The world is over as I know it.

I clutch the edge of the toilet—cold porcelain against the pads of my fingers—and vomit into the bowl. Red wine, tequila, Grey Goose, vermouth, brown bits of olive in the liquid swirl. I didn't eat much tonight.

Someone's hands are scraping back my hair. Grant? McKay?

"Hey." It's McKay's voice, from very far away. "Sit up. Here. Rinse." She hands me a tall, clear glass. The water looks like a distorted fishbowl, and my arm won't move, a heavy weight at my side.

I close my eyes and all I see is Ella. Her round blue eyes, pudgy cheeks, the gummy smile that sets my heart on fire every time. The flat spot on the back of her head where her light brown hair is sparser. The way her chubby little fist grabs for the collar of my shirt when she feeds.

Ella. Gone.

I don't want to exist in a world without her. I won't. I refuse.

I screw my eyes shut tighter, and fresh tears leak through, dripping down my face and onto the bathroom tile. I think of the last excruciating minutes of labor, how my body felt like it was shattering on the side where the epidural hadn't worked. Unbearable agony, but nothing compared to the pain I feel now.

My phone is on the floor and I reach for it, try Billie one more time. But the call just rings and rings until it hits voicemail. Where is she?

McKay's voice again. "Why do you keep calling Billie? Here. You need to rinse."

I let McKay pull me up, and I take the glass, swish some water around my mouth, and spit it into the sink. She hands me a towel, and I brush it across my lips. I don't care if I smell like puke. I don't care about anything other than finding my daughter.

I stumble out of the powder room.

Grant, Lillian, and Reed are all sitting on the living room sofa, stone-faced. Everyone else appears to have left, but I hear the faucet running in the kitchen, a couple of pairs of feet shuffling around.

Lillian glances up at me, her eyes bloodshot. "Grant kicked everyone out, but I told the caterers to stay and clean. We'll all be able to think more clearly if the apartment is spick-and-span."

Grant's face is red, his eyes pinched slits. "Christ, Mom."

"And I called down to the doorman and told him to send the police right up. They should be here any minute."

McKay pats my arm. "Do you want to lie down for a sec?"

Falling. The weight of my body gathering speed as it spins and sinks through the air. There is only one way for this to end, but the end won't come. I will fall forever, waiting for the devastating blow.

This is a nightmare, I'm sure of it. A hellish, lucid nightmare that won't release me. I blink my eyes, willing myself to wake up, to leave this terrorizing incubus. But the trap persists. Grant and Lillian and Reed are still sitting there, staring ahead like zombies. McKay's hand is on my arm again; she's repeating her question. Do I want to lie down?

"No." My voice sounds like it's grating through gravel, like it belongs to a machine, not a human. I can't bring myself to look at McKay. I hate her for knowing her own children are safe in their beds, for being a mother who hasn't lost her baby. McKay would never do what I did. She'd never be idiotic enough to leave her infant unattended on a terrace in the middle of a fifty-person party. No one would. I am despicable. I deserve this.

Returning to the scene of the crime, are we?

The crime. My crime. And now *this* crime, Ella, tonight. There's a reason I've felt a constant, haunting anxiety since receiving that DM last month, and now I know what it is. The two crimes are linked—it feels impossible that they aren't—and there is no one to blame but myself.

I would do anything to rewind time, to go back and undo my mistakes.

I don't want to be here if Ella is not.

A chiming sound. The doorbell.

Grant peels himself from the couch and shuffles to the foyer. I follow. He opens the door to two cops. One of them looks to be in his midfifties, with gray stubble and a paunch. The other is female and at least two decades younger, with short auburn hair. Her gaze is stern.

"Grant Adler?" The male cop's voice is clear and deep.

Grant nods. He rubs an eye and glances over his shoulder, where I'm hovering. "This is my wife, Cassie."

"I'm Officer Scott." His eyes find mine, briefly. "And this is Officer Gorski. I assume the baby is still missing?"

Grant nods again, checking his watch. "For almost forty minutes now."

"Why don't we sit." Officer Scott gestures toward the living room. "I'd like to ask a few questions."

The officers take the slipper chairs near the fireplace, and Grant and I sink onto the couch. Lillian pops up, and I hear her say something about lemon water and cookies before disappearing into the kitchen. McKay slides into the free armchair and tucks her legs under her knees. I've almost forgotten she's still here. I wish she would just go home.

I'm unable to speak without bursting into tears, so Grant continues to do the talking. He tells the cops about the party. He gives the details of Ella's disappearance and a physical description of our daughter, of the pink footie pajamas she was wearing. Our tiny, magical, beautiful daughter. It's torture to imagine her now, helpless and afraid. Is she in the arms of a stranger? Are they on their way out of the city, the miles between us expanding with every breath? I can't stand it, these seconds without her ticking by, each one a new level of hell.

I don't realize I'm crying again until I feel Grant's hand, warm on the back of my trembling neck.

"Mr. and Mrs. Adler." Officer Scott sighs, but not unkindly. "Do you have reason to suspect any of the guests at your party would have taken your daughter?"

"No." Grant's expression is adamant.

Dread engulfs me as I think of someone knowing, someone watching. I killed a man, and even if I never let myself think about it, even if I believe in my heart he deserved it, it still happened. And now there is a price to pay.

I force my mind to slow down, to fight through the paranoia. Because the truth is this: no one at our party tonight knew me back then. No one in my *life* knew me back then—except for my parents and Mara. And Billie, who isn't answering her phone.

I lift my gaze. What I need to do is concentrate on the police in front of me. The people who are trying to help.

"Mrs. Adler?" Officer Scott is watching me. "What about you? Can you think of anyone here tonight who could be responsible for this?"

I give my head a small shake, my voice barely a whisper. "No."

Officer Scott frowns, jots something down in his notebook. He says nothing for an extended moment. Then he nods, clicks his pen closed, and stands. Officer Gorski—who has yet to speak—does the same.

"We're going to do a thorough search of the apartment," he says.

Grant leans forward, rests his forearms on his knees. "But we've looked everywhere."

"Yes, well, more eyes can't hurt. It isn't uncommon that young children go missing in their own homes. She could've crawled under a bed or hidden in a closet and gone to sleep. It happens more often than you might—"

"That's ridiculous." I clear the tears from my throat. "Ella's not a young child, she's four and a half months old. She can't walk or crawl or even sit up yet. We told you, she was lying in her stroller—"

"Cassie." Grant puts his hand on my leg. Tears leak into the crevice of my nose, spilling from my chin.

"Mrs. Adler." It's Officer Gorski speaking, and her voice—snappy, a bit raspy—bothers me instantly. "I promise we'll be quick. In the meantime, do you have a photograph of Ella you can find for us? A physical copy, ideally. We'll need one for the report."

I can't bring myself to enter the nursery, let alone look through pictures of Ella, so McKay tackles this while the cops search the apartment. Lillian has placed a pitcher of water and a plate of shortbread cookies on the coffee table. I study the glass she's poured for me, the limp slice of lemon floating on the surface. I watch Reed take a cookie and pop the whole thing in his mouth, and wonder how he can possibly think of food at a time like this. But then I feel my own body respond to the sight of the cold water, the dry strip along the back of my throat, the physical thirst. It feels like mockery that bodily needs persist in the face of such unthinkable devastation. I think of Billie, then, of what it was like the first night Wade ever touched her. How long did it take for her to feel thirst in the aftermath of that horror?

I reach for the glass and chug it down, the icy water a relief even though I wish it weren't. Even though I wish I could feel nothing at all.

Twenty-five minutes later, the police have concluded their search. They didn't find Ella, like I knew they wouldn't. I'm her mother. If she were in this apartment, I'd know. I can feel that she isn't here.

McKay hands Officer Gorski the photograph. It's the most recent one I've had printed—a shot of Ella on a blanket in our yard in East Hampton. She's wearing a pale pink bubble romper, and her eyes look especially blue against the white quilt, her mouth curled into a small smile. It's a beautiful photo, a five-by-seven I'd placed in the engraved silver frame on top of her dresser, beside her changing station.

Officer Scott hands Grant his card, but his gaze is fixed on me. "We're going to hand our report over to a detective from the Major Crimes unit, who will conduct an area canvass. You know, talk to neighbors and others in the surrounding buildings, in case anyone saw anything suspicious. You'll be contacted shortly. If anything comes up in the meantime, you have my number."

After they leave, the apartment feels heavy and still, the air thick with something uncanny. Something more twisted than fear. It's past eleven by the time Lillian and Reed head back to Lillian's Central Park South pied-à-terre, eleven thirty by the time we finally convince McKay to go home. She keeps offering to stay, to sleep in the guest room. I don't understand why she assumes we still want her here.

I crawl into bed without bothering to take off my dress. I feel the emptiness of everything around me—the bottomless void that Ella has left in each of my cells—and sob into my pillow. Grant curls himself around my body and holds me, but the feel of him is an invasion, and I'm glad when he rolls off to his side of the mattress.

I close my eyes and see Ella's face. I hear her gurgles and babbles. I smell the warm, milky top of her head, and I feel as though my heart has split right down the center, a clean break. My mind wanders to its darkest corners; I arrive at the place where Ella becomes a headline, Grant and I a cautionary tale.

At some point, I blink my eyes open and fumble on the nightstand for my phone, which is somehow in its usual place, plugged into the charger.

There's a new text from Billie. Finally.

> Sorry I missed your calls! Home tonight with a terrible migraine, will try you back soon. x

I check the time on the screen. *12:07*. It's my birthday.

Chapter Twenty-eight
Billie

October 13, 2023
2 hours after

Ella sleeps soundly in my arms. Her soft, even breathing soothes me, stills the panic that threatens to bubble over in my chest.

The city is quieting down around us. It isn't *quiet*—New York never is—but the frequency of horns and sirens has lessened, more lights have extinguished in neighboring buildings. I still have the window cracked. I need to be ready for whatever comes next.

I glance down at my phone, at my text conversation with Alex. I finally responded to him, half an hour after we were supposed to meet at Westville.

> So sorry. I came down with an awful migraine and it hurts
> to look at the phone screen. I drifted off for a few and just
> woke up. Need to rain check tonight. Sorry again.

Alex, gentleman that he is, hadn't given me a hard time for standing him up. He'd even offered to come over, to stop at the pharmacy for Excedrin PM, but I'd insisted all I needed was to be alone in my dark bedroom. I promised to call him in the morning.

So now, it's just Ella and me in Jane's apartment. I haven't heard a peep from upstairs, but I imagine Cassie and Grant have closed the windows and terrace doors and are inside, waiting in wrenching terror for the other shoe to drop. I can't imagine the depth of Cassie's pain in this moment. I'm not a mother.

Bye, Baby.

For some reason, I can't stop hearing Cassie speak those words. Seventeen years ago—that old nickname from high school—and yet it feels like just yesterday.

She called me again, a little while ago. I can't help but wonder if she suspects something, but then I remember the desperation in her voice on the terrace: *Billie. I need Billie.*

Cassie needs me. Just like she used to. The idea warms my nerves with pride.

I didn't want her to keep calling, obviously, so I sent a text explaining that I was in bed with a migraine and couldn't talk. The same thing I'd told Alex. It's important to keep my story straight.

Jane's apartment is eerily still, the air around me humming with something ominous. I wish I could get the hell out of here, but I'm trapped by the weight of this sleeping baby. The weight of the decision that created these circumstances.

I close my eyes. I don't know how much time passes. It seems impossible that I've drifted off, but I startle when Willie Nelson leaps from the couch, his padded paws thudding against the wood floor. He begins to circle my legs in figure eights again; the end of his tail swishes against Ella's cheek. She stirs, her face scrunching, her mouth twisting against the pacifier. *No.*

Her eyes blink open, absorbing the unfamiliar sight of my face, of her surroundings, and I don't have time to prepare for what's next. The noises start slowly, little whimpers at first, but then the pacifier falls out and Ella's cries become louder, higher in pitch. My heart picks up speed; I try to push the pacifier back between her lips, but she isn't having it. *Shit.*

If I were a mother—if I had any kind of maternal instinct—I would have understood the inevitability of this moment. I would have been ready, would have formulated some semblance of a plan in advance.

Maybe Ella is hungry. Does Cassie feed her in the middle of the night? I have no idea. I check my phone, which tells me it's past one in the morning. I realize, with a pang, that it's Cassie's birthday. October 14.

I hold Ella to my chest and rush to the kitchen. I'll check to see if there's milk—babies drink milk, right? I fling open the refrigerator door, but all that's there is a bottle of white wine and a jar of olives. *Jesus, Jane.*

Ella is really crying now, and I can't do this, I really can't. It wasn't like I was trying to kidnap this child, anyway. I *haven't* kidnapped this child. None of this was supposed to happen. I'm not a criminal.

I weave through the rest of the apartment until I find the master bedroom. There's a king mattress and headboard, but the rest of the room is just boxes. Only a couple have been opened, and I begin to rummage through them, unsure of what exactly I'm looking for. Some kind of disguise, maybe—a wig; a hat? I would laugh at myself if I weren't physically shaking, a wailing baby in my arms.

Nothing in the open boxes is any help to me—one contains just bedding, and the other is full of shoes. I swing open the door to the closet, which is mostly empty, save for a few dresses and shirts on hangers. Then, something on the top shelf catches my eye. It's a wide-brimmed felt hat with a small feather in the band, the kind you might wear to go apple picking. I've never seen Jane in anything like it, so maybe it's Sasha's. Regardless, it'll have to do.

Three minutes later, I'm out the door. Ella is miraculously quiet—I've managed to get the pacifier back in her mouth—and I'm praying to a God I'm not sure I believe in that this building is too ancient to have security cameras. I tiptoe down the hallway, clutching Ella tightly inside my coat—the pleather jacket I bought at H&M earlier this fall—and keep my eyes peeled for the stairwell. My heart is beating so hard I can hear the pounding blood in my ears. Sweat slicks the back of my neck, slides down my spine.

There's a door at the end of the hallway, and I push it open as softly as possible. When I see that it's a stairwell, my entire body floods with relief. I can do this.

Ella begins to fuss again, the corners of her lips twitching, and I'm running out of time. I reach the ninth-floor landing and nudge the door open with my hip. It creaks on its hinges, and I wince, brace myself for someone to emerge from Cassie's apartment and find me, guilty, a deer caught in headlights.

But the coast is clear. Still, Ella's whimpers are growing more audible by the second, and I'm sick with terror as I speed down the hall, my body pulsing with a panic so intense I think I'll burst into a million pieces if I stop moving. I place Ella on the floor in front of 9A, Cassie's apartment. I wish I had a blanket or something to wrap her in, but I don't, and this is it—all I can do is accelerate forward, propelled by the surreal, subconscious choices I'm forced to accept as my own.

I sprint for the stairwell. I no longer care how much noise I make—I just need to count on the fact that most residents of 27 Gramercy Park

South are sound asleep and get myself out of this building as fast as physically possible.

I dash down the stairs like I'm running for my life—which, in a way, I am. I don't slow down until the stairwell spits me out into the lobby, where the doorman—a different guy from the one here hours earlier—sits behind the front desk. The felt hat is secure on my head, and I've twisted my hair back into a tight bun at the nape of my neck, but still—I keep my gaze straight ahead as I walk toward the lobby doors. I'm not even sure the doorman notices me, but then I hear his voice at my back. A thick Irish accent.

"Have a good night, miss."

I hold up a hand. I don't turn around. I don't let out the breath I've been holding until I'm safely on the sidewalk, the night air shrouding me in sharp, cool solace. With the city cloaking me in anonymity, I remember: this is New York, where I am one of millions. Worse has been done here.

Chapter Twenty-nine

Billie

Fall 2006

My freshman-year roommate is a girl named Becca from New Jersey. She has long, flaxen hair and is so tall that she doesn't need to stand on anything when she hangs a bohemian tapestry beside her bed. It's purple and turquoise and takes up the whole wall; she says it belonged to her mother in college.

Becca is carefree and almost fanatically outgoing, which makes her easy to be friends with right away. There's a girl down the hall who we've clicked with, too. Esme lives in a single, but she spends most of her time in our room. I can't be sure, but I suspect this is partially due to the fact that I'm often gone, especially on the weekends. When Cassie calls, I go.

Without traffic, I can get from Northeastern to Harvard in eight minutes in a taxi. But cabs add up, so I usually ride my bike, Mom's old ten-speed that I snagged from the garage before I left for college. It's red and rusty, but it does the trick. I've come to enjoy it, my rides across the Charles River and into the heart of Cambridge.

Cassie doesn't like her roommate, a mousy Midwesterner named Flora who she claims has nothing to offer. She prefers a group of girls on the floor upstairs—they're all tan and pretty and from places like Marblehead and Fairfield County—so most Friday and Saturday nights when I visit Harvard, that's where we go. It feels like Cassie is chasing them, this clique, like they're hesitant to carve out a place for her. But I suspect she senses this, so I don't bother telling her what she already knows.

In December, there's an ugly sweater party at one of the frats, and we're pregaming with the cool girls upstairs. McKay is beautiful and rich, with a curtain of blond hair and tan legs that poke out from underneath her oversize reindeer sweater. If she's wearing shorts, I can't see them.

"You should fuck Harrison tonight," McKay tells Ava, who is so thin she looks like she'd break in half if I touched her. I've never seen her eat anything, and she only drinks vodka mixed with Crystal Light.

"Maybe I will." Ava gives a wild laugh, throws a shot back. She hands Cassie the handle of Popov.

Cassie thanks her, takes a pull, winces. "Who should I fuck?" she asks the room.

I've been with Cassie at Harvard enough times to know that she only wants the blue-blood guys. The WASPs from Connecticut or the North Shore with summer homes on Nantucket and airtight lineage. They have to be decent-looking, yes, but pedigree is more important than appearance. Earlier in the fall, Cassie slept with a sophomore named Luke, who looked like Joshua Jackson during his prime Dawson's Creek days. She liked him; they went out to dinner at a Mexican restaurant in Cambridge. When she saw his license and discovered he was from rural Maine, she stopped responding to his texts.

"There's no point," Cassie said when I objected, pointing that she could have her own real-life Pacey Witter, our ultimate TV crush from middle school. "I know what I want in life, Billie. And it isn't a poor kid from Bumfuck, Maine."

I said nothing, her words sinking my heart. I was reminded of Kyle all over again.

"Hmm." A girl named Adair considers Cassie's question as she gazes into the mirror above the dresser, painting her lips in pink gloss. "There's a junior named Phil on the lacrosse team who's single and gorgeous. He went to Deerfield with Ava's brother."

Cassie perks up at this. I can feel her salivating at the mention of an elite boarding school. "Tell me more."

Someone hands me the vodka, which is ice-cold and slushy from the freezer. I take a small sip, chase it with an open can of Diet Dr. Pepper. All of us are on our way to being drunk.

McKay twists around, her gaze narrow, pinning Adair's. "Phil Anderson? I told you last weekend I thought he was hot."

Adair's blithe smile drops. "Oh. Right. I completely forgot, Mick."

Beside me, I feel Cassie deflate. It doesn't matter that McKay has a long-distance boyfriend; in twelve quick words, she has deemed Phil

Anderson off-limits, hers. The power she holds both disgusts and en-trances me.

McKay shrugs, but her eyes are still fiery, and they find Cassie. They linger there for a moment, a threat. I wish Cassie would look for a new group of friends.

I'm not sure if the ugly sweater shindig is even fun. I often feel this way at frat parties, when I'm so drunk on cheap liquor that the line between consciousness and oblivion blurs, a distorted wash of hours. The memory of these nights is always fuzzy: blaring music, sweaty crowds, the sour smell of keg beer that sticks to the bottoms of my shoes. I stumble around the creaky, thumping house in an inebriated daze until Cassie decides it's time to leave.

In the dorm kitchen, we microwave Celeste pizzas. We take them back to Cassie's room and devour them in drunken silence on her bed, two ravenous zombies.

Ten feet away, Flora is asleep; she never goes to parties. Even though she hardly talks, I can tell she dislikes Cassie and that she dreads when I visit. I don't exactly blame her. After midnight, we turn into vultures.

Cassie and I wipe our greasy hands on her blankets, toss the empty pizza boxes on the floor. We climb under the covers of the twin bed, too exhausted and wasted to change into pajamas or brush our teeth. It's disgusting, but this is how these nights go.

"Thank you for coming every weekend," Cassie says. Her voice is so close to me—we share the same pillow—but as sleep tugs at the edges of my brain, she feels far away.

"Do you think McKay hates me?" she is asking.

I want to tell her that it doesn't matter. That McKay is poison. But I do what I have always done. I lift her up.

"Of course not," I mumble. "She was just pissed at Adair tonight. She seems to really like you."

"You think so?"

"She always invites you to pregame upstairs."

"I guess." Cassie is quiet for a long stretch. "Really, though. I don't know what I would do if I didn't have you in Boston."

A pause. "You're the reason I'm here, Cass."

When I make comments like this, it's the closest we come to talking about Wade, about last spring. But the truth sits between us, constant, binding. The authorities never questioned our claim that his death was an accident when Sandra called 911 just after the fall. Rotten railing, drunk man known around town for being a clumsy boozehound. He had family in Albany; they buried his body up there. How Mom could've loved a person like Wade is something I'll never understand. And something she'll never be able to explain.

Cassie nuzzles in close, adjusts her head on the pillow. We barely fit in this tiny twin, but she never lets me sleep on the floor.

Torpid quiet permeates the room. Sleep is heavy and welcome, an undercurrent that pulls me toward blissful nonbeing.

Chapter Thirty

Cassie

October 14, 2023
5 hours after

I am nibbling the inside of Ella's foot, teeth on chubby flesh. It sounds ridiculous, but it's the one thing that makes her laugh uncontrollably, every time. And Ella's laughter is the most magical sound in the world.

The space around us tilts, the edges cloudy, but there's grass, lots of it, and Ella is wearing her pale pink bubble just like in the picture McKay gave Officer Gorski. Stalks of wildflowers bend toward our faces like they're reaching for light, and we're the sun.

Ella squirms on her back, caught in a fit of giggles, and there is nothing but this bright, blissful moment, orchestrated only for the two of us. But suddenly, my teeth are clenching harder on her foot—too hard, I can feel it—and I can't control it, and her giggles are quickly morphing into terrified wails. Shrill, piercing screams that send my heart into my throat, and even as I taste the metal of her blood in my mouth, I can't stop, and before I know what's happening, the ground is opening underneath the grass, quivering a little before gravity pulls Ella under, her fleshy toes sliding off my tongue, and all I hear is the echo of my daughter's cries as she disappears.

I jolt up in bed, shaken by the nightmare, but the crying won't stop. I hear it even now, when there's no doubt in my mind that I'm awake. It feels impossible—vaguely sociopathic—that my body was even able to fall asleep in the midst of such circumstances. I blame the alcohol.

I'm on top of the covers, still in my black silk dress from the party. Grant is beside me, passed out like a log, a sight that sparks anger. How can he have drifted off, too? What is wrong with us?

The sound of Ella crying persists, an echo of the dream that rings in my ears. Or perhaps it's my own deluded brain, still trapped in the nightmare. I'm struck with a fresh wave of misery at the memory of this new reality, the one where Ella is gone. My heart drops into my stomach, then lower, out of my body. All that's left is agony, too heavy to carry. How am I supposed to exist when I don't know where my own baby is?

I tap the screen of my phone, which lights up to tell me that it's nearly two in the morning. I slide off the bed and leave the room, eager to shake the haunting sound of Ella's cries. Maybe walking around will help.

But as I pad down the hallway and approach the living room, the crying only grows louder. It's coming from the foyer. It's coming from the front door of the apartment. Maybe I'm in a lucid dream. Maybe I've lost my fucking mind. Maybe my brain is stuck in a loop in the past that will hear the ghost of Ella forever.

Or maybe . . .

I sprint to the door, swing it open with extra force, and there she is. My daughter.

The relief that warps every inch of my being feels imagined, some kind of cruel joke from the universe distorting reality. But I see her. This isn't a mirage or an apparition. Ella is really there, lying on the floor as if the stork dropped her off in the night.

Everything that happens next is involuntary. The tears, pouring from me like a flash flood as I scoop my daughter off the floor, clutch her to my chest, smash my nose against the top of her head. In all my life, there has never been such a euphoric moment.

She is howling, her face scrunched, beet red. I lock and dead bolt the front door, then settle down onto the couch and hike my dress and bra all the way up. Ella is on my nipple like a magnet, like she hasn't eaten in days, my breasts engorged and tingling from the let-down. I haven't fed her in so many hours. There is so much milk, and it flows out of me like the ocean feeding a river, mixing with the tears that continue to fall. My body shakes with relief.

Relief.

Relief.

Relief.

I call for Grant. He deserves to feel this, too.

We sit with Ella for hours, until a pale orange glow begins to leak through the darkness, slivers of shadowy light reaching across the living room floor. Neither of us sleeps for the rest of the night. We can't do anything but stare at Ella, at the soft flutter of her closed eyelids, her perfect, peaceful face. The relief of having her back persists like a strong drug, blocking out the questions I'm not ready to face.

Ella wakes at seven, hungry again, and I feed her while Grant goes to the kitchen to make coffee. I hear the beans grinding, the suctioning sound of the refrigerator opening and closing, the low drone of Grant's voice—it sounds like he's on the phone. Minutes later, he brings me a steaming cup of coffee, with whole milk and sugar, the way I like it.

His lips meet my cheek. "Happy birthday, beautiful." He slides my phone out of his pocket and sets it on the couch. "Thought you might want this. It's blowing up."

I shake my head and glance down at Ella. "Maybe later. Right now, she's the only thing I want to look at."

Grant takes a sip from his own mug. "I called Officer Scott and told him the good news. He said they'd already handed our case over to the detective he mentioned last night. Someone more adept at handling kidnappings."

Kidnappings. The word is a knife in my stomach. A scary story you read about in the back pages of *People* magazine. Not something that happens to me.

Grant sits beside us. He places his hand on the back of Ella's head while she feeds. "He's on his way over now."

"The detective?"

"Yes. He's going to find out what happened to Ella, Cass. Who took her. Who brought her back."

I close my eyes, tears leaking through. I know in my gut that I'll never stop being scared. That the torture of five hours without Ella—without knowing if I'd ever see her again—will stay with me for the rest of my days.

"Hey." Grant smooths the hair back from my forehead. "Ella's home safe with us, honey. She's not going anywhere ever again. We're going to find out who did this. And why."

Out of habit, I scroll through my messages while I wait for the detective to show up. There are too many notifications—texts, emails, DMs. I've almost forgotten it's my birthday, and that's the reason my phone is blowing up even more than usual. Normally, I would care; normally, I'd luxuriate in the new posts and story mentions and gushing sentiments from followers, eyes glued to my phone screen for a blissful thirty minutes while I drink my morning coffee.

But today, my phone means nothing. It's an empty rectangle, metal and glass, and I could toss it off the terrace without giving a damn. And maybe I will. I gaze down at Ella, snug beside me on the couch in her DockATot. The fact that she's here at all feels like a miracle. Nothing else matters. Nothing else will ever matter again.

I stuff my phone between two couch cushions and stare at my daughter while she sleeps. The slope of her tiny button nose. The tuft of wispy hair at her temple. The way the corners of her lips twitch intermittently, like she's smiling at something in her dream.

"Cassie." Grant's hand is on my back, startling me. "This is Detective Barringer."

I look up to see a small man with thin, dusty blond hair, a boyish face. I hadn't heard him come in.

He gives me a tight smile and takes a seat in one of the slipper chairs, bends forward so his elbows rest on the knees of his navy slacks. Grant offers him a coffee, but he shakes his head.

"I max out after one cup," he says, and already I know he'll be useless. I can't stand when people are fussy about their caffeine consumption.

Grant tries again. "Water? Herbal tea?"

Detective Barringer flaps his hand against the air. "I'm all set. Have a seat, Mr. Adler. I'd like to talk to you and your wife."

Grant sits down at the other end of the couch, sleeping Ella wedged between us.

"Maybe I should put her in the crib," he says.

I cast him a hard glance, like he's got to be joking. I'm never letting this baby out of my sight, and Grant is smart enough to know that.

Detective Barringer clears his throat. "I'm so happy your daughter has been returned to you safely. This is what we like to see. Now, the officers you met last night caught me up on the details of your case. But can you walk me through the past few hours? How you found Ella, where she was, her condition?"

I nod. The words are a struggle to get out at first, but I tell him everything. How I woke to the sound of Ella's cries, how I found her outside the door in the middle of the night, how I stripped her down and checked every inch of her body—her armpits, the cracks between her toes—for signs of physical harm.

When I've finished speaking, Detective Barringer sits in silence for several moments. I reach for my coffee and take a shaky, lukewarm sip. Waiting.

Finally, he exhales. He looks vaguely bored. "Is there anything else you think I should know?"

"There is one thing." Grant rubs the soft part of his throat, stealing a quick glance in my direction. "Cassie . . . she's an influencer. She has a good number of followers on Instagram. We forgot to mention that to the officers who came by yesterday, but it's something that could be . . . relevant."

"I see." Detective Barringer nods as though absorbing this, though I doubt he knows the first thing about Instagram. "How many followers are we talking?"

"Forty-eight thousand." My voice is hoarse. "Give or take."

"Wow." His pale eyebrows jump, and I'm almost embarrassed for him, or maybe I'm embarrassed for myself as I watch this inept man attempt to indulge my so-called popularity.

"That's a lot of people," he continues. "Did they all know about the party?"

"I—well, I posted some stories. You know, pictures and videos and stuff—earlier in the night. So, feasibly, yes. But none of my followers know our address. Obviously."

Grant frowns. "But are you sure about that, Cassie? Are you sure there isn't a way they'd be able to find out?"

"Let me look into it," Barringer offers as if that isn't already his job. "I'm in the process of questioning the other residents in the building, but I'd also like you to send me a list of every guest that attended your party. Names and contact information. I'll conduct some interviews, get my hands on any security footage that's available, but I'll just say off the bat: I've been doing this a long time. From what I'm hearing and seeing, there's no evidence of foul play. This is likely a misunderstanding."

"A misunderstanding?" I place my mug down on the table, harder than I mean to. Coffee spills over the rim, pooling around the base. "Detective Barringer, someone *took* our daughter."

"And someone brought her back." He looks from me to Grant, then back to me. "I'm going to find out what happened, and I'm only saying this to try to put you at ease."

"At *ease*?" Fresh tears sting the corners of my eyes; panic curdles like poison in my stomach.

Barringer blinks, and I notice the sharp lines around his eyes, the one area of his face that makes him look like he might possibly be older than thirty. He appears as tired as I feel as he hands a business card to Grant—safer to approach the composed husband than the verge-of-hysterical wife—and tells us he'll be in touch soon.

I'm glad when he's gone—this useless, indifferent, childlike man—and I sink back into the couch and let myself sob. Grant disappears into the kitchen and when he comes back, he hands me a plate of breakfast. Sourdough toast with the crunchy almond butter I like, honey drizzled on top. But I push the food away—the thought of eating repels me.

"Cassie." Grant sighs. "Why don't you take a shower? Change out of your dress from last night? There's makeup all over your face."

There's a buzzing sound coming from the couch again—my phone. It's been buzzing all morning. I dig my hand between the cushions and fish it out, ready to power the dumb thing off and stick it in the back of a dresser drawer for the rest of the day. For the rest of eternity. But then I see her name.

Billie West.

Finally, Billie is calling me back.

Chapter Thirty-one
Billie

October 14, 2023
The day after

I toss and turn through the night. I don't know why I bothered trying to sleep at all, come to think of it. At seven, I give up entirely and shake the covers off. My eyes sting from lack of rest, but it is what it is. Shutting off my mind is impossible.

I put water on for the french press and wait impatiently for it to boil, tapping my fingernails against the granite countertop. The kitchen window is speckled with rain; outside the morning is gray, drizzly.

I close my eyes and hear Cassie screaming. I hear Ella crying. I listen to the kettle begin to whistle, and I feel like the water trapped inside: gurgling, suffocating. I can't stand it a second longer. I switch off the burner and reach for my phone.

Jane answers on the second ring, her voice chipper.

"Billie! Sasha and I are about to ride Icelandic horses through a field of snow."

"Wow."

"You would fucking love it here. It's beautiful and everyone minds their own business."

"Mm."

A beat of silence passes. "Bill? You okay?"

"Fuck, Jane." A rush of tears climbs up my throat, pricking my eyes. "I need to tell you something."

"Hang on a sec." There's a rustling sound, followed by the murmur of voices. "Okay, I stepped outside. But I only have a few minutes. Sasha and our guide are waiting."

I take a deep breath. Some subconscious part of me knows there's no way I'll get through this without Jane's help. Without Jane knowing what really happened last night.

So I tell her. I explain the whole thing, from start to finish—finding out about the party, going to Jane's apartment, feeding Willie Nelson, hearing Ella on the terrace upstairs, taking Ella, returning Ella.

I wait for Jane to say something. I feel as though I'm suspended in midair, the gravity sucked up around me. My heart is in my mouth.

"Christ, Billie," she says when she finally speaks. Her voice is fragile, lacking its usual zest.

"I just—I had to tell you. They have Ella back now, but still. What if the police get involved? They might start questioning the neighbors."

Jane snorts. "What *if* the police get involved? Billie, do you seriously think Cassie and Grant are going to let this slide? That they're going to let their infant daughter go missing for *hours* and not care to find out what the fuck happened?"

"I know. I know you're right. I just haven't slept, I haven't thought it through."

"What were you *thinking*, Billie?"

"I wasn't thinking, Jane! I was just mad. And frustrated. I was reacting; it wasn't even conscious—"

"It wasn't conscious and you took someone's *baby*? Hang on." There's background noise again—it sounds like a horse's neighing—and I hear Jane tell Sasha that she'll be right there. "Billie? I have to go."

"Jane—"

"Look." The resolve is back in her voice. "I know Cassie is a terrible bitch. And I know you two have your fucked-up history. And even if I don't understand it, because you've never actually explained to me *why* it's so fucked up, you're—you're still my people, Billie. If anyone calls and asks about last night, well . . . you weren't at my apartment. No one was."

My eyelids fall shut, a few tears snaking down my cheeks. "Thank you, Jane."

"Now, I really do need to go. Try to get some rest. I'm sure you didn't sleep all night."

I feel a little better after talking to Jane. But only a little. I take her advice and abandon the coffee, climb back into bed. I huddle under the sheets with my phone and open Instagram, navigate over to Cassie's page like a preprogrammed robot. The act isn't even conscious.

@cassidyadler hasn't posted anything new since the night before. Since the terrace selfie with the two women smoking cigarettes, a shot that somehow makes the disgusting habit appear chic, European. Three martini glasses clinked together, joyful smiles.

A wave of exhaustion slides over me, heavy; the phone goes limp in my hand as my eyelids droop closed. Finally, my brain and body settle.

I don't know how much time has passed when I wake up, but it still feels like morning. A wave of anxiety barrels across my chest, and I fumble for my phone, which is tangled in the sheets. The screen tells me it's almost eleven. I can't drag this out any longer; I have to call her back. It might look suspicious if I don't.

She answers almost right away.

"Billie? Jesus. I've been calling you." Cassie's voice is a panicked croak. She sounds worse than I imagined.

"I'm sorry. I'm—I'm just coming out of this migraine fog. I've been in bed since 6:00 p.m. yesterday."

"Billie, I—look, can you come over? Something happened."

I sit up in bed, rubbing my eye. It feels swollen and bruised at the corner, like maybe I'm getting a stye. I didn't take off my makeup last night.

"Wait, Cass. Happy birthday."

"Fuck my birthday. Come over."

I draw in a breath. I have to tread carefully. I don't know what she knows. "Cassie. What's going on? What happened?"

"Someone took Ella."

My heart stops pumping. I'm not prepared for this. I *should* be prepared for this. But I can't crack. I need to act completely normal in this moment; I need to act as shocked as she expects me to feel.

"What do you mean, someone took Ella?" I infuse my voice with feigned horror. "She's gone?"

"No, I have her now." Cassie begins to cry. I picture her thin shoulders rattling with each racking sob. "But someone took her last night, at this party at our apartment. Grant—he threw me something last-minute. It was low-key."

A sliver of anger burns hot behind my rib cage. We both know she's lying—whatever party Grant threw her was not last-minute or low-key—but there's nothing I can say about it. Not right now.

"But then someone brought her back, in the middle of the night, left her right outside our front door. Bill, I've never been so scared in my whole life. And the thing is, I'm still just as scared. Even though Ella is right here next to me, sleeping peacefully. I'm so fucking terrified, I feel like I'm losing my mind. Please come over. There's something I . . . I just—I need you."

The anger in my chest softens, morphs into tenderness. Those three words again. *I need you.* Like magic. A time capsule that brings us back, to before Grant and Ella and McKay and Ava, to when it was just Cassie and me—two best friends who needed each other, who carried each other.

I rub my eye again, feel last night's mascara crusted to my lower lashes. I slide my legs off the edge of the bed and lower my feet to the floor, flooded with conviction, purpose. Cassie needs me.

"Of course I'll come over. I'll be right there."

I turn on the shower when we hang up. I wash the past fourteen hours from my body, my hair, turning the water hotter than I normally like it.

I throw on jeans and a striped sweater, dab a little cream under my eyes. I have a bunch of missed texts from Alex, asking how I'm feeling, if I need anything. Guilt pricks my stomach—I hate lying to him—but I can't tell Alex the truth. I just can't.

I craft a quick text.

> Just woke up. I feel much better, thanks. I know I said I'd call you, but Cassie is having an emergency, and I need to go over there. Ella went missing last night, but they found her. I promise I'll call and fill you in soon.

Uneasiness wobbles through me, but I tap Send, anyway. Then I grab my jacket and rush out the door.

Chapter Thirty-two

Billie

Fall 2007

I see him naked before we've ever spoken.

Becca, Esme, and I have signed up for Figure Drawing to fulfill our studio art requirement. Our preference was Intro to Ceramics, but we waited too long to enroll, and by the time we visited the registrar, Ceramics was full. Figure Drawing is the only course left that aligns with all three of our schedules.

I'm wary of the nude male form. The only man I've seen naked is Wade, and recalling his body makes my stomach turn rancid, prompts every excruciating memory of the basement to come rushing back. An old nightmare sinking its teeth in.

I don't tell Becca and Esme, obviously. Only Cassie knows about Wade, and I intend to keep it this way. It's just art class, *I tell myself.* I'll have to grin and bear it.

The studio in Ryder Hall is a large space with high ceilings that smells of oil paints and charcoal pencils. The wood floor creaks as the model makes his way toward the center of the room, a small platform serving as a makeshift stage. He sheds his robe, lets it pool on the floor beside his chair.

There are at least two dozen of us in the class; two dozen easels facing this naked stranger. No one giggles or bristles. There is an air of maturity in the room, of respect, of art. The professor—a woman with a long gray braid who insists we call her Wanda—directs the model into position. He stands face-forward, left arm on his hip, chin pointed to the right.

He is tall and rangy like a string bean, with wild, nut-brown curls that cascade around his face. His body is nothing like Wade's, and I find myself assessing him as an artist, observing the way his arms arch into his shoulders as I capture the lines of his form with my charcoal nub.

Twenty minutes tick by, and the man doesn't move a muscle. Questions swarm my mind. Does he have to pee? Is he tired? What if he has a terrible itch?

Half an hour in, Wanda tells him he can take five. The spell breaks; the wax figure turns human again. He reaches for his robe, jostles his legs and arms. He sits down in the folding chair, rolls out the kinks in his neck. I can't stop watching him. He is long and lean everywhere, even his fingers and toes.

I glance over at Esme's easel. Her shadows are smooth, blended, her lines natural. My own drawing looks like something out of a fourth-grader's coloring book—all jagged edges and bold strokes, like I'm trying too hard. Wanda weaves through the easels, hands laced behind her back as she absorbs our progress. She speaks to us about proportion, alignment of the joints.

Five minutes later, the model is naked again. Frozen in place. For the second half of class, he lies reclined on the floor, one knee bent, chin propped up by a fist.

I'm relieved for him when the hour is up. He gives Wanda a brief nod, then grabs his robe and heads for the door. I stare at his butt cheeks as he walks away. They are taut and smooth but jiggle slightly—the only fleshy part of him. The air in the studio is warm, on the verge of hot. When I peel off my cardigan, my chest glistens with sweat.

Becca turns to me, one eyebrow raised. "Billie. Do you have something you want to tell us?"

I find him outside Ryder Hall, propped against the trunk of a leafy maple, his long legs extended, one crossed over the other. He reads a paperback while eating a sandwich, a smear of mustard above his lip.

I shouldn't speak to him. Rationally, I understand that it would be crossing a metaphorical line. But there is something about him, about the way I feel in the dizzy aftermath of those surreal sixty minutes in the light-filled studio. A momentum that carries me toward his tree.

"Thank you," I hear myself say.

He peers up at me, swallows his bite, wipes the smudge of mustard from his face. "No problem." His voice is low and calm, but confident. It matches him perfectly.

"Is it uncomfortable?"

"Posing naked in a roomful of strangers?" His gentle gray eyes don't move from mine.

I feel my face flush. "Holding the same position for that long. Without fidgeting."

He shrugs. "It's worth it, for the money."

I rub my arms through my thin cardigan. "Do you go here? To Northeastern?"

He shakes his head. "I went to BU. I'm an artist, and Wanda is married to my old advisor. That's how I got the gig."

I'm not sure what to do with my hands, so I stuff them in the pockets of my jeans. I have so many more questions. But it dawns on me then how intrusive I'm being. Inappropriate. This quiet, hardworking artist just wants to eat his lunch in peace.

"Ah. Well, enjoy your book. Sorry to disturb." I give an awkward wave, begin to turn and walk away.

"Hang on," he calls behind me, and something flickers low in my stomach. I glance back over my shoulder. He isn't smiling, but his eyes are curious, watching me.

"I'm sorry," he says, balling up the wrapper of his sandwich. "Students from Wanda's class don't usually approach me."

"No, I get it, I shouldn't have—"

"Are you an art major?"

I shake my head. "I'm deciding between history and business. Or I might double. But I need an art credit."

He nods. A few curls have fallen in front of his eyes, and he brushes them back.

"I'm not very good," I add.

"You'll get better." He gestures to the spot beside him, a flat patch of earth among the gnarled roots where the light is dappled through the leaves. "Do you want to sit?"

I have East Asian Studies starting in ten minutes on the other side of campus. In my year at Northeastern, I've never missed a class. But I know, with simple clarity that cuts through my hesitation, that staying here with this man, under this maple tree, on this particular afternoon, is what I must do. That whatever is happening inside of me in this moment is tinged with magic I can't turn away from.

I place my backpack on the ground and sink down beside him, tucking my knees to my chest. I inhale the sharp scent of rotting leaves and pastrami from his lunch.

Up close, I can see a single dark freckle on the side of the long pitch of his nose. When he smiles, it feels like something I've been waiting for, something I've earned. His eyes move over my face.

"I'm Remy," he says.

Chapter Thirty-three

Cassie

October 14, 2023
The day after

I open the door and she is standing there, all five feet five inches of her. Her eyes are wide and clear like pools of honey, a color that nearly matches her hair. I've forgotten this about Billie's eyes—the way the hazel looks almost clear in the right light.

She hugs me without saying a word. A long, silent hug that erases the need for an explanation. The absurdity of her being my first phone call in a moment of crisis isn't actually absurd. Billie and I understand this.

I inhale the scent of her hair, which is damp and smells like Paul Mitchell. Billie has used the same lemon-sage shampoo since high school.

The pads of her fingers dig into my shoulder blades, which signals the end of the hug.

I wipe my eyes. "Thanks for coming."

"Stop." Billie shakes her head. "Where is she?"

I lead her to the family room off the kitchen, where Ella is bouncing in her activity center. She bats her tiny hand at a row of plastic trees.

Grant is slumped on the couch, eyes glued to his phone. A bolt of resentment pierces my chest, and I call his name. He startles, sits up straighter.

"Hey, Billie." His voice is scratchy. He's wearing sweatpants and a tattered New York Rangers T-shirt. We both must look like such wrecks.

"I'm so sorry about everything. I'm so glad . . ." Billie stuffs her hands in the back pockets of her jeans, her eyes traveling to Ella. "She's okay."

Grant reaches for a glass of water on the coffee table. I watch the liquid move over his throat as he drinks.

"You should go lie down," I tell him. "Billie and I will hold down the fort."

He rubs his eye and stands. "How about I make some sandwiches first?"

"I'm not hungry." I sit where he just was, on one end of the love seat we recently had upholstered. I think of the hours I spent perusing fabrics on Pinterest, agonizing over the options. In the end, a designer friend of McKay's helped me decide, and I run my fingers over the winning textile—Lisa Fine, small blue flowers block printed on cream linen. How little it seems to matter now.

"You have to eat, Cassie." Grant frowns. "Billie, tell her she has to eat."

"Grant." I pin him a look, a silent order to drop it. "I'm fine."

When he wanders off to the bedroom, Billie curls up on the couch beside me, tucking her legs underneath her. We sit like this, without speaking, for several minutes. Ella manages to slap a red plastic button, and "The Wheels on the Bus" begins to play through the staticky speakers. Her little knees bounce up and down; a gummy smile fills her face.

I don't realize I'm crying again until Billie plucks a Kleenex from the side table and hands it to me. Her eyes are full of sorrow, and something else, too. She looks worried. But empathy has always been one of Billie's strong suits.

"We don't have to talk about it, Cass," she says. "But if you want to, I'm here."

I nod, press the tissue to my leaking face. "I'm just so scared, Bill. I mean, *who* would take her? And then just bring her back? It had to be some kind of threat, right? Some kind of warning? Whoever it was, I know their business is unfinished. I just know it." I pause, lowering my voice. "I have to tell you something."

"What?"

I swallow, then draw in a nervous breath. "About a month ago, Grant and I drove up to Red Hook to have dinner with my parents. And I posted a story of the Hudson River—like, a super-generic picture of the water, it was nothing, and I didn't geotag. But some random account replied and said, 'Returning to the scene of the crime, are we?'" I scan Billie's face. "*The crime*, Billie. Isn't that weird?"

"Maybe a little." She scrunches her nose.

"What if somebody knows? About Wade, I mean. What if this thing with Ella . . . what if it's . . . retribution?"

Billie says nothing for a long moment. Finally, she sighs. "Cassie." She bites her bottom lip and tips her chin forward as if searching for the right words. "If you want my honest opinion, that theory seems like a stretch to me. What if what happened was just an accident? What if someone at your party was drunk and did something by mistake . . ." She gives her head a little shake. "I just think, if someone actually wanted to take Ella . . . they would've taken her. You know?"

I swallow the lump in my throat, a hard mix of tears and mucus. "You sound just like the detective."

"Who?"

I tell her about Detective Barringer, about the way he looked at me with bored, tired eyes and muttered the words: *likely a misunderstanding.* I can't believe it was only a few hours ago that he was here in the apartment. It feels like an eternity has passed since he walked out the door, promising to be in touch soon.

"He's a detective, Cassie. He knows what he's doing."

When I scowl, Billie's gaze softens. The damp hair around her face has dried, curling slightly. The tiniest freckles dust the bridge of her nose. "Hey." She touches my arm. "You know I'm on your side."

I do know it. It's the reason that immediately after Ella went missing, my subconscious reached for Billie. It's how I imagine it would feel to be on a plane that's on its way down, seconds from nose-diving into the earth. The clarity of perspective as the rest of the world evaporates into thin, meaningless dust. What matters is distilled.

"I'm so sorry I didn't invite you last night." I sniffle, wipe my nose with the tissue again. I feel like a child, but it's easy to be vulnerable with Billie when I let my guard down.

"Don't worry about that." She glances over my shoulder toward the window. "It's turned into such a nice day. Should we go for a walk? Maybe get some lunch?"

My windpipe tightens. "I can't. Ella—"

"We'll bring her. Obviously."

"Billie, I *can't*." I use the nail of my index finger to pick away the polish on my thumb. Little flakes of crimson fall to the couch. "I'm not leaving this apartment."

She nods. "Okay. I'm sorry."

"You don't have to be sorry—"

"Cass, I get it. We're not leaving the apartment."

Warm relief fills my chest. Ella begins to fuss in her activity center, the lines beside her eyebrows scrunching.

"Shoot, what time is it? I should feed her." I hook my hands under Ella's armpits and pull her to my lap. Instantly, her nose nuzzles in toward my breast. I lift my shirt and hold her body close to me, feeling her warmth, her weight, the movement of her lips as her little hand flings against my collarbone. But the peace that normally washes over me during our feeding sessions isn't there. Nothing can blot out the anxiety that curdles behind my ribs like a tumor, festering, fattening.

"I'll make us a couple of coffees, okay?" Billie stands, brushes the front of her jeans.

I nod. "Ella should nap after this."

"Should I forget the coffee, then? Maybe you want to lie down, too."

"No." My response is quick, certain. "I won't be able to sleep. Coffee sounds good. There's whole milk in the fridge."

"We can turn on a movie or something," Billie offers. "*You've Got Mail?*"

I smile. The Nora Ephron rom-com was always one of our go-to flicks. I think of all the Friday nights Billie and I stayed in to watch a movie, a stainless-steel mixing bowl of popcorn between us, two glasses of ginger ale. The memory is a comfort.

We're settled on the couch, coffees in hand, watching Meg Ryan clack away on her laptop next to a bouquet of daisies, when the doorbell rings. I startle, my gaze darting toward the baby monitor on my lap, the handheld screen I've been checking nonstop throughout the film. My brain knows it's illogical—that the doorbell would somehow be connected to any disturbance of Ella napping in her crib—but all rationality has slipped from my mind, leaving my senses on high alert.

Coffee sloshes over the rim of my mug, camel-colored liquid sliding down my knuckles. "I'll get that," I say, bringing the monitor with me. Through the grainy black-and-white rectangle, Ella sleeps peacefully on her back, a little indentation forming in the fabric of the sleep sack as she breathes.

Inhale. Exhale. Inhale. Exhale.

I remind myself to do the same.

Billie pauses the movie, adjusts herself on the couch. Her presence in the apartment is like armor; it makes me feel safe, protected. I never want her to leave.

I open the front door slowly, cautiously. It's McKay. She holds a small Jo Malone shopping bag tied with a pink ribbon.

"Happy birthday, Cass." She smiles, but her eyes are pools of concern. "Grant texted Tom." Her voice wavers. "Ella's—*back*?"

I nod, on the verge of tears again. We move inside, and I dead bolt the apartment.

"I'm so, *so* relieved, Cassie. Jesus Christ . . ." McKay hesitates, and I know what she's going to say before she asks the question. "I've called you a dozen times. Why didn't you tell me?"

The answer I *want* to give runs through my head: *This isn't about you, McKay. Don't make this about you, and me, and what I did or didn't tell you.* But I don't have the nerve or the energy to speak it out loud.

McKay seems to catch her mistake. "Sorry—forget it. It doesn't matter." She sweeps a tendril of hair off her face and spots Billie, who's standing in the doorway to the kitchen, holding her coffee.

"*Billie?*" McKay spins her name into an alarmed question.

In normal times, this dynamic would have paralyzed me with self-consciousness. But normal times are a thing of the past.

Billie holds up a hand. "Hi."

McKay turns to me, her eyes demanding an explanation. Her being here feels toxic, at least with Billie in the same room, and I wish she'd just leave. I can't handle the two of them together. Not right now.

"We're just watching a movie." I reattach my eyes to the screen of the baby monitor, where they belong.

McKay says nothing for several long seconds. Then her mouth spreads into a conclusive smile, like she's decided to move past the abnormality of the situation.

"Great." Her teeth are wide and gleaming, incisors pointed. Even in leggings and an oversize button-down, she looks polished and perfect.

I have yet to wash last night's makeup off my face. "Are you hungry, Cassie? What are you in the mood for?"

I shake my head. I wish people would stop trying to force-feed me. I've never had less of an appetite in my life.

"You're the birthday girl, after all." McKay's Cheshire Cat grin persists, and she waves the Jo Malone bag in my face. It's a candle, obviously—English Pear and Freesia is our favorite scent—and I can't believe I have to pretend to care about a fucking candle in this moment. The tears erupt before I can stop them.

"Hey." McKay's palm is on my back, rubbing in small circles. "I'm sorry, it's just a stupid present. I picked it up a few days ago."

I use the sleeve of my sweatshirt to wipe my face. "Don't be sorry."

"Can we talk about it? Let's just sit down and go through the whole thing. Grant's text was vague. Tell me what happened."

"Mick—" My throat feels impossibly compressed, like its stuffed with cotton.

McKay takes my hand and leads me to the family room, lowers us to the couch. She cradles her chin in her hand and blinks expectantly, like we're two sorority girls on the verge of sharing our juiciest gossip.

"Cassie." Billie has taken a seat in the adjacent armchair, legs crossed. "If you want me to explain, I can."

I nod gratefully, half listening as Billie recounts the details of Ella's return. I can't see McKay's eyes, but I imagine they've narrowed into a confused glare, trying to pinpoint what the hell Billie is doing here. I suppose if I were her, I'd wonder, too.

When Billie has finished speaking, McKay flips around to me, her jaw on the floor. "*Christ*, Cassie. Thank God she's back safely. That's all that matters."

It isn't all that matters—*who took her and why, who took her and why*—but I don't have it in me to challenge McKay. Instead, I pick up the remote and unfreeze Meg Ryan.

McKay grabs the remote from my hand and presses Pause again. "Cass. The rain has cleared, it's a beautiful day outside. It's your *birthday*."

"I don't care, Mick."

She sighs. "We can't just sit indoors and watch mediocre rom-coms on your birthday."

"Mediocre?" Billie raises an eyebrow, and I can't help but crack a smile.

McKay ignores her, thumbing through her phone. "Ah! Boucherie has a rez for three in twenty minutes. I'll book it, yes?"

"McKay." I shoot her a pleading glance. "I can't go to a restaurant right now. I just need to be home. With Ella."

"All right, well, we can all go when she wakes up. You need an old-fashioned and a cheeseburger, stat. My treat."

"*McKay!*" Something inside of me snaps, a rubber band that's reached its breaking point. "I am not fucking leaving this apartment."

I watch her shrink, her spine curling back into the couch one vertebra at a time.

Billie stands, holding her phone. For the first time since she arrived at the apartment, I notice how exhausted she looks, her eyes red-rimmed.

"I need to make a quick call," she says. "Be right back."

Once Billie has wandered off, McKay picks up the remote. A few beats of silence pass between us. Finally, she turns to me. "I'm sorry. I know you've been through hell. I don't really know what to say or do."

I know she wants to ask point-blank what Billie is doing here—I can see the question itching to escape her lips—but she holds her tongue.

"Do you want me to leave?"

I do, but I shake my head. If I tell McKay to go, it'll just create more conflict in my life, more drama I can't handle.

"I just need to have a quiet afternoon. I need the hours to pass. But you should stay." My stomach folds in on itself, twisting into a pit of fresh dread. I can't envision a reality where it will ever be possible not to feel like this. Not to be trapped in a flooded cave of worry, the water level rising higher and higher, the last of the oxygen on the precipice of slipping away. My own pain will suffocate me.

McKay nods and settles back into the love seat, taps Play on the remote. Tom Hanks slinks into a coffee shop, casts Meg a flirtatious smile. I grip the baby monitor, the pads of my sweat-slicked fingers smudging the screen. I watch my daughter's slow, steady breathing, a relentless stream of paranoia swarming my brain. I am haunted by the burning desire—the vehement *need*—to know whose hands touched my baby sixteen hours earlier. Who snatched her, right from under my nose.

Chapter Thirty-four

Billie

October 14, 2023
The day after

I am slumped against the wall outside Cassie's apartment, phone glued to my ear. After dodging Alex's calls all day, I finally rang him back. I've just finished explaining everything.

Well, not everything. Just the version he needs to know. Stolen baby. Missing baby. Returned baby. Terrified parents.

I've skipped the part that involves me.

"Holy shit, Billie. Cassie must be losing her mind."

"She is." I glance to my right, palming the carpeted space directly in front of Cassie and Grant's front door. The place where I lay Ella last night, like some kind of demented stork.

"Damn." Alex sighs through the phone. "This is heavy."

"I know. I'm dying to see you, but . . . I think I need to stay here with her." I pause. "I know it's confusing . . . me being here with Cassie, after everything I've told you about her. About us . . ."

Alex is quiet for a moment. Then: "Your friend needs you right now. I'm not judging you, if that's what you're thinking."

I consider this. If Alex were to judge me, would I even care? Despite the circumstances surrounding our reunion, being *needed* by Cassie this way has left me almost giddy, infused with the feeling that something in the universe has been righted. It's been years since the two of us sat on the couch and turned on a movie. No agenda, no hard stop. I didn't think it would ever happen again.

"So this detective. Do they think he's any good?"

I bite the inside of my bottom lip, hard. Sometimes I forget that Alex is a cop. Of course he's going to ask these kinds of questions.

"Um, I think Cassie likes him." I unbend my knees and stretch my legs out into the middle of the hallway, feel my calf muscles loosen with the blood flow. I hate lying to Alex, but confessing that Cassie has dubbed Detective Barringer a worthless bozo—her words—feels like an invitation.

"That's good to hear. I could see a case like this being a real drag for some detectives."

My ears perk up. "A drag?"

"Well, an annoyance." Alex pauses. "That's not really the right word, either. I just mean that it's resolved, in some senses. It's no longer a missing persons case. The baby has been returned, safe and sound, without a threat of ransom or signs of foul play. So for a lot of cops—"

I finish his sentence. "There are bigger fish to fry."

"That's how I'm worried some officers might see it."

"Well, you're kind to worry. But Cassie seems to be in good hands with this Barringer guy."

"Glad to hear it." A beat passes. "How's the head feeling?"

It takes me a minute to register what he means. "Oh. My migraine's gone, thank God. Last night was pure hell. That pain is no joke."

"Damn. I didn't even know you got migraines. I'm so sorry."

"I don't. Not often, at least. That was maybe the third one I've ever had in my life." I can't believe how easily the lies drip out. Like I'm made of them. "I think I should get back to Cassie, Alex. But I miss you."

"I miss you, too." His voice is low, husky, and I can feel through the phone how much we both mean it. How, if we were physically together in this moment, we'd curl around each other like mating lions, high on each other's pheromones.

"Come over later, okay?"

I swallow. "I want to. I just—I don't know when it will be. I'll check in with Cassie, see how long she wants me to stay."

"All right."

"Don't be annoyed."

"I'm not annoyed. I'll probably go grab a beer with my brother. Just text me when you're free."

For some unfounded reason, I think he's about to add *I love you*, even though we haven't said that yet. Haven't even hinted at it.

After Alex and I hang up, I peel myself off the floor and have to ring the doorbell to get back inside, since Cassie has dead bolted the apartment. I can't exactly challenge her paranoia.

She greets me with Ella in her arms, the baby's eyes bright from her nap. Cassie's face is flushed with a bit more color; she looks relieved to be back with Ella in the flesh, rather than staring at the monitor like it might sprout wings and fly. I see it now, more clearly than ever: how at home Cassie is as a mother. I respect her for not checking her phone today. Finally, something is grave enough to pull her away from the shallow world of self-promotion.

Grant appears behind Cassie and plucks Ella from her arms. Alarmingly, he starts to cry. I am not prepared for this. Arrogant, sardonic Grant, of the Stiff Upper Lip New England Adlers, is shedding tears in the presence of three women, and without an iota of self-consciousness. He presses his wet face to Ella's, suddenly humanized.

"My baby girl." He chokes back a sob, and McKay runs off for Kleenex.

Now Cassie is in tears, too, and it's just the three of us standing in the living room, husband and wife smothering their child with salty kisses. I've never felt like such an intruder. Perhaps this is my cue.

"Cass," I say quietly. "I should probably get going."

"No!" Her response is instant, unequivocal. I'm caught off guard, but the shock quickly morphs into that warm, fuzzy feeling, little sparks sizzling behind my chest.

Cassie blinks, the ends of her eyelashes damp. "You can stay, right?"

Grant doesn't seem to consider Cassie's sudden interest in having me around as anything unusual. His eyes are closed, his nose pressed to the top of Ella's head as he rocks her back and forth. She grabs a fistful of his hair.

"I can stay," I tell Cassie. It's the only answer, and it comes easily.

It's a joint effort, but the three of us finally convince Cassie to shower. She emerges clean, in a rose pink sweat suit—one of those trendy sets I could never pull off—her damp hair combed in two long sheets that run past her rib cage. The smudged mascara is gone from under her eyes. She looks beautiful again, and healthier; much less like the female version of Heath Ledger in *The Dark Knight*.

"How about Thai for an early birthday dinner?" Grant suggests, the baby propped on his hip. "The place we love that delivers."

Cassie reaches for Ella, distracted, stroking her daughter's pillowy cheek. "Sure. Whatever."

Grant slides a hand into his back pocket and produces Cassie's phone. I recognize the case, matte lavender with her initials in black: CBA. Cassidy Barnwell Adler.

"I really don't want to look at my phone, Grant." Cassie cuddles Ella, planting little kisses all over her face.

"It's blowing up, though."

"It's all birthday messages. I don't care."

Despite the circumstances, I'm stunned. The Cassie I've known and watched behind a screen for the past three years hasn't gone eight hours without filming the most banal moments of her daily existence. Her followers might think she's dead. I steal a glance at McKay, who looks equally shocked.

"Your mom has called twice," Grant presses. "Don't you want to tell her what happened?"

Cassie scowls. "God, no. My mom wasn't even here last night. You think I want her *involved* in this? She'll just drive down here in a panic and get in the way."

My heart sinks. *There are worse things than having a mother who's here, who cares, who wants to be included in your life,* is the protest I want to fling in Cassie's face. I've always liked Mrs. Barnwell. I haven't seen her in years, but she always treated me like a third daughter. She still calls me on my birthday.

"If we figure out who took Ella, then maybe I'll loop my family in. But in the meantime, it's too much stress," Cassie insists.

"*If,* Cassie?" Grant turns to her, his eyes hardening. "We *will* figure out who took Ella. There's a detective on the case now. It's only a matter of time until we get answers."

My stomach lurches, clenching violently. I excuse myself to the bathroom. I need a minute. Inside, I clutch the edges of the porcelain sink and taste acid creeping up the back of my throat.

What if Grant is right—what if it's only a matter of time? What if there *are* security cameras in the hallways of this building? What if Detective Barringer gets his hands on the footage?

What if, what if, what if.

I retch into the sink. It's just coffee and bile—I haven't eaten to-day. Afterward, I rinse my mouth and splash some water on my face, dabbing my chin with one of Cassie's scallop-edged, mono-grammed hand towels. Like the rest of the apartment, the powder room is luxurious and perfect. I admire the screen-printed wallpaper, a jade-green-and-blue depiction of what look like upside-down lotus flowers. A gold bamboo mirror hangs above the sink, and there's a single white rose in a small glass vase, perched beside a bottle of Ac-qua di Parma hand soap.

When I emerge from the bathroom, McKay is standing a few feet from the door, arms folded.

I startle, attempt a smile. "Are you waiting?"

Her mouth is a rigid line, her eyes suspicious pools of clear, Ca-ribbean blue. "It sounded like you were sick. I wanted to make sure you were all right."

I feel the blood drain from my face. "I'm fine," I manage. "But thanks."

Her gaze lingers, narrowing, beyond it a series of thoughts I can mind-read: *You shouldn't be here. Why are you here? What does she want from you?*

My stomach grumbles noisily, and McKay smirks, flips her blond locks. "We're all starving, aren't we? Grant just ordered takeout. It'll be here in less than an hour."

Somehow, it's past four by the time Grant is spooning shrimp pad Thai into bowls. Ella is down for her afternoon nap, and Cassie is twitchy, like an addict, the way she keeps adjusting the screen of the baby monitor, as if a slightly different angle might keep her child safer.

We eat in the family room, afternoon light glowing behind the wo-ven wood shades. Grant asks Cassie what she wants to watch, and when she doesn't answer, he turns on *Mare of Easttown*. McKay eyes Grant and drags a flattened hand through the center of her neck, as if to say: *What the hell are you thinking turning on a show about a murdered daughter and abducted children,* and it might be the first time I've ever agreed with her. Grant catches his mistake and switches to *Curb Your Enthusiasm* while Cassie is still busy inspecting the monitor, the plate of oily noodles untouched on her lap. Larry David insults a pregnant woman running on the treadmill at the gym, and I can't help myself, I laugh.

I've lost track of how many episodes we've watched, when McKay stands and stretches her arms overhead. The motion reveals a sliver of her stomach, which is taut and smooth like Cassie's, even after pregnancy.

"Tom is bombarding me with texts," she groans. "I think he's losing his mind; a solo day with two kids, no nanny. I bet *Encanto* is playing on repeat. Anyway, I might need to show my face at home."

I resist the urge to make an off-the-cuff remark about Tom's ability as a parent, or lack thereof, fueling the Disney+ machine.

"That's fine." Cassie is adjusting the brightness setting on the baby monitor and doesn't look up.

"Are you sure? Honestly, I can stay. Or I can just zip home for bedtime and be back in a couple of hours."

Finally, Cassie lifts her chin. She moves her untouched plate of food to the coffee table.

"Don't worry about it. Go home to your kids. I'm zonked, anyway."

McKay seems dissatisfied with this response—slightly maimed by it—and better than anyone, I understand. I know all too well what it's like to be needed by Cassie, then suddenly not.

But McKay plays it cool. She tells Cassie she'll be back in the morning, that she'll bring coffee and scones from Ralph's. Once she's gone, something in Cassie's posture changes, almost like visible relief. She picks up her plate and twirls her fork into the pad Thai, takes a small bite.

"I'm sorry, but this tastes like rubber." Cassie swallows, her eyes filling. "I'm just not hungry at all."

"Come on, babe. Just try to eat a little more." Grant stands and stacks my empty dish on top of his, walks off toward the kitchen. We hear the sound of the faucet running, stoneware clinking in the sink.

"Hey." I take the plate from Cassie's lap and slide it back onto the coffee table. "Don't worry about food. If you're not hungry, you're not hungry."

"God, I'm such a wreck." She sniffles, rubs an eye with the sleeve of her sweatshirt. "Thank you for being the only one who understands."

As nonsensical as this statement is—I don't understand; I'm not a mother, let alone one who's child went missing—I know what she's saying. In a pre-language sort of way, I do get it. Unlike Grant, unlike

McKay, I know trauma. Trauma that takes your skin and turns it inside out, so the world hits you raw.

My phone vibrates against my thigh—a new text from Alex.

Hey, you. How's it going over there?

When I glance up from the screen, Cassie is watching me. In the rose pink sweat suit, she resembles a piece of mochi. "You're not leaving, are you?" She fingers a piece of her hair, which is completely dry now, pin straight from whatever smoothing treatment she uses. I miss her curls.

"I don't have to leave." I hold up my phone. "Alex was just checking in."

"Billie." Cassie's eyes grow wide, almost feral. She hinges forward and reaches for me, her nails digging into my jeans. "Please. Please don't go. You can stay in the guest room. Okay? *Please.*" Her voice is pained, desperate.

There is too much irony surrounding me; I taste it, I am swimming in it.

I glance at Alex's text on my phone. I'm falling in love with him—oddly, in this moment, I feel the truth of this. But it doesn't hold weight against the knowledge that Cassie wants me here—*me,* not McKay. I feel pleasantly hot, like I've just lowered myself into a steaming bath after a frigid day in the snow.

"Of course I'll stay, Cassie," I tell her. "I'll stay as long as you need."

Chapter Thirty-five

Billie

Fall 2007

The first time Remy and I have sex, I'm not expecting it. He takes me to a launch party in Beacon Hill for his friend Antoine's photography exhibit. The photos are of assemblages of repeated objects that are meant to challenge our perception of dimension, Remy explains. I sip luke-warm pinot grigio and stare at an abstract black-and-white image of what he says is an aerial view of hundreds of plastic straws.

"Do you like it?" Remy asks. He wears a white linen top with half the buttons undone, cropped pants, paint-splattered Birkenstocks. It's November.

"I'm not sure," I answer truthfully.

My phone buzzes in my pocket, and when Remy drifts over to the next photograph, I pull it out. A series of texts from Cassie.

> Where are you?? I thought you were coming tonight.
>
> Tell me you're not on a date with that nude model who looks like the reincarnation of Jesus.
>
> Bc you can do way better . . .

I glance over at Remy, who's chatting with an older woman in denim overalls and combat boots.

I don't know what's wrong with resembling Jesus, but I'm sure Cassie would love to tell me. Anyway, I'm doubtful that this is a date. Remy had me meet him here, and he hasn't touched me all night. Every time we get together, it's for a reason that could be platonic—a friend's art show, a midday walk along the Charles, a new exhibit at some gallery

*that's supposed to be cool. Add to that, Remy has never kissed me. He's
never so much as held my hand.*

It's not a date, *I type back.* But I'm in Beacon Hill. I can't make it to
Harvard tonight. Tomorrow I'll be there!

"Hey." *Remy appears beside me, and I slip my phone back in my
pocket. He leans closer, and I can smell the wine on his breath, the clove
cigarettes he smokes. His eyelashes are long and darker than his hair.
"They're all going to a bar down the street, but I'm not sure I'm up for it."*

*I nod, swallowing my disappointment. I'm not ready to leave him. I
never am.* "Yeah, I should head back—"

"How about a nightcap at my place? It isn't far."

*Remy's place in Back Bay is nicer than I'm expecting. I've envisioned
messy bookshelves, an empty fridge, a mattress on the floor. But the studio apartment is civilized, with framed artwork and a pine headboard
and ivory curtains flanking the tall windows. There's a bowl of fresh
fruit in the kitchen, a well-stocked bar. A small alcove off the main room
contains an easel and a neat row of oil paints lining the window ledge,
a few blank canvases propped against the wall.*

*Remy mixes us Campari sodas, and I've only taken one sip when his
fingers graze my forearm, my skin burning all over from the single point
of his touch. His face moves toward mine; he's so tall he has to stoop to
kiss me. When his lips brush mine, I feel my whole body quiver.*

"Is this okay?" *His voice is low, nervous.*

*I nod. I had a couple of drunken make-outs at parties last year, but
there's been nothing like this. Not ever.*

"Why wouldn't it be?" *It's my bold attempt to sound flirty and coy,
the way Cassie does with guys.*

Remy hesitates. "I get the feeling you don't want me to touch you. I've
wanted to, for a while now, but you seem tense . . ."

*I shake my head, pissed at myself for whatever it is I can't get right. I
don't want to come off this way; I don't want to be tense. Not with Remy.
Remy isn't Wade. No one is Wade. Wade is gone.*

*I think of Remy's body, the naked being I've seen so many times in
Wanda's class this fall. His long, sinewy muscles, the nest of dark hair
that trails south from his belly button. It isn't sexual, not even slightly,
and perhaps that's what has allowed me to come this far. Maybe what*

drew me to Remy is the vulnerability he offered from that first moment; the way he placed a sexless lens over my fears without even trying. His body is just a body. So is mine.

Slowly, I unclasp the buttons of my shirt. I reach for his hand and place his warm fingers against my chest, feel them slide underneath the fabric of my bra, over my nipple.

"Billie," he says. "You're shaking."

I close my eyes, will the panic down.

"I'm okay," I tell him as he works my shirt off. "This is my first time."

"It is?"

"Yes. But I want you."

At least all of it is true.

Cassie has always been adamant that when I finally have sex, I shouldn't tell the guy I'm a virgin beforehand. She says it might scare them off, that it's too much pressure.

But Remy isn't scared. Instead, he gives a gentle nod and leads me to the bed. A beam of streetlight shines through the window above his nightstand, illuminating the sheets, which are soft and smell faintly of cloves.

He lays me down, removes the rest of my clothes, then his own.

"You're beautiful," he whispers, his mouth working mine open as he enters me, a shot of pain mixed with relief that it's ending, that it's over, that someone else now has access to these parts of me. That my own shame hasn't been enough to brand me. That Remy sees a beauty I cannot.

Afterward, he holds me close, our skin humming and hot, and more than happiness, more than exhilaration, what shrouds me is the feeling of safety. The sense of something being accepted, possibly forgiven.

Chapter Thirty-six

Cassie

October 15, 2023
2 days after

I'm nursing Ella in her room when Billie wanders in, bleary-eyed from sleep. The nostalgia hits me like an unexpected wave—vicious, unrelenting—as I remember all the mornings we've woken up in the same place. Sleepovers in high school, Billie sprawled on the blow-up mattress on the floor of my childhood room, her legs tangled in the yellow jersey sheets. Then in college, the two of us squished into the twin bed in my Cambridge dorm, thirsty and hungover, but content to be together. And then in New York, in that shoebox of an apartment we shared in the East Village when we first moved to the city. The way we'd huddle on the threadbare couch before work and sip percolator coffee; the feeling that our four hundred square feet was a palace for no other reason than that it belonged to us.

I'm tempted to miss those days, but I don't. I couldn't. It wouldn't be possible to genuinely yearn for a time in my life before Ella.

Billie drops to her knees beside the glider. She's wearing my pajamas—an old gray set from Eberjey—and the white fuzzy robe I keep on a hook in the guest bathroom. "How'd you sleep?" she asks, yawning.

"I didn't." I glance down at Ella, adjust her against my chest. "I got maybe an hour."

Billie sighs. "Me, too."

I look up, surprised. "Really?"

She nods, pulling her hair loose from the collar of the robe, a little color flushing her cheeks. "Yeah—I mean, with everything going on. With you, that is. I just couldn't get my mind to shut down."

"Same." I study her face, the youthful quality it still possesses after all this time. I know without asking that she's never tried Botox or fillers—Billie wouldn't. The years have simply been good to her.

"I'm so glad you're here." I give a small smile, meaning the words.

Ella unlatches from my drained breast, satisfied, blinking up at me with blue doe eyes. I hold her close, willing the oxytocin to replenish the dark, ever-deepening pit in my stomach.

Who took her? Who brought her back? Why?

"Me, too." Billie matches my smile as she stands. "How about some caffeine?"

We're on our second cups of coffee when Grant trudges into the kitchen in boxers and nothing else, hair rumpled, one patch of it sticking straight up. He seems to have forgotten Billie stayed the night.

"Oh. Hey." His voice is husky, like he's just woken from deep REM. I listened to him snore for half the night, wondering then and now: How can Grant sleep so soundly at a time like this? How can he tamp down the panic and fear enough to turn off his brain? Even Billie can't.

"Babe." He gives me a wet morning kiss—the kind I used to cherish when we first started dating. Now, I wish he'd wait till after toothpaste to get near me.

Grant turns his focus to Ella in the bouncy chair, and I use the opportunity to wipe his saliva off my face, hoping Billie doesn't notice.

"How'd you sleep?" Billie asks him.

Grant reaches for the cabinet where we keep the mugs. "Like I was dead, honestly." I bristle at his figure of speech. "And I needed it," he adds, pouring his coffee. Grant drinks it black, sugarless, and I wonder sometimes if he likes it that way, or if he's trying to prove something. I study his bare stomach, the hairy paunch spilling over the waistband of his boxers. I wish he'd put a shirt on in front of company. He's gained weight since our wedding.

Suddenly, the doorbell rings, a shrill chime that causes me to jump.

I glance at my phone on the counter to check the time, ignoring the swarm of notifications, mostly from Instagram. *9:08.*

I shuffle toward the front door, praying it isn't McKay. I just can't deal with her, not right now. I can't force the smile I know she wishes would magically appear on my face, like everything that happened was a bad dream, well on its way to being forgotten. She hasn't said it out loud, but I can tell—she wants normalcy restored.

When I swing the door open, it isn't McKay. But I'm not exactly relieved by the sight of Detective Barringer, hands in his pockets, his mouth a colorless slash across his face. He doesn't look like the bearer of good news.

I hug my robe tighter around my body, covering my chest—I'm not wearing a bra, or even my usual nursing tank.

"Morning, Mrs. Adler. Your doorman sent me right up."

"You can call me Cassie."

"All right, Cassie." There's a sly humor to his tone that I don't appreciate. None of this is funny. "Can I come in? I have some information I think you and your husband will want to hear."

I situate Detective Barringer in the living room while Billie gets him a mug of coffee—apparently, he's not yet consumed his daily cup—and Grant runs off to put on clothes. I pluck Ella from the bouncy and settle her onto my lap with Sophie the rubber giraffe, which she gleefully gums.

Detective Barringer sips his coffee. He drinks it black, like Grant. Like all men, it seems, as if acquiring the bitter taste is some sort of power statement. "Is she teething?" he asks, gesturing toward Sophie the giraffe. "I remember my son had one of those."

"We think she has a tooth coming in on the bottom." I pause. "How old is your son?"

"Six. First grade."

Grant has returned, wearing jeans and a navy half zip, perched on the other end of the couch. I wonder if he's thinking what I am—that a guy with a six-year-old can't possibly be experienced enough to do this job. Detective Barringer looks younger than I am. I wonder if he's still with the kid's mother, or if she's just some girl he knocked up who decided to keep the baby, resulting in joint custody he never wanted.

"So what's the latest, Detective?" Grant shifts forward in his seat, forearms propped on his knees.

Barringer clears his throat. "I was able to get a look at the security cameras."

I brace myself. *Cameras.*

"I'll give the bad news first. The footage we have is minimal. There are no cameras in the elevator, stairwells, or residential hallways—as is often the case with buildings this old—so unfortunately, there's no footage of Ella being returned to your doorstep."

Grant runs a hand through his disheveled hair. "How about some good news?"

There's a subtle lift to the corners of Barringer's mouth. "The interior footage that does exist—there's a camera in the lobby—revealed no suspicious activity. So that's positive."

I shake my head. "But how would you know what's suspicious activity? It would just be a person entering or leaving the building or whatever. You can't necessarily tell from security footage if they're suspicious."

Barringer holds up a palm; I can practically feel the condescension seeping from his pores. "Cassie. Here's the *really* good news. There's a pole camera just across the street, and it happens to capture activity on the fire escape of this building."

Beside me, Billie lets out a little yelp. "Sorry," she says. "I'm just—wow. Someone climbed up the fire escape? That's so creepy."

Barringer nods. "Friday-evening footage shows a couple of kids—teenage boys, from the looks of it—screwing around on the fire escape just after eight o'clock. An hour before Ella went missing."

My cells freeze, every atom inside of me tensing. "You—you saw these kids on camera? They climbed up to our terrace?" My voice is shaking, crumbling, barely audible. "They—they took her?"

Barringer rests his hands on his lap, interlaces his fingers. "The camera's range only extends to the third or fourth story of the building. But we can conjecture."

"*Conjecture?*" Anger crashes through my veins, nudging out the fear.

"Yes, it means we can assess—"

"I *know* what the word means."

Barringer sighs. "Cassie. I looked through several weeks' worth of footage. There's not *one* other instance of activity on the fire escape. Not one, in all those weeks. That tells us something."

I glance over at Grant. He's chewing the edge of his thumb, his eyes cloudy and glazed over, the way they are when he's processing.

My gaze darts back to Barringer. "Is that it, though? What about the footage from the lobby? Did it show those same kids later in the night? If they took Ella from the terrace and then managed to put her in the hallway outside our door, they would've left the building after that."

Barringer hesitates. "No," he answers carefully. "Like I said, there was no suspicious activity gleaned from the lobby camera. No one directly resembling the kids from the fire escape. But it's an older surveillance system. The quality isn't the best."

"This sounds like a bullshit theory to me."

On my lap, Ella starts to whimper. I sometimes forget how in tune she is with my energy, the symbiotic nature of our relationship. We rely on each other's well-being.

Grant presses his index fingers to his temples, agitated. "Cassie, come on. Just try to listen to Detective Barringer. He knows what he's doing."

"I am listening, Grant—"

"I think what Cassie is trying to understand—what we're *all* trying to understand here, Detective—is if what you're saying about these kids on the fire escape is conclusive, given the lack of . . . evidence?" It's Billie who's posed the question, catching me off guard. I've almost forgotten she's here.

Detective Barringer cocks his head. "I'm sorry. Who are you?"

"This is Billie," I say, before she has a chance to answer herself. "My—oldest friend. She stayed over last night."

Barringer's gaze remains fixed on Billie. "Were you at the party on Friday?"

The question is followed by heavy silence, the moment too surreal to be awkward. Nevertheless, I can't do this to her; I can't sit here and watch her squirm, not after the way she's shown up for me. I open my mouth to respond, but she beats me to it.

"I couldn't make it on Friday," she says evenly. "I came down with a terrible migraine."

"I see." Barringer gives a sympathetic nod. "My wife gets migraines. Agonizing."

So he is married.

"Yeah, they're not fun."

I steal a glance at Billie, a silent expression of gratitude.

Barringer continues. "To answer your question, Billie, yes. This is *mostly* conclusive. I've spent the past twenty-four hours watching security footage, interviewing guests who attended your party—"

"You have?" My eyebrows knit together. "I didn't know you'd been talking to our guests."

"I believe I mentioned yesterday that I'd be contacting everyone who was in attendance Friday night. Grant sent me the list."

Grant sighs. "You haven't looked at your phone all weekend, Cassie. Plenty of people have been texting us, checking in, letting us know they've been contacted."

"Anyway." Barringer swallows the last of his coffee, the liquid moving against his Adam's apple. "I haven't gotten hold of everyone yet, but give me another few days. But of the twenty or so couples I have spoken with, well—no one saw anything suspicious. No one has reason to believe that anyone else who was present at the party would've taken Ella."

I shake my head, fighting tears. "This doesn't make sense, though. Why would two random teenage boys take my baby? And then bring her back?"

"It was probably an accident. There was likely alcohol involved. Possibly drugs."

Probably. Likely. Possibly.

"Listen." Barringer places his empty mug on the table and stands, smoothing the front of his khakis. "I'm going to get in touch with the rest of your guests this week. If anything comes up, I'll call right away. And vice versa. You have my number." His gaze trails from Grant to me. His eyes are puffy and slightly bloodshot, like perhaps he didn't sleep last night, either. "For what it's worth, I hoped this information would put you at a bit more ease. It's extremely plausible that these kids are responsible. That they were screwing around, wasted or high, and things got out of hand. I can show you the footage, if it would help. Think about it."

When Detective Barringer is gone, Grant turns to me, irritation creasing his brow. "You know, Cassie, it wouldn't hurt you to be a little more receptive to this guy. He's the *police*. He's helping us."

I scowl. "He's clearly written off what happened as an 'accident,' Grant." I use air quotes around the words. "You heard him. He said his theory about the teenagers is 'mostly conclusive.' And you want to know why? He's tired and lazy, and we have our baby back, so what does it matter? This case is probably a joke to him, to the whole department."

Grant is silent for a moment. "It's Sunday morning, Cassie. He's clearly been at work on this all weekend—did you see how exhausted he looked?"

I say nothing. I can't argue that.

Grant presses on, and I can see the wheels turning in his head, almost like he's trying to convince himself that what he's telling me holds merit. "He didn't have to show up here. He could've just called. And moreover, he could've waited until Monday to contact us at all. You heard the guy—he has a kid, a wife. If this weren't a serious case, he'd be home with them."

Grant's phone begins to vibrate, and he slides it from the back pocket of his jeans. "It's the pediatrician. I have to take this."

"The pediatrician?" My stomach sinks. "Why is she calling?"

"Because I texted her yesterday to ask if they could see Ella on Monday." Grant stands, impatient. "I figured it was a good idea, after what happened. Not that there are signs of physical harm, but still."

"It is, but why didn't you—"

"I included you on the text, Cassie. Which you'd know if you checked your phone." Grant slides his thumb across the screen to take the call, his voice buoying as he greets the doctor and walks toward the other end of the apartment.

Ella is growing fussy. I bounce her on my knees, an attempt to avoid her first nap for as long as possible. To delay those excruciating two hours when she's out of arm's reach.

I glance over at Billie, who's sitting cross-legged on the couch. She looks vaguely shell-shocked.

"Grant can be such a dick," I mutter half-consciously.

Billie's eyes lift to meet mine. "I know." She hesitates. "I mean, I'm sorry. He's probably just processing everything in his own way."

"I guess."

Her phone vibrates on the side table. She leans over to check the screen, her expression unreadable.

"Everything okay?"

Billie nods. "It's Alex again. I should probably go call him."

Alex. In the twenty-four hours Billie has been at my apartment, I've completely forgotten about her boyfriend.

"Shoot, Bill, I'm such a jerk. You've probably blown him off all weekend to be here."

She shakes her head. "Cass, are you kidding? This is so much more important."

"And I haven't even asked you how it's going with him."

"Well, to say you've been preoccupied is an understatement. But it's going . . . well. Really well." A demure smile spreads across Billie's face, her cheekbones reddening.

"Oh my God. You *love* him!" A small laugh escapes my throat.

"I don't know . . ."

"You do, I can tell. This is great. You haven't loved anyone since Remy." I pause. "Why don't you tell him to come over?"

"Here?"

"Why not? I'm about to put Ella down for her morning nap, and I could use the distraction. We can order brunch or something. Besides, I bet you miss him."

One end of Billie's mouth curls. "I haven't seen him since Thursday. It feels like an eternity."

"Because that *is* an eternity in the beginning." I lean my head back into the cushion, thinking of those early days with Grant. The way my stomach used to dip and twirl while I'd wait for him to come over after work, my eyes perfectly lined, my lingerie carefully chosen in anticipation of his arrival—of the things we would do once our bodies could touch again.

"God, I miss that feeling." I haven't meant to speak the words out loud, but there they are. An admission.

I blink, lowering my chin to meet Billie's gaze. "Tell Alex to get over here."

She smiles. "Yeah. I'll text him."

Chapter Thirty-seven

Billie

October 15, 2023
2 days after

Alex gets to Cassie and Grant's around dinnertime. I invited him over earlier, when Cassie told me to, but he had plans to go surfing with Dave again, so we postponed to dinner instead of brunch. Alex arrives with a bag of takeout from Novitá, a hesitant smile on his face. I can tell he feels like an intruder, the way I did not long ago. But Cassie greets him warmly, her mouth spreading into a wide, genuine smile.

"You're sweet to bring dinner." She's wearing leggings and an old flannel with misaligned buttons, no makeup, hair twisted back into a messy bun. She looks like a completely different Cassie from the one Alex met back in September, and I'm grateful he's seeing this side of her. Maybe it will help him understand.

Cassie unpacks the takeout in the kitchen, and Alex pulls me in for a hug. He's showered since surfing, but I can still smell the salt water on his skin, in his hair.

"God, I've missed you," he whispers. Goose bumps prickle the space behind my ear.

Cassie takes four plates from the cabinet and sets them on the counter a bit roughly, a loud clink ringing through the room. "Help yourselves. We can just eat on the couch, right? I don't have the energy to set the table." She darts to the fridge and plucks a bottle of rosé from the side door, already uncorked. Her movements are frenzied, slightly manic. "If you'd prefer red, I'll let Grant deal with that. He's all finicky about his wine."

Grant frowns, but says nothing as he scoops heaping piles of carbonara and pesto gnocchi onto his plate. Cassie serves herself a pea-size portion of gnocchi and goat cheese salad, which I know she won't touch. All I've seen her consume this weekend are a few Wheat Thins.

We eat in the family room, the last of the dusky light filtering in through the blinds, which Cassie still refuses to open. It occurs to me that I haven't left this apartment in nearly thirty-six hours, and I've hardly seen the sun in that time. But it hasn't felt claustrophobic. On the contrary, aside from missing Alex, and aside from the unnerving presence of Detective Barringer, I've been strangely at peace.

"This is delicious," Grant remarks, his mouth full, carbonara disappearing from his plate at the speed of light. "Thanks, Alex."

Cassie pours more rosé into her goblet, gulps it down like it's water after a sweaty session of cardio. Her mood, which seemed more optimistic earlier in the day, has returned to a state of bleak desperation. The baby monitor sits on her lap, volume at the max. Ella went down half an hour ago.

"It's really nice of you to have me over." Alex shifts beside me on the love seat. "Given the circumstances."

Cassie gives a lost smile. "I'm holding your girlfriend hostage. It's the least I can do."

"I'm so sorry about everything." Alex's voice softens, and I feel it again, the thing I do so often around him—his pure goodness. Nothing crooked or ambiguous about his psyche, not like mine. "How are you guys holding up?"

"We're okay." Grant swallows another bite of pasta. "The detective who's working on the case, he came over this morning with an update that helped settle some nerves."

Cassie chokes on a sip of wine. "Speak for yourself," she sputters, pivoting her shoulders to face Alex. "This guy, he's worthless." She proceeds to tell him about Detective Barringer, slurring her words a little as she recounts the details of his investigation, the teenagers he thinks are responsible.

"He's not basing any of this on hard evidence," she says, pouring herself more rosé. The blush liquid clunks through the nose of the bottle, sloshing into the bowl of her glass. "It's all speculation. He doesn't *care* who took Ella or why, because we have her back. And yet he *pretends* like he's killing himself over this case, even though it's only been two days and he's basically implied that it's all wrapped up."

Alex is quiet for a few moments, his lips pursed in thought. "I was worried something like this might happen," he says eventually. "I mentioned it to Billie."

Cassie's eyebrows knit together. "What are you talking about?"

"I just mean, I'm not entirely surprised to hear this. When it's no longer a missing persons case, well, some detectives feel pressure to move on. To tackle homicides, burglaries. More . . . pressing cases."

"But this *is* pressing!" Cassie's eyes fill, her voice edging toward hysteria. "Someone took our baby and we don't know who and they might come back and it *fucking matters!*"

"Hey, hey." Alex holds up a hand. "I'm with you, okay? I'm on your side. I'm just telling you what I know, from my own experience with some guys in the department."

Cassie blinks and cocks her head, mouth agape as she studies Alex. Suddenly, she starts to laugh. Real, unadulterated, erratic laughter that makes me nervous.

"Oh my God." She covers her mouth, tears still dripping down her face as she giggles uncontrollably. "You're a cop. I'm sorry, I completely forgot you're a cop. Honey—" She stabs Grant's shoulder. "He's a *cop.*"

Grant rubs his jaw uncomfortably, then gestures to Cassie's untouched plate on the coffee table. "Babe. Why don't you eat some dinner?"

Cassie ignores him, turning her focus back to Alex. "Wait, so do you know him? Detective Barringer? Blond? Short and kind of baby-faced? Looks like an ugly version of Matt Damon?"

A laugh escapes me, despite myself.

"Can't say I do," Alex replies with a hint of amusement. "But we're in different divisions, so it's not surprising. The NYPD is massive."

Cassie nods, wiping her cheeks. The skin under her eyes is mottled and dark. "I'm sorry. You probably think I'm completely unhinged. I just . . . I thought the police would be able to do more. I've told Grant I think we need to hire a private investigator."

My heart stops beating; my breath is trapped in my lungs.

"I have a lot of social media followers," Cassie continues. "Almost fifty thousand. And I'm worried it might've been one of them. Some crazy person who hates me. I get messages from trolls all the time, you know." She pauses. "We mentioned this to *Detective* Barringer, but he doesn't seem to think it matters. I told you, he's worthless."

Alex interlaces his hands across his lap, thumbs circling. "I hear you, but you know, it's possible that this Barringer guy might be right, Cassie. If weeks' worth of footage shows nobody scaling the fire escape except for *one* night—the same night Ella went missing—well, that might not be a coincidence."

I release the air I'm holding, possibly more grateful for Alex in this moment than I've ever been.

Cassie sips more wine. "True. It *might* not be a coincidence." She sets the glass down on the side table, her eyes watery and fixed. "But this is my baby. *Might* isn't good enough. We need a PI."

Alex nods. "I understand." A few long beats of silence pass, the only sound in the room the crunchy static of the baby monitor. "Hey." He shifts forward on the couch. "Before you hire a PI, why don't you let me look into this?"

I stiffen, every cell in my body switched to high alert.

"Oh my God." Cassie's voice fills with tears again, her words raspy and thick. "You would do that?"

"Of course." Alex picks up his wineglass. "I can't promise a different answer from the one you've been given. But Barringer—well, you're right. It's possible he was rushed, that he overlooked something. What I can promise is that I'll be thorough."

My heart is in my throat.

Grant gives an appreciative nod. "That's very kind of you."

"It's nothing." Alex moves the wine toward his lips. "I'll give Barringer a call tomorrow and have him loop me in on everything."

Out on the street, I gulp for oxygen like I've just emerged from a windowless cell and not a lavish penthouse. Alex and I left the apartment just after dinner, Grant insisting we go enjoy the rest of the night together despite the pleading urgency in Cassie's eyes.

Call me in the morning, she'd whispered as the door closed, the desperation in her expression warping me with a fucked-up mix of guilt and pride. I'm the reason for her suffering. I did this. But if I hadn't, I would just be a forgotten contact in Cassie's phone like I was two days ago. A once-upon-a-time friend not worthy of a party invitation or even a text response.

"Are you okay, Billie?" Alex reaches for my hand and starts to walk us down the block, which is quiet and lamplit. "You look a little pale."

"Yeah. Just a weird weekend." I interlace my fingers through his. "I missed you."

"I missed you, too. It's kind of crazy how much." At the corner of Nineteenth and Park, he turns to face me, his eyes glowing green in the lamplight. "We don't have to talk about it, if you don't want to."

I manage a tiny smile, grateful for this offer, my stomach full of pasta and wine and stony dread. "I really don't. Not right now."

He nods, his eyes clipping mine, brimming with so much compassion I feel like a viper even before he speaks.

"Billie," he starts. An MTA bus speeds by, my ponytail whipped back by the hard rush of air. "I get that it's a weird friendship, but I understand how much you care about Cassie. And I want you to know, I meant what I told her. I'm going to do everything I can to find out who took her baby." He pauses, his gaze unflinching, on the brink of promising me something I couldn't want less. "You have my word."

Chapter Thirty-eight

Billie

December 2009

Senior year, McKay Adler invites seven girls from her sorority to spend New Year's in St. Barts at her family's villa. Cassie is not one of them.

I can tell Cassie has been crying when she calls me to vent. I'm sick of her being so obsessed with McKay and her cohort, but there's no point in relaying this. It's been more than three years, and Cassie is still trying to worm her way into their inner circle. Some days, they seem to want her around. But mostly she remains on the periphery of whatever big thing it is they have going on, orbiting like a pesky mosquito. I can't stand watching it.

"Honestly, fuck McKay." Cassie's voice is hoarse, a little wobbly. "Jay says we can do New Year's at his parents' ranch in Aspen."

Jay Crowley is Cassie's boyfriend. He's an econ major at Harvard, like all the guys that capture her attention. They've been dating for eight months, Cassie's longest relationship since Kyle Briggs in high school.

"That sounds awesome," I tell her. "Who needs St. Barts? You guys will have a great time."

"No, Billie. I said we. You and Remy, too."

I pause, digesting this. "Jay wants Remy and me to come to Aspen?"

"Yes. He said the more the merrier."

I'm stunned. In the two years I've been with Remy, Cassie has never suggested doing a trip together. She's mostly ambivalent to Remy's existence.

"I don't know, Cass." I sit down on the edge of my twin bed. I'm in a

single this year, though I end up spending most nights at Remy's in Back Bay. "I told Becca and Esme I would go to New York."

Cassie huffs. "What's in New York?"

"Esme's sister is having a party. Remy and I were going to stay at his aunt's apartment in Queens."

"Billie. How can you even think about turning down an invitation to Aspen to sit in a dumpy apartment in Queens?"

A long beat of silence trickles by. I sink back into the pillows. "I can't afford to fly to Aspen. I doubt Remy can, either."

I imagine Cassie rolling her eyes at the reminder that my boyfriend is a poor artist. It's the last thing she wants for me.

"That's such a cop-out, Billie."

"It really isn't."

She exhales, annoyed. "If we fly into Denver instead, the flights will be cheap. I'll rent a car and drive us all to Aspen."

It's impossible to argue with Cassie when she gets her mind set on something, and besides, the invitation is certainly appealing. I don't ski, but sitting around a cozy fire drinking red wine with Cassie and Jay and Remy while we gaze out at snow-covered peaks sounds like heaven.

Remy puts up a fight, like I knew he would. He doesn't ski, either, and he hates when I get roped into what he calls "Cassie's pretentious bullshit."

"You hardly know Jay," I counter. "How can you claim he's pretentious?"

"Because everything Cassie likes is pretentious." Remy's eyes move over my face. "Except for you." He sighs, his expression a blend of frustration and tenderness. "If you really want to go, Billie, we can go. I'll tell my aunt we're bagging New York."

I buy our plane tickets. I get a monthly stipend from Mom—well, from an account that was set up for me when the house sold. It isn't much—most of the money was set aside to cover Sandra's wages and Mom's new place in Poughkeepsie. But it's money I've been extra careful with, so I can justify cutting into my savings for a special occasion like this one.

Pointlessly, I wish I could call Mom and thank her. That I could tell her about my plans for New Year's, about Remy, how much I love him. It would make her happy, I know. But it's been years since Mom has remembered my voice, my name, and calling the one-bedroom apartment *where she now lives is futile. Sandra would be the one to answer, and most days, her cheery demeanor is too much for me to bear.*

I spend Christmas with Cassie in Red Hook, like I have every year since Mom moved to Poughkeepsie. As usual, Cassie is cranky around her family. The Barnwell home feels festive; it smells like warm sugar, and Bing Crosby floats through the living room speakers, but Cassie doesn't appreciate any of it. She rolls her eyes when her mom gives us fuzzy socks and gift cards to Aéropostale.

"What makes my mother think I shop at such skanky stores?" Cassie asks me when we're done opening presents. It's just the two of us in her bedroom, getting ready for dinner. She's wearing fitted black pants and an ivory silk blouse with sequins lining the collar, black kitten heels. It's the kind of outfit McKay and the girls from Harvard would wear—conservative with a stylish edge. Preppy with sex appeal. It's overkill, of course. I doubt Mara will change out of sweats.

"I don't think Aéropostale is skanky," I offer, mostly in defense of Mrs. Barnwell.

"You can have mine, then." Cassie tosses the gift card on the bed and sighs. "Christmas presents suck without my grandmother."

Grandma Catherine passed away earlier this year. She had a stroke in her sleep and never woke up, which sounds like a nice way out if there is one. She didn't leave Cassie anything except the rest of her college tuition money, which Cassie claims was an oversight. If Grandma Catherine had known she was dying, she would've updated her will.

In the mirror above her dresser, Cassie paints her lips in clear gloss. Her eyes find mine. "Sorry," she mutters. "I don't mean to sound like a brat."

I shrug. We both know she doesn't care if she sounds like a brat, not around me.

"Did Remy get you anything good?" she asks.

"A scarf. And tickets to a Bruins game. We're going with his parents and siblings in January."

Cassie snorts. "You don't even like hockey."

"His family loves the Bruins. They go every winter, and he wanted to include me." I bite the inside of my cheek, annoyed.

"Right. I forgot he has that big Boston family."

"Yeah." A moment passes. "What'd Jay get you?"

Cassie screws the top on the lip gloss and flashes a shiny smile. "I don't know yet. I'm sure I'll find out when we get to Aspen. Jay is already there."

Cassie has booked the same flight as Remy and me, and the three of us arrive in Denver a few days after Christmas.

"Are you nervous to meet Jay's parents?" I ask Cassie on the drive into the mountains. Independence Pass is closed for the season, so we loop through the high, majestic canyons of I-70. The sky is overcast, knotted with cottony clouds.

"A little." Her eyes are glued to the road as she steers the rental car around a sharp bend. "Especially since the Crowleys are loaded." Her mouth curls in profile, and she turns up the music. For some reason, we're listening to Cher.

I glance over my shoulder, grateful that Remy is passed out in the back seat, oblivious to our conversation. We stayed out late last night at a gallery opening that turned into a bar crawl, and he's been a zombie all day. I watch him for a moment, the way he's slumped against the window, lips parted, and feel a warm stitch of affection at the sight of his eyelashes fluttering softly against his cheek. Remy and I almost never leave Boston, and it's exciting to be somewhere new with him. I crack my window, and cold air whips in, the smell of pine and fresh snow.

I turn back to Cassie. "How do you know the Crowleys are loaded?"

"Haven't you seen Dumb and Dumber? Only rich people own vacation homes in Aspen." A pause. "Plus, with Jay, I can just tell. He golfs. He skis. His mom's name is Tinsley, okay?" She laughs.

Once again, I'm glad that Remy is asleep.

As it turns out, the Crowley home isn't in Aspen. It's in a town called Carbondale, thirty miles northwest of the ski area. This is something we learn when Cassie calls Jay from the road to get the address.

"It's a ranch. I guess it makes sense that it's out of town." She shrugs, but I can hear the nerves in her voice.

It's dusk by the time we pull into the Crowleys' driveway. Jay is sitting on the front stoop, forearms resting on his knees. Cassie isn't wrong about him—objectively, he does look like a kid with money. Good, symmetrical face. Patagonia jacket. One of those preppy wool hats with the ear flaps and tassels affixed to his head. His cheeks are pink from wait-

ing out in the cold for us to arrive, a chivalrous act that doesn't surprise me. Jay is nuts about Cassie.

Cassie puts the car in park, frowning. I know right away what the problem is. The property is not at all what she expected. When Jay said his parents owned a ranch in Aspen, he didn't mean a glitzy compound with horses and snowmobiles and hundreds of acres of coveted mountain terrain, like we'd imagined. He meant this: a one-story ranch house in a dirt cul-de-sac full of identical structures. Even in the dim light, I can see that the home is small and unremarkable, the siding cheap, paint-chipped.

I watch Cassie's jaw clench; a muscle pulses along her neck. Jay stands and waves, approaches the car. His smile is wide as he opens Cassie's door and pulls her out into his arms. He looks so genuinely happy, and I feel so badly for him in this moment. I know what's coming. I can already see what he doesn't.

The inside of the house is as basic as the exterior. Dated kitchen, small windows, a drably decorated living room with low popcorn ceilings and a shag carpet. I watch Cassie as she peers around, horrified. I watch Jay, on the verge of shame as he registers her disapproval. Remy yawns and squeezes my shoulder, oblivious to all of it.

"It's not much." Jay shrugs awkwardly. "Just a simple mountain house. My grandfather bought it for next to nothing in the seventies."

After what feels like an eternity of silence, Cassie speaks. "I thought you said your place was in Aspen." Her mouth is a hard line. "We're an hour from there."

Jay fidgets with his hands. "It's Carbondale, technically. It's forty minutes to Aspen proper without traffic. I'll show you tomorrow." He gives a strained smile, looks toward the kitchen. "You guys must be wiped from all the travel. How about a drink?"

"Where are your parents?" Cassie asks, ignoring him. I sense the challenge in her voice, the need to prove something to Jay, to herself.

"They flew back to Chicago. They're dying to meet you, Cass, but they knew all three of you were coming. There's obviously not . . . a ton of space. They didn't want to get in our way."

I clear my throat to break the tension and announce that I'd love a shower. Jay, who seems grateful for the interruption, shows Remy and me to our room at the end of the hall. We crash down on the double bed, and I bury my face into his chest, relieved that we're alone.

"*Maybe this was a mistake,*" I tell him.

Remy laughs. "*And I was about to say that it feels nice to be in the mountains.*"

I inhale the warm, clovey smell of his neck. "*I didn't know you'd spent time in the mountains.*"

He nods, playing with my hair. "*My grandparents rented a house outside Burlington for a couple of summers when I was young. Not quite the Rockies, but beautiful.*"

I close my eyes and picture Remy as a child. Small but still lanky, curls untamed, same wild laugh.

"*I bet you were a cute kid.*"

"*Oh, I was the cutest.*"

I smile against him. "*Cuter than I am?*"

"*Hmm . . . not possible.*" A beat of silence passes. "*We'd make pretty cute babies, Billie.*"

There's a punch of panic in my chest, unexpected, languidly morphing into something that resembles fear. I say nothing, and eventually Remy's fingers stop looping through my hair. His breathing grows heavy and even; I listen to the thumping beat of his heart as his chest rises and falls. He's asleep. A few minutes later, so am I.

When I wake, it's dark, and someone is shaking my shoulders. I blink, my eyelids heavy with sleep. My vision slowly adjusts as I remember where I am.

"*Billie.*"

Cassie is standing beside the bed, the outline of her body barely perceptible. "*We need to go,*" she says.

"*Now? What time is it?*"

"*Late. Jay and I had a fight. We're done. We can't stay here.*"

Beside me, Remy begins to stir.

"*Cass.*" I rub my forehead. "*Tell me this isn't because of the house. It's just a ski house.*"

"*Jay lied to me, Billie. He said his parents' place was in Aspen, and it's not. Not even close.*"

I groan. "*Maybe he was just trying to impress you.*"

"*And it's not a ski house. Get this—Jay doesn't even ski.*" Cassie switches on a lamp, harsh yellow light stabbing my eyes. "*He says his family comes here in the winter to go snowshoeing in the woods. Like, what the actual fuck?"*

I sit up, swing my legs over the side of the bed. I feel grubby and hot, still in my clothes from the plane. I'm tempted to remind Cassie that I don't ski, either. That neither does Remy. But it feels pointless.

"Where are we supposed to go in the middle of the night?"

Cassie lets out a shaky breath, and I absorb the sight of her. Blood-shot eyes, blotchy skin, long, tangled hair. Broken, yet somehow still so undeniably beautiful.

The mattress squeaks as Remy rolls off the other side of the bed. He rubs his eyes and doesn't so much as glance at Cassie as he walks into the bathroom. Through the awning window, the outside lights illuminate fat flakes of snow dancing down from the sky.

"We can find a hotel," Cassie says. "I have my parents' emergency credit card."

"You're not supposed to use that," I remind her.

"I can't stay here, Billie." Her voice is suddenly panicked, thick with tears. "This feels all wrong. How did I get this so wrong?"

I shrug, already defeated. Already knowing, as I have for so many years, that I'll follow her wherever she needs to go.

As we're loading our bags into the trunk of the rental, Cassie turns to me, snow swirling in front of her face, the fresh powder squeaking underneath her boots. Remy is a few steps behind us, shutting the Crowleys' front door, ready to snap.

"You're so lucky." Cassie's breath clouds the freezing air as her gaze moves from Remy to me.

I'm not sure what she means, or perhaps I wonder if what I think she might mean can possibly be true. That she sees her own demons, that she's tired of looking for something she might never find. Of trying to become someone she might never be.

The thought sparks my heart with an involuntary flicker of hope. I pretend not to notice the tears that stream down her face as she drives us into the dark, frigid night.

Chapter Thirty-nine

Cassie

October 16, 2023
3 days after

"Well, your girl is as healthy as a horse." Dr. Marconi touches Ella's head, casting Grant and me a reassuring smile.

I despise these kinds of platitudes, particularly right now, and am about to object when Grant thanks the pediatrician for her time, and she slips out the door. Every doctor in this city is always rushing, always pulled in a new direction that's more pressing and important than wherever they've been.

Grant turns to me, his expression soft with relief. "That's great, right?"

I shrug, zipping Ella's fleece jacket and securing the pink hood over her ears. It's a cool morning. "No signs of foul play." I repeat what Dr. Marconi said, what Detective Barringer has said, as if somehow the truth of that statement is supposed to erase the trauma that leaches into my veins like a toxin.

We grab coffee from Ralph's on the way home from the pediatrician. I stir milk and two Sugar in the Raw packets into mine while Grant sips his usual black, Ella nestled in the carrier strapped to his chest. An older woman with a short gray bob tells us what a beautiful family we have. She grabs one of Ella's feet and squeezes, and I'm not ready for this, not prepared for what the sight of a stranger touching my baby does to my emotional state.

"You need to get your hands off her," I snap. The color leaks from Grant's face.

The woman bristles as if I've just slapped her, which maybe I should've. She rushes out of Ralph's without a word, a few customers staring in my direction, their expressions alarmed, judgmental.

"Jesus Christ, Cassie!" Grant barks when we're out on the street, the late-morning sun strong overhead. "You can't talk to people like that. That woman was like eighty years old."

"It's not okay to just touch people's babies. She should know better."

"She was just a sweet old lady. She probably has grandkids of her own."

"You don't know *who* she was, Grant!" I storm a few steps ahead, sensing my own unraveling as it's happening, powerless to stop the psychosis taking over my brain.

Back at the apartment, I startle when I walk into the kitchen and see Lourdes bent over the sink, up to her elbows in soapsuds.

"Oh my God, Lourdes, you scared me." A hand flies to my collarbone, my heart racing. "I—I forgot it was Monday."

She smiles brightly, turns off the faucet, and dries her hands with a dish towel. "Morning! How was the party?"

The tears press against my throat like it's a pipe about to burst, but I won't let myself cry. It's too much to explain to someone who wasn't there that night. Grant walks in behind me, unclips Ella from the carrier. Lourdes reaches for her excitedly; she adores Ella, she's fantastic with her, but it's no longer enough.

I want to scream, to evaporate into nothing as I watch Lourdes take over, whisking Ella off to the nursery for a fresh diaper.

"I'm going to work from home for as much of the day as I can, but I have a meeting uptown at two—" Grant stops short when he sees my face. "Cassie. What is it?"

"I forgot she was coming." My face burns with shame, with fear, with helplessness. "Did you?"

Grant sets his cardboard cup on the counter. "No. I texted to let her know we were taking Ella to the doctor and would be back around ten."

I screw my eyes shut, the tears spilling over. "I don't think I can do this, Grant."

"Do *what*, Cassie?"

I shake my head. "I don't want anyone else in the house."

"But it's just Lourdes. I have to work. *You* have to work."

"I *can't* work, Grant. Not right now." My voice is squeaky, tight.

His arms fall open at his sides. "Look, I don't know what to say to you. I get that you're freaked out, but Cass . . . you have to try to pull yourself together. Ella is safe. There were some drunk kids climbing up the fire escape—"

"You honestly believe that's what happened?"

"You don't?"

"I don't *know*, Grant!" The tears drip down my cheeks, my neck. "I really don't know. What if Lourdes—"

"Oh my God, you can't think what happened has anything to do with *Lourdes*!" Grant gives an exasperated sigh, pinching his sinuses in a way that makes me feel asinine, invisible. "Cassie, if you don't want to work today, go shower. Lie down. Take a minute for yourself. If you're worried about Ella, just tell Lourdes not to take her out. And for Christ's sake, I never thought I'd have to persuade you to do this, but check your goddamn phone."

My phone is plugged into the charger on my nightstand; I don't remember putting it there, so perhaps Grant did. I'm aware that avoiding my emails and texts and direct messages isn't going to help me, that I have no choice but to at least *peek* at the notifications I've ignored all weekend. My phone, which used to be my greatest source of dopamine besides Ella, now feels meaningless in my hand, an irrelevant object I could toss in the trash and forget.

I have one hundred and fifteen text messages, thirty-three missed calls, eighty-seven direct messages on Instagram, and so many DM requests that the app merely reads "99+" in the upper-right-hand corner. I scroll through my texts, past the names of close friends I haven't thought about in days: Ava, Evelyn, Allegra, Kate, Lisette. There are birthday wishes from my parents, and even Mara.

My email isn't terrible—mostly a bombardment of junk mail from the weekend. But now that it's Monday, there are a bunch of recent messages from Violet and Wendy that spike my blood with fresh anxiety. As if I can even think about Cassidy Adler right now. Just then, a new text from Violet flashes on top of the screen:

> Did you see my email about Johanna Ortiz? Also, are you
> ok? You've gone dark on Insta . . .

And then a text from McKay:

Picking up Sweetgreen for lunch! Kale Caesar for you?

My forehead prickles with sweat. I can't do this. I can't do life—not right now. Without really thinking, I craft a message to Billie. I just know, with certainty, that she's the only one who will help me without asking any questions. I send her contact information for Violet and Wendy at the SoHo and East Hampton stores, ask her to tell them there's been a family emergency, that everything is all right but I'm taking a few days off. I'll be in touch as soon as I can, but in the meantime, I trust them to make any and all decisions.

I navigate over to Instagram, where my feed provides me with the most important updates first. A girl I knew peripherally at Harvard had her second baby. A Malibu-based workout guru I follow has just announced her pregnancy, a boy due in March. Grant's younger cousin Sophie is engaged, her manicured hand slabbed against the fiancé's chest, ring finger glistening with a massive, emerald-cut diamond.

Normally, I would freak over something like this. I'd leave a supportive row of exclamation points and heart emojis under the photo with the subconscious hope that Sophie's friends would see my comment and recognize my handle, ask her how she knows me. *That's my cousin's wife,* I'd imagine Sophie explaining, secretly proud. *She'll be at the wedding.*

I tap the upper-right-hand corner of the screen to check my direct messages. I won't read them in full—there are too many—but I glance through the names. Most of the older messages from Friday and Saturday are replies to my stories from the party, friends and strangers wishing me a happy birthday. The more recent DMs are mostly from people I don't know, users who think it's appropriate to write things like: *Where are you??? You haven't posted all weekend! Come back to us!*

It strikes me now, how creepy it all is. How little it actually matters, the validation of these strangers. Faceless usernames that covet my clothes, that think my daughter is cute, that want to know what serums I use to battle sun damage and fine lines. But each seemingly inconsequential interaction has amounted to something valuable, forty-eight thousand followers who define me, who've granted me a kind of power I could never fathom abandoning.

Until now.

I scroll further through my DMs. I know which message I'm looking for; I know rereading it is only going to induce fresh panic, but it's
like googling medical symptoms: I can't help but terrorize myself to the
max.

birchballer6: *Returning to the scene of the crime, are we?*

Just then, a response from Billie appears at the top of the screen:
Done! How are you feeling today?

I place my phone back on the nightstand, scoot forward on the
rumpled duvet. The door to our bedroom is ajar, and I notice, suddenly, how silent the apartment is. It's so quiet I can hear my own
heartbeat, the even thump of my pulse.

Panic scrabbles in my chest. I dart out of the room, each of my
senses shot awake as I run through the apartment, searching for a sign
of them. I find Grant in his office, peering at his extra-wide monitor,
the screen covered in charts and graphs I don't understand.

"Have you seen Ella and Lourdes?" I'm panting, out of breath.
"They're not in the kitchen or the family room *or* her nursery!" Tears
are leaking down my face—sudden, uncontrollable.

Grant spins toward me in his swivel chair, ankles crossed. "Did
you tell Lourdes to stay in the apartment? If not, maybe they went
for a walk."

"I didn't, but—she usually tells me before they leave." Stabs of fear
slice through me, taking me straight back to Friday night, to the gutting memory of Ella's empty stroller.

Grant hands me a box of Kleenex from his desk. He puffs air into
his cheeks, looking vaguely annoyed. "I'm sure everything is fine,
Cass. Just call Lourdes if you're worried."

"I'm obviously worried!" I press a tissue to my face, feel it grow
soggy with tears. "My phone is in the bedroom."

Grant picks up his own phone, tapping the screen to put the call to
Lourdes on speaker. It rings several times before going to voicemail.

I feel as if I'm floating, absent from my own body except for the
terror. How could I have been so stupid as to leave Ella with a stranger,
not even three days after she was kidnapped? I make my way back into
my body, into my voice, and say as much to Grant.

"Lourdes isn't a stranger, Cassie. She's been with us for months. She adores Ella."

I shake my head. "We need to call the police."

Grant's jaw clenches as he stands, a muscle twitching along his neck. He brushes past me in the doorway, inadvertently knocking the box of Kleenex from my hand.

I follow him as he paces down the hallway, past the powder room and the kitchen and Ella's nursery and her bathroom, stopping to check each space. When he reaches the master at the end of the hall, he turns around and heads back to the other end of the apartment, toward the foyer. He pauses outside the living room, his gaze lingering on the windows. No, not the windows. The terrace doors. The blinds are still closed the way I left them, but one of the doors is cracked. Grant gets there before I do, pushing it all the way open, sunlight pouring through the apartment in thick golden rays.

And there is Ella, cooing happily in her BabyBjörn chair while Lourdes bounces her, carefree smiles on both their faces.

I race toward my daughter, crouching beside her chair and smothering her with kisses. If Lourdes notices I've been crying, she doesn't say anything.

"It's such a nice day!" Lourdes reaches an arm up toward the cloudless blue sky. "Baby girl needs fresh air."

But the terrace—why the *terrace*? And today of all days. I twist my neck back, my eyes landing on Grant's. He is staring at me, frowning, hands in his pockets. A silent order passes through his clipped gaze: *Get your shit together, Cassie.*

"Great idea, Lourdes." Grant's frown flips into a warm smile. "Enjoy the sunshine. I need to get back to work."

I linger near Ella, her tiny fist wrapping my pointer finger as my heartbeat slows back down. Normally, I pride myself on being a relaxed employer, the antithesis of a helicopter mom. I give Lourdes free rein to take Ella wherever she wants—the park, the playground, lunch dates with other nannies and their charges. It's a system that's allowed me to do my job, often from the quiet solitude of the apartment, while knowing my daughter is safe.

Except now, I don't know. Now, she isn't safe with anyone except for me. Not actually.

I hear Grant calling my name from inside. Reluctantly, I stand, and just untangling my finger from Ella's grasp is enough to fill my throat with more tears.

I find Grant standing in the foyer with McKay. She looks rested and polished, her hair cascading past her shoulders in perfect, Airwrap-blown waves. She flashes me a wide smile, a paper bag from Sweetgreen hooked in the crevice of her elbow.

"McKay says you two are having lunch," Grant says impatiently. "Now, I *really* have to get back to work."

Fuck. I forgot McKay said she was coming over with Sweetgreen. Now that I think of it, she didn't even *ask* if she could come over, or if I was available for lunch. What makes her so presumptuous, so entitled to my time?

"You never answered my text," she's saying, kicking off her Chanel flats and making her way into the kitchen. "So I got you your usual Kale Caesar. The order of a true basic bitch." She looks over at me and laughs, inviting me to join, but the joke falls flat.

"Wait." She pauses as she's unpacking the salads. "Let's eat these in the park instead. It's fucking gorgeous out. Indian summer."

My stomach drops, churning. "You're not supposed to say shit like that anymore. And I'd rather just eat here."

McKay glances up; her eyes search my face. "Oh, Cass. You're still a full-on mess, aren't you?"

Frustration simmers behind my sternum. "McKay, of course I'm a mess. What do you expect?"

She sighs, popping the plastic top off my salad, then her own. She reaches into the silverware drawer and hands me a fork.

"Grant was just telling me the good news from the detective." She slides onto a counter stool and digs into her food. The only time I truly see McKay eat with abandon is when it's a salad. Even if there are big chunks of feta and oily croutons and the lettuce is minimal. It doesn't make much sense.

I lower myself onto the stool beside her, trailing my fork through the dark lettuce. The Kale Caesar was always Billie's order at Sweetgreen, too. When we were broke twenty-two-year-olds living on East Eleventh Street, she'd sometimes bring a single salad home and we'd split it for dinner. We'd throw in a few hard-boiled eggs to make it more filling.

"I wouldn't necessarily say it's good news," I tell McKay.

"Why not? It seems like they solved the mystery. I mean, it makes sense, right?" She shoves a wad of arugula down her throat. The way she chews reminds me of a farm animal, a cow in a pasture ripping grass from the ground with its teeth. I watch the bite travel down her neck. "A couple of drunk kids dicking around, maybe one of them dares the other to take the baby. Then they realize their dumb mistake." McKay shrugs. "Sounds plausible."

I shake my head. "Not to me. Whoever brought her back . . . they knew which apartment was ours. A couple of drunk teenagers stupid enough to take someone's baby wouldn't be smart enough to figure out which terrace correlates with apartment 9A."

McKay stops chewing, swallows. She studies me carefully, the way she always does when I've said something that surprises her.

"Maybe it was one of your followers. Some psychopath troll hater on the internet."

"Yeah. I'm worried it might've been." Fear opens in the lowest part of my stomach as I think about how much I've shared on social media, the access I've given thousands of random people into my world.

McKay turns back to her lunch. "Well, whatever happened, here's the good news: if the person in question had actually *wanted* to kidnap Ella, they would've done it."

I resist the urge to scream. "Why does everyone keep saying that?"

"Because it's true, Cass."

"Not necessarily." I dig my nails into the soapstone counter until pain shoots up toward my knuckles. "If it *was* a follower, it would've been premeditated, not random. So maybe the person was trying to fuck with me, and this is only the beginning. And if so, it's only a matter of time until they come back for more." As these sentences leave me, I understand with crystalline clarity: *this* is the reason I'm truly afraid. This is why I can't sleep, can't eat, can't do anything but stare at my daughter and make sure she continues to breathe.

McKay scrapes the last bit of goat cheese from the bottom of her bowl. "God, I was starving." She drops her fork on the counter and peers over at my untouched salad. "You have to eat, Cassie."

"I don't *have* to do anything," I snap, shocking myself. I'm almost never short with McKay. "Sorry, I just . . . I'm not hungry."

She says nothing as she goes to the refrigerator and plucks two lemon Spindrifts from the side door. She holds one out to me. "Thirsty?"

"Thanks." I wrap my palm around the ice-cold can.

McKay leans against the center island and takes a small sip of seltzer. "So," she says, wiping her mouth with the back of her wrist. "Are you going to tell me what Billie was doing here the other day?"

I shrug. I know I should feel embarrassed, hypocritical—these are the emotional buttons McKay is trying to press—but I don't. Instead, I'm protective of whatever piece of my heart needs Billie right now, needs her for a reason I could never explain and don't fully understand.

"I'm just going through a lot," I manage, nibbling the edge of a parmesan crisp. It tastes terrible, like a chunk of salt, and I toss the rest back onto the bed of kale.

"Yeah, but *Billie*?" She isn't letting this go. "You don't even want her around during normal circumstances."

I say nothing, working to deflect the shame of this truth. This is the drawback of closeness with McKay: she knows her way under my skin and has no problem going there.

"Look, I'm sorry to say this, but someone has to." She pauses for a beat. "Is it possible Billie had something to do with Ella's disappearance?"

I frown. "McKay. Just stop."

"I'm serious, Cassie. You guys have this weird, one-sided friendship, she's obviously obsessed with you, she could've been angry that—"

"McKay!" My pulse hammers against my throat. "You don't know Billie, all right? What you're saying is completely unfounded, and—and—*offensive*. Billie would never in a million years have been the one to take Ella."

McKay rolls her eyes, but she drops it. "I'm here for you, Cassie. We all are." She gives a tender smile that feels simulated, like she's comforting a child. "Ava's super worried—she says she keeps calling and texting you but hasn't heard back. I guess you're not checking your phone, huh?"

"I can't deal with my phone right now."

"Well, a social media break never hurt anyone. But for *you,* it's different. I mean, you have a brand image to uphold. Your followers are going to wonder where the hell their fearless leader has run off to." McKay drinks more Spindrift. "Anyway, since you've been living under a rock, I *have* to catch you up on Adair's totally insane news . . ."

McKay shifts into gossip mode, recounting the latest update on Adair, who now lives in Charleston and who I've all but lost touch with, who I really only pretend to care about because McKay still seems to. McKay's hands move wildly as she shares that Adair, the mother of two-year-old twins, has recently discovered she's pregnant with another set of twins. "That'll be four two and under!" she shrieks. "Can you imagine?"

From there, McKay launches into an anecdote about Juliette's preschool teacher, who apparently read the class a wildly inappropriate book about sex and now isn't allowed to read the kids anything without approval from the preschool director. McKay speaks quickly, moving from story to story in a way that leaves me dizzy and numb, half listening to the words that fly from her mouth. But I nod along, managing to hum in agreement at most of the right moments, until finally she glances at her watch and announces she needs to get home.

"I forgot Hadley is coming over with wallpaper samples." She sighs as if meeting with her decorator is a chore. "Did I tell you we're redoing Finn's room? I hate everything I picked out when I was pregnant." She laughs, a hollow cackle that I can't match.

When she's gone, I find Lourdes vacuuming in Grant's office. He must have left for his meeting.

"Baby girl is happy today," Lourdes sings, powering off the Dyson. "She drank eight ounces before her nap."

I nod, the mention of milk bringing my awareness to the full feeling in my bra. I usually breastfeed Ella if I'm home when she needs to eat, but Lourdes must've assumed I was busy with McKay. I should go pump.

"*Gracias,* Lourdes." I stare at the oriental carpet, the thick red and gold fibers that cushion my feet. I'm afraid if I look up and meet her warm, cheerful gaze, I'll fall apart.

"You okay, Mrs. Adler?"

I force my head to lift. Lourdes's dark eyes study me, full of concern.

"Actually, Lourdes . . ." My chest tightens with shame, but I know what I have to do. "We're all set this week. I—I'll still pay you, but you should leave early today. Take the rest of the week off."

Her lips part in confusion, but I don't have the energy to try to translate. Lourdes's minimal English is one of the reasons Grant and I hired her—she primarily speaks to Ella in Spanish, which we always saw as a bonus. Perhaps our daughter could grow up bilingual, be capable of more than the occasional *gracias* like her parents.

"I'll text you," I tell Lourdes as I walk her to the foyer, her brow furrowed with uncertainty, or maybe worry. Guilt clobbers my insides at the knowledge of what I'm going to say in my text message, but I can't think about that right now. In some moments, all you can do is keep moving forward, turn a blind eye to the collateral damage of your own twisted circumstances.

After Lourdes is gone, I lock the dead bolt and wander back toward Ella's room, savoring the quiet of the apartment. I nudge the nursery door open, just enough to slip inside. When I peek over the edge of the crib, my whole body unclenches at the sight of her: eyes closed against flushed round cheeks, lips suckling the pacifier. The whole of her like a ripe, tender peach.

I curl into a ball on the soft carpet beside the crib, my own eyelids drooping with exhaustion. The white noise is heavy and peaceful, like rainfall. My daughter is here. Her scent, her body. The room is warm. For the first time in three days, I dissolve into a deep, dreamless sleep, where I'm free.

Chapter Forty
Billie

October 20, 2023
7 days after

"What a week."

Alex pours more wine into my plastic glass, then settles back onto his forearms. Dappled sunlight washes through the oak tree beside our picnic, shimmering gold against the red-checkered blanket. Scents of autumn in the city roll through Washington Square Park: dry leaves, sharp air, spicy meats from the halal truck on University Place.

It's Friday afternoon, and Alex and I have both ducked away from our jobs early for wine and cheese in the waning sun. I take a long sip of malbec, willing the alcohol to dull the guilt that worms through my system after the least productive workweek I've had in years. I nestle against Alex's chest, feel the soft cotton of his shirt, the strong beat of his heart.

"I'm so happy," he says, his fingers playing with my hair. "You make me so happy, Billie."

I want to respond with the words I really feel: *You make me so happy, too, Alex. You might make me too happy. Do you ever worry about that—about the price of becoming too happy?* But I'm paralyzed. The knowledge that he's looking into Cassie's case is like an invisible barrier between us that only I can detect, that forces my guard to stay put.

"I meant to tell you," he continues, sitting up and reaching for the cheese platter, my head sliding to his lap. "I had kind of a weird call from Barringer yesterday."

It's as if he's reading my mind. I watch him break off a piece of crumbly Boursin with a cracker, shove the whole thing in his mouth.

I sit up, too, adjusting my sunglasses. "What do you mean?" I will the nerves from my voice. I've made a point to try to avoid nudging him for updates on the case. The last thing I need is to appear over-curious.

"It was strange. He finally called me back to loop me in on his case notes. I guess he finished talking to everyone who was at the party last weekend, and nothing noteworthy or suspicious came up." Alex reaches for another cracker.

"Huh." I sip my wine, relieved. "So he's sticking with the drunk teenagers?"

"Seems like it. But that wasn't the weird part." Alex pauses, squint-ing into the sun. "He said he got a call from Cassie's friend McKay. Do you know her? She was one of the women at the dinner party, right?"

I nod. "She and Cassie are close. She's Grant's cousin."

"Right. Well . . ." Alex turns to face me, rubbing his jaw. "She told Barringer something about you, actually."

I freeze.

"Me?"

"This is off the record, obviously." The warm lines around Alex's eyes soften, his gaze growing intense. "But McKay told Barringer that the only person she could think of who might've had any motive for taking Ella . . . was you."

A combination of anger and fear simmers against my collarbone. "That's ridiculous. Why would she say that?"

"I guess because Cassie didn't invite you to the party?" Alex pauses, swirling the wine around in his cup. "I know it's ridiculous, obviously. I told him you were home with a migraine that night, that you bailed on me—and Jane—because you felt so awful."

"Jane?"

"Yeah." Alex stares at me blankly. "You were supposed to feed her cat."

"*Oh*. Right."

"And Jane backed up your alibi to both Barringer and me, so there's really nothing to worry about."

My heart turns to stone. "You talked to Jane?"

"I had to, Billie. I wanted to nip any unfounded accusations in the bud." He refills his glass, then mine. "I didn't realize she'd moved to the same building as Cassie, though. That's a pretty fucking crazy coincidence."

I feel paralyzed, suctioned to the picnic blanket, like if I wanted to jump up and run away, my synapses wouldn't fire.

Alex runs a hand through his hair and laughs, and I feel it then: the certainty that he suspects nothing. That he's genuinely shocked by the coincidence of Jane and Cassie's shared address, just as I was.

"*So crazy, right?*" I raise an eyebrow, cracking a smile. I need to match his energy. "I thought I'd told you that."

A couple of girls on Rollerblades speed by, pigtails flying underneath their helmets. I think of the time Cassie and I went Rollerblading on her street, how I lost my balance on a hill and slid down the asphalt, a giant raspberry scorching the side of my thigh. I remember the pain when she lowered me into the bathtub to wash the cut, how I screamed so psychotically we both started laughing, even as tears of agony streamed down my face.

"There's more, though," Alex is saying, breaking off another hunk of Boursin. "Barringer mentioned that when he met you at Cassie's the other day, you told him you weren't at the party because you had a migraine. So he was confused when he heard from McKay that you hadn't been invited at all." Alex swallows the cheese, his eyes on my face. "And he asked me directly, so . . . I told him. Not that I think anything else McKay said to Barringer is credible, but I told him I didn't think you were invited. 'Cause you weren't, right? Otherwise, wouldn't we have planned to go?" The corners of his lips curve. "Unless you have some other boyfriend I don't know about, who you were planning on taking instead."

I glance down into my glass of malbec, a few pieces of pollen floating in what little remains. I'm tipsy, but I have to answer his question, and I can't waver. I have to be solid, certain, clear. I dig through the wine fog for the right response, reminding myself that Alex is on my side.

I draw in a deep breath. "No, I wasn't invited. I only said that about having a migraine because Cassie was sitting right there when the detective asked." I close my eyes behind my sunglasses, remembering the way Cassie introduced me to Barringer. *This is Billie. My oldest friend. She stayed over last night.* "I could sense she felt awkward admitting she hadn't invited me, especially after giving Barringer the impression that we were close."

Alex nods. "Okay. That makes sense." He hesitates. "Kind of rude she didn't invite you, though. Right? From what I gather, it wasn't a small party."

At first, his words are salt in a wound. Then I remember: everything is different now. Cassie needs me again. The salt doesn't stick.

"You know we have a complicated relationship," I offer.

"Yeah. I'm still trying to figure out exactly what that means." Alex taps my temple. "Want to tell me what's going on up here? You've been off all week."

"I—well, I just feel so badly for Cassie." I shrug, redirecting the conversation and hoping he doesn't notice. "What she's going through is heavy. And I'm trying to be there for her, but also . . . her energy affects me, you know?" The sun moves behind a thick cloud, leaving us in cool shadows.

"You *are* there for her, Billie. You've been over at her place every day after work."

Because she needs me, I think, unable to quell the sense of victory that sparks in my chest. Alex is right. I've spent the past week shuttling between my place and his and Cassie's. And even though work has taken a hit, I feel a sense of purpose I haven't had since before Cassie met Grant. A sense of duty to our friendship that fulfills me like nothing else can.

"Well, I wasn't there today," I remind Alex, reaching for his hand. I interlace our fingers, run my thumb in circles through the center of his palm. "So, what's your next move with the case? How much longer will you spend helping Cassie?" I shouldn't be asking, but the wine has left me loose, uninhibited. I'm not ready to drop the subject.

"I can't say I've really helped her at all." Alex stretches his legs out long on the blanket. "I still have to look into the Instagram stuff—Cassie sent over a list of haters, a.k.a. followers who've sent her disparaging messages over the years. And I need to go through all the security footage."

I stiffen. "The footage Barringer already checked?"

"Another set of eyes can't hurt." He sighs. "There's not much else I can do, but I promised Cassie and Grant I'd try." He picks up the bottle of malbec, peers into the empty base. "It's getting kind of cold. How about we go for one more drink? Maybe an early dinner?"

I nod, and he leans in to kiss me, his tongue sliding past my teeth. I savor the taste of him, salt and hints of cherry from the wine.

The next morning, I'm leaving Alex's apartment when he presses a silver key into my fingers.

I glance up at him, waiting for an explanation. He tucks a loose strand of hair behind my ear. "I thought it might be convenient for you to have this. So you don't have to wait next door at the bodega if I'm stuck somewhere for work." He shrugs, as if we both don't know that happened only once. "Don't overthink it, Bill." His lips brush mine, and there's an intimacy in the way he speaks as someone who really knows me. Who gets me.

My walk home from Alex's is chilly, the sky a pale mass of white overhead, a few drops of rain leaking through. I grab a second coffee from Starbucks, which I drink in bed, huddled under the covers with my laptop as wind whistles against my poorly insulated windows. It's Saturday morning, but I have so much email to catch up on that the sight of my inbox is dizzying, and a few of my clients seem legitimately annoyed. I normally pride myself on being ultra-responsive.

I sip my latte and tackle a reply to an angry client currently on vacation in Anguilla. He's an angel investor named Emerson who's reaming me out because his room at the Malliouhana—which he claims was supposed to boast ocean views—tragically faces the garden. I call the hotel, and after an hour and a half, we finally get it sorted.

This is the shit part of my job—indulging rich people like Emerson who will always find a reason to be angry, even while vacationing at a five-star resort in the middle of paradise. I think of my proposition to Jane, of the legitimate possibility that The Path could become a charitable company, one that would make me feel slightly better about catering to the Emersons of the world. I make a mental note to follow up with Jane when she's back from Iceland on Monday.

I spend the next few hours in a blur of emails and spreadsheets and phone calls to high-end properties, my coffee growing cold beside me, too in the zone to make myself an actual meal. Eventually, I pull a bag of cinnamon rice cakes into the bed—a habit I can't get away with at Alex's—and eat them mechanically, crumbs falling to the sheets.

By two, my inbox is manageable again, and my reward is my phone. There's a message from Alex, asking where I want to meet for dinner before the Comedy Cellar tonight. We have tickets to the nine thirty show.

Minetta Tavern? I reply. I can never remember if they take reservations.

My only other text is from Cassie, a Spotify link to an Alanis Morissette album we loved in high school. Been listening to this all morning! I think Ella loves her as much as we did.

My chest warms, and I send back a few heart emojis.

I open Instagram next, greeted by a boring feed, the recent highlights of people I don't particularly care about. Esme's sister had a bridal shower at Brooklyn Winery; an old coworker traveled to Ireland and has shared ten identical photos of the Cliffs of Moher.

Instinctively, I narrow my eyes and search the top of the screen for her avatar—long brown hair, white strapless maxi dress—but of course it isn't there. She hasn't posted in a full week now. The account has gone silent, and I realize, with a pang of irony, what a dull place Instagram has become without @cassidyadler. The source of so much eye-rolling intrigue, so much angst and frustration—vanished. I lie back against the soft pillows and close my eyes, wondering why I miss it.

Chapter Forty-one

Billie

2010–2011

After graduation, Cassie and I move to New York. It isn't up for debate; we've both wanted to live in Manhattan post-college since seeing Working Girl *in seventh grade. We envision ourselves as young Melanie Griffiths—minus the perm—riding elevators up skyscrapers and taking the workforce by storm, Carly Simon's "Let the River Run" booming in the background.*

Cassie uses her English degree to get a job as an editorial assistant at Elle, *a highly coveted position that somehow pays less than minimum wage. I manage to land an entry-level sales role at Expedia, where my salary is hardly higher. Together, the only living situation we can afford is a four-hundred-square-foot studio on East Eleventh Street in Alphabet City. We make it work by shoving two twin beds against the far wall, where the windows look out at the adjacent building, a panorama of brick. There's a mini fridge and a two-burner hot plate in the minuscule kitchen, a bathroom so narrow that the shower hangs over the toilet.*

But the apartment is ours. We've made it to New York.

Everyone else seems to have a lot more money. Becca and Esme live in a sleek, newly renovated building in the Financial District with a gym and in-unit laundry. But their rent is subsidized by their parents, who recognize that surviving in Manhattan on an entry-level salary is next to impossible. Cassie and I are in a different boat. I still get my monthly stipend from Mom, but it's barely enough to cover a grocery run.

Being scrappy and poor doesn't bother me. It feels temporary, like buying Two Buck Chuck and being strict about taking the subway are all part of a rite of passage. Financial security seems like something that comes later.

On the best nights, Cassie and I bring a bottle of wine up to the roof of our building and watch the sunset. We're not technically allowed on the roof, but no one ever seems to notice. Our eyes gaze out over the urban sprawl as the orange sun drops behind the skyscrapers, bathing the city in a wash of gold. We talk about everything and nothing, conversations that flow into the darkness without structure or time constraints. The weight of real adulthood looms, not yet ours to carry. There's a precious transience to this time, the bittersweet sense that it won't always be this way. That it can't.

Remy and I are doing long distance, for now. He'll move to New York in the summer, after his lease is up in Back Bay.

One Friday in April, he comes down from Boston, and the next morning, we take the train up to Poughkeepsie to see Mom. She hasn't met Remy, and even though introducing them feels pointless, I still want to. I've spent loads of time with Remy's family in Winchester, so it only seems fair. Besides, no one knows how long Mom has left.

Remy and I leave the apartment for Grand Central as Cassie is putting on makeup in the bathroom. McKay is having a birthday brunch—some day-drinking thing at the Frying Pan—and Cassie got the invite. She's been giddy all week.

"Have fun," I call on our way out.

"Thanks," she mumbles, not peeling her gaze from the mirror as she dusts her face with bronzer. Cassie gets grumpy when Remy stays over, which I understand. Our apartment is too tiny for guests. It's why Remy hardly comes here. Most of the time, I'm the one visiting him in Boston.

On the train, I drink an iced latte and devour the new issue of Condé Nast Traveler while Remy naps. I swear, that man could fall asleep in the middle of an earthquake.

Mom's apartment is walking distance from the train station. Sandra opens the front door when we arrive. Her appearance is permanently unchanged; she looks exactly the same as she did six years ago. I'm hit with a sudden wave of affection for Sandra, for devoting so much of her life to Mom. For being here all this time. When she throws her arms around me, I fight back tears.

We find Mom out on the deck, which has a view of the river. She's sitting in front of a small terrarium, peering inside. When she hears our footsteps, she looks up. A childish grin spreads across her face.

"Hello." She turns back to the terrarium, taps the glass. "This is my frog, Frank. Want to meet him?"

It's a short visit, as it has to be. Mom doesn't have much stamina for visitors these days, and it's still painful for me to see her like this. Time hasn't softened the blow of becoming a stranger to the person I love most in the world.

Remy suggests grabbing a drink or a late lunch in Poughkeepsie, but I just want to go back to the city. He holds my hand on the train, his eyes fixed to my face. I can feel his concern, an amalgamation of shock and sympathy.

"She's beautiful, Billie." His voice is heavy, like it's holding something. "You look just like her."

I try to smile, but the corners of my mouth won't lift. "That isn't Mom."

"I know." He squeezes my fingers. "But still. Thank you for letting me meet her."

"Of course. I wanted you to."

We sit in silence for a few minutes as the train roars south.

"It must never get easier," Remy says after a while. "Seeing her like that."

I rest my head against his shoulder. "I think what I hate most is that she can't know the person I've become. She can't be proud of me. And she can't know the people who have become everything in my life. Like you."

"Yeah." He pauses. "Like your future kids. Our kids."

I freeze. The punch of fear in my chest is back, the same one I felt in Carbondale two years ago, the night Remy said we'd make cute babies. But the punch is stronger this time.

"Rem." I can't help but pull away from him; it's instinctual, the sudden impulse to need my body to myself. "We're a little young to be talking about kids. I'm twenty-three."

"Yeah, and I'm twenty-seven."

The panic unfurls, leaching into my veins. "So?"

"So, I'm not saying we're ready to be parents now, or any time soon. But it's a given part of our future, even if it's distant."

"What do you mean, it's a given?"

Remy rakes a hand through his curls, his eyebrows knitting together.

"I'm moving to New York in two months, Billie. I have a whole life in Boston, my family is there, and I'm leaving all of it, for you."

My throat feels tight, my breath stuck there. I don't realize I'm crying until I feel the tears dripping down my face, the taste of salt in my mouth.

"Remy—" My voice cracks, and even though it's wrong, I know I can use the circumstances of this moment to my advantage. I can buy myself more time. "I love you, and I'm counting the days until we're in the same city, but can we just . . . not do this right now?" I wipe my face with my sleeve. "It's been a rough day."

His gray eyes soften, and for a moment, I almost feel guilty.

"Of course." He wraps an arm around me, pulls me close. "I'm sorry, Bill. I love you, too. Just close your eyes. We don't have to talk."

In the blackness behind my eyelids, I see Mom out on the deck in Poughkeepsie. The way she hardly looked at Remy or me, her gaze passing over us with minimal interest before turning back to Frank the Frog.

And then—perhaps because of the topic Remy just tried to broach—I realize something else. I can't remember the last time I had a period.

Chapter Forty-two

Cassie

October 21, 2023
8 days after

A scream rips through me. The woman is ahead, a flash of dark hair, fitted black dress slowing her down, her steps little shuffles. Sunlight steals through the next cross street, illuminating the pilled fabric of her tight dress. She is slow, but I am slower, my legs dragging through water as I fight to keep up, reaching, wailing. I see my daughter's chubby thigh wrapped around the side of the woman's body, Ella's perfect face peering back at me, brow furrowed, lips parted as if she wants to call out, as if she'd speak if she were able.

Mama.

Mama mama mama mama mama mama mama.

They round the corner. By the time I do, too, they are halfway down the block. The air is cold and smells chalky, like imminent rain. I am gaining on her, steadily. Because I'm still running, even against the pounding wind that feels like molasses sinking into my limbs. Because I'm not done fighting, because I'll never be done fighting. As long as I live, I will be a mother, and this will be my purpose.

I look for Ella, but she isn't there, no longer on the woman's hip. Cold panic opens in my chest. Where is Ella?

Then I see.

The stroller.

The woman is pushing the stroller now; the street is crowded, but I see the pale blue canopy, the wheels moving against the bumpy sidewalk several feet ahead. I have to be faster. Braver.

The muscles in my legs burn with fatigue, but I push through, weaving between a flock of children in plaid school uniforms. I reach out, my fingers like tentacles as I clamp them into her hair, yanking her back by the roots.

She cries out in pain, her grip on the handlebar loosening, her long swan neck twisting around. Her eyes—wild, liquid blue—land on mine.

My eyes.

Mara's eyes.

But then Mara's face is changing, nose beginning to bulge, eyes shrinking to small, black beads. Sweat slicks her puffy skin, pores gleaming. It's no longer Mara.

It's Wade.

You know you killed me, right? He is amused, his fleshy chin quivering with laughter.

You killed me.

The voice echoes, but it doesn't belong to him. It's the voice of someone I love—clear, modulated, a little throaty. The voice belongs to Billie.

You killed me, she is singing, he is singing.

I glance down just as his fingers release the handlebar, and the stroller moves forward with an icy puff of wind. Blood zips back into my legs. Awareness, energy. I sprint after the stroller, catching it just before it descends over a small pitch.

My heart lifts as I bend toward the bassinet, ready to scoop her into my arms, to smell her skin, to become whole again.

But she isn't there. The bassinet is empty. Ella is gone.

Bye, baby, calls a voice that belongs to Wade, then Mara, then Billie.

This time, the sound of my own howling jolts me awake. Sweat runs down my forehead, through the hollow between my breasts. I glance to the left, shaken by yet another iteration of my new recurring nightmare—the fifth in a row now. But Grant's side of the bed is empty, the duvet smooth where his slumbering body should be, and then I remember: he slept in the guest room. He couldn't stand another night of interrupted sleep, of being woken to the sound of his wife's piercing screams. I'm alone with my own terror.

I take the baby monitor and go to the kitchen, where I find Grant reading *The Times* and drinking a green juice. He's dressed in gym clothes, his neon sneakers laced. He does this sometimes—acts healthy on the weekends. Pretends to be the kind of man who likes jogging and liquified spinach, instead of an overworked investor with high blood pressure who guzzles scotch at night and hits the midtown halal cart more days than not.

"You're up early," I say. Morning light sluices through the kitchen windows, reaching across the wood floor in wide beams.

"I'm meeting Tom for a run at eight." Grant doesn't glance up from the paper.

"Impressive." I pause. "So, I had the nightmare again—"

"Cassie." Grant holds up a hand, his tone brusque. When he finally looks at me, his gaze is glacial. "I texted Lourdes."

I draw in a breath, brace myself. "Okay."

"I asked her if she could come early next Monday, since I have an eight o'clock meeting and I know that's the morning you like to do CorePower Yoga with McKay and Ava."

"I can skip CorePower—"

"And do you know what she said?" Grant's eyes narrow, his jaw clenched. "She informed me that she no longer works for us."

I say nothing, remembering the message I sent Lourdes last week.

"What the hell, Cassie? You told me you'd given her a few days off while you got your shit together. You didn't tell me you *fired* our nanny."

Grant's use of the word fills me with shame. I think of the text I carefully crafted, how I used Google Translate to explain to Lourdes that in a turn of events, we no longer needed her at all. I stressed that it wasn't her fault, that I would be working fewer hours and no longer required full-time care for Ella.

"This is insanity," Grant snaps. "You've really fucking lost it, haven't you?"

A headache sits behind my eye sockets, little throbbing clenches of pain. I'm in desperate need of coffee after sleeping like shit again.

"You've taken it too far," Grant is saying, and I wish he would stop speaking.

The baby monitor emits a low crackle in my hand, and I jump, check the screen to make sure Ella is still asleep. Still breathing. Still there at all.

"I was going to tell you." I sigh. "You don't have to guilt-trip me, Grant. I feel terrible, but I let Lourdes go for my own well-being—"

"That's exactly the problem, Cassie." Grant stands, slams his hand on top of the counter. "You just think about *you,* but what about me? What about Ella? You're too self-involved to realize that she loves Lourdes, that having help is good for our whole family. It wasn't just your decision to make. And putting the poor woman out of work—"

"I'm giving her two months' pay while she finds another job!"

"Oh, that's a great use of my money. Thanks."

"*Your* money?" A bolt of anger surges in my chest. My eyes burn with exhaustion.

"Okay, our money. But it wouldn't be ours if it weren't for me, would it, Cass?" Grant's words are snide, dripping with derision.

"Fuck you," I spit. "Don't stand there and pretend like you did anything to earn your trust fund. Like you did anything other than be born lucky."

Grant's gaze hardens; a muscle pulses along his neck. "I'm getting really, *really* worried about you," he says, but his voice is full of condescension, not actual concern. "You need to talk to someone. I'll give Tom's guy a call on Monday. You know he went through some stuff last year, after his dad died."

"You're delusional if you think I'm seeing Tom's therapist."

Grant shakes his head, grabs his phone from where it lies beside the newspaper. "I'm leaving."

"It's not even seven. You said you're meeting Tom at eight."

"Then I'll take a walk around the block. I can't be here right now. I can't even look at you." He turns away from me, storming out of the kitchen before I have time to respond.

"Wait!" I call behind him. "Can you at least start the coffee before you go? My head is killing me."

"No," he barks, his voice fading as it disappears down the hall. "You can make your own fucking coffee, Cassie."

I hear the jingle of his keys, the hard slam of the front door.

I close my eyes, succumb to the pain that snakes itself around my brittle heart. I agree with Grant on one thing, at least. I can't be here right now, either.

Chapter Forty-three

Billie

October 21, 2023
8 days after

I've just gotten out of the shower when the buzzer sounds—a scraping, offensively loud noise that makes me jump every time.

I press the gray button beside the speaker. "Who is it?"

"It's Cassie. And Ella!"

I glance at the time on the intercom—it's just after three. I buzz them up. Leaving the door cracked, I throw on leggings and a sweater and am running a comb through my hair when Cassie appears in my bedroom, Ella snug in the carrier against her chest.

"Hey." I flash a perplexed grin, thrown by the sight of Cassie standing in my apartment. This is the first time she's set foot here. "I'm surprised you know my address."

"Christmas card spreadsheet." Her expression is contrite, hands on her hips. Something about her body language is slightly off. "I should've come to see your new place a long time ago."

"Well, it's not really new anymore . . ."

"Right." She glances around, taking in the details of the room. My stuff is mostly a hodgepodge of Facebook Marketplace finds, a cheap cream rug from Wayfair. Nothing in my bedroom is particularly nice, except for the walnut dresser, an antique from our house in Red Hook. It used to be Mom's bureau, and it's one of the only pieces of furniture I opted to keep when the house sold.

Cassie runs her hand along the glossy wood surface. "I remember this dresser." She reaches for a small silver frame, a picture of Mom and me from forever ago. I can't be older than five, and I'm lying against her on the hammock in the backyard, Mom's arm wrapped around my chest. My smile is sleepy and content, but hers—as usual—is big and bright, creasing her eyes. When I study the photo, I can almost smell her cucumber face cream, can almost feel the sensation of being tucked in the warmth of her soft neck.

"Thinking about you and your mom always makes me hope I get to have that with Ella. It makes me hope she loves me as much as you loved Lorraine, I mean." Cassie places the frame back where it was.

Ella. For a moment, I've forgotten she's here. My gaze drops to the carrier, to the baby's fat cheeks, the wide set of her eyes a replica of Cassie's. She's watching me, and I have the unnerving sense that she recognizes my face. And why wouldn't she? We spent almost five hours alone together.

"So!" I shake off the unease, tossing my comb on the unmade bed, the ends of my hair still dripping as I move past Cassie into the tiny living room. Her Gramercy apartment could swallow this one whole. "Were you in the neighborhood?"

"Not exactly." She follows me, leaning against the back of the couch. "How fast can you pack?"

"Huh?"

Cassie's eyes glitter, her mouth splitting into a lopsided smile that's so bizarre I almost ask her if she's on something. We once tried LSD in college, but Cassie was so freaked out by the trip that she swore off drugs for good after that, even when McKay and her crowd were deep in their cocaine phase senior year.

"I booked us a suite at the Mayflower Inn. With Ella, too, obviously." She taps her shoe—a beige, expensive-looking sneaker— against the hardwood floor. "I just need to get the eff out of the city."

"Tonight?" I stare at Cassie. She's wearing jeans and a baggy white sweater that's bunched at the waist where the carrier buckles. I can tell, even through her clothes, how much thinner she is than she was a week ago.

"Yes! A girls' weekend, like old times. Maybe Sunday night, too, okay? The driver is waiting downstairs." She adjusts the carrier, Ella's socked feet tapping against her hips.

"You—you want me to go with you?"

"*Yes.* You'll love the Mayflower, Bill. They have an amazing restaurant, a spa—"

"Cass, I have plans tonight." I wrap my arms around my chest, suddenly cold. "Alex and I have had these tickets to the Comedy Cellar for weeks."

A wounded expression crosses her face, like my words are a gut punch. "Please, Billie." Her voice, which was brimming with manic excitement just moments before, is barely a whisper. "I need this. I need time away from Grant, time to be with Ella, and you—"

"You weren't even speaking to me ten days ago!" I blurt, without really meaning to.

An extended moment of silence sits between us. "That isn't true," she says quietly, ineffectively, the things we both know but won't express sitting between us like a rotting wall. A flimsy barrier that's easy to break down, pretend was never there.

I sigh, glancing out the rain-speckled window, powerless against my own loyalty, my own love. I turn back to her, our eyes locking. We both know what I'm going to say before I say it.

"I'll go pack," I tell her, defeated but strangely exhilarated. I can't remember the last time it was just Cassie and me—no Grant, no McKay. This is a gift.

I text Alex from the West Side Highway. Cassie emergency, I write. We're heading to the Mayflower Inn in Connecticut, just for a night or two. I'm so sorry to miss the Comedy Cellar. I'll make it up to you, I swear.

Traffic creeps out of the city, but we're cruising by the time we pass Yonkers and merge onto the Cross County Parkway. Whatever car we're in isn't an Uber; it's a black Mercedes SUV that smells like new leather, with an array of Lifesaver mints and bottles of Poland Spring up for grabs in the spacious back seat. Cassie seems to have an established relationship with the driver, a middle-aged man named Malcolm with a Scottish accent, and I get the feeling he's someone the Adlers employ with frequency.

Malcolm doesn't say much, and I suspect Cassie likes this about him. Ella falls asleep in the car seat, and Cassie peers over at me, across her napping daughter.

"Thank you." Her voice is sincere. "I thought I might die if I didn't leave that apartment. And I don't feel safe anywhere in the city."

I nod. "Is everything okay with Grant?"

She shakes her head. "Not really. He's beside himself since I let Lourdes go."

"You let Lourdes go? Like, you fired her?"

"I had to, Billie. I don't trust anyone right now. I mean, I trust Grant, I trust you . . . and even though I thought I trusted Lourdes, well . . . this isn't even about her." Cassie glances down into the car seat, swipes a tear from her lower lashes. "I know I'm a terrible person. I know that. But I can't leave Ella alone with anyone, not right now. Maybe not ever."

"Cassie." My heart wrenches, an elaborate form of guilt worming through my arteries.

"I gave her two months' pay. I promised her a glowing reference. Finding a good nanny is like striking gold in this city. Lourdes will land another job in half a second." She chews her bottom lip. "Grant doesn't understand."

I reach for hand. "You're not a terrible person." I squeeze her palm, force her eyes to lift, to meet mine. "You're not, Cassie."

The drizzle has stopped by the time we reach the Mayflower Inn, which a quick Google search on my phone describes as an "exquisite country retreat nestled in fifty-eight acres of beautifully landscaped gardens and woodland." I know the Mayflower, of course, but I've never had to go for work. Being just a couple of hours from Manhattan, the property isn't exactly a travel destination for most of The Path's clients.

The inn's exterior is all white paint and pale wood shingles, a stunning structure dropped smack-dab in the rolling hills of peak New England foliage.

Cassie thanks Malcolm for the ride and says she'll be in touch when we're ready to return to the city, Monday at the latest. I open my mouth to tell her I really need to get back tomorrow—Jane lands Monday morning and we have a Zoom call with a hotel in Big Sur that afternoon—but the words won't come. Instead, I follow Cassie and Ella and the bellhops into the lobby of the Mayflower, which I recognize instantly.

"Oh," I say out loud to no one.

Cassie eyes me, Ella propped against her hip. "What?"

I glance around the familiar room, which is wrapped in that prominent wallpaper: blue-hued with white feathery vines crawling up toward the high ceilings. A vibrant Turkish rug covers the floor in splashes of color.

"I've seen this lobby a thousand times on Instagram. Isn't it a rite of passage to post that wallpaper if you stay here?"

"Do you even know how to post an Instagram story, Billie?" Cassie cracks a smile, clocking the joke.

"Yes! I post when I'm on work trips. Just not from my personal Instagram—I do it from The Path's account."

Cassie shrugs. "Well, *I'm* certainly not posting. I may never post again."

Fifteen minutes later, we're settled into our suite, which is lavish and sprawling and as Instagram-ready as the lobby. Cassie breastfeeds Ella on the sitting room couch, like there was never a time when it was weird for her to be half-naked in my presence. I flip through the room service menu—we've decided to save the restaurant for tomorrow, when we're not so tired—and read the options aloud.

"Order whatever you want," she tells me. "This weekend is my treat."

We opt for fancy cheeseburgers and truffle fries and a bottle of pinot noir that's pricier than anything I would normally choose. The food arrives, and I watch Cassie eat—really eat—for what feels like the first time since Ella went missing.

"This is fucking delicious," she says half audibly, her mouth stuffed with food. She wipes a smear of grease from the edge of her lips. "Sorry." She swallows and glances down at Ella, who's propped against a pile of pillows on the floor, gumming her rubber giraffe. "I shouldn't swear in front of the baby. I always nag Grant about that, and then I do it myself."

"It's probably hard not to slip." I bite into a truffle fry, which melts in my mouth. "I'm glad you're eating, though. You need the calories."

"I know." Cassie nods. She's wearing a black nursing tank, the bones in her chest sinewy and protruding, her arms like two long twigs. "This is the first time I've felt hungry since . . . before."

"I guess you really did need to get out of New York."

It's eight thirty by the time we finish the food, and Cassie goes off to put Ella down and shower. I pour myself a glass of wine and settle onto the couch, use the time alone to check in with Alex. But he doesn't answer when I call, and I notice that he hasn't responded to my text from earlier. I write him again. How's your night? I really am sorry . . . call me when you're free.

I set my phone on the arm of the couch and open the paperback I brought—an old Lisa Jewell novel I've been meaning to read for years.

It hooks me instantly, and I'm forty pages in when Cassie emerges from the other end of the suite. She's wearing a pale blue pajama set, her long hair damp from the shower. She runs a brush through the ends. "Good book?"

I dog-ear my page and close the paperback. "You know I love my psychological thrillers."

Cassie reaches for the pinot noir and pours her own glass, burgundy liquid climbing toward the brim. "I don't think I've ever been so full. But now, it's time to drink."

Her phone, which is lying faceup on the coffee table, begins to vibrate, Grant's face filling the screen.

"Are you gonna get that?"

Cassie emits a small, joyless laugh, then chugs half her glass of wine in one gulp. "Fuck Grant," she mutters, her cheeks already flushed from the alcohol. "He's an asshole. Don't you think I married an asshole?"

I say nothing—we both know I can't answer that question truthfully.

"I know he thinks I'm weak, that I'm not *handling* this." She drinks more wine. The glass is empty. "I know he agrees with the detective that it was those kids, but guess what?" Cassie takes the bottle and pours herself a second, bigger glass. Her eyes clip mine, wild but certain, drilling into the center of my soul. "I *know* it wasn't those kids, Billie. I know it in the marrow of my fucking bones."

For a brief, absurd moment, I'm convinced that she's onto me. That it's the reason she's brought me here, to the middle of nowhere Connecticut, to confront me and—possibly—murder me? But then I remember that this is an Auberge resort, and the thought of Cassie killing me and draping my bloodied corpse over a Schumacher-upholstered ottoman is so preposterous it's hysterical.

Once I start laughing, I can't stop, and Cassie studies me quizzically for a moment, but then she is laughing, too. We're both on the floor, howling, and I'm hit with a pounding wave of déjà vu that stops me in my tracks: this is how we used to be. Two best friends losing our minds over some unknowable source of humor, the laughter contagious, unrelenting, legitimately hurting our stomach muscles. I think of the time Cassie cracked up so hard she peed on the floor of her parents' room, and how we had to go out and buy rug cleaner, and how when her mother asked about the stain later that night, we blamed it on the dog. I share this memory with Cassie, and it does us in. She spits her wine back into her glass and flaps her free hand in front of her face, keeling over.

When we finally stop laughing, Cassie tips what's left of the wine into each of our glasses, but it's only droplets.

She lifts an eyebrow. "Another bottle?"

I'm heavy with sudden exhaustion, like I've come up against a wall. "I don't know if I can drink more."

Cassie groans. "You're right. I'm already drunk. When did we become such lightweights? We used to split, like, five bottles of Two Buck Chuck and rage until dawn."

We brush our teeth and crawl into the king-size bed. The sheets are buttery and crisp at the same time, heaven against my skin. Cassie switches on the television, where *Dirty Dancing* is playing on AMC.

"Oh my God!" she exclaims. "What are the chances?"

We keep the volume low; Ella is asleep in the Pack 'n Play on the other side of the room.

At some point, Cassie turns to me, nestled against the pillows. "Thank you for being here," she says, her voice hushed. "I needed this."

I study her face in the soft glow of the TV, the unmistakable pain that wasn't there before. The way her eyes and cheeks appear sunken, the dull pallor of her skin. She'll never not be beautiful, but this isn't the Cassie I know. It's like a light has gone out inside.

I wish I could tell her, suddenly. Just spit out the truth, save her from whatever psychological damage is still to come. But what would I say? *It was me, Cass, all right? Ella was crying and no one was paying attention and I was pissed at you for excluding me, for making me feel like a speck of dirt, yet again. So I took her, in a fit of emotion, and then I realized my stupid mistake and I brought her back. I'm sorry.*

And then what? Cassie and Grant would press charges, because why wouldn't they? I could wind up in prison. At the very least, our friendship—this restoration of closeness—would be over in an instant. Cassie would never speak to me again.

"I'm still worried about that Instagram message," she says. "'*Returning to the scene of the crime.*' I've tried so hard to figure out who birchballer6 is, but the account is private, and we don't have any mutuals, so it's a dead end."

I nod. "Is Alex looking into it? He mentioned you sent him a list of followers who've creeped you out in the past."

"No way. I know you say it's a stretch, but I really think that DM has something to do with Wade. I haven't told anyone about it. I *can't* tell anyone." She blinks. "Except you."

"Wait." I pause, digging through the wine fog. "Did you say birchballer6?"

"Yes. Why?"

I prop myself up higher in the bed. "You didn't tell me that before. Cassie, birchballer6 is Owen Birch, from Red Hook. He was our year."

Her forehead creases. "How do you know that?"

"Because he was the basketball captain, and I used to think he was cute."

"But you don't follow him, do you? Otherwise, I would have seen we had a friend in common."

My cheeks grow hot as I think of my tendency to lurk on social media. "No, I don't. I've just seen him tagged before. In some pictures Ashton posted, probably."

Cassie's hand flies to her chest. "Oh my God. So it wasn't anybody fucking with me? It wasn't someone who knew Wade?"

"Nope. Just Owen noticing that Red Hook's biggest influencer was back in town. I'm sure that's all he meant by 'the scene of the crime.'"

"You have *no* idea how relieved I am." She laughs, then cringes. "What a dorky username. Guess he's still riding on basketball captain status."

I shrug. "He's married with kids now."

"You would know." She says nothing for a long moment. Then: "Sometimes I can't believe what I did to Wade. That I'm a person who's capable of . . . that."

"Cass. It was complicated."

Her eyes fall closed for a few seconds before fluttering open, latching onto mine. "Red wine confession?"

I adjust my head against the pillow. "Okay."

Cassie swallows. "There's a huge part of me that's always wanted to forget it ever happened. Not just Wade but all of it—my years in Red Hook, that whole past life. And I think when I met Grant, when he pulled me into his world and gave me the chance to start fresh, to escape . . ." She pauses, her eyes shiny. "I think it just felt easier to push you away, too."

There's a dropkick in my gut, but I'm not sure if it's hurt, or shock that Cassie is suddenly being so honest.

"Because you're really the only person I'm close with who knew me then, Billie. And you're the only one who knows what I did on that roof."

I release a long breath. "I don't know what to say."

"I'm so sorry. I truly am."

Cassie's eyes rest on mine, heavy with the apology. I can tell she means it.

"Thank you," I say eventually. "For admitting that. For . . . acknowledging that we stopped being close. It's the first time either of us have said it out loud."

She nods, and something in the air between us has shifted; the elephant in the room is finally fading. I bask in the relief of the honesty.

"It feels like I'll never be able to stop reliving the night Ella was taken," Cassie says, chewing her bottom lip. "Do you . . . do you still think about Wade?"

I'm quiet for a moment. I think of the trauma he left in my body, how so little helped for so long. Then Remy, and the healing power of time.

"Sometimes," I answer truthfully. "But when he does come to mind, I mostly think about you. What you did for me. That's the way I want to remember the story."

Cassie blinks, her nose inches from mine. "Does it work? Does it make it hurt less?" She pauses. "Reframing the story to remember it how you want?"

An old, unwanted memory of Wade stretches across my mind. The musty smell of the basement. The sound of his belt buckle clinking, pants dropping to his ankles. The cold terror in my body. That's the problem with trauma. You can decide to change how you think about it, time can fade it, but it's never going to disappear.

But the trepidation in Cassie's eyes makes me nod against my pillow. I want to be the one who tells her something good. "It helps," I say. "It helps as much as anything can."

On the television, Patrick Swayze finds Jennifer Grey at the dance recital and takes her hand. *Nobody puts Baby in a corner,* he says, pulling her up. It's the end of the movie and the very best scene, but my eyelids are drooping as if they hold weights, and I let them fall closed as I listen to Cassie say something about making up for lost time, about being made stronger by what almost breaks us.

"You're my best friend, Baby," she whispers, and this is the last thing I hear before sleep pulls me under.

Brassy light filters in through the drapes the next morning, bathing the backs of my eyes in a warm red glow. I blink them open, disoriented for a moment before I remember where I am.

I find Cassie in the living room. Ella is perched on her lap, a board book open in front of them.

"Hey." Cassie glances up when she hears me come in. She looks rested, her eyes a little brighter than they were yesterday. Ella flashes me a gummy grin. "Aw, look at that big smile! You love your auntie Billie, don't you?" Cassie beams, rubbing her daughter's cheek.

My stomach clenches with unease.

"How'd you sleep, Bill? I ordered coffee and croissants." Cassie gestures toward the round dining table, where there's a tray with breakfast. The smell of rich coffee seeps into my nostrils.

"I slept great." I pour myself a cup with milk and sugar, then savor the first couple of sips. "How about you? What time did Ella wake up?"

"Seven, like clockwork." Cassie kisses the back of Ella's head, where her light brown hair is soft and wispy. "Ooh. Someone needs a diaper change."

I watch Cassie hop up from the couch, overtaken with purpose. "Here." She presses the baby into my arms. "Hold her for a sec."

I set my mug down and readjust my grip, propping Ella against my hip bone. The warm weight of her in my arms is hauntingly familiar, a memory from a lucid dream. She reaches for one of my small hoop earrings and yanks, letting out a little giggle when I wince.

"She's started laughing *so* much lately," Cassie says, digging through her stuff and pulling out more items than the task of changing a diaper can possibly require. "Thanks." She takes Ella from me and lays her on the waterproof pad. I exhale relief, reach for my coffee.

Cassie unzips Ella's onesie and changes her with so much care, so much attention. Wipes and cream and Aquaphor and belly kisses and singing. She dresses her for the day, in tiny pink pants and a white knit cardigan embroidered with rosebuds, her feet wrapped in little fleece booties. Everything Cassie does for Ella radiates love and tenderness. I tell her she's a great mom, meaning it.

"You'll be a great mom, too," she says, then catches herself. She smiles kindly, her eyes rising to meet mine. "If that's something you decide you want."

After breakfast, we take a long walk around the property, Ella strapped to Cassie's chest like a baby kangaroo. The day is gorgeous, just a few wispy clouds knotting the rich blue sky. The trees around us glow like they're on fire, swirls of gold and orange and red. It all looks like a painting, and I take out my phone and snap a few pictures. I send one to Alex, the ratio of blue to gray in our chat disconcerting. He still hasn't called or texted me back.

When Cassie takes Ella back to the room for her afternoon nap, she insists I head to the spa for a facial. I object, but she says she's already booked me an appointment and that she's paying. What this really means is that Grant is paying—I saw his name on the credit card she gave the front desk when we checked in—but I can live with this. There are worse things than using Grant Adler's money to tighten my pores.

I haven't had a facial in years, and the esthetician is merciless. She drowns my face in piping-hot steam, then stabs at my skin with her fingernails, a tiny drill excavating my epidermal layer. She grates my cheeks and chest with goo that feels like sandpaper and lectures me in a thick German accent about all the ways I've wronged my skin.

"You're glowing," she pronounces at the end, holding up a mirror. My face is red as a lobster and slick with grease, but I nod gratefully and ask if I can charge the tip to the card on file.

"You're glowing!" Cassie echoes when I'm back upstairs.

"Am I? I look like I've been under a broiler."

"Oh, that'll fade in a couple of hours." Cassie comes closer, inspects my face. "She did a great job."

Cassie's appointment is next, which means it's my turn to stay in the room with Ella.

"You sure you want to leave her?" I ask, instantly regretting the question. "I only mean . . . I don't want you to be stressed."

Cassie peers at me oddly, then shrugs. "It's just you. It's not like you're going to leave the room. Ella should stay asleep the whole time, anyway. If she does wake up, there's a bottle in the mini fridge. I'll have my phone on loud. Just call if you need me."

I sit on the couch in fear while I wait for Cassie to come back, counting the minutes she's been gone. The bedroom door is cracked, the static rhythm of the white noise machine whooshing through. Cassie told me the machine is designed to mimic the sound of the mother's heartbeat in utero, to comfort the baby. *Whoosh, whoosh, whoosh.*

I fidget with the piping on the couch cushions. Is it possible I don't trust myself to be alone with Ella? Am I right to wonder if something inside me could snap, like a rotten tree branch, a lingering, latent anger that would send me off on another subliminal, blundering quest toward nonexistent justice? Is this fear unfounded?

I thumb through my messages again. Still nothing—*nothing*—from Alex. My heart shrinks to a small, hard mass as I consider the possibility that he could be done with me. I try calling, but voicemail picks up. I call again, and this time leave a rambling, shaky message. I say something about being extremely sorry, about missing him, about my shit skills when it comes to relationships.

Cassie is back forty-five minutes later, her skin dewy and pink, not blisteringly red like mine. Ella is still fast asleep in her Pack 'n Play, and relief shudders through my body. Cassie doesn't even go in to check on her; that's how much she trusts me.

Neither of us really ate lunch, so we opt for an early dinner in the hotel restaurant. The space is light and airy, with pale wood floors and lots of greenery, the walls hand painted with garden-inspired flora and fauna. The restaurant opened at five thirty; we're the first ones here.

"Honestly, Grant and I do this all the time," Cassie says when we're seated, Ella dressed in an adorable yellow jumper on her lap. "Eat at five thirty, home by seven, in pajamas by eight. Early bird special!" She laughs, bounces the baby on her thighs. "God, this has been the nicest day. I wish we didn't have to leave tomorrow." Her eyes find mine. "Hey. What's wrong?"

I shake my head, shifting forward in the rattan chair. "Nothing."

"Billie. Just tell me."

I sigh. "I think Alex is really mad at me." I tell her about all the unanswered texts, how I haven't heard from him since I bailed on our Saturday plans.

"Well," Cassie says, when I'm finished. "If he's pissed, it's my fault for kidnapping you. Obviously."

I wince at her word choice.

"Next time, Alex will come with!" She sips her ginger margarita. "Actually, what if the five of us went to St. Barts for a few days? Maybe next weekend?"

"Are you serious?"

"Completely." She squeezes a wedge of lime into her drink. "Being here, I've realized how much it helps to get away. The city freaks me out right now."

I let the scene play in my mind. Alex, me, Grant, Cassie, and Ella relaxing on a wide white deck overlooking the turquoise sea. I've heard about the Adlers' hillside villa in St. Barts, seen endless pictures of the idyllic setting on Instagram. When Cassie first started dating Grant, I assumed it was only a matter of time before she asked me to join one of their weekend getaways to the island via Grant's father's private jet. But then everything changed so quickly, and with each passing month, the invitation seemed less and less likely until I knew for certain it would never come.

"That would be incredible." I feel the corners of my lips lift, unable to hide my excitement. "If Alex can get off work. And *if* he decides to forgive me."

"Of course he will." Cassie gives a supportive nod. "Just talk to him. Explain what a catastrophic mess your best friend is. I promise we'll head back to the city first thing in the morning. I'll text Malcolm tonight."

Your best friend. It will never get old, hearing Cassie say this.

A smile moves across her face. "You know how much I want things to work out between you and Alex." Her words reverberate, and I sense the missing half of this statement, the part she isn't saying: *I hope it works out not just for you but for me. I need Alex, too. I need him to tell me who took my daughter the night of October 13.*

Cassie keeps her promise. We're on the road by eight the next morning, coffee in to-go cups, Malcolm and his black Mercedes at her beck and call. Ella is already passed out in the car seat between us by the time we hit Route 7, eyelids fluttering softly as she dreams.

I sip my coffee and stare out the window as rural country speeds by, the foliage brightening as we move south. In a matter of weeks, most of these trees will be bare—the stark landscape that precedes winter. I nibble on a blueberry muffin—homemade, compliments of the inn at checkout—and do my best not to think of what's to come.

Traffic is miraculously sparse, and we make it back to Manhattan just after ten. Alex's shift doesn't start until three on Mondays, so I have Malcolm drop me at his place in Chelsea. Cassie hugs me goodbye on the street.

"Keep me posted, okay? Nothing a little sex marathon can't fix. Mention St. Barts, too." She hesitates, squinting in the midday sun. "And will you let me know . . . if he says anything about the case, I mean . . ."

"Of course, Cass." I force a reassuring smile. The irony strikes me then: the minute she finally stopped pretending, I started.

Given the circumstances, it feels strange that this is the first time I'm using Alex's key. I let myself into his apartment and find him in the kitchen, scrambling eggs. He doesn't look surprised—or happy—to see me.

"Hi." I set my tote bag on the ground, nervous. "How was your weekend?"

Alex is silent. He sprinkles some shredded cheese on top of the eggs, lowers the burner to a simmer.

"Alex. Come on."

"Stop." He pivots around, holding the spatula out in front of him, a runny piece of egg dropping to the floor. "Don't waltz in here and ask me how my weekend was, like everything is normal."

"I'm not saying everything is normal—"

"My weekend was *shit*, Billie." He tosses the dirty spatula on the counter, brushes a hand through his golden-brown hair.

I stuff my hands in the back pockets of my jeans. "I'm so sorry."

"I mean, what the hell? You didn't even call me on Saturday to talk to me about whatever came up for you. You just sent a text, casually canceling our plans. Plans I was excited about, tickets I bought for us weeks ago. You were sorry to 'miss' the Comedy Cellar? As though I would just go without you, no big deal?"

"I figured you could bring someone else! Your brother or your friend Simon? You guys all love comedy shows." I screw my eyes shut, knowing in the tenderest corner of my heart that I've played this all wrong.

"It doesn't work like that, Billie." Alex folds his arms across his broad chest, his mouth a sharp line. "Relationships don't work like that."

"I told you in my message, I'm bad at relationships, I am, really—"

"Then what?" Alex throws his hands in the air. I see the pulse at his neck, the artery leaping furiously.

This is it, I realize. *This is how it ends. This is how I fuck it up with the only man I've cared about in years.*

"Then *what*?" He is saying, angry. "Then I'm just screwed, because my girlfriend is 'bad at relationships'? And it's too late now because I'm already falling in love with her so this is just something I'll have to deal with?"

The air in the room stills, the only sound the faint sizzling of eggs in hot butter. Every word I'd been ready to use in my own weak defense is suddenly gone from my mind, evaporated, irrelevant. A small bead of hope springs in my chest.

"What did you just say?"

Alex's lips are parted, his eyes hard orbs of shock that soften as they latch mine. His shoulders drop away from his ears. "You heard me. I love you."

Tears run down my face, a salt river of clashing emotions, so many from the past forty-eight hours—from the past ten days—that I'm no longer sure what or who it is I'm crying for.

But the one thing I do know finds its way into the smooth muscle of my vocal cords, out into the space between us. I tell Alex the irrevocable truth: that I love him, too.

Chapter Forty-four
Billie

2013–2015

"It's the end of an era!" Cassie pops the cork, champagne spraying across the tar rooftop.

We weren't organized enough to remember glasses—and besides, most of our stuff is packed—so we drink straight from the bottle. The carbonation inflates our cheeks.

It's been three years since Cassie and I moved into our Alphabet City shoebox, and now, it's time to part ways.

The decision wasn't contentious; it's just time. Cassie switched jobs and industries, and her new salary at Intermix means she can afford her own place, a studio on the Lower East Side. Meanwhile, Remy has been in New York for two years now, and we're itching to live together. I'm moving into his one-bedroom in Harlem.

"I never thought I'd say it, but I'm going to miss this place." Cassie passes me the bottle. She wears a sky-blue halter dress that matches her eyes, and trendy leather sandals with thin straps that wrap around her ankles. Her clothes and accessories have gotten nicer since she started the new job. Cassie has always viewed fashion as a status symbol, but now, with a discount at Intermix, her wardrobe has reached a whole new level.

I give a wistful smile, nostalgia churning through me as we watch the sun go down from the roof of our building one last time. "We had a good run here."

"We did. But I have to say, I won't miss showering over the toilet."

"God, me neither."

We laugh.

Cassie takes another swig. "I can't believe we've been in the city for three years already."

"Yeah. Time flies."

"I feel like nothing has even happened to me yet."

"That isn't true. You're figuring out your career. You know now that you want to be in fashion. You have this amazing gig at Intermix."

"I guess." She points her chin forward, gazing out over the city. "I meant my love life, though. I'm ready to meet someone."

"You know you could have anybody you want," I tell her.

She raises an eyebrow, but we both know it's true. Cassie is just picky. She goes on dates—plenty of them—but no one is ever good enough. The unspoken truth that sits between us, perpetually, is that she wants a man with money. Old money. The kind of wealth her family had before her father lost it. Before Grandma Catherine cut the Barnwells off for good.

Objectively, I understand that this desire of Cassie's makes her shallow. It makes her a gold digger. But it's been this way for so long that I have trouble seeing the quality as anything other than part of the fabric of Cassie. My best friend. And isn't that a requisite of loving someone—to grow complacent to their most fatal flaw? To suppress the urge to change them until it all but disappears? The practice resembles acceptance, but the process is more painful. It's more like sacrifice.

Remy's place in Harlem is only nine hundred square feet, but it feels like a palace after where I've been. Three tall windows overlook West 119th Street, flooding the apartment with afternoon light. The bedroom is substantial, big enough to fit an oversize dresser and a king. And while the location is far uptown—forty-five minutes on the subway to Cassie's on Delancey, half an hour to my office in NoMad—it's worth it for the cheap rent and extra space.

Life with Remy in our Harlem love nest is happy. He works thirty hours a week at a small gallery nearby and uses the rest of his time to paint in studio space he rents from his boss. Remy's paintings are layered and abstract and starting to gain recognition around the city. A collection of his work is featured at a prominent gallery in Chelsea; a social media influencer buys one of his landscapes and posts about it. It's been *years, but Remy is finally making a name for himself, more so than he ever did in Boston. I'm endlessly proud.*

In 2015, when we've been living together for two years and our lease is coming up for renewal, he suggests we look for a bigger apartment.

"We're both making a bit more money now," he reasons. "We could move to a neighborhood with more charm. Maybe somewhere in Brooklyn. Maybe get a two-bedroom."

"A two-bedroom?" We're at our favorite tapas spot in West Harlem, sipping sangria. "That seems excessive, Rem. I'm still underpaid at Expedia."

He shrugs, his shoulders dropping away from his ears. "If we can swing it, could be nice."

"What would you want with a second bedroom, anyway? Would it be your studio?"

"I'm not sure. Maybe." He pauses, drumming his fingers against the pine surface of the table. "Or, you know, maybe it could be a nursery. One day in the not-too-far-off future." His lips pull into a smile.

I reach for my sangria, chug the rest, then refill my glass to the brim.

Remy is thirty-one. I'm not quite sure how it happened, and so quickly—how he morphed from a twentysomething recent grad into an actual adult, a man in his thirties who thinks about being a father. But we've been together for close to seven years now, and his mentions of marriage and kids are growing more frequent. I'm running out of time.

I aim for a casual grin. "You think about babies an awful lot."

"You don't?"

I sip more sangria. I wish it were stronger, that it were pure liquor instead of all this sweet, limp fruit. "No. I'm only twenty-seven."

"My mom had me when she was twenty-five."

"Good for her."

"Billie." Remy folds his arms across his chest, his gaze narrowing. "What's going on here?"

The alcohol sits heavily in the base of my stomach, clouding my head. "Nothing." I focus on breathing. "I just—I guess I didn't realize you were so traditional." As soon as I speak the words, I know they're true. I hadn't expected this of Remy. Perhaps it's what drew me to him all those years ago.

He frowns. "Does wanting a family someday make me traditional? A family with the woman I love?"

Bile burns the back of my throat, and I'm worried I'll be sick.

"Is there something you're not telling me, Billie?" Remy leans forward; his eyes grow more serious than I've ever seen them.

My mind feels waterlogged as the restaurant noises around us— plates clinking, spirited conversations competing with lively flamenco music—drown into silence. I think of the things I haven't told Remy about. Wade, for starters, but that's a secret I'll take to the grave. And then, the pregnancy. The baby that could have been.

I swallow the lump in my throat; some subliminal part of me understands that I have come to the end of a road. That I can no longer go on this way. Perhaps, subconsciously, I sense what's about to happen. Maybe I tell Remy because of how deeply I love him. Because I know it will be easier for his heart if it can hate me.

My eyes sting, and I clear my throat. Sound rushes back in.

"Three years ago, just before you moved to the city, I had an abortion." I shift into a state of autopilot as I explain the rest. How Cassie took me to the clinic, how they told me I was already eleven weeks along. How she held my hand while they did what I knew in my gut was the right thing, and how afterward, I was filled with unimaginable relief. How I didn't tell him because I was too scared it would break us, that it would cause him to look at me the way he's looking at me now.

I'm weeping into my plate of garlic shrimp, my shoulders trembling. Remy is silent as he digs into his wallet and pulls out some cash, throws it on the table. I follow him out of the restaurant and into the bright, October day.

When we reach the end of the block, he turns to me. His face—like magic to me, always—is contorted with pain and shock.

"I'm going to ask you something, and whatever you do, please don't lie." He squints into the sunlight, his eyes wet. A cab speeds by, blares its horn at a couple of jaywalkers. "Do you ever want to have children, Billie?"

I blink. This was the part of the story I had yet to share: how when Cassie came with me to the clinic, I hadn't corrected her when she assured me there would be another chance. A better time for a baby. When I wasn't so young. When I was ready.

But now, in a refreshingly clear moment that cuts through the san-

gria and the bullshit I've heard all my life—one day you will, just wait, there's no love like it, you'll see—*I tell Remy the truth, the thing I have always known in the marrow of my bones.*

"No." *I shake my head.* "I don't want to be a mother."

As they say: when it rains, it pours. A week later, I'm packing up my half of the apartment when my phone rings. Remy isn't here; he's been staying with his aunt in Queens since we broke up. Tomorrow, I move to a spare room in Chinatown, a unit in a five-story walk-up with Craigslist roommates. It isn't ideal, but it's the only affordable option I could find on short notice. At least I'll be close to Cassie again.

I toss a pile of shirts into a cardboard box and reach for my phone, swiping across the screen to answer the call from a number I don't recognize.

"Hello?"

"Billie? It's Sandra."

She sounds uncharacteristically bleak. Right away, I know.

"I'm calling from the hospital," *she says, her voice breaking.* "I'm so sorry, Billie. Your mom is gone."

Chapter Forty-five
Cassie

October 25, 2023
12 days after

I meet Wendy and Violet for lunch at Palma on Cornelia Street. They greet me with identical, cautious smiles, their expressions equal parts sympathy and horror. It's been nearly two weeks since I've been off social media, since I've let days of carefully planned content fall through the cracks. I've barely been in touch with my store managers, and even in my warped emotional state, I know this isn't fair.

Our table is at the front of the restaurant, parallel to the paneled windows that overlook the charming West Village block. I've brought Ella along, obviously, and I park the stroller beside my chair, angle the sunshade so the light won't hit her eyes.

"Sorry I'm late!" I give a strained smile. "Traffic down Seventh was a nightmare."

"Don't worry. It's good to see you." Violet fidgets with the edge of her napkin, glances at Ella in the stroller. "Lourdes is off today?"

Thirsty, I take a long sip of tap water, crunch a piece of ice between my teeth. "Lourdes is no longer with us."

Wendy raises a thin, penciled-on eyebrow. She over-plucked in the nineties, and this is the consequence. "What do you mean, she's no longer with you?"

I take a deep breath. There's an open bottle of rosé in a marble cooler on the table, and I pour myself a glass, grateful for the presence of alcohol at noon. Violet can be a bit of a teetotaler, but Wendy would have wine with breakfast if she could.

"You look thin, Cassie." Wendy blinks, her eyelashes spiky with mascara. "Like you haven't been eating."

"I'm so sorry, you guys." I tip my glass back, close my eyes as the rosé runs down my throat, landing on top of the latte I drank in the cab. "I'm sorry for going dark. I'm not in a good place."

"Of course you're not," Violet says, her voice oozing with concern. "You've been to hell and back."

"That's the thing, though." I pinch the stem of my glass. "I'm still in hell. I haven't come back."

It's true. Despite the relief of discovering that birchballer6 is no one threatening, I'm still consumed by terror.

A lanky, handsome waiter comes by, and we order salads and the black truffle fettuccine to share. When he darts off, I fill Wendy and Violet in on everything that's happened since Ella went missing. The detectives, the nightmares, the gut-wrenching decision to fire Lourdes, the constant, interminable fear that whoever took my daughter had a reason, that they want something, that it's only a matter of time before they come back for more.

"Look." I swallow, cold nerves swimming in my stomach. "Cassidy Adler is everything to me, you guys know that. But I just need to be with Ella right now. I can't focus on work. I need . . . a few more weeks, maybe a month, or two—" I rub my temples, wishing I'd come better prepared for this conversation. "Is it too much to ask you both to step it up while I'm away? I trust you to finish ordering for spring-summer, you can run the Instagram, make whatever decisions you want. I'll pay you more, obviously. And, Wendy, I know we said we'd wait till next year to hire a store assistant for East Hampton, but you should go ahead and do that now, so you have more help out there—" My voice cracks, my eyes filling. "I'm so sorry," I add pathetically.

"Cassie." Violet reaches across the table and touches my arm. Her fingers are smooth and cool, her nails painted a deep shade of plum that matches her name. "You don't need to apologize."

Wendy nods in agreement. Her chin-length, bottle-blond hair looks almost white in the wash of midday sun that pours through the window beside our table, the fine cracks in her foundation illuminated. "You can count on us. We know how hard it's been. We'll do whatever you need for the business while you take time to . . . figure things out." She steals a glance at Violet, and it's suddenly obvious that the two of them have been talking, that they've been expecting me to drop a bomb just like this one.

In the stroller, Ella begins to fuss. I put the paci back in her mouth and hand her a toy from the diaper bag—the crinkle rattle she loves.

Violet takes the smallest sip of wine. "Cassie, I have to ask." She tucks a lock of silky dark hair behind her ear. "Have you considered therapy?"

I think of my fight with Grant a few days ago, how he broached the same topic, his threat to call "Tom's guy." I don't have a problem with therapy, but I'm not taking orders from my husband, and I'm certainly not seeing Tom's shrink—no doubt some ancient Republican on the Upper East Side who is Tom-approved solely because he went to Yale and doesn't take insurance.

"Yeah," I tell Violet, swallowing a forkful of fettuccine with effort. "I think I probably do need a therapist."

"Who doesn't?" Wendy tops off our glasses, emptying the bottle. "I see mine weekly ever since I walked in on Christopher whacking off to a picture of Judi Dench in *Skyfall*."

I laugh out loud, startling Ella, nearly choking my rosé at this image of Wendy and her teenage son. "Oh my *God*, Wendy."

Violet's shoulders are shaking—she can't contain herself, either.

Even if just for a moment, my heart feels full. For the grace of these women who care about me, about the well-being of my business. For the laughter that I can still find.

McKay has requested that I meet her in the park after lunch. She says she has "news." Briefly, I wonder if she could be pregnant again, but it seems unlikely. Finn is only six weeks older than Ella, and besides, the last time I asked McKay if she wanted a third baby, she laughed in my face and said Tom was seriously considering a vasectomy.

I meet her at our usual spot in Madison Square Park, the southeast entrance by Shake Shack. It's late October now—in less than a week, it will be November—and even though the sun shines high in the cobalt sky, the air is cold. I spot McKay on a bench beside a tall horse chestnut whose leaves have mostly fallen. She smiles, waves us over.

"Hey." I plop down next to her and press the brake on the stroller, adjust the cashmere blanket around Ella. Thankfully, she's fallen asleep. "Where are the kids?"

"With Mariana today." McKay rubs her hands together. "It's frigid, isn't it?" She's wrapped in a white faux-fur coat and black earmuffs—even as a born and bred New Englander, she's a drama queen about the weather when the temperature dips below fifty.

I haven't seen McKay in almost a week, not since before Billie and I went to the Mayflower Inn. She doesn't know about that, or that we're going to St. Barts this coming weekend, and I certainly don't plan on telling her about either Billie-involved excursion.

"I could've just called, but I wanted to see your face." McKay turns to me, removing her sunglasses. "I heard about what happened with Lourdes. Are you doing okay?"

I shrug. I don't want to talk about Lourdes or Grant, so I tell McKay about my lunch with Wendy and Violet, my decision to take some time off from work. I mention therapy.

She nods supportively. "You know Tom has a guy . . ."

"Right." I glance down at my hands, pick a strip of dried skin from the cuticle on my thumb. My gross habit. "I'd rather see a woman, I think."

"Look, Cass." McKay uncrosses and recrosses her legs. "I have to talk to you."

I brace myself for another lecture on how I need to "snap out of this funk" and "move on with my life," when McKay says something that catches me off guard.

"I met Detective Barringer for coffee yesterday."

An older couple strolls by our bench hand in hand. The man points to something up in the horse chestnut tree—a bird, maybe—and his wife gives a wrinkled smile. They must be in their seventies—even early eighties—and I wonder, passingly, if Grant and I will be like that one day. Old and happy. Somehow, I have trouble picturing it.

"I had a weird feeling, so I decided to follow up with him," McKay is saying, pulling me back to the moment.

"A weird feeling?"

"Yeah." She pauses. "About Billie."

"Oh come *on*, McKay." Frustration batters my chest. "You've got to give up this Billie thing. She's my oldest friend. She wouldn't kidnap my child!"

"Well, the detective mentioned something about your oldest friend that he thought was quite strange." McKay's tone is suddenly clipped, laced with derision. "And I'm only trying to help you, Cassie. But if you don't want to hear it, I won't mention Billie's name again."

I close my eyes for a moment, let the sun hit the backs of my lids, a muted red glow. I blink them open. "Obviously, you should tell me anything that might be important."

McKay presses her lips together, watching me. "Barringer thought it was strange that when he first met Billie at your apartment—when she said she wasn't at your party because of her migraine—she never mentioned the fact that she was supposed to feed her boss's cat that night."

I feel my brow scrunch in confusion. "What?"

"Her boss, a woman named Jane, lives in your building."

"I know who Jane is. She's Billie's boss and also one of her close friends." I shake my head. "She definitely doesn't live in our building."

"She does, though. Apparently, she just moved in a couple of weeks ago."

I pause, trying to make sense of whatever the hell McKay is describing. "How do you know all this?"

"Because Barringer talked to Billie's boyfriend, Alex—you know, the cop. Apparently, he offered to be another set of eyes on the case."

"Yeah, he did offer. He's helping us out."

"So anyway, when Barringer called Alex to fill him in on the investigation thus far, he used the opportunity to confirm Billie's alibi. Because Barringer was obviously made aware that Billie and Alex are a couple."

"I know. Grant and I never tried to hide that from him. Nobody did."

"Right. So Barringer ran Billie's alibi by Alex, who confirmed it. He said she bailed on dinner with him that night because she had a migraine."

"So *what*, McKay?" I throw my hands in front of me, the irritation building behind my sternum. "If her alibi checked out, what does this have to do with Billie's boss—"

"I'm getting there, Cassie, you just need to listen." McKay draws in a breath, her gaze growing stern, serious. "Alex *also* happened to tell Barringer that Billie bailed on feeding her boss's cat that night, for the same reason, a migraine. And Barringer asked for her boss's name—you know, to further confirm the alibi, as is protocol. So Alex told him:

Jane Falkenberg. That's not exactly a *common* last name, so it wasn't hard for Barringer to put two and two together. He'd already done a thorough investigation into everyone in your building—to get alibis, to see if anybody heard or saw anything that night." McKay pauses for a beat as if to make sure I'm listening. "According to Barringer, as of earlier this month, Jane Falkenberg and her wife are the current owners and residents of 8A, the apartment directly below yours. They were out of the country on vacation the night Ella was taken. But Barringer contacted Jane, who confirmed what Alex told him: that Billie was supposed to stop by 27 Gramercy Park the evening of October 13 to feed their cat."

My blood is suddenly icy, churning with a new strain of unease. I rub my arms through my flimsy trench, wishing I'd worn something thicker. "Well—well, did she? Did Billie stop by and feed the cat that night?"

McKay hesitates. "Apparently not. Jane confirmed Billie's migraine alibi."

"So what, then?" I ask, even though I already know.

"So it's *weird*, Cassie!" McKay's voice is frenzied, agitated. "Wake the fuck up. It's really fucking weird that Billie didn't tell you any of this. That she's never even *mentioned* the fact that her boss moved to your building! Especially since you just told me they're close friends."

I say nothing. For once, I can't argue with McKay.

"I don't know, Cassie." She picks a piece of lint off her fuzzy coat. "It seems like . . . Billie might be hiding something."

I press my palms together, thinking. "If Barringer agrees that it's strange, why won't he look into it?"

"Because Billie's alibi checked out. Twice. What more can he do?" McKay shrugs. "I had to let you know, Cass. I really think you should talk to her."

I don't tell McKay that in forty-eight hours, Billie, Alex, Ella, Grant, and I will be on our way to Teterboro, where Grant's father's plane is waiting to jet the five of us to St. Barts for a long weekend at the villa.

I think of Billie's familiar face—big hazel eyes, the way her mouth opens when she smiles. The face that's always been home to me, even when I didn't want it to be. Even when I willed the loyalty out of my psyche, desperate to run as far as I could from all the things our friendship would never let me forget. But hers was the first face I saw when Ella went missing, the person my heart has reached for in its deepest, most vulnerable grief. Billie couldn't have had anything to do with Ella's disappearance. The thought feels ludicrous, impossible.

And yet, as I push the stroller home from the park, McKay's words reverberating in my mind, my blood is cold with fear.

Chapter Forty-six

Billie

October 26, 2023
13 days after

To make it up to Alex for missing the Comedy Cellar, I buy us last-minute tickets to see Zac Brown Band at Madison Square Garden. He thinks we're just going out to dinner around the corner from my apartment, but I surprise him when he walks in the door, waving the Ticketmaster app in his face.

"Are you kidding me?" Alex loops his arms around my waist and picks me right up off the ground, spinning us in circles. He's been obsessed with Zac Brown Band since college.

"I love you," he says. "I love you, I love you."

"I love *you*," I parrot, my chest fizzy with warmth.

Since Alex first dropped the L-bomb a few days ago—albeit mid-fight—neither of us have been able to stop repeating the words. I do love him. And being able to tell him that, and to know it's reciprocal, is everything. I haven't been this content in years. And with Cassie back in my life, the world feels close to perfect.

The guilt keeps me up at night, but if there's one thing I know about guilt, it fades with time. Already its descent feels less abrasive, less consuming. In a matter of weeks, Cassie will be okay again. She'll come to trust that what happened was a terrible mistake, to believe Detective Barringer's verdict—just a couple of dumb teenagers screwing around on the fire escape. And as for Alex, he won't find anything Barringer couldn't. He'll try his best, but ultimately, he'll tell Cassie what everyone else has, and she'll have no choice but to accept it.

This is what I force myself to believe. This is how I keep moving forward.

Alex flops down on my bed while I finish getting dressed.

"Seriously, I needed this. It was a rough day in the Twenty-sixth Precinct. Armed robbery up by Columbia, a pedestrian in critical condition."

"God. That's terrible." Sometimes I forget how heavy Alex's job can be, the traumatic events that are commonplace in his daily work. And yet, he stays so cheerful, so grounded. I don't know if I could do it.

I put on high-waisted light-wash jeans and an ivory peasant top from Free People. My hair is still damp from the shower, but I'll let it air-dry.

"Has there been anything further with Cassie's case?" I ask, dabbing concealer under my eyes in the mirror above my dresser. It's been several days since I've inquired, and I can't help myself. Besides, it would be weird if I *weren't* asking for updates about my best friend's case.

Alex clasps his hands across his torso. I love the sight of him on my bed, the way his strong legs stretch the whole length of the mattress.

"Honestly, nothing new." He chews his bottom lip. "I've scoured every bit of security footage, multiple times, and I can't identify anything strange."

I nod, lining my eyelids with dark brown pencil, careful not to overdo it. I look like a raccoon when I wear too much eye makeup.

"And I've contacted everyone on that list Cassie gave me—you know, the people she's gotten hate messages from on social media. Only a few of them even live in the city. But regardless, all of them had an alibi, and every alibi checked out." Alex sighs. I can tell my question has gotten him worked up. He sounds frustrated, hopeless.

"Hey." I glance at him in the mirror, our eyes locking. "Thank you for being so invested in this. Seriously, you're amazing. But if no new evidence is emerging, it's okay to drop it. Barringer very well may be right about those teenagers, and everyone knows that."

"Not Cassie." Alex frowns.

"Look." I sit down at the edge of the bed, place my fingers underneath the top of his flannel, where the first two buttons are undone. His chest hair is light brown, coarse. "Cassie wasn't vibing with Barringer. She just didn't trust him. But *you*—well, she'll listen to you. I know it. And the two of you will have plenty of time together in St. Barts this weekend."

A beat of silence passes. Alex rubs the back of his neck. "It's pretty nuts that we're flying to St. Barts on a whim on your friend's private plane."

I nod. It's certainly wild. After so many years of empty promises, I wasn't fully expecting Cassie to follow up on the invitation, but the day after we got back from the Mayflower, she did. She called and said she'd talked to Grant and that everything was arranged. Her father-in-law's jet would be waiting for us at Teterboro on Friday morning. Tomorrow. In spite of how much I travel, I can't remember the last time I was this excited for a trip.

I study Alex. "You want to go, right? It's going to be amazing."

He shrugs. "I'm sure it will be. It's just—" He hesitates, his eyes moving over me as though he's weighing the consequences of saying what's really on his mind. "A private jet? A St. Barts villa? I mean, the Adlers are *stupid* rich, right? I don't know. I can't pretend the idea of spending an entire weekend on their turf doesn't make me a little uncomfortable. And frankly, I thought their whole scene made you uncomfortable, too."

My stomach clenches as I think back to the dinner party at Cassie's apartment. At how out of place Alex and I had both felt; at how, in an unspoken way, that mutual feeling had bonded us.

"It's complicated," I tell him after an extended pause. "And Cassie didn't grow up like that."

"So you keep saying." He sounds unconvinced.

"Alex." I tilt my chin up to look at him. "I know the Adlers have fuck you money, and I get that it's all a little much, but . . . you already took your weekend shift off. Let's just go and have fun and not think too hard about it." I rest my hands on his chest. "Please. Cassie and I are finally in a good place again. It would really mean a lot to me."

Alex nods slowly, exhaling. "Okay. I guess you're right—we should just enjoy it." He pauses, the corners of his mouth tugging into a grin. "And it'll be our first time away together." He pulls me in for a kiss. His lips are warm and smooth and leave my body wanting more.

"I love you," he whispers.

In this moment, I know, like I've known before, that I need to tell him. That I need to bite the bullet and say the words out loud: *I love you, and I'm probably getting ahead of myself, but you should know, before we take this any further, that I don't want children. I don't want to be a mother.*

And possibly, understandably, that will be a deal breaker for him. But maybe—*maybe*—it won't. Either way, we'll both be free.

He moves his hands down to the waistband of my jeans, his mouth working against mine. He smells like his usual Old Spice.

"Later." I pull back, tousling his hair, my whole body turned to putty from his kiss. "It's almost seven, and the doors opened at six thirty."

He watches as I slide my feet into a pair of suede-heeled booties. "You look hot." He tilts his head. "That outfit is very . . . country concert appropriate."

I toss him his jacket from the end of the bed. "Thanks. I tried."

"But I feel like it's missing something." He goes over to my closet and begins riffling through.

I glance at the time at my phone. "If we don't leave now, we'll miss their opening song."

"Aha!" He grabs something from a shelf at the back of my closet, and before I know what's happening, he's securing Jane's felt hat to the top of my head.

"Perfect." He smiles, that faint dimple appearing on one cheek. "Now you look like a real cowgirl."

I startle, touching the wide brim. I've completely forgotten about this hat, the one I'd snagged from Jane's apartment and worn in that awful blur of minutes when I'd dashed up the stairwell and brought Ella back. The memory, the irony of Alex finding the hat now, is enough to drain the color from my face. I meant to get rid of it.

"This isn't a cowboy hat, you know."

Alex shrugs. "It's close enough. You look awesome."

I want nothing more than to rip the hat from my head and shove it down the garbage chute, a reminder of the worst night of my life that I never want to see again, but I know that isn't an option. If I draw attention to the fact that I don't want to wear it, Alex will remember. He'll register this piece of information somewhere in his cop-investigator subconscious, and I don't need that. I can't risk making it a thing.

"Are you sure you're all right? You're really pale."

"Yeah, I'm just—I just got light-headed. I think I'm hungry." I slide my arms into the crunchy, cheap sleeves of my pleather jacket. "Maybe we can grab a slice of pizza on the way?"

Traffic is a nightmare getting up to Madison Square Garden, so we don't have time to stop for food. Alex grabs us a couple of draft beers on the way to our seats, and we make it into the arena just as the fiddle picks up at the beginning of "Knee Deep."

Alex grins and bops his head to the beat, and I love this about him, this fusion of contrasting traits and hobbies, the way it's impossible to put him in a box. A cop from Long Island who surfs and reads political thrillers and loves country music. An enigma, maybe, but mine.

Zac Brown Band plays most of their hits, songs I haven't heard in years. Alex loops his arms around my neck, and we sway through the haunting lyrics of "Colder Weather," a slow ballad that reminds me of college and Boston and Remy. The crowd goes wild when the band finally gives us "Chicken Fried" as the encore, thousands of phones glittering toward the stage to capture it.

I'm tipsy after two beers on an empty stomach as Alex and I make our way out of the Garden, shuffling down the escalators in a noisy, packed sea of concertgoers that feels more like a herd of cattle.

"I'm *starving*!" I yelp once we're out on the street. It's chilly, the lights from the Empire State Building shining a few blocks away, its golden spire piercing the inky sky.

"Come on." Alex interlaces his fingers in mine. "One of my favorite pizza joints in the whole city is right around the corner."

There's already a line formed at Pizza Suprema, but Alex promises it's worth the wait. The smell of fresh dough and sweet tomato sauce makes my mouth water. When we finally reach the register, I order two slices of mushroom and onion, and Alex asks for pepperoni. I lean against the counter and watch the guy slide our slices into the oven to warm them, my stomach growling.

"Billie?"

Someone calls my name from behind, a startlingly familiar voice that I can't immediately place. I turn around, and then—of course, of *course* I know this voice—I see that it's Jane. She and Sasha are sitting at a booth, a couple of grease-puddled paper plates between them, empty except for Jane's discarded crusts.

"Jane!" For some reason, my insides flip. Maybe it's knowing she's talked to Alex and Detective Barringer on the phone, or perhaps it's just seeing her in the flesh for the first time since admitting what really happened the night of October 13—our private understanding that she's the only other person in the world who knows the truth.

"What are you doing here?" I shift my weight to one hip. "Did you—were you at Zac Brown Band?"

"We were!" Sasha's face breaks into a smile. "I'm a huge country fan. Explains why I've got a cat named Willie Nelson. And why I've dragged Jane out on a Wednesday."

"Alex is a fan, too." I reach for his arm beside me, make the necessary introductions. *Alex, this is Jane and Sasha. Jane and Sasha, this is Alex.*

"It's crazy we're only just meeting in person." Jane is speaking to Alex, but her eyes are still fixed to my face, narrowed, her head tilted as if she's deep in thought. Something feels off between us. Jane and I are not the type of friends who run into each other after a concert. We're the type of friends who *know* when the other person is going to a concert, who would never normally have this type of coincidental encounter. We're looped into each other's lives almost intimately, perpetually at the top of the other's most recent texts. At least we were until these past couple of weeks. Until Cassie came roaring back into my orbit.

I nod. "I know, right? So how amazing was that encore—"

"Is that my hat?" Jane's finger is pointed directly at my hairline. She's looking at me funny, with a slight frown, but then her eyes grow wide in recognition. "That *is* my hat!"

My heart jumps into my throat, stops beating. I'm so hungry and tipsy, so distracted by the awkward circumstances of this unexpected run-in, I've completely forgotten that I'm wearing Jane's stupid hat.

"I'm not sure." I feel my face flush crimson. "I don't think so."

"I'm almost positive it's mine." Jane is standing now, plucking the hat from my head. "I got one exactly like this when Sasha and I were in Jackson Hole last summer, with this little black-and-white feather in the band and everything."

"Didn't you have it monogrammed?" Sasha asks.

"I *did* have it monogrammed!" Jane flips it over, runs her index finger over three gold-foiled letters on the underside of the brim. *JEF.* Jane Elizabeth Falkenberg. The letters are small, but perfectly legible. Of course, in the blur of everything that happened, I never noticed.

Jane pokes my shoulder, her jaw dropping. "You little thief. I've been *looking* for this hat. When did you borrow it?"

I want to melt into the floor and vanish. Evaporate from my own existence. I feign an innocent laugh that sounds more like a wheeze. "Honestly, I don't even remember. I forgot it was yours."

"Well, I'm taking it back." Jane slides into her seat, affixes the hat to her own head. She's frowning again. "That's really so strange, because I could've sworn I left it out to bring to Iceland. I didn't pack it with the rest of our stuff before we moved—I could've *sworn* I wore it in the U-Haul that day so I wouldn't have to dig through boxes later."

The inside of my mouth is bone-dry. I stare at Jane, willing her to turn her face half an inch and meet my gaze. When she does, I give my head a tiny, barely perceptible shake, praying she'll receive the silent message and understand. That she'll cover for me, or at least drop the subject.

"Wait." Sasha raps her knuckles on the linoleum tabletop with excitement, as if she's just remembered something. "I *did* see that hat in our new place, Janie. I remember because it was basically the only thing in the closet. I bet you meant to wear it on the plane, then just forgot when we were rushing out the door."

Jane's eyes lock mine, blooming in sudden comprehension, but it's too late. I feel Alex's gaze ping-ponging between the three of us, his brain at work connecting the dots.

And then Sasha—blameless Sasha, who knows nothing of the consequences of her unintentional sleuthing—poses the final question, the one that will flip the world as I know it on its head.

"But then Billie . . ." She glances at me, her lips pursing in genuine curiosity, like we're all just pals trying to solve some fun, unimpeachable mystery. "You didn't end up feeding Willie Nelson, right? So how did *you* get Jane's hat from our new apartment when we weren't even there?"

I don't want to look at Alex, but it doesn't feel like a choice. When

I do, when I see his eyes—stunned, horrified, registering all of it—I know in my bones that everything is different now.

The man behind the counter calls my name, hands me a paper plate, the base warm. Melted cheese slides off the end of the slice, staining my fingers with orange grease. Moments earlier, I would've killed for this pizza. But my appetite is extinguished.

Chapter Forty-seven

Billie

Summer 2020

Just when I think it's never going to happen, it does: Cassie meets some-one. Someone, finally, is good enough.

The minute I hear his name, I know why. Grant Worthington Adler. It isn't just a collection of WASPy consonants irresistible to the most blue-blood-sucking corner of Cassie's heart. No, the pull extends beyond that. He's an Adler. McKay's first cousin.

Cassie is euphoric.

They've been dating for a month when she finally decides it's time to introduce us. It's a sticky August night, and one of Grant's friends is having a birthday party, some drinks thing at the Wren.

PLEASE COME, *Cassie texts. Her use of all caps tells me she means it.*

I write back that I'm finishing up at work and have happy hour plans with my new boss, Jane. Cassie replies in seconds.

BRING JANE!

It's my second week at The Path, a boutique luxury travel service Jane founded after leaving Mince, a larger agency in midtown where I worked briefly, too. We'd both hated it, and when Jane left Mince to start her own company, I was her first hire. And even though The Path is only the third place I've worked in my eight years out of college, something about it already feels right. Finally, I'm building my own itineraries for clients. Finally, I'll have a real opportunity to travel, to scout properties and destinations all around the globe. I'm no longer just a cog in the wheel of some corporate entity. Thanks to Jane, I might actually have my dream job.

Jane agrees to check out the party at the Wren, and we meet at Astor Place to walk there together.

"If it's awful, we can go somewhere else," I promise as we stride down the Bowery. We pass a smoke shop, and I inhale the unmistakable scent of cloves, a whiff of spicy-sweet vanilla that stops my heart. This smell is the ghost of Remy, every time.

"You okay?" Jane is looking at me funny.

I think of my new job at The Path, of my fast friendship with Jane, the way she feels less like an employer and more like a kindred spirit I've known all my life. I think of Cassie finally being excited about a romantic interest, a man I'm moments away from meeting. I shake off the gutting nostalgia and shift my focus away from the pain of the past, toward all the ways I'm supremely lucky in the here and now.

"Yeah." I nod. "Come on. It's right up here on the corner."

When we walk into the Wren, the first person I see is McKay. Her glossy blond hair cascades down her tanned back like something out of a commercial. She wears a red silk camisole and white shorts, a collection of gold bracelets clinking on one of her twiggy wrists. She got married, I think, and when my eyes find her left hand, it's confirmed, a gold band nestled against a three-stone diamond ring that lets the world know. McKay's arms are looped around someone's neck—another woman's— and when she pulls back a little, I see that it's Cassie.

There's a dropkick in my stomach because I just know that something is different; the air is charged with an unfamiliar vibe. Cassie's smile is giddy and wide as McKay whispers something in her ear, and for a surreal moment, I feel the phantom sensation of someone whispering in my own ear. Microscopic hairs rise along the side of my neck.

"Is it me, or did we just walk into a Harvard frat house?" Jane peers around at all the people, most of them young and attractive and preppy and drunk. Someone spills their drink on my foot, liquid soaking my toes and the leather strap of my sandal. Macklemore thumps from the speakers. Jane beelines for the bar, promising to return with tequila.

I move to find Cassie, who is still physically attached to McKay. They are laughing, hugging, and I've never seen McKay like this before—so receptive to Cassie. The degree of intimacy between them unnerves me.

"Hi."

The music is so loud, I have to repeat myself. "HI!"

I tap Cassie's shoulder, and she spins around. Her cheekbones are flushed; she's wearing heavy eye makeup and a pair of diamond studs I've never seen before. A slinky black minidress that shows off her body.

"Omigod, hiii." She peels herself off McKay, wraps her arms around me instead. "I'm so fucking glad you came." Her voice is a high-pitched squeal. Drunk Cassie. "You remember McKay."

I resist the urge to say obviously, and force myself to wave. "Of course."

"And Ava and Adair and the crew from college. They're all around here somewhere. It's Ava's fiancé's birthday. He went to business school with Grant. Such a small world."

"Ah. Got it. Fun!" I rearrange my mouth into a smile. "I like your earrings."

Cassie beams. "They were a gift from Grant."

"Wow." There's a pause. "So, where is Grant? I'm dying to meet him."

McKay folds her arms and shoots Cassie a sly grin. "Yeah, where is my cousin who's head over heels in love with you?"

I bristle at the word love, at McKay's use of it. I feel edgy and tense, like I'm on the outside of a big circle with no way in. I crane my neck toward the bar, searching for Jane. Tequila will help.

I finally spot her, a flash of strawberry-blond hair at the end of the bar. She's clutching two drinks, and she isn't alone. She's talking to someone, a guy I recognize instantly because Cassie has shown me a thousand pictures. It's Grant. And before I can process what's happening, I'm watching Grant lean in toward Jane, so close to her face that their noses touch. Another inch and they'd be kissing. I freeze.

But Cassie and McKay are deep in conversation again, oblivious. I clear my throat and gesture toward the bar. "Jane has my drink. I'll be right back."

By the time I push through the packed crowds and make it to the other side of the room, Jane is alone.

"Double tequila soda with lime." She hands me the drink, and I take a long sip.

"*Thank you.*"

"*I may need to get out of here,*" Jane says dryly. "*I just ran into the sleaziest old client.*"

"*Huh?*"

"*This douchey rich boy who was a client at Mince, before I left to start The Path. He hired us to plan a trip for him and his fiancée, then shamelessly asked for my number.*" Jane frowns. "*And he just hit on me* again. *He knows I'm in a relationship, too. Pervert.*"

"*Wait.*" My stomach sinks. "Grant *hit on you?* Grant *was your client?*"

"*You know Grant Adler? The guy who was just, like, breathing on me?*"

"*Jane.*" I shake my head. I feel like I might pass out. "*Grant is Cassie's boyfriend.*"

"*Shut the fuck up.*"

"*I'm serious.*"

"*Are you sure? The guy over there, in the pale pink button-down?*" Jane glances toward the other end of the bar, where Grant has reunited with Cassie. He slings an arm around her shoulders, plants a kiss on the side of her head.

"*Never mind, I believe you.*" Jane winces, clinks the ice around in her glass.

"*What happened? When he was a client, I mean.*" I study her, the way her big doe eyes pop in the dim light of the bar. She isn't wearing makeup—she never seems to—but there's something perpetually sexy about her effortlessness, her air of indifference. I'm sure Jane gets hit on all the time.

"*He wanted to surprise his fiancée with a post-engagement trip to Mallorca,*" she starts. "*We had a lunch meeting to go over the itinerary. He kept ordering more wine, and he was blatantly flirting. He asked if he could call me sometime, take me out. It was . . . so awkward. When I told him I had a girlfriend—and reminded him that he had a fiancée— that really got him going. He was like, maybe all of us can hang out sometime.*"

"*You're joking.*"

"*I wish.*"

"*I had no idea he was engaged before Cassie. When was this?*"

"*Two years ago?*" *A sour expression morphs her face.* "*Yikes, I'm sorry. I know Cassie's your best friend. But that dude is obviously bad news. Better she find out sooner.*"

"*You think I should tell her?*"

Jane stares at me like I have two heads. "*I think you* have to *tell her. Wouldn't you want to know?*"

"*I guess.*" *I chew my thumbnail and watch Cassie knock back a shot at the other end of the bar. Grant picks her up and spins her around, and she's laughing so hard her eyes are dewy. I don't know if I've ever seen her look so happy.*

The next morning, I pick up iced coffees and deli bacon egg and cheeses. I've planned to meet Cassie in the park by the East River, but when I text that I'm outside her building, she says she's too hungover to see the sun.

Come up, *she writes.* Grant just left.

Cassie still lives in the same apartment on Delancey, a second-floor studio with east-facing windows. Her place is always immaculate and smells like the black currant Diptyque candles she splurges on.

"*Savior,*" *she says when I hand her breakfast.* "*I feel so ill I could perish.*"

"*Late night?*" *We plop down on her couch. The blinds are still drawn, and the apartment feels like a shadowy cave. The AC window unit hums in the corner.*

Cassie tucks her long legs underneath her and sips her iced coffee. She's wearing a silky green pajama set that must be new. "*So late. But that was a blast, right? Did you and Jane have fun?*"

"*Yeah,*" *I lie.* "*I was tired this morning.*"

"*But you met Grant?*" *Cassie can't suppress her smile.* "*Honestly, I was so drunk I can't remember exactly when I introduced you guys.*"

"*I—yeah, I did. Briefly, right before Jane and I left.*"

"*And? What did you think? I know it's crazy fast to say this, Bill, but I really think this is it. Grant's the one I've been waiting for all along.*" *She unwraps her bacon egg and cheese and takes a bite. Melted cheddar smudges her upper lip.* "*He invited me to the Hamptons for Labor Day weekend. To meet his* parents. *They have a place right on Hook Pond. Apparently, it's massive.*"

"Wow." Nerves crawl into the pit of my stomach.

"So? You're not answering my question. What did you think of Grant, Billie?"

"I—well, I thought he seemed nice."

"Nice?" Cassie wipes her mouth with a paper napkin. "You can do better than that."

Jane's words sit at the front of my mind. They won't budge, and I know she's right. What kind of friend am I if I don't tell Cassie the truth?

I place my iced coffee on the side table, press my hands to my thighs to keep them from quivering. "Um, I don't know how to say this . . ." I pause, draw in a breath. "Grant hit on Jane."

Cassie snorts. "What?"

"Last night, but also a couple of years ago, I guess." I stare into my lap.

"You guess?"

I blink up at her. "Grant was Jane's client at Mince. He—did you know he was engaged before?"

She scowls. "Yes, obviously. He was engaged for like three months, then broke it off because he realized she wasn't the one. They hadn't even planned the wedding. What does this have to do with Jane?"

"Nothing! I mean, he was supposedly planning a trip to Mallorca with his fiancée—ex-fiancée—and was working with Jane. And came on to her at the time. And was flirting with her last night, too."

Cassie's eyes narrow. "I'm supposed to believe that Grant came on to your gay boss?"

"What does it matter if she's gay or not? It happened, and I'm sorry. I just thought you should know. I would want to know if it were—"

"It's impossible for you to be happy for me, isn't it?" Cassie stands.

"What? Of course not. I want you to be happy; that's why I'm telling you."

"That's such a load of crock. McKay is totally right about you."

I freeze. "McKay? What do you mean?"

"You're obsessed with me, Billie. You want to be the only one who loves me, and you don't want me to love anyone else."

I feel my face crumple. "Are you kidding right now?"

"No." Cassie folds her arms across her chest, shoots me a death stare. "I see it more clearly than ever. And it's pathetic."

A fire catches in the pit of my stomach. It climbs up into my throat.

"You want to know what's pathetic? Turning a blind eye to Grant's character just because you finally landed a guy with a trust fund."

She gives an ugly, disdainful laugh. "Wow. You're so jealous, and it's really so sad."

"You're a gold digger." I swallow. Blood beats in my ears. "You always have been."

Cassie moves toward the door, swings it open. "Get the fuck out of my apartment, Billie."

I say nothing. My knees shake as I stand, my mind frantically searching for a way to draw back, to restabilize. "Cassie."

"Get out." Her eyes are like ice. "Now."

I pause in the doorway for a moment, praying she'll change her mind. But Cassie's gaze is unyielding, and I know there isn't a way to reverse whatever big thing I've just put into motion. My regret eclipses my anger; it pools in the base of my gut as I make my way down the stairs and back out into the city heat, alone.

Chapter Forty-eight
Cassie

October 26, 2023
13 days after

Grant watches me toss bathing suits and cotton dresses into my open suitcase, a couple of pairs of flat sandals. I used to pack for St. Barts with so much intention—curated outfits for each day and night and everything in between—but now that I'm not using Instagram, what I wear hardly seems to matter. I'm no longer the star of my own show—just an exhausted mom who wants to be comfortable. If I'm draped in an Ulla Johnson crochet cover-up while carrying a Prada tote on the beach and there's no one there to see it—no photographic evidence to share with the world—did it even happen? I've realized the answer is no. It didn't.

"Excited for this weekend?" Grant is lounging on the chaise in the corner of our bedroom, thumbing through his phone. We leave for St. Barts tomorrow, but he won't bother to start packing until the last possible second. There's no point in nagging him. Sixteen months of marriage has taught me as much.

"I *was* excited." From my cross-legged perch on the floor, I look up at my husband. Things have felt fragile and tense since our fight over Lourdes, but there's so much I haven't told him, and I'm tired of keeping it all inside. I need an ally. I thought my ally was Billie, but now, I really don't know.

"I saw McKay yesterday. She told me something weird." I fiddle with the zipper on my suitcase, wait for Grant to ask me to elaborate. When he does, I tell him what McKay said about Jane living in our building, and how Billie was supposed to feed Jane's cat the night Ella went missing.

"I don't know who to trust, Grant." The tears come suddenly, a stinging sluice behind my eyes. "I thought I could trust Billie. I *always* thought I could, even these past few years when we weren't as close, when things between us changed. They changed because of me, I'll admit—but even so, I never questioned Billie's loyalty. Is that naive?"

Grant moves to the floor beside me, wipes my cheeks with his thumbs. His eyes meet mine—that deep blue gray, like the ocean when it storms.

"No," he says after an extended pause. "But people don't always turn out to be what you decide they are when you're younger. Even your closest friends. Loyalties can shift. Yours did."

The truth of Grant's words slinks behind my chest, a heavy weight there. And I know in this moment that at least I've done one thing right: I've married a man who isn't afraid to challenge me, to hold a mirror up to my face and demand I study my own reflection. The vulnerability burns, an open wound, but my subconscious tells me it's something I need to feel.

"So you think McKay's telling the truth?" I ask him. "You think Billie's lying? We leave for St. Barts tomorrow. How can we spend the whole weekend with her if we think she might be hiding something?"

Grant considers this for a moment. "I think we should call Barringer," he says. "See if he confirms McKay's story. Then we'll know."

But somehow, going to Barringer feels wrong. I shake my head. "I'm so sick of it being this way. All this secretive behavior. I'll just ask Billie directly. She won't lie to me—not if I look her in the eye and demand the truth."

If Grant finds the contradiction in what I've expressed, he doesn't say so. Instead, he massages the back of my neck and asks me when I'm going to do it.

I glance toward our bedroom windows. It's been dark for hours already, too late to try to see Billie tonight, and I don't want to confront her on the phone. When I do, I want to see her face, the lines and contours of the initial reaction that will tell me everything.

"Tomorrow morning," I say, hugging my knees to my chest. "We're meeting at the airport at ten. You and I can go a little early, get Ella settled on the plane. When Billie and Alex show up, I'll tell her we need to talk."

Grant nods. "Okay."

I swallow. "I'm scared."

"Me, too."

"You are?"

"Yes, Cass. I've been scared for the past two weeks." He blinks. "Just because I don't always show it doesn't mean I haven't been terrified."

On the nightstand, the sound of Ella fussing crackles through the baby monitor. I startle—I can't help it—as Grant reaches for the monitor and tilts the screen in my direction. She's fine, snug in her sleep sack at one end of the crib, already quieting. But Grant knows me; he knows what I need.

"Come on." He takes my hand, leads me down the hallway. We pause outside the nursery. Grant gives the door a soft nudge, and we tiptoe in.

Our daughter is asleep, undisturbed, peaceful. Grant doesn't let go of my hand as we watch her in the dimness, transfixed, the gentle rise and dip of her tiny chest as she breathes. Our perfect, magical creation. Grant squeezes my palm. For the first time in a long time, it feels like we're on the same team.

Chapter Forty-nine

Billie

My Uber speeds through the Lincoln Tunnel on the way to Teterboro Airport. I try calling Alex again—my fourth attempt this morning—but he doesn't pick up. I don't know why I'm remotely surprised, but my stomach plunges into a new wave of misery all the same.

I lean back into the stiff leather seat and close my eyes, the horror of everything that happened last night rushing back to my consciousness, like remembering a nightmare. Alex and me standing face-to-face on Eighth Avenue, the street congested with foot traffic from Madison Square Garden around us, our pizza forgotten.

Have you been lying to me? he'd asked. *Were you in Jane's apartment that night? Is that when you got the hat? You didn't miss our dinner because of a migraine, did you?*

In that instant, in my delirious fog of cheap Bud Light and looming panic, I considered more lies I could tell him. More ways to fabricate the story I'd already spun. But what was the point? Even if Alex wasn't a cop—wasn't a person with the training and resources to eventually determine the truth—what was the use in continuing to lie to someone you love?

If I confessed, I could wind up in jail. I could lose my job; most certainly, I would lose Cassie. But none of that seemed to matter anymore, not if it meant being eaten away by my own dishonesty, peering over my shoulder for the rest of my life, waiting in a permanent state of shame and fear for the truth to catch me.

So I told Alex. I confessed everything. And when I finished, I watched his eyes glaze over as he told me never to contact him again. Then he turned and walked away, disappearing into the cold, crowded night.

And now what? I have no plan. I don't know why I'm still on my way to the airport, but Cassie is expecting me at ten, and a subconscious momentum propels me forward.

The Uber reaches the end of the tunnel, the car emerging back into the bright light of day. I glance out the window at the cloudless blue sky; a line of birds runs over it in one long thread. We're not far from Teterboro; I take a tissue from my purse and wipe the crusted mascara from underneath my eyes, dab some concealer there. Still, I know I look like shit. I didn't sleep a wink.

My phone buzzes on the seat beside me, and I lunge for it, praying it's Alex. But it's yet another text from Jane, asking me to call her back. She's called a handful of times since last night, since watching me chase Alex out onto the street after the excruciating exchange at Pizza Suprema.

But I can't talk to Jane right now. I just can't.

My heart is in my mouth by the time the Uber pulls to a stop in front of the airport, the wrenching sickness in my gut growing more unbearable by the second. It's possible that Alex has called Cassie and told her everything. It's more than possible. It's his goddamn *job* to do so.

The driver removes my suitcase from the trunk, tells me to have a safe flight. I manage to thank him in a small, weak voice.

The sunlight stabs my eyes as I glance around the outside of the terminal, searching for Cassie. I can't remember where she told me to meet her, and I'm about to read through our messages when I spot the familiar line of her shoulders, hunched on a wooden bench near the automatic doors. She's alone.

I wheel my suitcase over to the bench and hold up a hand in greeting—a limp, pathetic wave that feels all wrong. I can sense her staring at my pale, swollen face, and I wish so badly I was wearing the sunglasses that are buried somewhere deep inside my bag.

"Hey," she says. "Where's Alex?"

I shake my head. "He's not coming."

Cassie looks genuinely surprised, which catches me off guard. Perhaps he hasn't called her, after all.

"Something came up with work last minute," I add quickly. "He's really sorry not to be here."

Cassie says nothing. She's wearing her dark cat-eye sunglasses, black leggings, and a sherpa jacket. Her long, silky hair is loose around her shoulders.

"Where are Ella and Grant?"

"They're waiting on the plane." Cassie's voice is uncharacteristically clipped, and it's then that I feel it, as perceptible in the air as the smell of smoke. Something is wrong.

"I need to talk to you, Billie."

My breath is shallow, barely reaching my lungs. "Okay." I lower myself onto the bench beside her. My legs are trembling; I pray she doesn't notice. "What's up?"

"I was hoping you could tell me." She pivots her shoulders so that I'm forced to do the same, then slides her sunglasses to the top of her head. Her eyes are wide, clear, blue as ever. "I'm only going to ask you this once, and whatever you say, I'll believe you." She pauses for what feels like an eternity. Finally, she clears her throat. "I heard a rumor that Jane—your boss—moved to our building. And I heard that you were supposed to stop by and feed her cat the night that Ella went missing. Are those things true?"

My temples pound as the sounds around me drown into silence. I feel too numb to cry, but when I close my eyes, hot tears slide through. I let them drip down my cheeks, wishing everything were different— wishing I could wake up two weeks in the past and do it all over the right way. And what would that look like?

I imagine myself watching Cassie's Instagram stories on the subway and swallowing the pain of being excluded from her big showy birthday party. I do what Jane and Alex and so many others have told me to do: I make the decision to forget her, to move on with my one wild and precious life. Then I go to 27 Gramercy Park South with my head held high and I feed Willie Nelson, and when I hear Ella crying from the terrace upstairs, I let it be someone else's problem. I get out of there as quickly as possible and I show up to Westville on time, brimming with excitement to be meeting the man I love for dinner.

But that isn't what happened. And now, I have to live with the choices I made. I have to own my mistakes.

I wipe my face with the back of my hand. "Yes, those things are true." I blink, lift my wet eyes to Cassie's. "It was me."

"Well, what the fuck, why didn't you tell me about Jane before—"

"No, Cassie, it was *me*. I'm the one who took Ella."

The world stops on its axis. Cassie says nothing for an eternal moment. The seconds tick by, agonizing. Finally, she shakes her head, her
gaze unflinching. "That's not true."

I nod. I have to do this. "Yes, it is. Jane did move to your building.
I had only just found out earlier that day, and I'd already committed
to feeding her cat that night, and then I saw on Instagram that you
were having a birthday party—clearly, a big one—and I was so hurt
that you lied to me about it, that you didn't invite me. *Hurt* isn't the
right word, Cassie. I was blown apart. You didn't want me in your
life anymore—you haven't wanted me in your life for years, not in
a real way, not since you met Grant, and maybe even before then.
You just cut me out. Until now, for whatever twisted reason you've
decided you need me again." I pause, feel a wave of unexpected anger
build in my chest, clashing with the guilt. "And it's not like I came to
your building *planning* to take Ella. I was at Jane's, out on the terrace
directly under yours, and I heard her crying. Wailing. It went on and
on and no one was paying attention and you kept uploading your
fucking Instagram stories and your daughter was hysterical, and in a
fit of rage and emotion, I climbed up the fire escape and I took her,
just to calm her down, really, and I didn't think it through. And it's the
most insane, idiotic, thoughtless thing I've ever done in my life and I
regret it every second of every day, but it's the truth, and you deserve
to know. I should have told you earlier, and I'm so sorry I didn't. But I
missed you, and having you back in my life these past two weeks—in
spite of the circumstances—has been . . . everything. I'm so fucking
sorry, Cass. You don't know how sorry I am."

Cassie's face is unreadable. She's not looking at me anymore; she's
staring straight ahead at nothing, her expression glassy, trancelike.
And then suddenly her mouth opens wide, her eyes screw shut. She
hinges forward, dropping her face into her hands, and at first, I think
she's bawling. But then I realize she's laughing. Howling. I sit, frozen,
listening, watching her shoulders shake, her whole body convulse.

Finally, Cassie sits back, the laughter draining from her body.
She turns to me, her gaze narrowed to slits. "Fuck you, Billie." Her
mouth twists, an expression of pure disgust. "This whole time . . .
this *whole* time, I thought some psychopath was lurking around the
corner in the city, following me, fucking with me, waiting to come

back and kidnap Ella for good." She shakes her head, her voice rising in pitch, full of venom. "I haven't been able to work. I haven't been able to sleep. I haven't been able to eat. And all this time it was just . . . *you*. And all because I didn't invite you to a stupid birthday party. You pathetic, demented child."

Cassie stands, tears falling from her eyes now. She shoves her sunglasses back down, masking herself.

I think of the past two weeks, all the time Cassie and I have spent together. Curled under a blanket on the couch watching *You've Got Mail*; drinking red wine and talking late into the night like we used to; eating buttery croissants in our suite at the Mayflower Inn; blasting Alanis Morissette on the ride home. The way I was suddenly plugged into her daily world after being kept so long in the dark; how effortless it felt to need each other again. And I think of Wade; I always think of Wade. Cassie's hands pressed to his shoulders, the rage in her eyes as she shoved him into the rotten wood.

And then, out of nowhere, I remember something. From a tiny, forgotten corner of my subconscious, Wade's words to Cassie come back to me, moments before she pushed him. I hear the spite in his voice like it was yesterday.

You only think *you're better; that's what makes you so insufferable. You think you have an exit plan . . . that your years here won't matter. But guess what? This place . . . this shit town that you want to forget? It runs in your fucking blood now, Cassie Barnwell. It's who you are. Whether you cover it up or not.*

And what hits me, suddenly, is the tragic irony of it all. Cassie didn't push Wade for me. Cassie pushed Wade for Cassie.

"You know this is it, Billie." She wipes her cheeks, drawing me back to the present, to this harrowing moment. "You're not coming to St. Barts."

"I know." I stand, too.

Cassie's face is inches from mine, so close I can smell the stale coffee on her breath, the Altoid she ate to try to cover it up. "This is a line in the sand. This is friendship-ending. It can't be anything else."

I nod. My senses feel dead, trapped somewhere, but I know this anesthesia is temporary. When it wears off later, the pain will find me. And though I suspect the sensation will be unbearable—the loss of

Cassie a hollow, cavernous pit of grief—a small part of me wonders if maybe it won't hurt as much as I think. Perhaps people have been right. Perhaps I don't really need her.

"I'm so sorry," I repeat, the words useless. "Are you—are you going to turn me in?"

Cassie scowls. "Shouldn't I? You kidnapped my baby."

An awful silence hangs in the air between us. By the time I open my mouth to respond, she is already walking away, the back of her dark hair shining in the sun. Her slim form disappears into the automatic doors of the terminal, and then she is gone.

I wait awhile before I call an Uber to take me back to the city. I sit down on the bench and watch the planes take off, imagining which of them holds Cassie. A small white jet launches into the clear cobalt sky, and it's just a feeling, but I'm almost certain that's the one. Its wheels tuck under its body as it whirs through air, receding south into the horizon, away from me.

Chapter Fifty
Billie

2022

"So you're not even going to consider bringing a date?" Jane examines Cassie and Grant's wedding invitation. Ivory, thick as plywood. The heavy card stock screams bottomless wealth. "Because it says here Billie West and guest."

I shrug. "Who would I bring?"

I date sporadically, but there hasn't been anyone serious since Remy. Not even close.

Jane sips her iced tea. It's the first truly warm day of spring, and we're sitting on the patio at Café Standard, sans jackets. The sun feels like heaven, its rays thawing our faces after an extended winter. We're meant to be meeting about work travel—a trip to Bali coming up next week—but the conversation took a turn when I showed Jane what arrived in the mail.

"I just think it would be good for you to have someone there," she presses. "A WASPy wedding at a golf club in East Hampton isn't exactly where I see you thriving solo."

I roll my eyes. "I'll be fine, Mom."

"Just looking out for you, apprentice." Jane sighs. "This is all my fault, isn't it?"

I swallow the dregs of my latte. "Stop. Don't even say that."

"But it's true. Partly."

"No, Jane. Cassie's like a whole different person than she was before she met Grant."

"But things haven't been the same between you two since you confronted her."

I shake my head. "I didn't confront Cassie. I just told her the truth about Grant. And she didn't want to hear it."

We didn't speak for weeks after our fight. When we finally made up over dumplings at Vanessa's, Cassie said it was wrong to call me pathetic, and I apologized for calling her a gold digger. But I promised I hadn't been lying about Grant, about the things Jane told me. Cassie had shrugged, her gaze drifting down toward our shared plate of sesame pancakes.

"Grant didn't deny an innocent flirtation with Jane back when he was her client," she'd said. "It was wrong—he was with someone else— but that girl wasn't me, Billie. I know Grant would never do that to me. When you meet the right person, you change."

I'd fallen silent, considering whether this was true.

"And that night at the Wren . . ." Cassie had sighed, her eyes rising to meet mine. "Grant was wasted. He's in love with the world when he's drunk, he's a close talker, and honestly, he doesn't even remember seeing Jane at the bar. Maybe it looked like flirting to you, but it wasn't." She'd paused, her expression filled with conviction. "Everyone has a list of past mistakes at this age. But Grant loves me, Billie. We're grown-ups, and we're moving forward with a clean slate."

"Bill." Jane's voice jolts me back to the present. She squeezes a wedge of lemon into her tea, swirls it around. "The wedding is still a couple of months away, right? Maybe Cassie will still ask you to be her maid of honor."

I'm wearing sunglasses, so Jane can't tell when I close my eyes. My mind floods with another memory: Cassie on the floor of our old apartment in Alphabet City, pizza crumbs dusting the front of her shirt. Nine years ago now, but I hear her voice like it was seconds ago. You'll be my maid of honor, right? Whenever I do find someone in this crazy world who will have me. It'll be you, right?

I blink my eyes open and find Jane staring, waiting for me to say something.

"Maybe she will," I tell her, though we both know it isn't true.

I call Cassie on my walk home from Café Standard, but she doesn't pick up. She never used to screen my calls, but over the past few months, I've started to feel genuinely lucky if I get to talk to her. My best friend in the world.

It's my second month in the new apartment on Christopher Street. The Path is doing well, and after Jane gave me a sizable raise last year, I can finally afford to live on my own, and in one of the most charming neighborhoods in the city. It has yet to get old, climbing the three flights of stairs and opening the door to this place, knowing I have it all to myself.

I fill a glass with water from the tap and sink down onto the couch. I turn Cassie's wedding invitation over in my hands, tracing my fingers along the ridges of the engraved lettering.

Mr. and Mrs. Eric Barnwell request the honor of
your presence at the marriage of their daughter.

I almost can't digest the irony. Cassie has spent most of her life running from her parents, and now, etiquette demands their presence. But knowing the Barnwells like I do, I can't imagine they're paying for this wedding, even if the invitation suggests it.

I dig my phone out of my bag and scroll through Instagram. I lose myself in the mindless, addictive task of letting other people's highlight reels make me feel something.

Cassie has posted a story, a video of herself working out. The clip has been edited to increase the speed. It looks like a Pilates sequence, but it's hard to tell with how fast everything is moving. Cassie lies on a mat in a matching crop top and leggings, her skinny hips humping the air at the speed of light.

Cassie has been doing something bizarre on Instagram that I can't figure out. It started last year, just after Grant proposed and she quit her job at Intermix to start her own retail business. Cassidy's Closet, she named it, changing her handle to reflect the online clothing boutique she's curating, with a brick-and-mortar store in SoHo slated to open at the end of the summer. One night over strong margaritas a few months ago, Cassie confessed that Grant was bankrolling the whole thing. He'd even hired some top-notch publicist who was getting Cassidy's Closet a mention in Vogue, *and who also suggested that Cassie change the name of the store to something less quirky. "Cassidy Adler" is supposed to sound more upscale and aligned with her brand, whatever that means, so they're making the switch after the wedding, when the Adler surname is officially hers. I don't know why she needed to be drunk to tell me all of this, but she hasn't shared anything as personal since.*

On my phone, the Pilates video ends and Cassie's face appears on camera, her hair scraped back into a topknot. I can tell she's sweaty, but her skin looks flawless. Maybe there's a filter.

"Melissa Wood kicks my ass every time," she pants, catching her breath. "But I'm getting married in eight weeks, you guys. If not now, when, right?" She smirks. "Also, I'm seeing some questions about this set, so I'm gonna link it in the next slide. It's Alo, and it's soft as butter. An amazing selection of colors, too. How gorgeous is this purple?"

I click on Cassie's profile—@cassidyscloset, soon to be @cassidyadler. She's gaining followers quickly—she's up to eleven thousand now. It feels like she's trying to be an influencer, which leaves me perpetually confused. I make a mental note to ask her what's going on, the next time I have the chance. She's been so crazed with wedding stuff lately.

Cassie and Grant are tying the knot over Fourth of July weekend, which Becca says is unforgivably obnoxious.

"The hotels are more expensive—well, everything is more expensive— and it's just a pain in the ass to have to devote an entire long weekend to a wedding." Becca sips from her water bottle. "Sorry, I'm hormonal as hell right now. But it does piss me off when people get married on holiday weekends."

It's June, and Becca and I are walking down Park Avenue. She's newly pregnant with her second baby, and even though she moved to Bronxville last year, she's still wedded to her obstetrician on the Upper East Side. I make an effort to see her when she comes into the city for appointments—it's part of my private pledge to do better with Becca. Esme, too. I feel like I've been making that pledge since I met them, since Cassie's the one I've always put first. Somehow, in spite of this, Becca and Esme are still there for me. It's a loyalty I'm not sure I deserve.

I wrap my arms around Becca outside Grant Central. "Bye. I hope the nausea improves . . ."

"Oh, it won't. With Milo, I was sick as a dog until fourteen weeks. This one's bound to keep me suffering for at least another month."

I give a consoling smile. "It'll be a blip in time, Becks."

"Yeah. Have fun at the wedding, okay?" Her expression is tender. "I know Cassie's been . . . distracted. Off in her own world lately. But I'm sure it'll be a beautiful weekend. Just try to enjoy it."

I nod, my throat suddenly full of tears. I hug Becca one more time. I don't let myself cry until she's through the revolving doors of the station and I'm safely alone on the street.

The day of the wedding is hot, high eighties, but a breeze rolls in from the ocean and burns off the humidity. I wear a lavender slip dress—silk, borrowed from Esme—and carry a small gold clutch that belonged to Mom. I blow-dry my hair and run a straightener over the ends so it looks bouncy and longer than usual.

At the church, I slip into a pew and try not to think about how odd it is that I hardly know anybody here. I spot the Barnwells up front, Mara seated beside her mother, but other than Cassie's family and a few of the girls from Harvard, I recognize almost no one.

A string quartet begins to play; instrumental versions of "Wild Horses" and "Here Comes the Sun" fill the nave of the packed church. In these moments before the processional, I feel sick to my stomach; I know what's coming, even if I've pretended to hope that I might be wrong. I think of all the weeks and months I spent waiting for Cassie to say something about my involvement in the wedding, to ask me to do a reading or give a toast, or to explain that she decided not to do the bridal party thing, after all.

But of course she never said anything, and it's too late now. And suddenly, the sight I'm not ready for: McKay, cascading down the aisle in a pale green dress, her hair swept up, a proud smile splitting across her face. She carries a creamy bouquet of peonies, and it must be her—it has to be her—and it occurs to me for the first time since I sat down to glance at the program that was handed to me on my way into the church. The wedding party is listed on the second page. Just two names.

Best Man: Reed Adler
Matron of Honor: McKay Adler Morris

Before I have time to think about how this happened, how Cassie and I have reached a place where I am one of two hundred unremarkable guests in attendance at her wedding, just another pair of eyes watching the ceremony but removed from the intimate details, from all the fuss and stress and anticipation that led to this moment, Canon in D begins to play. Everyone stands as the delicate, glassy notes of the violin float through the church. Even in middle school, Cassie knew she wanted to walk down the aisle to Pachelbel.

I crane my neck around, and there she is, elbow hooked through her father's. The dress is perfect, the kind of simple yet elegant crisp white gown I always pictured her wearing, and for a passing instant, this makes me happy—the fact that she chose this timeless dress and not some trendy, over-the-top confection that would've been all wrong.

Tears spring to my eyes at the same time waves of anger beat against my chest. Cassie reaches the altar, where Grant waits with a steady smile, hands clasped behind his back. I watch McKay—horrible McKay, who never gave a shit about Cassie until Grant did—as she adjusts Cassie's veil, as she fluffs out the skirt of her gown. The sight is too much. It should be me. How is it not me?

An older man to my left hands me a cloth handkerchief, and I realize I'm weeping. But it's okay, it's appropriate to cry at weddings, I'm not doing anything wrong. He can't see the hurt and rage inflating inside behind my sternum, the expansion there, something gummy and sick ballooning, stretching, on the verge of breaking.

The truth I've tried so hard not to see for so many years has finally forced me to look it straight in the eye.

Cassie isn't mine. She's never belonged to anyone but herself.

Chapter Fifty-one

Cassie

October 28, 2023
15 days after

I slide my heel through the soft, powdered sugar sand. The air is warm, the sound of waves lapping gently against the shore like a tonic that slowly melts away my anger. I open one eye and see Grant dangling Ella above the shallow ocean, her little feet skimming the surface of the water. She giggles. She loves it.

I don't know the time, but the sun has dropped low in the sky and the light possesses a magical quality, bathing everything it touches in gold. *Fillet of the day,* that's what McKay calls it.

McKay. Loyal, perceptive McKay. I see it now, how wrong I was to doubt her. How warped my mind has been these past two weeks, how out of whack I allowed my priorities to become. Billie might have been the friend who shaped my youth, but McKay is the one who will be by my side for the future.

Grant strides out of the water with Ella in his arms, his body dripping, his smile broad. At the sight of them, I am floating on a cloud of love. Debilitating, blissful love that carries everything inside of me— all the pain, the anxiety, the brokenness—to a place of joy.

The three of us go back up to the house, where we can see the sun setting from the deck, dipping toward the ocean beyond the red flamboyant trees and turquoise infinity pool. There's no doubt about it; St. Barts is my happy place.

Grant starts dinner in the kitchen while I give Ella her bath. I put her in a fresh diaper and a onesie and feed her lying on the bed, a soft gust blowing through the open window, the white drapes dancing. Ella's body is warm and clean as she suckles against my chest, and I hope I can preserve this forever, long after it stops being a physical need—the memory of our bodily connection. Sometimes the tenderness feels so fleeting, I want to cry.

I put her down in the Pack 'n Play in our bedroom, close the curtains, and turn on the white noise. I find Grant on the deck, in one of the chaises overlooking the sea. The sun has disappeared; above the horizon, the wide sky lies in stripes of orange and magenta. The balmy breeze coats my skin like velvet.

"Here." Grant hands me a rum punch—his signature recipe—with a Mount Gay floater. I slide onto the chaise beside him and take a sip; the combination of strong liquor and sweet juices tastes like heaven.

"Dinner is on the stove," he says. "I made pesto linguini."

"You're an angel. I'm starved."

"I thought we could have this drink first. Watch the sky."

"Mm. It's so perfect here. I wish we could stay for a month."

"Cass." Grant turns to me, brushes a hand through his hair. His nose and cheeks are pink from a day in the sun. "You didn't bring the monitor out."

"You're right." I sip more of my cocktail, already feeling the buzz, my limbs warm and mollified. "We'll be able to hear her, though. She's just through the window."

"Yeah, but Cass . . ." Grant is grinning. And I realize he's making a point, not an accusation.

"I know." I grin back. "I'm not scared anymore."

And it's true—I'm not. In the day and a half since Billie confessed what really happened—what she did that night—my fear has evaporated. Because no one is following me. No one is searching for Ella, waiting for the right moment to take her again. We are safe. We were never not safe.

"I still can't believe it." Grant shakes his head. "Fucking Billie."

"Don't even say her name." I close my eyes and drink, the sugary rum running down my throat. "She doesn't get to steal this moment."

"We should talk about it, Cassie. When you're ready."

"What is there to talk about?"

"Pressing charges, for one. I was too rattled yesterday, but I'll call Detective Barringer first thing Monday morning. And the lawyer."

I blink my eyes open. The crazy colors have faded from the sky, but the ocean still glistens in semidarkness, the tips of the waves golden. "I don't want to press charges, Grant. What's the point?"

He gives a wry laugh. "Um, justice?"

Justice. I sit with the word.

There are countless instances when fighting for justice feels like the way to morph anger into something useful. But when I think of Billie, I think of Wade, of what he did to her in that basement. I think of Lorraine, a mother not recognizing her own daughter. And I think of myself, of the ways I've treated Billie that I'm not proud of—of the wrongdoings I can only acknowledge in this moment of post-shock, rum-induced clarity. I cut her out of my life when it stopped feeling easy to be her friend.

I know I'll never speak to Billie again—the image of her snatching Ella from the stroller will never allow me to—but I also know that pressing charges won't help either of us.

I explain as much as I can to Grant, omitting the part about Wade. And it strikes me, suddenly, that with Billie gone from my life, so is what happened on that roof in 2006. No one else knows what I did, and they never will. It's a secret Billie and I will take to our graves.

I brace myself for Grant's rebuttal, his insistence that we take legal action. But shockingly, he doesn't fight me. Instead, he drains the rest of his drink and moves over to my chaise, curling against me. I'm still wearing my bathing suit under my cover-up, and he works the bottoms off slowly as he plants soft kisses along the back of my neck. He enters me from behind, his hands pressed to the front of my hips as our bodies fall into a familiar rhythm, and it feels so good I don't even try to stop myself from moaning like it's the first time I've ever come.

Afterward, our limbs tangled, heartbeats slowing, I laugh out loud. I can't help it. The two of us, drunk off one rum punch, having sex outside on the deck like a couple of teenagers. Above us, the sky is an inky bed of bright stars.

Grant kisses me deeply, holds me in this postcoital moment like he did when we first started dating, before there was always something to rush off to. Shower, phone, work, baby. My stomach grumbles, and we remember the pasta.

Grant serves the linguini into bowls, and we eat inside on the big white sofa in front of the television. I don't care what we watch, so Grant turns on a documentary about cults that his coworker claimed to be riveting. Thirty minutes in, Grant is passed out against one corner of the couch, head slumped back, mouth gaping. I take the empty bowl from his lap and rinse our dishes at the sink, find Tupperware for the leftover pasta. Then I mix another rum punch—mine are never as good as Grant's, but I try—and wander tipsily through the house.

Grant and I have never been here alone—always with his parents or McKay or other Adler relatives—and I admire the interior—all Brazilian hardwood and limestone bathrooms and white, airy décor. The villa is built into the hillside, so you can see the ocean from almost every window. It is the definition of paradise.

I wind up back on the main deck, where it's dark and peaceful, the sea shimmering in soft yellow moonlight. I find my phone on the chaise, where I left it earlier, and sit down on the ledge of the infinity pool with my feet in the water. A balmy breeze that smells of salt and sweet flowers coats my skin like velvet.

Without thinking twice, I open Instagram. It's surreal to be on the app—it's been over two weeks since I've posted anything or even glanced at my feed. I check my stats, relieved to see that my follower count hasn't dropped in my absence. On the contrary, I'm now up to forty-nine thousand.

They are loyal, my followers. They deserve more from me.

I tap my avatar at the upper-left corner of the screen, check my reflection in the camera. The lighting is dim and my hair is a little wild from the humidity, but I look good. My face has some color, which brightens my eyes. I tap the button at the bottom of the app to record a video.

"You guys . . . I'm back. I'm so sorry for disappearing on you, I truly, truly am. One day, I'll explain everything, but for now, all you need to know is I had to take care of a family emergency, and everything is okay, I promise. We actually flew down to St. Barts this weekend for a last-minute getaway, and it's pure heaven here . . . Grant is already asleep, but I'm sitting out on the deck, having a drink, watching the full moon, and God, I could stay here forever. But we're heading back to New York on Monday, and I promise you guys a slew of store updates from the past two weeks, because I know we have a lot of catching up to do. In the meantime, I hope you're having an amazing Saturday night, and I'll check in tomorrow. I got Ella the cutest bathing suit from Maisonette—her little buddha belly is to die for—and I'll have to jump on here and show you in the morning. Okay, that's all. Sweet dreams, loves."

I don't even rewatch the video before I post it to my story. Almost instantly, replies from strangers flood my inbox.

Omg thank god ur back queen

where the f have you been!!! missed you! need more content asap!

You look soooo beautiful and tan

Love that cover-up, details pls!

Hallelujah, have been eagerly awaiting your return!!

But they aren't strangers, I remind myself. They're *followers.* Forty-nine thousand people who indulge me, who watch me, who are there to lift me up every moment of every day.

There's a sudden rumble of thunder in the distance and I lift my eyes to see storm clouds gathered on the horizon, their bellies swollen and black. I don't remember rain in the forecast, and it catches me off guard. But then my phone vibrates again, and again, story replies accumulating faster than they ever have before. I forget the storm as I read each one, my eyes glued to the screen as I savor them all, my heart dancing inside my chest.

Chapter Fifty-two

Billie

November 17, 2023
35 days after

Rain speckles the window of the car Jane and I are sharing home from the airport. We're just back from four days in Cuba, a trip we'd been looking forward to for ages.

I want things to be normal between Jane and me, but something still feels off. I imagine it will for quite a while. Our time in Cuba was so jam-packed with meetings and property tours and other activities, we hardly had a chance to talk about anything personal. I haven't gotten much sleep lately and my eyes sting with exhaustion, but I clear my throat.

"Jane." I glance across the empty middle seat. "Are we okay?"

She's typing something on her phone. When she finishes, she looks up at me. "Yes, Billie. We're okay."

It's been five weeks since the night I took Ella; three since the day I told Cassie the truth outside the terminal at Teterboro. And for the past twenty-one days, I've been waiting for the other shoe to drop. For Cassie's lawyer to call, citing the charges she and Grant have decided to press; for Alex—or someone in his department—to bring me in for questioning and a written statement. But no one has contacted me. If not for the reverberating guilt and wrenching anxiety—and the fact that both Alex and Cassie have left my life for good—it would almost seem as though the night of October 13 never happened.

The car slows into a clogged sea of traffic on the Long Island Expressway, and I tell Jane what I already have countless times over the past three weeks. "You know that if anyone contacts you, if anyone tries to implicate you . . . I'll take the fall for everything. I'll say you weren't home, that I snuck in using the key you gave me. You know that, right?"

Jane sighs. Her eyes are red around the rims; she looks as tired as I feel. "Billie, as I've said, let's just cross that bridge if we come to it, okay?"

"But I don't want you to—"

"*Billie.*" Jane's expression grows stern, her mouth a thin line. She tosses her phone in her bag, pivots toward me. "You need to think about yourself, too, okay? You made a huge mistake, but I have your back. And I've watched you sitting in the hell of limbo these past few weeks, torturing yourself, and I don't want to do it anymore."

"What are you saying?"

Her eyes rest on mine. "You need to talk to Alex."

Alex. An image of his face lands in the center of my mind, slicing into my heart. I bite the inside of my lip so hard I taste blood, willing the pain of missing him to relocate. I shake my head. "He doesn't want to hear from me. He's made that clear. And after everything I put him through, the least I can do is respect his space. He deserves that."

"But *you* deserve to know if and how he's planning to move forward with the case. Because right now . . . you're living in fear. I can see it on your face, in the way your shoulders are always hunched, in how you've barely smiled in weeks. I can tell you're not sleeping. And I know how much you still love him."

I say nothing for a few long beats. I glance out the window at the spitting rain, the gray blur of Long Island City as we crawl toward the Midtown Tunnel. "I fucked it up, Jane."

"Maybe." She tucks a loose strand of hair behind her ear, draws in a breath. "But a wise friend once told me that you can't fuck up what's meant for you."

I close my eyes. A lone tear slides through, snaking down my cheek.

"You deserve to talk to him," she says again.

"Why do I deserve anything, Jane?"

The traffic begins to ease as we merge into the mouth of the tunnel, finally cruising.

Jane shakes her head, her expression lined with frustration. "If you can't figure out why, then at least try to realize that it's not just your well-being at stake here. It's also mine. It's Sasha's."

"I *know.* That's why I'm reiterating all this, to make sure you know I'll have your back whenever it's—"

"Stop." Jane holds up a hand. "Stop going there. I want you to talk to Alex. And if you won't do it for yourself, then I demand that you do it for me." Her gaze is firm, unflinching.

"Okay," I whisper, defeated.

The corners of Jane's mouth lift, if only slightly. She looks toward the front of the car. "Excuse me," she calls to the driver. "My friend here needs to change the address of her stop."

Fifteen minutes later, when the car pulls to the curb in front of Alex's building on West Twenty-fourth Street, Jane touches my shoulder. "Wait," she says. "I meant to tell you that I heard back from Craig."

"Consultant Craig?"

Jane nods. "We had a call last week, and he emailed me this morning. He loves your idea of incorporating a charitable component to The Path's services, just like I do. And financially, he thinks it's feasible. He basically reiterated what you said about a philanthropic business model giving us an edge in the industry. He thinks we should go for it."

I am not expecting this. "Seriously?"

"Yes. He wants to meet with us—you and me together—early in the new year. To go over everything in detail and talk about how to get the ball rolling."

"Wow. That's . . ."

"It's incredible, Billie. I'm proud of you."

Perhaps it's all the emotion from the past few weeks gathered right on the surface, but my eyes fill with tears again.

"Hey." Jane wraps her arms around my neck, pulls me in for a tight hug. "I *am* here for you. No matter what happens with Alex, with the case . . . it's going to be okay."

I still have Alex's key, but using it is obviously out of the question. After the car pulls away, I linger outside his building for a full ten minutes, working up the nerve to approach the front door. The rain has let up, but the darkening sky is still overcast, the air chilly and damp. I sit on the stoop and watch pedestrians pass by, their heads down, AirPods secured. None of them notice me as they rush toward whatever is next.

When I finally muster the courage to get up and ring the buzzer, there's no answer. I wait a few minutes, then try again. Nothing. It's nearly five o'clock; I figured he'd be home—he has Fridays off—but maybe not. Maybe he's at happy hour with colleagues. Or out on a date. Any number of things is possible. At least I can tell Jane I tried.

I'm halfway down the block, about to request an Uber when I hear the sound of my name.

"Billie?"

It's Alex's voice, unmistakable. I turn around to see him, my stomach flipping with a sharp mixture of fear and longing. He's wearing his navy overcoat, his hair disheveled and longer than I remember it being just a few weeks earlier. He rakes a hand through it, and all I want in the world is to run to him, to collapse into his arms and pretend the last five weeks never happened.

"What are you doing on my street, Billie?"

I glance down at the suitcase at my feet, my heavy workbag perched on top of it. I try not to think about how awful I must look—beyond sleep-deprived, greasy from the plane. "I—I came from the airport. I just got back from a work trip in Cuba."

Alex casts me a puzzled look.

"I rang your buzzer, but you didn't answer. I didn't think you were home."

He stuffs his hands in his pockets. "I'm just getting in from the precinct."

"Oh. I thought you had Fridays off."

"I had a meeting with my supervisor about doing some time on the narcotics unit."

"You mean, to try to make detective?"

"Working toward that. What do you want, Billie?"

I swallow the lump in my throat. "I was hoping we could talk."

He's silent for what feels like an eternity. Finally, he sighs. "Not at my place. We can walk toward the river."

Alex insists on carrying my workbag while I wheel my suitcase across the West Side Highway. We don't speak until we reach the path, the Hudson River dark and glossy ahead of us, settled in dusk. I think of all the mornings we ran here together, my heart thrashing against my lungs as I fought to keep up with Alex's stride. The way we'd stop and catch our breaths, smiling at each other's sweaty faces, the smell of salt rolling in off the water.

Now, Alex places my bag down on the pavement at our feet. He leans against the railing and gazes out over the river, doesn't look at me.

"I'm so sorry about everything," I say. The apology feels pathetic, pointless. "I've missed you so much. But I know you can't forgive me. Obviously. And I understand."

Alex says nothing, but he finally turns to me. His gaze pierces mine, and I feel a jolt of heat at the base of my spine.

"I need to ask you something." I pause. "Not for my sake but for Jane's."

Alex nods for me to continue. A gust of wind whips off the surface of the water, the cold stinging my ears and cheeks. It's a terrible night to be outside.

"Can you tell me how you're planning on . . . moving forward? With the case, I mean. I haven't heard from anybody. Not from you, or Cassie, or any of the detectives. Jane is worried, after everything I put her through . . ." I rub my temples, try to focus. "What happened was my fault alone. Jane played no part in any of it."

Alex looks back toward the Hudson. On the other side of the river, Hoboken glows in a sea of twinkling lights. "And what about you, Billie?"

"Me?"

"You said Jane is worried, but what about you? Are you worried?"

I close my eyes for a moment. "Honestly? At this point, I'm mostly just numb. I've spent weeks regretting what I did, wishing more than anything that I could undo it . . . but what's the point of that now? It happened. I *did* do it. And I've lost you, I've lost Cassie. I'm just trying not to lose Jane, too." My eyes fill. "Am I scared of going to jail? Of course. Terrified. I'm a wreck, Alex. But it's been weeks of limbo, and I just want to know."

Something in his face softens, his gaze meeting mine again. "You know, that night we ran into Jane in the pizza place after the concert, the night she confronted you about the hat . . . I asked you afterward, on the street, if you'd been lying to me."

"I know."

"But the truth is, Billie, I knew you'd been lying. I knew it right when Jane recognized her hat on your head. Because the only thing from the lobby security camera that ever really gave me reason to pause was footage of someone—a woman, presumably—leaving Cassie's building at one thirty that morning. And she was wearing a hat that looked exactly like the one you wore to Zac Brown Band."

I let this sink in, attempt to process what he's implying. "So you . . . you suspected something from the security footage? Something about me?"

"No, I had no idea it was *you*. I just always thought it was strange, someone wearing a big wide hat indoors, and at that hour. And the timing lined up with whoever put Ella on the Adlers' doorstep in the middle of the night. But it wasn't like I could've investigated anything based on that footage. The person's face and hair were completely shielded." He pauses. "Now, I see that was intentional."

A fresh pang of remorse seizes my insides, and I'm suddenly so sick of feeling guilty for the same regrettable five hours of my life, over and over again. The sensation edges toward anger. "Why are you telling me this, Alex?"

I'm not expecting the smile that plays at the edges of his mouth, the light that comes back into his eyes. "I asked you because I wanted to see if you would tell me the truth. And you did."

"You were testing me?"

"I guess I was. I think part of me wanted to know if it would ever be possible to forgive you. To trust you again."

The slightest stirring of hope buds behind my chest.

Alex rubs the back of his neck. "I do understand why you didn't tell me at first. I mean, the whole thing is epically fucked up, but it's not so black and white, is it? We hadn't been dating for very long. I work in law enforcement. You broke the law."

I nod. "My friend had you looking into the case."

"Yeah. It was messy."

"It doesn't matter, though. I should have just told you. And Cassie."

"You should have." He sighs, his gaze heavy. "I thought about calling you a lot these past few weeks. But I just . . . it's complicated, you know? I need more time."

I grip the icy metal of the railing, resisting the urge to reach for him, to wrap my arms around his warm, good-smelling neck. "I get it. I really do."

"I did call Cassie, though. I had to."

My cells freeze, and I brace myself for the worst. The inevitable price that must be paid when you cross the police and a family like the Adlers.

Alex continues. "I was really relieved to learn you'd told her the truth as well. She's not going to press charges."

For a moment, I'm sure I've misheard him. "What?"

"The Adlers aren't pressing charges, Billie." Alex smiles, and I wonder how he can possibly be happy for me. "They've claimed what happened was a misunderstanding. You can put this behind you and move forward."

I shake my head. "But how . . . but why—"

"I don't know Cassie like you do." His eyes latch mine. "Your relationship is clearly twisted. But she did say to tell you that you're even now."

I think of Wade, of the fall, his head hitting the slate, me lying to the cops all those years ago. I think of the basement, of what he did to me, of Cassie keeping it all in a locked corner of her heart. Of the love between two best friends that dies but doesn't disappear. There's still the soul of that love. It goes somewhere.

"So maybe it's her way of taking responsibility for the things that brought you to your breaking point," Alex adds. "The things she could never own verbally."

I nod.

"But she doesn't want you to contact her ever again." His smile wavers.

"I won't," I say, too saturated with relief to really process the implications of his statement. Of a life without Cassie, her presence forever a ghost. And yet, in some increasingly conscious crevice of my mind, I know I'll be okay without her. "It's for the best," I tell Alex, surprised to find that I mean it.

"I think so, too."

"And us?" I reach for his hand before I can stop myself. His fingers are warm despite the cold. "I love you. I don't want this to be over before it even really starts."

I'm startled by the words coming out of my mouth. I feel them markedly; I haven't expected to speak them out loud.

Alex swallows. I watch the movement of his Adam's apple against his throat. "I love you, too," he says, and the words are a ripple of light through my body. "And I don't think . . . I don't think forgiving you is completely impossible."

I feel it, then: the certainty that this is the moment. I have to say it. Now, or never.

"I don't want kids."

Four words. They sit between us. Irrevocable. True.

Alex stares at me, confused.

"Sorry, I know that came out of nowhere. But I'm telling you now, because if you really do think forgiving me might be possible, that's the best thing I've ever heard, but you should know that I don't want to be a mother. I just don't. For so long, I thought the reason might be my parents' divorce, or the pain of losing my own mom so young. But I've been turning it over in my head for years, and I've realized it's not that simple. I've just always known on a gut level that I don't want children. Partnership, yes. But not motherhood. And I know myself well enough by now to be sure that I won't change my mind."

Alex is quiet. He gazes out over the still surface of the water, where a sliver of moonlight floats. When he looks back at me, his eyes are tender.

"The relationship you told me about. The one you said that you screwed up, because you couldn't be what he wanted you to be." He pauses. "This is what you meant, isn't it?"

I nod slowly. "He wanted children. I couldn't commit to giving him that."

Alex's silence is heavy, fraught, but I push past it, fighting against the pit in my stomach.

"I wish I could change my mind for someone I love, but I can't. And I'm sure you're at a point in your life where you need to be able to see a future in a relationship, and I understand, I truly—"

"Billie." Our hands are still interlaced, and he squeezes my fingers. Moves closer. I can smell his Old Spice and the lingering scent of aftershave in the creases of his neck. "I don't need to have kids to be happy," he says.

The words are a shock to my system. The moment feels like a dizzy, surreal dream. "For real?"

Alex shrugs. "I want partnership, too. If I were to end up with a woman who was set on having children, I'd be on board with that. But I would also be fine with not having them."

"So you—you don't think it's weird that I feel this way?"

"Weird? Billie, the world is a lot bigger than the young moms in the West Village and Gramercy Park. I know you, I've been with you. I've watched what you see. You look at the strollers and the tiny little outfits, and it makes you feel like you should be dying for a baby, right? But there are plenty of people who choose not to have kids. And there are plenty of reasons why. I would never assume that you—or any woman—wants to be a mother."

I study Alex's face, floored by the sentiment of his response. I'm so touched I can't speak.

"Look." He withdraws his hand from mine, rubs the side of his jaw. "You and I have a lot to work through, and I'm not sure—"

"I know." I shake my head. "I'm sorry. Maybe I shouldn't have said that. I wasn't trying to imply anything; I just thought—"

"No, Billie. I'm really glad you told me." His eyes brighten a little, flecks of green shining in his irises. One corner of his mouth twitches. "What are you doing right now?"

"Right now?" I sigh. "Nothing. Going home to shower and unwind and hopefully find a way to get some sleep."

"You have to eat, though, don't you?"

I tilt my head, unable to suppress the grin that slides across my face. "I do have to eat."

"There's a diner on the corner of Twenty-second and Tenth. They have famous french fries. And really big booths for people dining with luggage."

Another cold gust spins off the river, whipping our faces, but my body is warm, a fizzy glow behind my collarbone. "Famous french fries, huh?"

"World-class."

"Wait." I reach down, digging through the inside pocket of my workbag until I find what I'm looking for. "Here." I hand Alex the silver key he gave me a month ago. "I shouldn't have this. Not . . . right now."

Alex nods, his expression straddling the intersection of disappointment and acceptance and hope. It's where we are.

He carries my bag on his shoulder as we head east, and I'm acutely aware of the proximity of our hands, the possibility that he might reach for mine again. As we cross back over the West Side Highway, he does, bridging the gap with a leap of faith. It's cold, but the city is bright, and we walk toward what comes next. Behind us, the river rests in darkness, on its way to becoming an old memory.

Acknowledgments

Allison Hunter, I sent you the first half of this novel in early 2022, not knowing if it was anything, and your enthusiasm is what gave me the drive and the confidence to write the rest. You are a treasure, a wonderful friend, and always the agent of my dreams.

Sarah Cantin, I'm convinced that no editor is kinder, smarter, cooler, or better at her job. One of the best decisions of my life was emailing you in 2010, and again in 2015. Thank you for believing in this book and using your magical powers to make it shine. I cherish you and Allison and our three-way love.

To the magnificent team at St. Martin's Press, thank you for backing this novel with such passion and excitement from the very beginning. I'm especially grateful to Katie Bassel, Lisa Senz, Marissa Sangiacomo, Jennifer Enderlin, Drue VanDuker, Olga Grlic, Kejana Ayala, Brant Janeway, Tom Thompson, Kim Ludlam, Alexandra Hoopes, Sara Ensey, Carla Benton, Lizz Blaise, Michael Clark, Kiffin Steurer, Kerry Nordling, Anne Marie Tallberg, Gisela Ramos, and Ally Demeter.

To Natalie Edwards, thank you for the careful early read, and notes that made all the difference. I'm grateful to you, Allison Malecha, and everyone at Trellis.

To Jason Richman, Addison Duffy, Maialie Fitzpatrick, and the team at UTA: enormous thanks for being in my corner, and for all your hard work on my behalf.

To the teams at Belletrist, Rebelle Media, Refinery29, Hulu, 20th Television, 51 Entertainment, and Fifth Season: thank you for championing my work and helping my books reach so many more readers. I'm especially grateful to Karah Preiss, Emma Roberts, Matt Matruski, Meaghan Oppenheimer, Shannon Gibson, Laura Lewis, Stephanie

Noonan, Sam Schlaifer, Lauren Thorpe, Adelis Riveiro, and the ex-
traordinarily talented cast and crew behind *Tell Me Lies* at Hulu. I still
pinch myself.

Thank you to Kate Hodgson and everyone at *GMA*.

Joycie Hunter and Amelia Russo—forever my earliest readers—
thank you both for your intelligent feedback and continuous encour-
agement. Love you long time.

Avery Carpenter Forrey, I have much to thank you for—like your
helpful notes on this novel—but most of all for being my writer friend
who is also just my friend. Your positivity and warmth are contagious.
I'm incredibly lucky to be on this journey with you.

Colleen McKeegan, I'm very grateful for our friendship (writerly
and regular). Thank you for feedback that keeps my writing on the
straight and narrow. There was a Suburban Scrivener–shaped hole in
my life before you and Avery filled it.

Jamie Cheney, huge thanks for your thoughtful, comprehensive
answers to my many questions about the Hudson Valley. If anything
about Red Hook rings false in these pages, the fault is my own.

Ben Wallace, your feedback on all things related to police and detective work was invaluable; thank you for being so generous with
your time.

Mom and Ellie, the degree to which I value your opinions in all
areas may border on dysfunctional, and this book is no exception.
Thank you for being my best friends and for your brilliant notes that
improved these pages.

Thank you to all the independent bookstores and booksellers, especially the lovely women at Elm Street Books, Barrett Bookstore, and
Athena Books.

Thank you to my readers. I've said this before, but it remains true:
you allow me to keep writing.

To Silvana Valverde, immense thanks for taking such good care of
my children while I dove into my writing cave. I couldn't have finished
a single sentence without you.

To my parents and siblings: thank you never feels like enough, but
I'll say it anyway. You know the rest.

Rob, thanks for sticking with me through another book, my love.
It's not easy being married to a writer! I spend a lot of time in my
head, but when I blink my eyes open and you're there, I'm home.

Jamesy, I fall in love with you a hundred times a day. What a gift it is to watch you grow into the sweetest little boy. Lila, it's true what I said in my dedication: you and I wrote this book together. You were there all along, growing and preparing to make your way into the world as *Bye, Baby* did the same. So, thank you for the joint effort. My love and gratitude for you and James is boundless.